Mistress of the Sun

Also by Sandra Gulland

THE JOSEPHINE B. TRILOGY
The Many Lives & Secret Sorrows of Josephine B.
Tales of Passion, Tales of Woe
The Last Great Dance on Earth

Mistress
of the Sun

a novel

Sandra Gulland

HarperCollins*Publishers*Ltd

Published by HarperCollins Publishers Ltd.

HarperCollins books may be purchased for educational, business,
or sales promotional use through our Special Markets Department.

HarperCollins Publishers Ltd, 2 Bloor Street East, 20th Floor,
Toronto, Ontario, Canada M4W 1A8.

Mistress of the Sun is a work of fiction inspired by the life and times of
Louise de la Vallière, mistress of Louis XIV, the Sun King.

Grateful acknowledgment is made to the following for permission to reprint an
excerpt from the poem "Hall of Mirrors" in *Some Other Garden* by
Jane Urquhart © 2000. Published by McClelland & Stewart Ltd.
Used with permission of the publisher.

www.harpercollins.ca

Library and Archives Canada Cataloguing in Publication

Gulland, Sandra
Mistress of the sun : a novel / Sandra Gulland.—1st ed.

ISBN 978-0-00-200775-7

1. de la Vallière, Louise-Françoise La Baume Le Blanc, Duchesse de Vaujours,
1644–1710—Fiction. 2. Louis XIV, King of France, 1638–1715—Fiction.
I. Title.

PA8563.U643M58 2008   C813'.54   C2007-906574-0

RRD 9 8 7 6 5 4 3 2 1

Design by Sharon Kish
Maps by Paul J. Pugliese
Printed and bound in the United States

With longing for my celestial family—
grandmother May,
cousin Linda,
and now, sadly, my mother, Sharon

I wanted you three, more than anyone, to read this.

I am blind
from staring too long at the sun

—FROM "HALL OF MIRRORS"

BY JANE URQUHART

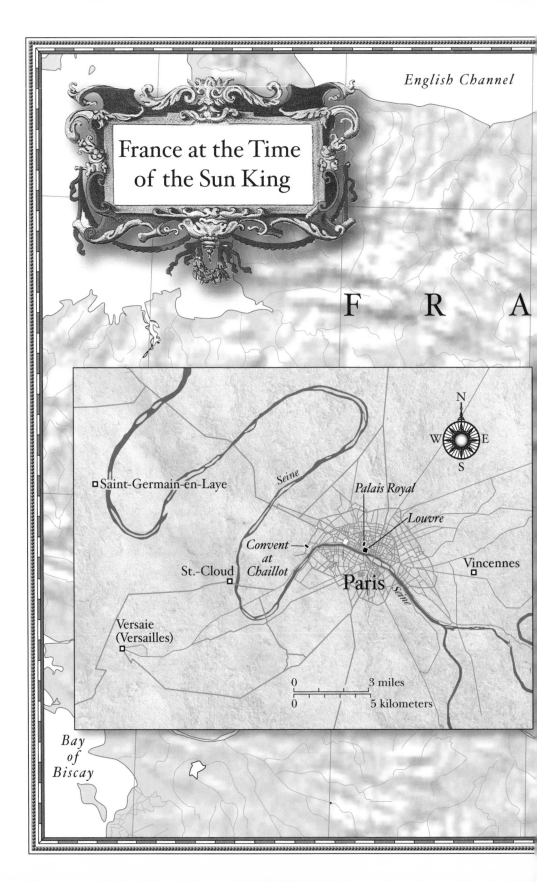

France at the Time
of the Sun King

English Channel

F R A

Saint-Germain-en-Laye

Seine

Palais Royal

Louvre

Convent at Chaillot

Vincennes

St.-Cloud

Paris

Seine

Versaie
(Versailles)

N
W E
S

0   3 miles
0   5 kilometers

Bay
of
Biscay

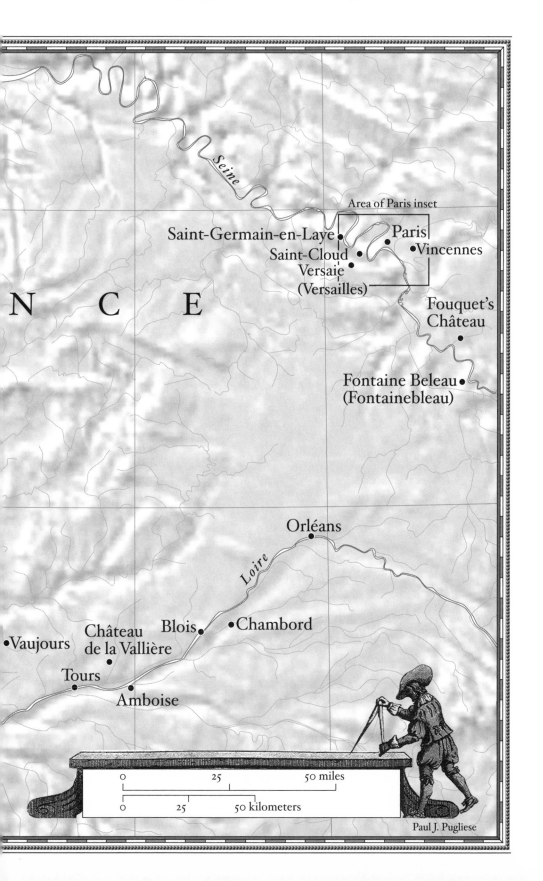

N   C   E

Seine

Area of Paris inset

Saint-Germain-en-Laye •   • Paris
Saint-Cloud •   • Vincennes
Versaie •
(Versailles)

Fouquet's
Château •

Fontaine Beleau •
(Fontainebleau)

Orléans •

Loire

Blois •   • Chambord
Château
de la Vallière •

•Vaujours

Tours •
• Amboise

0	25	50 miles
0	25	50 kilometers

Paul J. Pugliese

Contents

Part I

BONE MAGIC

Chapter One

A Romany woman *in a crimson gown flashes by, standing on the back of a cantering horse. Her crown of turkey feathers quivers under the burning summer sun.*

"The Wild Woman!" announces the showman, flourishing a black hat.

The crowd cheers as the lathered horse picks up speed. It tosses its big head, throwing off gobs of sweat and spittle. Its tail streams, and its hooves pound the dust.

The Wild Woman puts out her hands, her diaphanous skirts billowing out behind her. Slowly, she raises her arms to the cloudless sky and shrieks a piercing war cry.

A pale girl—barely tall enough to see over the rails—watches transfixed, imagining her own thin arms outstretched, her own feet planted on a horse's broad back.

She presses her hands to her cheeks in wonder. Oh, the wind!

It was 1650, year eight in the reign of young Louis XIV—a time of famine, plague and war. In the hamlets and caves and forests beyond, people were starving and violence ruled. The girl had just turned six.

She was small for her age, often taken for a four-year-old—until she spoke, that is, with a matter-of-fact maturity well beyond her years. She wore a close-fitting cap tied under her chin with ribbons, her golden curls falling down her back to her waist. Her gown of gray serge was adorned with a necklace she'd made herself from hedgehog teeth. A pixie child, people sometimes called her, because of her diminutive size, her fair coloring, her unsettling gaze.

The girl followed the Wild Woman with her eyes as she jumped from the horse and bowed out. Waving her feathered crown, she disappeared from view. The girl pushed her way out through the crowd. Ignoring two jugglers, a clown walking on sticks, and a tumbling dwarf, she circled around to the sprawl of covered wagons on the far side of the hill. There, she found the Wild Woman, pouring a leather bucket of water over her tangled hair. The tin spangles on her gown caught the light.

"Thunder, it's hot," the woman cursed. Her horse—a piebald with pink eyelids—was tethered to an oxcart close by. "What do you want, angel?" she asked through dripping tendrils.

"I want to ride a horse like you do," the girl said. "Standing."

"Do you," the woman said, wiping her face with her hands.

"I'm horse-possessed," the girl said soberly. "My father says."

The woman laughed. "And where be your father now?"

The horse pawed at the dirt, kicking up clouds. The Romany woman yanked its frayed lead and said something in a foreign tongue. The horse raised its ugly head and whinnied; a chorus answered.

Horses.

"They're in the back field," the woman told the child, shooing her on.

The girl crept between the wagons and tents, making her way toward a clearing where four cart horses, a donkey and a spotted pony were grazing. The tethered bell mare looked up as she approached, then returned to chewing the loaves of moldy bran bread that had been thrown down in a heap. The summer had been dry, and grass was sparse.

It was then that the girl saw the horse standing apart in the woods—a young stallion, she knew, by his proud bearing. He was fenced off from the others, one foreleg bound up with a leather strap.

He was a White, high in stature. His neck was long, slender at the head, and his up-pricked ears were small and sharp. Words from the Bible came to her: *I saw Heaven open, and behold: a White horse.* His eyes looked right into her. *Sing ye!*

She thought of stories her father had told her—stories of Neptune, sacrificing his Whites to the sun, stories of winged Pegasus. *Worship him that rides on clouds.* She thought of the King, a boy not much older than she was, stopping the riots in Paris by riding into the fray on a White. *He who rides him is faithful and true.*

She knew this horse: he was the horse in her dreams.

She picked her way across the clearing. "Ho, boy," she said, her hand outstretched.

The stallion pinned back his ears, threatening to strike.

Laurent de la Vallière turned his squeaky wagon into the rock-strewn field. He eased himself down off the driver's bench and straightened, one hand on the small of his back. His military hat was plumed but stained, and he wore a cracked leather jerkin with patched woolen sleeves laced on at the shoulders. His quilted knee breeches and sagging trunk hose, out of fashion for over a half-century, were well patched and darned. Booted and spurred and with a sword at his side, he had the air of a cavalry officer who had seen better days.

He tied the cart mare to a scrubby oak and headed toward the crowd in the field. At the top of the path, a big Romany woman sat on a stump: the gatekeeper, he surmised. Not all gypsies were hedge crawlers, but most were a rum lot. He patted his leather doublet, feeling for the rosary he kept next to his heart, a string of plain wooden beads touched by Saint Teresa of Avila. *O God, chase from my heart all ominous thoughts and make me glad with the brightness of hope. Amen.*

"Monsieur de la Vallière," he said, tipping his hat. He was well respected in these parts, revered for his doctoring and charity, but the Romas were a traveling people; they would not know him. "I am looking for a girl," he said.

A sudden breeze carried the scent of urine. "A *girl*, you say?" The woman grinned, gap-toothed.

"My daughter." Laurent held out his hand, palm down, to indicate height.

"Fair, two front teeth missing?"

"She is here, then." *Praised be my Lord.* He had been looking all afternoon. After searching the manor, he had combed the barn, the dovecote, the granary, the dairy and even the henhouse. He had walked the woods and fields beyond, and fearfully paced the banks of the river before harnessing the cart mare and heading into town. It was at the dry goods store in Reugny that he heard talk of Romas with trick ponies. The girl was a fool for horses.

"She's in the far field—with Diablo," the woman added with a throaty laugh.

The Devil? Laurent crossed himself and made his way over the hill and through the tented carts to the field behind. There, he spotted his daughter crouched in the dust.

"Petite," he called out. She was surrounded by heavy horses.

"Father?" She stood up. "Look," she said as he approached, pointing to a white horse at the edge of the woods.

"Where have you been?" Fear overwhelmed him, now that he knew she was safe. "You could have been—" Vagrants were everywhere. Just last week, two pilgrims had been murdered on the road to Tours. He stooped beside his daughter and took her hand. *O Lord, I offer my ardent thanksgiving for the grace You bestow on me. Amen.* Her pale cheeks were flushed. "Little one, you must not run away like that." She was an impulsive, emotional child, full-hearted and independent, boyish in her ways. These were not qualities his wife appreciated. She was strict with the girl, making her sit for hours at an embroidery frame—but what could he say? Raising a daughter was a woman's domain.

"I'm going to stand on a galloping horse," Petite lisped through the gap in her teeth. She stretched her arms out, her wide-set blue eyes luminous.

Was it the Holy Spirit shining through her, Laurent wondered—or the Devil? It was easy to confuse the two.

"Like the Wild Woman," she said.

The girl's fantastical imagination was a concern. That spring, she had constructed a primitive hovel out of stones in back of the barn, her "convent" she called it. There she had nursed broken animals back to health, most recently a spotted salamander and a goshawk.

"They said they would teach me how."

"Let us go," he said, taking his daughter's hand. "I have bread rolls in the wagon." If the Romas had not stolen them.

"But Diablo," Petite said, looking back at the stallion.

"He belongs to these people here."

"They said they'd sell him cheap."

"We will go to the horse market in Tours next week. We will find you a pony, just as you have always wanted." As it was, the girl would ride anything with four legs. A year earlier, she had trained a calf to jump.

"You said the horses at the market can hardly walk. You said they are fleshless."

"It is not a good year for horses, true." Between the endless war with Spain and interminable uprisings, decent mounts were hard to find. Any four-legged beast left standing had been taken by one army or another. As well, the taboo against eating horseflesh did not apply in a time of famine. "But there is always hope. We will pray, and the good Lord will provide."

"I prayed for *this* horse, Father," Petite said. The stallion was standing still as a statue, watching them. "I prayed for this White."

Laurent stopped to consider. The stallion's legs were straight and his shoulders long. His head was narrow, like a ram's: perfect. Although thin, the animal was broad in the chest. Horses of that rare milk-white color were said to be like water, spirited yet tender. He would be a beauty, no doubt, once curried and combed. His daughter had an uncanny eye for a horse, in truth.

"How much did they say they wanted for him?"

It took four strong men—the muscle men of the show—to secure the stallion to the back of the wagon. The leg strap came loose in the tussle. "Stand back," one of the men yelled as the beast let loose, kicking out furiously.

What is wrong with that stallion? Laurent wondered. Even a horse born under a bad constellation would not have this degree of wildness. Had he been unsettled by battle? One saw that often of late, yet the White had no scars that Laurent could see, no telltale sword wounds.

"With respect, Monsieur—"

Laurent turned with a start. The young man behind him had a face as black as a raven's wing. His tunic was patched at the elbows and his head wrapped round with linen cloth. A Moor? A small fringed carpetbag was attached to a cord tied around his waist, but Laurent could see no sword or knife. He made a quick supplication to Saint James the Moor-killer and reviewed his state of arms: his rusty sword, the dull knife in his right boot. He breathed with relief to see a small cross around the Moor's neck.

"I advise you to be cautious," the young man said. "That stallion is uncommonly ill-tempered—evil, some say, although that is not a word I care to use, at least not with respect to animals."

The stallion gave a high-pitched whinny.

"Father?" Petite said uncertainly, half-hiding behind her father's legs.

The beast lunged for one of the muscle men, teeth bared, and the man fell, his leather jerkin torn. "The Devil!" he cursed, scrambling clear.

Three urchins gathered to watch and jeer, as if the scene were a bear-baiting, part of the show.

"He has been named Diablo for a reason," the Moor said, gesturing to the lads to stand well back.

Laurent rubbed his stubbled chin, in need of its weekly shave. He was puzzled by the Moor's use of intelligible language. He'd been given to believe that pagans were more beast than human. "I gather that you know this horse," he said. Perhaps the Moor was the groom—a poor one, if that was the case. The creature had not been touched for some time, to judge by his long splintered hooves and the mats in his mane.

"I am Azeem, a gentler. I train the horses."

Petite spoke up. "Did you teach the donkey to sit like a dog?"

"You liked that trick?" The gentler smiled; his teeth were white and straight.

"I taught a goat to climb a ladder," she said.

Laurent took his daughter's hand. Gentlers were born during the chime hours. Did they not have the second sight? "This horse looks none too gentled."

"The Romas stitched his ears together when he was a colt, but it only made him vicious."

Laurent made a sound of disapproval. Stitching a horse's ears together was believed to calm the animal—to keep it from kicking out while being shod, for example—but there was no magic in the practice, in his view. It served only to distract the horse, give it something to think about. Tying up one hoof did the job just as well. "Vicious, you say?" The rope was cutting into the White's neck. The stallion was pulling so hard, Laurent feared the horse might break his neck.

"Aye. Bone magic is about the only thing that would turn him now," the Moor said, signing himself.

Laurent frowned. He had heard talk of bone magic. One man he knew had used it to settle his horse, but then he himself had turned crackbrained. *Gone to the river, been around water and streams* was how the neighbors put it, whispering among themselves. The man had only to tap on his barn door and it would fly open, as if the Devil were behind it. He claimed he saw the horse by his bed at night.

"Charlotte's father used magic on his lame Barb mare," Petite told her father.

"Monsieur Bosse?" That horse had gone on to win three purses. Not that Laurent approved of gambling.

"Water magic, but maybe that's different from bone magic," the girl said.

"Forgive me, Monsieur," the Moor said, addressing Laurent. "I should not have spoken of it in front of a child." He stooped to face the girl. "Mademoiselle, whatever it is called—bone magic, water magic, toad magic—have nothing to do with it. Understand?"

"We do not hold with witchcraft." Laurent pulled Petite closer, away from the Moor. The horse was tied securely now. It was time to move on.

"You are wise, Monsieur." The gentler stood and made a graceful bow from the waist, his hand pressing the cross to his chest. "It is the Devil's power, and the Devil gives away nothing for free."

LAURENT'S STOCKY MARE pulled the cart down the rutted laneway. His daughter sat beside him, looking anxiously back at the recalcitrant White. At first, the horse had braced himself against the pull of the wagon, but the cart mare was strong and the ropes held. After being dragged for a time, the stallion relented and followed along.

Petite asked if she could climb into the back of the wagon. "So that he won't think God has forsaken him," she said.

"Leave the horse be," Laurent answered wearily. The stallion was a handsome creature, but his condition was pitiable. His wife would have a thing to say, that was for sure. "You will just unsettle him."

Petite sat back down beside her father and bit into a bread roll, swinging her feet. "Was that gentler a Moor?"

"I believe so," Laurent said as they approached Reugny. The spire of the little church could be seen over the treetops. He wondered if there would be news. The sun was at salute level—about five of the clock—and the mail rider from Tours might have arrived. Last he had heard, Bordeaux, to the south, was in revolt against the Court, and the King's forces had the city under siege. If Bordeaux proved victorious, anything could happen. The King might have to retreat behind the walls of Paris and abandon the countryside to the warring princes. What was left to fight over? France was like a shattered vase. The only thing people shared was poverty. Peasants were lucky to get fifteen sous for a day's labor, the price of a basket of eggs.

How was it possible to go on living with such discord? Laurent felt for the copper coin sewn into the lining of his jerkin, the one engraved with the image of Henry the Great. That good king's death had unleashed a century of mayhem. Every night Laurent prayed that their young and most Christian King would put an end to the eternal bloodshed. The King was God's representative; that was ordained. Surely he would triumph.

"I was going to the land of the Moors," Petite said, interrupting Laurent's thoughts.

"Oh?" he replied absently, pulling the wagon into a vacant lot across from the village green. Something was going on: a crowd had gathered to one side of the hanging tree. A great laugh went up and then a hiss. A cockfight, perhaps?

"This morning."

"You were going to the land of the Moors *this* morning?"

"To be beheaded," Petite said. "Like Saint Teresa in the book. But that Moor was a gentler, and he didn't have a sword. Or an ax."

"Saint Teresa's book?" Laurent asked, confused. Over time he had acquired a small library—some texts on husbandry and history, but largely religious and philosophical tracts. Among them was Saint Teresa's account of her life, a slim leather-bound volume. How did his daughter know of it? "Did Monsieur Péniceau read it to you?" His son's tutor had once been a Court scribe; he could read and write passably, but theology was certainly not his province.

"I've been reading it myself, but I'm only to page sixteen."

Laurent turned to stare at her. "You can *read?*"

"Some words are hard."

"Who taught you?" His daughter was precocious—that he well knew—but his son Jean, two years older, had yet to even learn his letters.

"I learned myself," Petite said, standing and surveying the green. "Someone's in the stocks."

"Stay with the wagon," Laurent instructed, making a mental note to inquire into this matter later. "I have to pick up some supplies at the apothecary."

"Will Diablo be all right?" Petite asked, looking back at the White.

"He cannot go anywhere." The rope was holding. "Do not let anyone near him."

Laurent had walked only a few paces when he heard "Papa!"

A strapping lad ran across the crowded square, an angle rod in one hand and a bait bag in the other.

"Jean," Petite called out to her brother.

"They've got Agathe Balin in the stocks," the boy told his father breathlessly. He turned and pointed at the crowd.

"Why?" Petite asked.

"No mind," Laurent said with a warning tone.

"For *fornicating,* Papa. With Monsieur Bosse, everyone's saying. Go look, Papa. She's covered in spit." Jean's freckled cheeks were flushed.

"Monsieur Bosse—Charlotte's father?" Petite asked.

Laurent glared down at his son. "You are supposed to be at your lessons."

Jean threw his sack and rod into the back of the wagon. "Where'd this horse come from?" He circled around to have a look. The horse snorted, white-eyed. "Is it wild?"

"Stay back, son," Laurent warned.

"Mother!" the boy cursed, jumping to avoid a smartly aimed kick. "That's one mean beast."

"He's mine," Petite said. "I prayed for him."

"Little one, he is not a horse for a girl," Laurent said, heading for the apothecary.

"What does 'fornicating' mean?" Petite asked, making room for her big brother beside her on the cart's bench.

"What good is a horse you can't ride or work?" Madame Françoise de la Vallière demanded, her hands bloody from killing a rabbit for Lord's Day dinner. She cut off the head and snapped the legs to remove the feet. She was a pretty woman with round cheeks and a dimpled chin. Deep frown lines separated her thin plucked brows.

"I have yet to meet a stallion I cannot ride," Laurent said with false optimism. He had needed the help of the ploughman and three field hands just to get the beast into the barn—with pitchforks *and* the whalebone whip.

"He tried to kick me," Jean said.

"No news yet out of Bordeaux." Laurent let his running hound in by the back door. The dog hurried to her pups in the basket by the fire.

"They've got Mademoiselle Balin in stocks in town," Jean said.

Blanche, the pock-scarred kitchen maid, turned her one good eye to stare. "*Agathe* Balin?"

Françoise raised her brows. "You don't say."

"For fornicating with Monsieur Bosse, everyone's saying."

"A married man." Françoise cut through the rabbit's groin. "That girl has had the Devil in her from the day she was born." She took out the waste tube and cut off the tail, then pulled the skin down over the body in one easy go.

"Everyone spat on her, and a dog was licking her face," Jean said as he emptied two eels out of his sack into a copper basin. "You should have heard her scream when I tickled her feet."

"Good catch," Françoise noted, gesturing to Blanche to take the eels outside to clean.

"And *you* should have been praying for the salvation of her soul, son, not tormenting the girl," Laurent said with a sigh.

"Everyone was doing it," Jean said, following the maid out the back door.

"He's just a lad, Laurent," Françoise said, cutting the rabbit's stomach lining and removing the innards.

"He was supposed to be studying."

"And *she* was supposed to be at her needlework." Françoise glanced over at Petite, who was stroking the hound by the fire. "She runs off, and the two of you come back with a horse. What kind of discipline is that?"

"A true White is rare," Laurent said. The stallion even had blue eyes, something he'd heard of but never seen. "A noble breed," he added, thinking of the ancient inscription etched over the bedroom mantel: *Ad principem ut ad ignem amor indissolubilis.* For the King, love like an altar fire, eternal. These were the first words he saw on waking, the last words he saw before falling asleep. It had been his family's motto for generations. His father's great-great-great-grand-father had ridden beside Jeanne d'Arc. The King could count on a Vallière in troubled times, but Françoise was not a Vallière. She was a Provost, a family that tended to profit in troubled times. She would never understand the value of a horse such as this: a true Blanchard, a beautiful cheval blanc, the mount of kings. Not everything could be measured and weighed, not everything had a price.

"And he has conformation," Petite said, nuzzling one of the pups.

"He has *good* conformation," Laurent corrected. His old cavalry mount Hongre could hardly manage a trot anymore. He fancied himself on the White.

"Father's going to breed him."

"It's not seemly to discuss such things with a girl," Françoise told Laurent under her breath. "As it is, she spends too much time with the horses. It's time she started acting like a lady." She plunged her knife into the breast of the rabbit, splitting it in two with one stroke.

THE NEXT MORNING, at the third cock's crow, Petite moved quietly out the back door, a dry crust of bread in her hand. It had rained in the night. The moon was still visible, illuminating the outbuildings, the misty kitchen gardens and the great trees beyond—a silent world of half-light. The cock crowed again, answered by a chirping starling. Petite put on her wooden sabots and picked her way across the puddled poultry yard.

She pried open the barn door, taking care to lift it as best she could so that the rusty hinge wouldn't squeak. She didn't want to wake the ploughman asleep in the loft. Three swallows swooped by her. She stood in the dark, inhaling the warm scent of the horses, feeling their alert presence. Old Hongre nickered softly. The ploughman stirred, then returned to snoring.

Dim light shone through the window at the far side of the barn. A moment passed before Petite could make out the shapes of the horses and the two milk cows. On the wall above the harnesses was a silver-birch switch that kept demons from riding the horses at night.

The White's head appeared in the corner stall and then disappeared. Petite groped her way along the feed bins and woodpile to where Diablo stood facing her, a ghostly apparition. "Ho, boy," she whispered. He tossed his head. Handsome he surely was, the most beautiful creature she'd ever seen. *Behold, thou art fair,* she thought, recalling a line from the Song of Solomon. She longed to comb his matted mane, wash and oil his long white tail so snarled with burrs. The scabs on his haunches would clear with care, if only he would let her near him.

"Beloved," she murmured, the word dangerous and thrilling.

The horse pinned back his ears.

She tucked the crust under her armpit to give it her scent, then held it out on her palm, both offering and bribe. He turned his back to her, tail swishing.

Petite popped a bit of the crust into her mouth and crunched it noisily, watching with satisfaction as Diablo's right ear swiveled back. Patience is the companion of wisdom, her father had often told her, quoting Saint Augustine. She held out her hand yet again.

The horse twirled and lunged, teeth bared.

Chapter Two

THE FALL WAS STORMY that year. On wet days, if she had to be indoors, Petite preferred dusting the books in her father's small study, and she liked best to do it while her brother Jean was at his lessons in the sitting room. That way, she could listen as she worked, learning Latin and even a little history. On this particular rainy November morning a fire was crackling in the hearth, and Monsieur Péniceau was reading aloud from *Consolation of Philosophy,* a translation of *Consolatio Philosophiae* by Boethius.

"'Happy is that death which does not thrust itself upon men in their pleasant years,'" the tutor recited, his voice high and strangled.

Through the open door Petite could see Jean resting his head on the table, one cheek on the back of his hands, his eyes closed. With his turned-up nose, dimpled chin and dark curls, he looked like a cherub, the very image of their pretty mother.

Petite opened the window shutters to let in light and pulled up a step stool so that she could scan the spines of the books nearest the window. One appeared to be a book of Latin verses on hunting. Another—*Histoire naturelle des quadrupèdes*—was a pigskin text with a gilt-stamped spine. As far as she could tell, the books on this shelf were the more practical texts: on animal husbandry, herbs and trees.

She took down the dog-eared text of medical recipes her father consulted when tending the ill and impoverished. Petite knew this book well, for she often went with him on his rounds. The day before, they'd been to see a woman and three children who lived in a cave in the rock escarpment. The youngest had cut his leg setting a trap, and Petite's father had bandaged it with clean linen. At the head of the boy's bed of dried leaves was a cross made from twigs. The woman had bowed low before her father as they left, pressing his hand to her forehead as if seeking benediction.

The book, so often used, wasn't dusty, but Petite wiped the cover with her rag anyway and slid it back into place.

"'While I was pondering thus in silence,'" the tutor whined on, "'there appeared standing beside me an old woman, whose face was full of majesty, and whose eyes shone with wisdom.'"

Petite took out the next book and held it to the light, examining it for grime. It was bigger than the others, but it had no spine—the sheets of thin, yellowed paper were attached at the back with twine. The title, *The Horseman*, was crudely stamped onto a pasteboard cover. The contents were printed, not written, making the words easier for her to make out.

Carefully, Petite turned the brittle pages: "The Horse-Breeder," "Horse-Ryder," "Horse-Runner," "Horse-Ambler," "Horse-Keeper." Many afternoons, in the quiet hour after the midday meal, she had gone to the barn where, with fistfuls of grain or a stolen lump of sugar, she had tried to woo the stallion. She had used caressing words, offered him loaves of horse bread she'd baked herself, and even so he threatened her. She prayed for him every night before going to bed, imploring the saints.

Why are my prayers unanswered? she thought as she thumbed through the pages: "How to Correct the Evil Motions," "Corrections against Restiveness," "Of the Witch and the Night-mare." Her breath quickened as she read "Of the Bone Magic."

Petite glanced through the door at her brother and his tutor. Jean was clearly asleep now, his mouth agape. "'Away with you, Sirens,'" the tutor read on, "'seductive unto destruction.'" Petite opened the book to the section on bone magic, its use and composition. *Beware*, she read.

She heard the entry door shut, and then voices: it was her father, returning from town. She slipped the book back onto the shelf and went to the study door. Monsieur Péniceau stopped reading and Jean sat up, rubbing his eyes.

"Wonderful news," Petite's father said as he entered the room. His long hair was dripping wet from the rain. "The King has won a victory over Bordeaux."

"Bravo!" the tutor exclaimed shrilly.

"Bravo," Jean said, standing. "Has the rain let up? Can I go fishing?"

"Not so soon, son. There is a great deal to be done. The Court will be stopping at Amboise on its way back to Paris."

"The King is coming to *Amboise?*" Petite asked, stepping into the room.

"Aye, little one. The King and the Queen Mother. I'm to put on a royal welcome. Your mother will have to come with me to help serve the Queen Mother, and—" He turned to Petite's brother. "You will come as well, Jean. It will be a good opportunity for you to make yourself known to members of the Court, possibly even the King and his brother, who are close to you in age."

"Not me?" Petite asked, crestfallen.

"YOU'RE TOO YOUNG to go, Louise, and that's all there is to it," Françoise said, rummaging through her trunk.

"But I'm six now," Petite argued.

"It will annoy the members of the Court to have children about. Blanche will look after you here."

"Jean is going, and he's only eight."

"Eight is mature, young lady, and six is not. In any case, it's different for a boy." Françoise shook out her mauve velvet skirt. "I'll have to wear my yellow silk," she said sadly, more to herself than to her daughter. "Why aren't you at your needlework?" she asked.

"The rain has stopped," Petite said. "May I go help Father with the horses?"

"Go, go," Françoise said impatiently, opening her strongbox of jewels. "Mon Dieu!" she gasped.

LAURENT DE LA VALLIÈRE was in the barn checking on his old cavalry mount when his daughter appeared and tugged at his sleeve.

"Mother said to tell you that her pearls are missing."

Laurent sighed. "I'll talk to her later," he said, picking up Hongre's front right hoof.

"I hope you're not going to ride the Hungarian to Amboise, Papa," Jean said from his perch on a stall rail. "He's old and has a flat face. Everyone would laugh."

"Hongre is a noble horse, son. He has served me well—but no, I would rather not take him to Amboise." Laurent set down the horse's hoof and stroked his shoulder. "He is getting too old for long rides."

A horse snorted and they all turned.

"Why don't you ride Diablo?" Petite asked.

"If I could tame him." Despite his best efforts, Laurent had not been able to get near the White.

Petite went down to the corner stall with a fistful of grain.

"Stay back from that horse," Laurent warned. "Go collect the eggs."

Petite tossed a fistful of grain into the stall and dashed out the barn door.

"And you," Laurent said, addressing his son, "clean up Hongre for tomorrow. I'm going to have to take him to Amboise."

"Why can't the ploughman do that?" Jean complained, jumping down and brushing the dust from his breeches. "Look at all the muck he's let heap up in the White's stall."

"Son." Laurent felt for his beads. "He's fixing a wheel on the cart." The corner stall *was* knee-deep in leavings. The barn, usually so tidy, reeked.

What is *to be done with that horse?* Laurent thought, heading back across the barnyard to the manor. From the day the creature arrived, there had been trouble. A pig died of the measles. One of the cart horses got mange, and the lumpy eruptions on her back oozed fluid, making her impossible to harness. Laurent himself had wounded his leg on the plough blade. The cut had healed, thank goodness, but only after he had appealed to Saint George and treated the plough blade with a nostrum, purchased at a stall in the Reugny market, made from moss off the head of an unburied male corpse. The ploughman, whose bones knew these things, was convinced that the White had let in evil spirits. His matted mane, twisted into witch locks, was evidence aplenty. Laurent had given Curé Barouche ten sous to disenchant the horse as well as the barn, but even that had done no good.

Diablo, indeed. *A devil of a beast,* he thought, pausing at the back door and recalling, with a sinking heart, the matter of his wife's pearls.

Françoise was in the kitchen, lifting green codling apples out of a pot of boiling water. "I am sorry about your pearls," Laurent said, placing his hat on a peg and taking off his greatcoat.

"It's the scullery girl's doing," she said, plunging an apple into a wooden bucket of water from the well. "She's got sticky fingers, that one."

"It wasn't the girl, Françoise," Laurent said, stepping out of his work boots. "I took them."

His wife twirled to face him, an apple in one hand and a knife in the other.

Laurent dipped his head apologetically. "I pawned them," he confessed.

"You pawned *my* pearls—the pearls I inherited from my grandmother?"

"I promise I will get the necklace back."

"You had no right," Françoise said, tears threatening.

"Calm down," he whispered, nodding toward the pantry, where Blanche and the scullery girl were working. "Someone needed the money."

"*We* need the money, Laurent."

"I am sorry—" Laurent's apology was interrupted by a banging on the kitchen door.

"Why must the ploughman always pound like that?"

"I'll get it, Françoise."

"Master, it's that White," the ploughman said, his breath misting in the cold fall air. "He's kicked out two of the stall boards."

"Is he contained?"

"Yes, but—"

"I'll be right there."

"That horse has to go, Laurent," Françoise said as her husband closed the door against the chill. "Sell him at the market."

"Getting the horse there is the problem," Laurent said, reaching for his coat.

"Then it's time to consider the obvious." Françoise deftly peeled an apple, its skin hanging down in one long curl. "I don't know why you object to feeding horseflesh to the help. It's good nourishment, and—"

"I will not do so, and that is the end of it."

Petite appeared at the door with a basket of eggs. "Are you talking about Hongre?"

"You are not to interrupt your elders, Mademoiselle," Françoise said, dividing the apple in half and cutting out the core. "And no, we're not talking about Hongre—although you should get rid of him as well while you're at it, Laurent. That old horse does nothing but eat."

"Not just yet, Françoise," Laurent said with a sigh.

"You were talking about Diablo." Petite set the egg basket down roughly.

"Careful, now." Françoise frowned to see two eggs cracked.

"Little one, your mother is right. She is only being practical."

"But not Diablo, Father!"

Laurent pulled his hat down over his ears. "We leave for Amboise tomorrow. When I return, it will have to be done."

Caw! A CARRION CROW called out in warning.

Petite, bundled in homespun wool, looked up. Three blue-black crows perched on the branches of an elm below a mass of stick-and-mud nests.

Caw! Caw!

Petite turned to watch as her father checked the harness of the four-wheeled open carriage. "When will you be back?" she asked, reaching to stroke the neck of her father's old horse. Hongre was sleeping in the bright morning sun, his reins looped through the spokes of a wheel. The covered donkey cart was ready to go, loaded with trunks and bedding.

"That depends." Laurent pulled the leather strap two holes tighter and tugged on it to make sure it was secure.

Petite looked into her father's pale eyes. "I don't want you to kill Diablo, Father."

"A horse must be of use."

"He can be tamed. I've been praying for him."

"He is dangerous. I do not want you fooling with him—understand? I forbid it." He bent down. "You are *not* to go near him. Now, get back inside. You'll catch your death out here."

Petite ran to the manor steps and crouched there, hugging her knees. The cobbles of the courtyard were strewn with bright autumn leaves. Through the bare tree branches, she could glimpse the river, edged with moss and ferns.

The big front door opened, letting out a waft of warm vanilla-scented air. "*There* you are," Françoise said with a scolding tone. She was wearing whalebone hip-hoops under her cloak and gown, so she had to turn sideways to get through the door. The tutor was behind her, followed by Jean, uncomfortably done up in his church clothes, a worn yellow velvet doublet and knee breeches that were somewhat too small for him now.

"I'm not cold, Mother," Petite said, her teeth chattering. She scooted over, to make room for them to pass.

"Jean, come here," Laurent called out, placing the whip in its socket.

Jean pushed past, and the tutor helped Françoise down the steps, her boned skirts lifting and settling with each step. She turned at the bottom.

"You be good, Louise," she said, pointing her spotted rabbit muff at her daughter. "No mischief. No climbing trees. No horsing around."

Caw! Caw! The carrion crows took flight.

Chapter Three

IT WAS QUIET after everyone had left. Blanche set a whitepot for Petite on the yellow painted table in the kitchen. Petite prayed as she spooned the silky custard: *O Lord, I am in need of guidance.* She closed her eyes and waited for a sign.

"Have you finished with your father's books?" Blanche asked, taking away the wooden bowl.

That book on horses. *Of course.* "I'll finish now," Petite said, jumping up.

Her father's study was dark. Petite groped her way to the window and fumbled to open the shutters. Sunlight illuminated the statue of the Virgin weighting down the papers piled at one end of her father's desk.

The Horseman was where she'd last seen it, tucked between *The Family-Physician* and *The Art of Horsemanship* on the shelf closest to the window. Petite made the sign of the cross and reached for it.

Although thick, the book was not heavy. Petite pulled a cane chair to the window for light and eased herself up onto the seat. She opened the book on her lap, turning the pages until she came to the one titled "Of the Bone Magic." Most of it she could read—enough, in any case, to understand how the enchantment was done. *Kill a toad or frog . . . Set it on a whitethorn bush . . . At the full moon . . .*

Beware.

She felt daunted—as well as uneasy. Was enchantment not the Devil's work? She recalled the cautions she'd been given, the snippets of conversations overheard, and she thought to put the book away. The fires of Hell burned darkly. *Have nothing to do with it*, the Moor had said.

But what of Diablo? How was she to save him? She'd lured him with grain, with bits of bread and apple. She'd prayed to Jesus, Mother Mary and every saint she could think of—and still Diablo lunged, struck out. Bone magic was the only thing that could turn him, the Moor had said. How could gentling a horse be a sin?

The next morning, after her needlework (embroidering a sampler of the three virtues: chastity, humility, piety), after her barn and kitchen chores, after standing in her ritual way in front of Diablo's stall, Petite headed down the narrow footpath to the river. The fog had cleared, but the day was overcast and unseasonably mild, threatening rain. The water's surface was silvery gray. A fisherman dozed in his plank boat on the far side of the bridge, his long line tangled in cattails.

Petite headed upstream to a spot around the bend where trees overhung the river, the place where her brother often set his nets. At the gnarled oak, she tucked her skirt up under her apron sash and made her way through the damp bushes. Close to the water's edge, she slipped off her sabots and stockings. The cold guck oozed up between her toes.

It was slippery. She'd been warned to stay away from the river, told stories of the Lady in White, the ghost of the brokenhearted woman from Vaujours who had drowned herself in sorrow. The Lady's woeful spirit lured girls into ponds and rivers, into a watery grave. A girl had died that very winter on the feast day of Saint Catherine, patron saint of spinsters. Petite's neighbor Charlotte had even seen the Lady in White near a cow pond, heard her sing out—a sound like an owl, she said. Charlotte had run, feeling ghostly fingers at her heels—"like tiger-beetle bites," she said.

Petite tucked her stockings into her sabots. According to the book, the first thing she had to do was kill a frog or toad. She was not squeamish about killing—she'd trapped chipmunks and mice for the animals in her care, had hunted deer, rabbit, otter and even cat with her father and brother—but this was different, this wasn't to eat.

She crouched in the weeds, praying. As if in answer, she spotted two toads, one close by on a clump of moss, another sunning itself on a rock. If she reached for the one close by—

It leapt into the water.

Patience, she reminded herself. She waited motionless and then slowly reached for the sleepy toad on the rock.

She had it! It struggled, but she held tight. She stifled a scream, repulsed by its slippery skin, its sluggish squirming movements, surprisingly strong. With a foot pinning one of the toad's legs firmly, she grabbed for a rock and brought it down. The toad squirmed violently to get free. She closed her eyes and struck, making solid contact. The toad twitched, then stilled. Shaking, she opened her eyes. Its skull had opened, oozed. One leg kicked out, and she jumped back. She retched into the reeds, tears streaming.

It took a few moments for the toad to stop moving. Petite waited to be sure. She picked it up by one leg, but dropped it when it kicked. She poked it with a stick. It was dead, surely. Again, she reached for it, using the hem of her smock this time so that she wouldn't have to feel its skin.

She headed back to the house. The toad's body had to be left on a bush overnight—a whitethorn bush, the book said. There was one by the henhouse.

The scullery girl was at the henhouse door when Petite entered through the back gate. Petite wrapped her apron around the toad's body to hide it.

"Blanche has been looking for you everywhere," the girl said, hens pecking at her feet.

"My brother asked me to take in his nets," Petite lied, tucking the toad deep into the branches of the whitethorn bush as soon as the maid wasn't looking.

In the morning, at dawn, she would bury the toad under an anthill. Then it would be a matter of waiting until the noontide moon was round and full.

The days—the nights—passed slowly. Often, in the dark, Petite slipped out of her bed to gaze at the moon from her attic window, as if watching would hurry it along. New moon, crescent moon, quarter moon, gibbous moon: the time drew near.

Finally, one night at sunset, Petite saw the full moon rise over the far hills. Later she said her prayers and lay in bed waiting for the scullery girl to fall asleep, for the house to still.

After what seemed an eternity of silence, she opened her bed curtains. She tiptoed to the window and opened the shutters. The moon was penny full, illuminating the landscape in a ghostly light. She reached for her sabots and felt cloak, and stole down the stairs.

The silhouetted trees stood like sentinels around the barnyard. Petite breathed in the night air, stilling her heart against the night phantoms. Three fence posts past the gate and two giant strides to the right brought her to the anthill. She dug down with her fingers until she found the toad, bones now. She was relieved: the ants had done their work. Shaking off a few clinging insects, she lifted the little skeleton and brushed off the dirt. She felt breath on her neck, heard a branch snap behind her. Trembling, she stopped herself from looking over her shoulder, remembering what the book had said about not taking her eyes off the skeleton, not even once.

It wasn't easy getting down to the river in this way, her eyes fixed on the little bones. She stumbled two times, once falling to her knees. The plaintive hoot of an owl chilled her—the call of the Lady in White!—but even so she did not avert her eyes.

At the river's edge, holding onto alder branches with one hand, she slipped the skeleton into the water. It floated downstream and disappeared. She crouched, praying, watching for it to float back toward her, against the current, but she could see nothing. The surface of the black water shimmered in the moonlight.

O God, Creator, all life is in Your hands, she prayed in despair. She knew Diablo's fate: his throat would be cut, or a pistol held to his head. She had seen it done before, watched her father's slow, determined moves, his clenched jaw, his reverent moment of silence after, his hand on the animal as he waited for it to still, for the bright pulsing blood to slow.

Did animals have souls? Would Diablo go to Heaven? *The purpose of living was to prepare to die*, her father had taught her, to escape Hell fire and to have a joyful death. Petite didn't want Diablo to die. She was wiping the tears from her eyes with the back of one hand when she saw a white speck at the water's edge, something stuck between rocks. "I thank You," she whispered, for it was a bit of bone—the crotch bone, just as the book had said.

"I heard at the market that the Queen Mother is sick as a dog in Amboise," the scullery girl said as she stoked the oven fire.

"So maybe Father will have to stay longer," Petite said, eyeing the oven door. She had tucked the bone in behind the cast-iron stew pot to bake, but now she had to get it out without the two maids noticing.

"You talk as if you don't want your family to come back," Blanche said, pinching Petite's cheek. "Don't think I don't see you sneaking around."

"It's that White," the scullery girl said, taking a sip of Petite's warm beer before putting it down on the table in front of her.

"That horse makes me quake for fear," Blanche said. "He's possessed."

"The ploughman says Master's going to cut the beast's throat when he gets back." The scullery girl wiped her mouth with the back of her hand. "He said the girl's been putting holy trinkets all around its stall."

"What are you up to?" Blanche grabbed Petite by the arm.

"Nothing," Petite said. *I will wait them out*, she thought.

Not long after, as Blanche and the scullery girl chatted at the door with a man selling tooth powders, ribbons and other household notions, Petite got her chance to retrieve the bone from the hot oven. How was she to know whether it had baked through? She sniffed it. It had no odor, but she decided to bake it again the next day, just to be sure.

The next morning proved to be more difficult. After the bread dough was put in the oven to bake, the maid and scullery girl busied themselves preparing chickens to be smoked for the winter. The big canning pot was steaming in the stone fireplace for scalding the birds. One basin was filling with feathers, another with innards, and a big vat by the door held the feet. The musky smell of feather dander filled the room.

Petite stayed out of the fray, picking over a barrel of crab apples in one corner and tossing the rotten ones into the pig pail, watching for her chance. She'd hidden the bone behind the jar of dried rosemary on the shelf beside the cookstove. She had to get it into the oven somehow. Finally Blanche ducked out the back door to answer nature's call, leaving only the scullery girl in the kitchen.

Petite picked up the runt they had kept from the hound dog's litter and pressed him to her face, growling with him playfully. "Oh! He nipped me," she exclaimed, dropping the puppy in the basin of feathers.

"What are you doing?" The scullery girl waved the flying feathers away with bloody hands. "What a mess."

As the girl lunged to catch the pup, Petite retrieved the bone from behind the jar. "Oh, how I love to see bread baking," she said, opening the great oven door and pushing the bone in behind the pans. "*Nec cesso, nec erro*," she whispered in Latin for good measure: I do not slacken, I do not lose my way.

As BLANCHE AND THE SCULLERY GIRL were hanging chickens in the smoker, Petite snuck back into the kitchen to retrieve the bone. She was alarmed to see three bread loaves lined up on the sill to cool. She opened the door to the oven. It was warm still . . . and empty.

Where was the bone? Petite pulled out a rack and felt along the greasy edges of the pan floor.

"Get out of there." Blanche's voice boomed behind her.

Petite stood, her hands covered in soot.

"What in God's name were you doing?" Blanche frowned down at Petite with her one good eye.

"Blanche," the scullery girl yelled from the poultry yard.

Petite stared down at the floorboards. There it was: the bit of bone, caught between the cracks. She slipped her foot over it.

"Blanche! The goat's going after the hound!"

"Mon Dieu, if it's not one thing, it's another," the kitchen maid said, slamming the back door behind her.

Hiding in the dark pantry, Petite crushed the baked bone into powder using the marble mortar and stone her mother used to grind herbs. She mixed in a bit of oil and spooned the mix into a pin case, which she'd emptied three nights earlier. Then she tiptoed up to her attic room and put the case into the toe of one of her sabots. *Tomorrow,* she thought, pushing the wooden shoes under her bed.

PETITE WOKE AT COCK'S CROW and slipped down the narrow stairs, taking care not to wake Blanche, asleep on a pallet in the kitchen. She stood shivering on the back step for some time, listening for spirits. Her breath caught at the sound of flapping wings, and she saw a great bird rise from the woods. Her heart was pounding. She put the pin case between her teeth and, forming a cross with her fingers, made her way across the farmyard to the barn. She creaked open the door and stepped inside.

The barn was dark as pitch. She couldn't see Diablo, but she could hear his tail swishing against the boards. The acrid smell of urine stung her eyes. Moon glow filled the tiny window, and the stallion's head appeared, shining in the light.

Petite felt her way along the woodpile to the corner stall. She paused at the gate latch, her eyes adjusting to the dark. Perhaps she should climb over the rails. That way she would be out of reach of his hind quarters—but closer to his teeth.

No, there was no easy way, no way that was safe. She said a prayer as she opened the latch and slipped into the stall, ankle deep in manure. The horse pinned back his ears, watching her with a wary eye.

Petite pried the pin case open. "Ho, boy," she said faintly, rubbing the oil on her fingers. "Don't be afraid." She held out her trembling hand. "I can save you," she whispered, taking one cautious step forward. And then another.

Finally, she was at his shoulder. He was taller than she had imagined. "Ho, boy." She *knew* this horse. "Ho, my beautiful brave boy."

Slowly, so as not to startle him, she touched an oily finger to his nostril. "Ho, my pretty one," she said. She reached her finger into his mouth and felt his tongue. "*Beloved,*" she whispered, rubbing her oily hand over his chin, his chest.

He bent his head around to her. She pressed her face into his neck, inhaled his scent, joy coursing through her. The magic had worked. Diablo was hers now. She had tamed him—now he would bend to her will.

O God, I thank Thee. Although she knew it was not God she should thank, but the Devil.

PETITE WAS ON DIABLO'S BACK when the old ploughman appeared.

"Wha—!" he cried out, dropping his bucket of water. "*Que diable,*" he said, crossing himself.

Petite sat up and stretched. The horse nickered softly, bending his nose around to sniff her foot. She stroked his ears, then grabbed his mane and slid down his side, feeling for her sabots in the muck.

"Now we can clean out his stall," she told the ploughman, reaching up to stroke Diablo's nose. "He'll like being outside today," she said, combing out a snarl in his forelock with her fingers.

The kitchen bell rang. "Mademoiselle, how . . . ?" the old man sputtered, speechless.

"I told you he could be gentled."

"Blanche will be none too happy about the state of your cloak." He frowned at the stains on the hem.

"I have to go for my porridge now," Petite said, but addressing the horse. "Come—I'll put you outside." She opened the stall door and the White followed her out of the barn into the morning sunlight, his nose at her shoulder.

The ploughman jumped back as they passed.

"I'll put him in the front paddock," she said, "where Hongre usually goes."

"Mademoiselle, you dropped something." The ploughman held up a pin case.

"Thank you," Petite said, running back for it, her cheeks bright.

LATER, AFTER PORRIDGE and small beer, after lectures and scoldings, after chores, chores and more chores, Petite washed and groomed her horse, combing his mane and tail and dressing the scabs on his haunches with liniment. Only reluctantly did she return to the manor for a meal, slipping out yet again before candle-lighting to bid him a good night, blowing into his nose and inhaling his warm, fragrant breath.

That night, she fell into a deep sleep, the pin case tucked under her pillow.

The sound of growling woke her—it was not as a dog growled, but deeper, and almost with pleasure. She sat up. Something was in her room.

"Mademoiselle?" she called out to the scullery girl, but there was no answer.

The growl had come from the foot of her bed. Petite called out again, but still there was no sound from the maid's bed under the eaves. She'd snuck out, likely, and now Petite was alone. Something swooshed by her head. Trembling, she groped for the wooden cross above her bed. She cowered under the covers, staring into the dark, clutching the cross to her.

In the morning, Petite woke, weakened by the faint memory of a dream of a winged creature with talons of iron. A demon had got into her head.

Before gathering eggs, Petite buried the pin case in the dirt of her stone hovel and covered it with rocks. *Saint Michel, protect me from evil spirits, I beg you. Amen.* And then she went to her horse.

Chapter Four

Laurent de la Vallière approached home on the back of old Hongre. Behind him, in the open carriage, sat his wife, his son and the boy's tutor.

It had been an eventful three weeks. The Queen Mother had arrived at Amboise in a burning fever and had had to be bled four times. The pain she suffered had been terrible to see. At one point she looked like one possessed, and her attendants had thought to bring in a priest to rid her of a demon. The Devil had been spotted in the shape of a goat in the village market the night before she arrived. Thanks be to Mary, Laurent had thought to bring a rabbit paw. He'd had the cobbles in front of the château threshold taken up and had buried the charm there. He thrilled at the thought that he may have saved the Queen Mother's life.

His wife's thoughts were not so kindly. Laurent had endured one of Françoise's tongue-lashings the night before. It had been unfortunate, true, that she had not been presented to Her Majesty—but how could it have been otherwise? The Queen Mother was suffering fits and fevers! As for their son, Jean, it was understandable that the King and his brother would be kept apart, not permitted to mix with the local gentry. Laurent himself had laid eyes on His Majesty only a few times. It was attested that the King, although yet a boy, had cured hundreds of people of the Evil, the disfiguring neck growths melting away at his touch. (What a thing that would be to see!)

And then Françoise had started in about money. True, he had spent quite a sum on the royal welcome—hiring musicians and having banners and caparisons made up—but it was a privilege to serve, an honor. This his wife would never understand: it was not in her blood. "If any money's to be spent, it's to get back my pearls," she'd told him, demanding that he petition the Queen Mother for favor. He *had* saved the Queen Mother's life and deserved some sort of recognition—but simply serving was reward aplenty, was it not?

Laurent had been awed to see the Queen Mother's famously fine hands clasped in prayer as she lay stretched out on a bed, propped up against tasseled silk pillows. Although aged now, and somewhat large, it was easy to see that she had once been a beauty. He had been asked to obtain finely woven covering-sheets for her. Another expense, Françoise had complained. But to think of it: the Queen Mother had slept on cloth he had touched with his own hands.

Laurent patted his leather pouch where he kept his rosary. He had put it with the coin the Queen Mother had given him. The gold louis had slipped from her hand, rolled across the floor, and the young King himself had scooped it up. The Queen Mother—saintly woman—had asked her son to give the coin "to this kind man here." The King's hand had brushed his own.

"Only one lousy louis? Is that all she gave you?" Françoise had wept. "You spent a hundred! We could have used that money to repair our leaking roof, or replace the broken window in the sitting room, or mend the chimney so we could burn a fire without being smoked out, or . . ."

Or buy back his wife's pearls. Laurent pressed old Hongre forward over the bridge with a touch of his spurs. Françoise was young and ever so pretty. He wished he could make her happy. Ever since the loss of the baby, her humors had been out of balance.

"Papa?" he heard his son call out as they approached the gates to the family manor.

Laurent looked back to see Françoise standing up in the carriage, holding onto Jean's shoulder for support. "Laurent, do something!" She pointed at the manor and burst into tears.

Laurent turned, and gasped, for there, at the entrance to their courtyard, was his daughter—riding the White.

He crossed himself. *Mon Dieu.* What a glorious sight! It *was* the White, surely, yet this horse was combed and groomed, his mane plaited with mismatched ribbons, his haunches draped with one of Françoise's old comforters, like a royal caparison. The steed lifted his hooves neatly, stepping lightly.

"Yes, Father—it's Diablo," his daughter called out, grinning proudly. She was riding astride without a saddle, her skirts bunched around her thighs. She looked like a pixie atop such a large animal—such a large *beast.*

"Laurent, that horse will kill her," he heard his wife cry out behind him.

"*Get off!*" he bellowed, finding his voice.

"Isn't he beautiful?"

"Fie!" he cried, panic filling him.

"But he's gentle now," his daughter said, holding the reins loosely. The White's head bent submissively, one ear pricked back.

"Get *off*, I say," Laurent commanded, a sudden pain piercing his heart.

"Father?" Petite called out as he toppled. "Father!"

PETITE WATCHED IN CONFUSION as her father slumped and slowly slid off his horse, his foot caught in one stirrup. She jumped from Diablo and ran to him. Her father was pale and clutching his chest.

"I will be fine, little one," he said slowly.

Petite wiped the beads of perspiration from his forehead with her hand.

Jean appeared. "Papa?" He let his father's boot out of the stirrup and took up Hongre's reins.

"Laurent!" Françoise cried out.

Petite looked up to see her mother running with her hoops lifted.

"That horse," her father gasped, struggling to sit.

Petite felt a warm breath at her shoulder: Diablo. "Ho, boy," she said, touching his nose. "Back," she commanded, holding up one hand. The White took five steps back, and stood.

Her father crossed himself, his eyes on the stallion.

"Laurent, you are not to die," Françoise said, panting from her run. She knelt beside her fallen husband, her face powder streaked.

Die? Petite closed her eyes, praying silently.

IN THE DARK DAYS that followed, Laurent slowly recovered. "I told you not to go near that horse," he reprimanded Petite from his bed.

"Forgive me, Father," Petite said as she stoked the fire in the massive stone fireplace. She stood, tracing with her fingers the words etched into the mantel: *Ad principem ut ad ignem amor indissolubilis.* For the King, love like an altar fire, eternal.

"Little one?"

Petite turned.

"Come here." He patted the bed.

Petite climbed up and sat beside her father, chewing on the end of one of her braids. An image of the Virgin had been propped on the candle stand next to the bed. Beside it was the stoppered bottle her mother had made of Laurent's water, a fingernail and a lock of his hair together with two nails and two rosebush thorns. It would vanquish the evil spirit that had tried to kill her father, she'd told Petite—but Petite feared that she herself was that evil spirit and had twice uncorked the bottle while her father slept.

"Tell me how it came about," he said, taking the braid out of her mouth. "With the White."

Petite shrugged one shoulder and grinned. (She knew she could charm him.) "I prayed, and it just happened," she said. It was a partial truth, but mostly a lie.

"Praise be," Laurent said. "But promise me this: don't ride him, not until I'm well enough to coach you."

THREE DAYS LATER, Laurent came slowly down the winding stairs, holding onto his wife for support. Jean, Petite, the tutor and the household servants all cheered as he emerged into the sitting room.

"Behold," Laurent said, like one risen from the dead. He lifted his nightcap as if it were a hat. He hadn't been shaven and looked like a ruffian.

Petite was filled with delight. Soon she could ride Diablo again.

IN THE CONFINES OF THE PADDOCK, Petite rode Diablo as her father watched. Proudly, she took the stallion through the walk, trot and canter. He went smoothly, without overreaching or striking one foot upon another.

"A horse for a prince," Laurent said, shaking his head.

My horse, Petite thought, for the stallion would not allow anyone but her near.

Thereafter, weather and her father's health permitting, Petite schooled Diablo every afternoon. He was not so much skittish as eager, and she learned to focus his restiveness, teaching him to tread in large rings, to stop, retire and advance. Much to her father's amazement, he learned to perform a capriole and could even bound aloft on all four (which Petite loved best). After each lesson, she rubbed his neck with a light, soft hand, stroking as the hair lay.

By mid-April, when the grass was green and full of sun, Diablo was put into the back pasture, his provender supplemented with baked loaves of peas and meal. There, following her father's instructions, Petite accustomed him to rough ground for an hour or two a day—first at a foot pace, and then at a trot, and finally at a swift trot mingled with a few strokes of gallop. Then, and only then, did Laurent deem the stallion ready to ride into a newly ploughed field, thereby teaching him to take his feet up roundly and set them down surely, never to stumble.

"But he is not to go hoodwinked," Laurent explained to Petite one day, lying abed with a hot wrapped brick on his chest. "That's what Monsieur Bosse and some of our neighbors do, I know, but depriving a colt of sight takes away his delight and stirs up an excess of fear."

"Yes, Father," Petite said, eager to get Diablo beyond the pasture. She longed to see how fast he could go.

"Enough of this horse-talk, Laurent," Françoise said, coming into the room with a basket of needlework. "Louise is almost seven now. It's time our daughter started acting like a girl." She handed Petite her unfinished sampler.

Chastity, humility, piety: Petite groaned.

PETITE SANG AS SHE CLIMBED the narrow path to the back field where Diablo grazed. The spring woods were sprinkled with lily of the valley, periwinkle, and, in amongst the holly, a blue orchid she called "wishes." She noted the narrow rabbit tracks running toward rock outcroppings and hoof-marks where deer had jumped the path. The melodic chirps of spring birdsong intermingled with the staccato tap of a woodpecker and the raucous calls of the jays.

As Petite emerged from the woods, Diablo whinnied. She climbed over the fence and stood as he cantered to meet her. She made a motion with her hand and—slowly, ponderously—he knelt before her. She pressed her face into his neck, stroked his velvety nose. Then she slipped onto his back and commanded him to stand, her bare legs hugging his sides. She sat for a moment, enjoying the vista, the gentle rolling hills, the river, the woods. She felt like the goddess Diana, fearless and strong.

It hadn't taken her long to learn that she only had to think *slow* and Diablo would slow, think *canter* and he would canter, think *gallop* and he would race like a courser. It hadn't taken her long to discover that she had no need of a bit, much less a bridle, that he responded fully to the slightest pressure from her legs. At her command he would jump any log, bush or gully. He trusted her. Today they would leave the confines of the pasture, go up the hill and into the woods.

She put him through his paces and then nudged him into a canter, steering him towards a low point in the fence. "Yep, yep!" she said, grabbing a fistful of mane as he surged over the fence and up the trail. The wind brought tears to her eyes. They were flying! At the crest of the hill, Diablo slowed, then stopped. Petite fell forward onto his neck, weak with the thrill of it.

A rustle made the horse startle, and Petite looked back. It was the runt, scrambling up the forest trail, panting and wagging its tail. Petite groaned: she would have to lead it back home. She turned Diablo around, toward a path that came out behind the barn.

Diablo's pace relaxed into an amble. As they headed back, she sang "Ave Maria," letting her feet swing with his steps. The puppy followed, staying out from underfoot as Diablo picked his way through brambles and then through a mud sink, a boar wallow Petite hadn't seen before. The boar must be of good size, she guessed—it had rubbed mud onto tree trunks fairly high up. She noted the location: about five strides northeast of a sweet chestnut tree felled for shingles. Her father would want to know. He and three companions, gentry of the neighborhood, went boar hunting on Michaelmas, when wild pigs were high in flesh.

"Pup," she called out, looking behind. The shadows were lengthening, and she knew not to be around a boar bog late in the day.

Diablo's ears swiveled. Petite turned the horse and trotted back. At the bend, she spotted the puppy, snarling and growling. Suddenly, a boar charged out of the bushes. It caught the pup with a cheek tooth and tossed it into the air, splattering blood onto the leaves. Diablo planted his feet, and Petite tumbled over his head.

Petite tried to rise, but her left leg collapsed under her. The boar lowered its head, its little pig eyes on her, one of its tusks bright with blood. Petite pressed her face into the dirt. It would kill her.

She felt the earth shake and heard thudding, and she looked up. Diablo was facing the boar, rearing and striking. With each blow, the boar grunted and staggered back. Then Diablo twirled and kicked out, catching the beast square in the head.

Even the birds were silent. Diablo ambled up to the boar's body, sniffed it, then turned back to Petite. She signalled him to kneel and, almost swooning from pain, she draped herself over his back. He headed slowly down the path, toward home.

IN THE LONG WEEKS that followed, Petite didn't know what was worse: her mother's fretful tongue-lashing or the painful ministrations of the town surgeon, who first braced her broken ankle to make it straight and then bled her from the foot. For over two weeks she lay on the daybed in the sitting room, her injured leg encased in splints and propped up on pillows. The days were long. Were it not for her father's tutoring (he had decided to teach her to read Latin), she would have been unspeakably bored.

And then, for over a month, she endured hobbling about the house on crutches, her leg strapped to boards. At long last, the splints came off. Leaning on a hickory crutch, she eased her weight onto both legs. She felt lopsided.

"Like the village idiot," Jean taunted.

"Son," Laurent said in his warning voice.

Françoise burst into tears.

Petite turned to face her mother. If only she could calm her as easily as she could calm a horse. The horrid brace was finally off and she was standing, at least. She took two careful steps.

"Why couldn't that surgeon have set it right, Laurent?" Françoise said. "We paid him good money."

"She will be fine, Françoise."

"But her left leg is *short*: she'll walk with a limp."

"She just needs a little practice. How does it feel, little one?" Laurent asked.

"It doesn't hurt," Petite lied. "May I ride Diablo now?"

"You're never to get on that horse again," Françoise said.

Laurent objected. "The White saved our daughter's life."

"I begin to think you're both bewitched," Françoise said, stirring the fire with tongs. "Nothing would have happened if she'd been at her needlework."

"Françoise, calm—"

Françoise banged the tongs onto the stone hearth. "Don't you be saying calm to me, Laurent. Nothing has gone right since you brought that horse home. First, you and your pains, and now our daughter with a limp. That horse brought a curse down on our house, and you know it."

PETITE WAS AT her embroidery frame in the sitting room when she heard a knock at the door. She was supposed to have been reciting the ten commandments as she worked *(no false gods, no misuse of God's name, honor the Sabbath, honor my father and mother, no murder, no adultery, no theft . . .)*, but instead she'd been dreaming of Diablo, imagining racing him at the village fair next week and winning the prize. She would give the money to her mother, and her mother would praise Diablo (as well as her).

The knocking kept up, insistent.

"I'll get it, Mother," Petite called out, looking for her crutch. It was a special day, the fifth of September, and she thought the knocking might have something to do with that. Today, the King turned thirteen. It was the day of his majority, her father had explained that morning before prayers: on this day the Queen Mother would kneel down before her son and kiss his hand. Even in their faraway village, celebrations were being planned.

"What a racket." Françoise came down the spiral stairs and reached the door first. It was the old ploughman, clutching the rim of his torn felt hat. "You need not pound the door," she said. "And you're to come to the back."

"Madame, I did, but nobody answered, so I came round to the front. It's Monsieur de la Vallière, he's in the barn, he's"—the old man hid his eyes in the crook of his arm—"dead."

Françoise stood motionless. "That's not so," she said with anger.

"I found him there just now—dead as a stone."

Petite overturned the embroidery frame in her bolt for the barn. She hobbled across the farmyard on her crutch. *May it not be true, may it not be true . . . Please, God, may it not be true.*

The barn door was agape. Petite stopped for a moment to catch her breath. The wind rustled in the trees. Three hens strutted close by, clucking, one eye to the sky. She thought she heard that low growl again and twirled, her heart racing. The shadow of a hawk skimmed the muddy yard.

She stepped through the barn door.

Her father was curled on the floor in his barn clothes, her brother kneeling beside him. Jean looked up, his eyes stricken.

"He won't talk," he said, his voice strangled. He sat back against a wall. "I think he's dead."

Petite steeled herself and looked at her father's face. His eyes were half open, staring at Jean as if in surprise. His mouth was open too, but in a grimace of pain. She saw something dark on his lips. *Blood.*

"And that horse of yours is gone," Jean said.

The gate to Diablo's stall hung open. Petite looked back down at her father. *Was* he dead? She opened her mouth, but all that emerged was a choking sound.

PETITE HID IN the dovecote, crouching in the dark. The doves' cooing paused, then started up again, a humming pulse. Her father was dead and Diablo had disappeared, and she knew she was somehow to blame. She wanted to cry, but could not. Her heart had turned to stone.

"Come on out now, Mademoiselle," she heard a man say. It was the old ploughman, standing in the sunlight. He brushed away a cobweb and stepped inside.

"They've laid your father out in the house. He looks at peace," he said. He took a deep, shaky breath. "Your brother's gone to town for Curé Barouche. I thought you'd want to be there when he comes, to say the prayers and all."

Petite opened her mouth, but no sound came out. She felt as if she were retching air, as if she might choke.

"Are you all right, child?" the ploughman asked, stepping in, looking down at her with puzzlement.

Petite made fluttering finger motions in front of her lips. What was wrong with her? She opened and closed her mouth like a dying fish.

"Can't you talk?" he asked, laying his hand gently on her shoulder.

Petite covered her face with her hands. Even her cries were silent.

Chapter Five

SHORTLY AFTER THE FUNERAL, Françoise sent her son off to school in Paris. As the orphan of a cavalry officer who had been wounded at the Battle of Rocroi, he qualified for a scholarship to the Collège de Navarre. "Your father's death got you in, but the rest will be up to you," she instructed her son, closing his worn leather valise. "The highest nobility send their sons to the Collège de Navarre. Do what you can to befriend them."

She carried his valise out to the courtyard herself. He was being sent off on old Hongre. She had made a futile search for the White, hoping to trade the cursed beast for a roadworthy pony; now Hongre would have to do. It was a long trip, but the boy was light to carry. He and the tutor, ignobly mounted on the donkey, would take it in easy stages. At the end of the journey, the old horse would be sold for meat; she could not afford his keep.

Jean grabbed on to the Hungarian's thick mane and climbed up into the saddle. "Aren't you even going to say farewell?" He made a monkey face at his sister.

Petite put her hand on Hongre's nose and stepped back.

"What's wrong with her? Why doesn't she talk?" Jean asked.

"It's just an ague," Françoise said, taking her daughter's cold hand. "Don't worry about us. We'll manage."

She waved until she could see her son no more, then turned back to the house with Petite. She was not, in fact, the least bit confident that she could manage. Her daughter's silence unnerved her. The curé suggested that the girl might be under some curse and had offered to perform a ritual to exorcise the demon, but exorcisms were costly—well beyond Françoise's means, especially now. She was furious at Laurent: for dying, for one thing, but mostly for leaving her impoverished. She'd brought sixty thousand Tournais livres into her marriage—a small fortune—but now, she'd been informed, there was a debt of thirty-four thousand. The reckoning was not difficult: her husband had robbed her.

Scores had spoken at his funeral. The little church in the village had been mobbed. He was a saint, everyone said, always helping the poor in need. He'd given the servants money freely. He'd given hundreds to his sister's convent in Tours, lent money to his hapless brother, Father Gilles. He'd helped found a hospital, a school for the blind, a bakery to serve the starving. He'd even given money to their neighbors!

Well, they could keep their pious condolences. That was *her* money he'd been giving away, and she wanted it back. If Laurent weren't already dead, she would kill him.

"There will be men coming here today, Louise," Françoise told her silent daughter, who had settled into a chair by a window with a book, the hound curled at her feet. "A notary and master-broker, coming to make an inventory." Coming to assign value to every threadbare curtain and chipped plate.

"I have to consider our future," she went on, examining her mourning weeds in a cracked looking-glass. She detested the little black cap widows were required to wear. Perhaps a ribbon around the rim—a peach silk? But no, the oh-so-pious neighbors would talk, the neighbors who held themselves to be virtuous, the ones who had borrowed from Laurent and never paid him back. The neighbor who had had two bastard children by Agathe Balin. The neighbor who had new brocade curtains, no doubt purchased with Laurent's money—*her* money. Fie on them all!

How was she to manage? Perhaps she should make a trip to the château at Blois. The Duke d'Orléans, the King's uncle, was back in residence there now. He might be interested in buying Laurent's musty books. "Especially *your* future," she said, turning to her daughter.

Petite looked up with a puzzled look.

In truth, Françoise worried herself sick over the girl. With no dowry, a gimpy leg and now mute; what man would have her? "You must begin school as well," she said, busying herself with the fire. She would have to get out into the world to find a new husband. She couldn't afford to be tied down, and it would be better for the girl, in any case. "I've arranged for you to board at the Ursuline convent in Tours." Laurent's sister Angélique was superintendent of novices there, and his brother Gilles the resident priest. Françoise expected to be able to negotiate a greatly reduced rate (considering all the money Laurent had donated to the place). "You are seven now, the age of discretion. They will teach you comportment." Turn her horse-crazy tomboy of a daughter into a proper young lady.

PETITE AND HER MOTHER, and the ploughman as driver, traveled to the Ursuline convent in Tours in the open carriage, following the rutted road south to the river. Petite sat silently beside her mother, staring out at the barren fields. Whenever she saw horses, she looked for the proud White: where could he have gone? She would never ride again, she knew.

The bridge over the river was rickety; the cart horse balked and Petite had to lead her across. Once over, Petite climbed back into the carriage and they wended their way through the busy, narrow streets of the city.

Two years had passed since Petite had been to the convent. She had come with her father and Jean. The flower-filled parlor had been crowded. She remembered her jolly uncle Gilles, priest to the convent, telling jokes as her aunt Angélique, a nun there, served comfits and fruit drinks. They had sung hymns together and laughed at Father Gilles's stories. Petite had been much fussed-over—she sang like an angel, they had exclaimed. "Just like your father."

It seems strange to be here without him, Petite thought as the convent gates opened onto the tranquil gardens. Footpaths led to a number of outbuildings she knew well: the apothecary, the infirmary, the butchery, wine cellar, bake house and laundry. At the eastern end was the sacristy, and to the south an orchard, a kitchen garden, a fishpond, a barn and a poultry yard. A world unto itself, her father had described it, "a bit of Heaven." She wondered if he was in Heaven now.

The ploughman deposited Petite's trunk outside the door of the main building. "Well, then," he said, shifting his weight. "I'd best guard the wagon." He cleared his throat. "You look after yourself, Mademoiselle." He touched his mitt to the rim of his cap.

Petite watched as he shuffled away. Sometimes she felt so full of words, she thought she might burst.

While her mother spoke with the Prioress in the convent office, Petite sat on the trunk watching the comings and goings. Nuns shuffled along in silence with their eyes lowered, or whispered quietly together, their hands tucked into their voluminous sleeves. One nun sat reading to a group of schoolchildren—now and then they all laughed. From somewhere came the sweet scent of fruit being boiled down for jam. She heard a lute being played, and a woman singing a madrigal.

Her mother emerged from the convent office, slamming the door behind her with an echoing whack. "Your aunt's waiting for us in the parlor."

The convent parlor was like a large sitting room, with wooden chairs and stools set against the walls. Two side tables held vases of flowers and dishes of comfits. Along one wall was an open grille, behind which Sister Angélique was sitting, tatting lace. Petite's aunt put her needlework aside and stood. She stooped down to unlatch the little door to one side of the grille.

"Welcome," she said.

"There you go, now," Françoise said, her hand on Petite's back.

Petite turned to look up at her mother.

"Angélique will look after you now." Françoise blinked. She tucked a wayward curl back under Petite's cap.

"You are doing the right thing, Françoise," Sister Angélique said. Her voice was low, melodic, reminding Petite of her father's. "How old are you?" she asked Petite, inviting her within. "Six?"

Petite put up seven fingers. Her aunt smelled of roses.

"She stopped talking," Françoise said, fastening the bone button of her cape at her neck. "The doctor said she lacks phlegm, that she should have more wine and water. Ale, as well."

Petite reached back to touch her mother's hand.

"Be good," Françoise told her, squeezing Petite's fingers, her voice suddenly husky. Then she turned abruptly and was gone.

"Well, now," Sister Angélique said, closing and bolting the door. "I could show you your chamber, but perhaps you would rather eat first."

Petite peered into her aunt's thin face, encircled by a starched white wimple. Sister Angélique looked a lot like her father: the same pointed chin and high cheekbones, that same gentle regard, the same smile lines at the corners of her blue eyes.

"Our cook makes wonderful little cakes."

Petite shrugged: she wasn't hungry. She followed her aunt into another chamber, and then another, trying not to limp. The Devil had been lamed by his fall from Heaven. She'd had her fall too.

"We have two horses in the barn here, one just a baby," Sister Angélique said as they entered a wide passageway. "Perhaps we could go visit them later. Your father always used to tell stories about you and the horses, how it was as if you were one of them."

Petite shook her head emphatically.

Sister Angélique stopped, regarding Petite thoughtfully. "So it's true: you have stopped talking." She put her hand lightly on Petite's cap. "You have suffered a great loss. Perhaps the good Lord, in His wisdom, has led you to silence, His own holy language." Bells rang. "And now He calls us to chapel. Perhaps you can sing? 'Let all mortal flesh keep silence,'" Angélique sang softly. "You know it? I know you do. Singing is not at all like talking."

Petite opened her mouth, then closed it.

"That was a start," Petite's aunt said, smiling. She took Petite's hand and led her into a corridor. "Come, my little angel—we sing day and night here. You will join us, and sing in your heart."

IN THE MORNING, as a lay sister lit the fire and took out the chamber pot, Sister Angélique woke Petite. "Lord, thank you for the glorious beauty of another dawn," she prayed aloud. "Thank you for this precious little angel. Look over her this day. Amen." Then she laid out a clean shift, two flannel petticoats, a plain wool bodice and skirt, and helped Petite out of her night shift and cap. Petite didn't mind. Back home, the scullery girl had been the one to dress her and had handled her roughly.

Home. It seemed far away to Petite now. She thought of her mother there, with only the servants and the hound for company. She thought of the past. She couldn't bear to remember her father's body stretched out on the big table in the sitting room. She had stood by his side as prayers were read, holding her breath. The Devil hovered at such times in the hope of stealing a soul. His demons dwelt in the air; they swarmed like flies. Prayers were spoken and incense burned to keep the Devil and his demons away.

"Now we put away your nightclothes," her aunt Angélique instructed, opening Petite's wooden trunk.

Petite folded her shift as told, wondering if she *had* been the cause of her father's death. She had made a pact with the Devil, and now she was his. At night, in the dark of her attic room at home, the Devil had crouched under her bed or behind her trunk. He had no eyebrows and his eyes glowed. He had a smoky smell.

Has the Devil followed me here? Petite wondered as Sister Angélique cleaned her face with a white cloth dipped in wine, and then combed out her hair, winding her long curls into a bun. There had been strange noises in the night, and that faint scent of smoke. Her room faced north: the Devil's dark domain. It alarmed her to think the Evil One might be in the convent with her. For protection, she'd slept clutching a statue of the Blessed Mother that her aunt had given her. It was made of betony wood, which had power over evil spirits, she knew. A wounded stag would search for betony, eat it and be cured.

"There, now." Petite's aunt looked into her face. "Such a sweet and serious soul," she said with a smile.

Laced and coiffed, her bonnet strings tied, a kerchief around her neck, Petite followed her aunt to Mass in the convent chapel, performed with great ceremonial drama by her bumbling uncle Gilles, his breath misting in the winter air.

Like spirits rising, Petite thought. *Like demons.*

EACH MORNING AFTER Mass, after bread and beer in the rectory, Petite went to her studies—long, absorbing lessons in history, geography and modern languages. She was an eager student, reading whatever texts she was assigned and writing out answers in response to Sister Angélique's questions. As for numbers, they were easy to master. She astonished her aunt by correctly calculating how much eight yards of lace cost at 3s/4d a yard.

When the weather was good, Sister Angélique allowed her to take walks in the frozen gardens while she attended to the day students from town. Petite loved these moments of solitude. The squares of bare ground were pristine in the bright winter light. From a pavilion in the center, through tree branches glittering with hoarfrost, she could glimpse fields. Squinting into the sun, she searched for a White.

Had her father's soul ridden Diablo to Heaven? she wondered as she paced, scuffing up snow with each step. Or had the Devil taken him, ridden him backward into Hell?

There was a great deal to learn and that helped. There was the Angelus, the litanies of Our Lady, the *Pater* and *Ave* to memorize. There were prayers for getting up and for every hour of the day, prayers for keeping away evil spirits, for undressing at night and for going to sleep, prayers for her mother and brother, and—especially—ardent prayers for the soul of her father. It tormented her to think that he died suddenly, without Confession.

Did I kill him? A choking feeling rose in her.

Back at her study table, the wood fire blazing, she wrote out questions on slate with chalk-stone: *Is Heaven really up in the sky? What does the Holy Ghost look like? What is it like in Hell?*

Sister Angélique closed her eyes before answering: "Heaven is far above the clouds, the Holy Ghost speaks through dreams and Hell is a place without love." She opened her eyes and watched as Petite wrote out her next question, the letters round and even: *What does the Devil look like?*

"That is not an easy question," Sister Angélique said, stroking the cover of her gold-tooled missal. "It seems that he takes on many shapes and forms, whatever suits his purposes. He might be a woman, a man, a child even. Saint Paul warned that he might even appear as an angel of light. Indeed, it is possible for him not to have a form at all, but to manifest himself as a dream, or simply a thought."

Petite frowned. It had never occurred to her that the Devil might not be flesh. She'd had a disturbing dream the night before about trying to speak—trying to scream, in fact. Had that been the Devil's doing? Had *he* taken her voice?

"Some believe that the Devil looks and acts like a goat, but he is rarely so playful. His heart is full of jealous suspicion, and the best way to recognize him, if he is in human form, is to look into his eyes, which are cold, without love or scruple."

Petite wiped the slate clean and wrote, crumbling the end of the chalk-stone: *Could the Devil ride a horse away?*

Sister Angélique took the slateboard from Petite and examined the words her niece had written. "Did something happen to you, my little angel?" she asked finally, setting the stone slab down carefully, as if it were fragile.

Petite shook her head.

"Are you sure? You can trust me."

Petite nudged the slate toward her aunt, her eyes imploring.

"Well. . . ." Sister Angélique pressed the palms of her hands together. "You mean the way a witch will ride a night-mare?"

Petite nodded, tearing.

"Well, then, yes, I suppose he could. There's nothing the Devil can't do—but love, of course. He can't do that, even if he wants to."

FRANÇOISE DE LA VALLIÈRE promised her daughter that she would come to visit every year on the sixth of August, the anniversary of Petite's birth. And she did, in spite of considerable hardship. The first year, the year her daughter turned eight, it was humid and hot, so scorching that the horse could barely pull the wagon. The second year, the year Petite turned nine, Françoise arrived in spite of a violent thunderstorm. But the third year she didn't arrive until the early days of September—a full month late.

"I've been to Blois," Françoise explained, examining her daughter, who had grown but was still small for her age. "You're too thin. Are they feeding you?" she demanded, as Sister Angélique and the Prioress appeared behind the grille. "My daughter has been here three years," she informed the two nuns, "yet she's still not speaking." She intentionally made her tone accusing. If there was fault, it would best be theirs.

"We've had your daughter examined, as you know, Madame," the Prioress said. "The problem is not with her throat or her tongue."

"She's far too quiet for a ten-year-old." Being silent was an important female virtue (along with chastity, piety and humility), but not speaking at all was another matter altogether. "Are you feeding her?"

"You need not concern yourself on that account, Françoise," Sister Angélique said. "The fig comfits on the side table were freshly made this morning. There are a few sugar-plums left, as well."

The Prioress leaned forward on her cane, a bent stick with a gold knob. "Madame de la Vallière, your daughter was silent when you brought her."

Françoise held her tongue. The Prioress was tough as a pine knot. She imagined her as a pure-finder, collecting dung from the streets as something nasty got thrown on her out a window.

"Her mastery of letters is outstanding," Sister Angélique said, "and her quill-work delicate. As for her mind, she's exceptionally quick. She reads Latin, and even a little Greek now. I've never seen a child so—" The nun smiled over at Petite, who was sitting quietly by the window. "So *bright*."

"What use is all that if she's to marry?" Françoise demanded. Nuns had no understanding of the world, her deceased husband's sister in particular. "I made it clear from the beginning that my daughter was to be groomed to marry a nobleman." Once she started talking again, that is. Surely.

"The life of a Religious might suit her," Sister Angélique suggested. "She is sincerely devout."

The Prioress gave her a warning glance.

Françoise paced in front of the smoldering embers, rubbing her arms for warmth. Much as she hated to admit it, her late husband's sister had a point. Perhaps a convent would be a solution. "Is that your wish, Louise? Would this life appeal to you?"

Petite wrote out on her slateboard: *It is my wish.*

Françoise turned to the grille. "How much would be required for my daughter to become a nun?" In addition to the dowry, there would be an entrance fee, the cost of a habit, a bed and various other furnishings, not to mention the expense of the feast on the bridal day and the fee for the priest who preached the sermon.

"It is not entirely a question of money," the Prioress said as the black-guard boy came in with an armful of wood and dumped it onto the embers. "The girl is devout, no doubt, but there is a fine line between devotion and obsession, and we've had some—" She waited for the boy to shut the door behind him. "Some *difficulties*, in the past," she said.

Françoise nodded. Years earlier, one of the nuns had begun to hear noises and see things at night. The Duc d'Orléans, the King's uncle, had come from Blois to expel the demon himself.

"As a result, we've learned to be cautious."

"But that was long before my daughter even came to this place."

"A postulant must be sound in both mind and body."

"Perhaps a cure can be found," Sister Angélique suggested, her voice tearful.

PETITE LAY LONG in her narrow bed that night, listening to the wind. She loved the silence of the convent, the heady swirl of contemplation and study, the daily euphoria of choir, Mass, prayer. She felt safe in this place; the Devil was not present. She knew that now. *It is my wish,* she thought.

Petite was reading *Compendium of the Nicomachean Ethic* in the scriptorium when a lay nun informed her that her mother awaited her in the visitors' parlor. She closed the codex, considering. It was winter now, and her mother came only in the full heat of summer; she wasn't expected for another six months. *Has something happened to my brother Jean?* Petite wondered, hurrying down the dark passages.

Françoise stood in the parlor window, striped by the dim shafts of light thrown through the bars. Dust motes swirled all around her as she fingered a single strand of pearls. She was wearing a fine Brussels head lace with a tucker to match.

Petite curtsied to the Prioress and Sister Angélique, sitting behind the grille, and then kissed her mother's powdered cheeks. She smelled sweetly of vanilla.

"You still walk with a limp," Françoise observed. "What about that surgeon who uses pulleys and weights? I paid him to pull you straight."

Sister Angélique looked chagrined. "The sessions were painful, Françoise. The girl could not bear it—"

"Is this true, Louise?"

Petite took the slateboard attached by a rope to her waist and began to write out an answer.

Françoise turned to the nuns. "My daughter's still not speaking? I paid a small fortune for special Masses."

"But only once a month," the Prioress observed, hooking her cane on the grille. "Once a week is more effective, as I previously advised you."

"This convent is not to get a sou more out of me. My daughter is coming home."

Petite looked up in alarm.

"But—" Sister Angélique pressed her hands over her mouth.

"You see"—Françoise smiled as she pulled up her lace gloves—"there has been a change of plans. I've accepted a proposal of marriage—from a *marquis*."

Part II

CONFESSION

Chapter Six

IT WAS NOISY on the street outside the convent. Cart and carriage wheels grated on the icy cobblestones. A hawker with a deep voice called out, selling meat pies and oatcakes. Three snarling dogs encircled a goat as a milking maid tried to beat them off with a stick. Two chimney sweeps stood by laughing. Petite looked for the sun, but it was blocked by tall houses.

"Come along, Louise," Françoise said as a man handed her into the hired carriage.

Petite climbed up and wiped the seat before sitting down beside her mother. She turned up the torn leather window-covering and looked back at the gateway to the convent. There, behind the decorative ironwork cherubs, stood her aunt. The carriage jolted forward. Petite pressed her hands against her heart.

As they headed north, the sun cast long shadows over the glittering winter fields. Petite squinted against the glare. She recognized some of the landmarks—a tower windmill, a graveyard—yet they seemed foreign to her now. She hadn't been out of the convent for four years.

"He's César de Courtarvel, Marquis de Saint-Rémy," her mother told her, positioning her feet on the foot-warmer, "chief steward to the Duc d'Orléans at the château at Blois."

Petite didn't know what to make of this information. Blois was some distance away, yet she knew it was good for her mother to marry a titled gentleman. Her father had tried to become a marquis, but had failed. Now her mother would no longer be addressed familiarly as "mademoiselle," no longer suffer the disrespect of being married to an untitled man.

"He's an older gentleman, a widower himself. He will be a good father for you and Jean."

Petite looked out the carriage window. Three heavy horses stood against the wind. One was a black, like old Hongre. She recalled riding behind her father as he went about his doctoring. She remembered leaning her cheek against the cold leather of his doublet, singing hymns in harmony with him as they ambled down the laneways. She didn't want another father.

"He might even be able to get Jean a position through his contacts at Court."

Her brother needed a father to help him make his way in the world, Petite knew, and she also understood that her mother couldn't live alone. Only witches and women of another sort lived without the protection of a husband or father.

"We'll be moving to Blois after the ceremony. I'll have you fitted for a proper gown. I need to find you a personal maid to keep you tidy and well turned-out. I'm sure the Marquis will be able to get you a position as waiting maid to one of the princesses. A good maid is silent, so one who doesn't talk at all might be considered advantageous." Françoise patted Petite's knee. "And who knows? Maybe he will even be able to find a husband for you some day."

They passed through the village and crossed the narrow bridge. The lower gardens on the opposite bank lay fallow. Petite's eyes filled as they pulled through the gates into the manor yard.

An old man hobbled from the wood shed, wrapped in woolens. The carriage rolled to a stop and Petite climbed down.

"Upon my soul—Mademoiselle Petite?" The ploughman leaned on a stout walking stick. He reached out one arm and embraced Petite, enveloping her in scents of damp wool and smoke. "What am I going to call you now? You're not so petite anymore—but pretty as ever, aye. Come now, won't you give us a word?"

Petite willed her mouth to open, but her tongue remained inert, as if under a spell.

"Louise, aren't you coming?" her mother called from the porch.

"Mind your mother, lass."

Petite sprinted across the yard. Inside, the manor smelled familiarly of tallow-candle grease. Embers were smoldering in the sitting room fireplace, the muzzle of the leather bellows tipped against the grate. The furniture had been changed. There used to be a bed in one corner, for company.

"I got one hundred thirty-five livres for it," Petite's mother said, removing her hooded cape, "and twenty-eight for the carpet." The gold Turkey rug had been replaced by one of knotted wool.

What else is missing? Petite wondered, alarmed. *What else gone?* The walls looked bare. Only the black-framed mirror remained.

"And seven hundred eighty for the tapestries."

The door to her father's study was open. The desk was there, but the shelves looked empty.

"Where does this go?" the driver demanded, standing in the entrance with Petite's trunk on his shoulders.

"Louise, show him to your room," Françoise said, pulling aside the red camlet curtains to let in light.

Petite climbed the narrow spiral stairs, the driver behind her hefting her trunk. At the second landing, she stepped into her garret room under the eaves. Her red-canopied oak bed was covered with the familiar red and black striped wool blanket. There, as before, was the little servant bed at the far end, under the eaves. There the trestle table, there the trunks for the maids. She went to the window. There, the farmyard, and there . . . the barn.

She turned away.

"Here, I suppose?" the driver asked, setting down her trunk and shoving it against the wall next to the others.

Petite sat bolt upright in her bed, her heart pounding. Something had woken her. Was the Devil in the room? Then she heard it again: a horse's scream. Trembling, she pulled back the bed curtain. The night air was chill. Her bonnet had slipped off her head in the night—she found it tangled in her bed linens and pulled it back on.

Again, she heard the horse. It was not a cry of pain, or fear, or even a cry of loneliness. It was an angry cry, a cry of protest—and it both thrilled and alarmed her.

It seemed to be coming from the barn. Petite reached for the shawl draped on the wooden ladder-chair by her bed and tiptoed to the narrow window. A crescent moon hung in the sky, illuminating the wisps of fog that lay over the dark fields. In the paddock at the side of the barn, the weak moonlight vaguely shone on the two cart horses standing together. A rooster crowed.

Picking up her wooden sabots with one hand and the night candle with the other, Petite slipped out the door, down the spiral stairs and through the sitting room, passing down the narrow passageway to the kitchen. She tiptoed around the yellow painted table, taking care not to wake Blanche, asleep on her pallet by the chimney. The bolt clanged as she slid it open. The maid stirred in her sleep, then fell to steady breathing. Petite stepped into her sabots and quietly closed the door behind her.

The ground was frosty; iced puddles cracked under her weight. She made her way slowly, holding one hand around the flame to protect it. It guttered and then steadied as she approached the barn. She pushed the door gently, testing it. It swung open.

She stood for a long moment in that familiar space, her eyes adjusting to the gloom. Her heart caught when she saw the shape of something white moving in the far stall, but it was only Vachel, the milk cow. A simple wooden cross had been nailed to the wall—at the spot where her father had died, she realized. Backing away, she tipped over a hoe.

"Saint Michel, defend me!" The old ploughman rose up from one of the grain bins. Trembling, holding onto the bin, he held up a metal cross. "Safeguard me against the Devil!"

"It's me," Petite croaked, her voice husky, strange.

"Saint Michel! I beseech you, cast Satan into Hell. Amen!"

Petite held her candle to her face. "It's me, *Petite*," she said. Her tongue felt like a live thing in her mouth.

"Mademoiselle?" The ploughman staggered forward, draped in ragged furs, oats spilling from him. "You . . . talked?"

Petite's candle guttered, then went out, and she was plunged into darkness. She felt something prickling at her ankles and thought she heard a hissing sound. She turned, fumbling for the barn door. Outside, she broke down and wept—shattering, gut-wrenching sobs. "I heard a horse," she told the ploughman, who had followed her. She'd heard *Diablo*.

"Mademoiselle Petite," the old man said, uneasily patting her heaving shoulder, "you'll catch your death out here. Come into the barn."

"No," Petite gasped.

"There, there." Smoke curled from the kitchen chimney. "Mademoiselle

Blanche must be up." He led Petite by the hand to the manor kitchen, now warmed by a crackling fire. "She can talk now," he told the kitchen maid.

"Can she now," Blanche said, her one eye wide. She had lost several teeth since Petite had last seen her.

"Go on, Mademoiselle," the ploughman said.

Petite stared. Behind Blanche, next to the pantry, was her father's old suit of armor, now hung with aprons. The dog's basket wasn't in its usual spot by the fire: her father's old hound must have died, she feared.

"Hot cider or a beer? I don't have all day," Blanche said, as bossy as ever.

"Cider," Petite said finally, her voice foreign to her yet, as if a spirit were speaking through her.

"Louise?" Françoise came into the kitchen carrying a night lamp. Her face was covered in a thick paste. "What are you doing in here? Why aren't you in bed?"

"She talked, Madame," Blanche said. "She just told me she wants a cider."

Françoise looked at Petite with astonishment. "Is that what you said, a cider?"

Petite nodded.

"Say something for your mother. Go on, show her," the ploughman said.

"Thank you," Petite said as Blanche handed her a steaming earthenware bowl.

"Praise Mary." Françoise smiled. "And perfect timing. A gentleman is bringing a maid for you this afternoon, Louise, and it wouldn't do for her to think you simple."

THE MAN ARRIVED on a donkey at midday, the maid (his sister) riding pillion behind him. They were shown into the sitting room, where Petite and her mother sat waiting in the two fringed armchairs.

"She is Mademoiselle Clorine Goubert of Tours," the man said, rocking on his heels. "She served as a fille de suite—or *suivante*, as they say in Paris—to a gentlewoman for eleven years, the wife of a magistrate, so she knows all about dressing hair and arranging a woman's toilette."

Petite glanced at the woman. She was tall, practical and strong-looking, in spite of the fussy gray taffeta gown she was wearing. Her teeth looked good, with only one missing. She had a pleasing horselike face.

"She is older than I expected, Monsieur," Françoise said.

"She is just above thirty years, but in health, I assure you. Unwed, and of an age not to be susceptible to notions."

"Why was her former employment terminated?"

The man looked perplexed.

"My mistress died, Madame de la Vallière," the maid spoke up, bending her knee in a curtsy. Her voice was steady and matter-of-fact. "Of broke ribs. She insisted I tie her traces tight and I do what I'm told—except, you should know, I would not permit it for a growing girl, for it would deform the bones, which are soft until the fifteenth year. A training corset is another matter, however, for it would get her to sit straight—"

"Mademoiselle Clorine is honest, a God-fearing girl," the man interrupted uneasily. "She does not steal. She was schooled at a charity convent and knows manners, I assure you. She does not speak coarse, or stand close. I need not remind you that it is not easy to find a maid in these times. The daughter of the deceased has provided a reference." A sheet of paper trembled in his hand.

Françoise looked it over and quickly handed it back. "Very well. She has her belongings with her?"

"I assure you," the man said, bowing.

CLORINE PUT DOWN her carpet haversack in Petite's attic room. "They didn't tell me that you have a limp." She looked around, her hands on her hips.

"It's always warm," Petite said. "You can use that trunk there, and that bed over there. The scullery girl used to sleep on it, but she ran away with a field hand."

"Is it true that your mother is to marry a marquis and that you will soon be moving to the château at Blois?"

"Yes," Petite said.

"Well, then." Clorine opened her haversack and transferred a nightcap, flannels, three aprons and small linens into the trunk. "It's said even the servants eat with prongs at Blois." She sat down on the bed, testing it. "I'll have to do you in curl-papers every night," she said.

PETITE SAT IN THE WOODEN chair in the sitting room, trying to read *Wisdom's Watch upon the Hours*. The maid Clorine had persuaded her mother that it was time for her to wear a training corset, and it itched, breaking her concentration. Furthermore, they were expecting a caller: the Marquis, the man her mother was to marry. The man who was to be her new father.

Her mother poked at the enormous log blazing on the hearth, then went into the room that used to be her father's study, a sewing room now, and looked out the window that faced the courtyard. "Maybe he won't be able to make it," she said, returning to her chair by the fire. It had been raining for days.

A horse whinnied, followed by the sound of carriage wheels. "That must be him now." Françoise took the book from Petite's hands and positioned her in front of the occasional chair. "Whatever you do, don't move," she said, "I haven't told him about your . . . you know." She glanced down at Petite's leg. "Mademoiselle Clorine, are you there?"

The maid, done up in a smock somewhat too small for her (the sleeves not reaching her stout wrists), poked her head from behind a door.

A loud knocking sounded. A field hand, dressed in a worn butler's jacket, darted into the entry. Petite heard the voice of an old man, followed by a belch. As the sitting room door creaked open, Françoise tugged down her bodice.

"Madame de la Vallière, I am come through blustery weather and squall to pay a visit upon you," the Marquis de Saint-Rémy announced, making a deep and ceremonious bow.

Petite's future stepfather was older than she'd expected. Under a powdered wig in the tightly curled style of Henry the Great, his face was a mass of wrinkles, the frown lines deep furrows between his blackened thin brows. He was short—about Petite's height—with a belly as round as an inflated ox bladder. His boots were covered in muck up to the ankles.

Françoise curtsied. "Monsieur le Marquis de Saint-Rémy, my waiting woman will take your sword and riding boots." She signaled to Clorine. "She will polish them for you while you relax by the fire with a cup."

The Marquis lowered himself into the best chair, the one with the tapestry footstool, as Clorine knelt to remove his muddy boots, yanking them free.

"I have noticed your fondness for vin sec and went to some effort to get in a cask," Françoise said, taking a wide-mouthed glass of liqueur from the field hand's tray and handing it to her intended.

"You are sympathetic, Madame de la Vallière." The Marquis took a sip and grimaced.

"May I introduce to you my daughter, Mademoiselle Louise?"

The Marquis craned his neck toward Petite. "That girl? I reflected her to be a domestic."

Françoise gestured at Petite to curtsy, using a sly downward movement of her right hand at hip height.

Petite made an obedient reverence. Everyone was behaving strangely, she thought, as if on a stage.

"She is ten and has just returned from the Ursuline convent in Tours where she was well trained in needlework and comportment, but she misses her brother Jean," Françoise chattered on nervously. "He's a student at the Collège de Navarre—in Paris—where all the noblemen's sons go. He gets an allowance of six sous a week and will earn even more upon graduation, no doubt."

The Marquis cleared his throat and looked about for a spittoon, which Françoise leapt to provide. "She's ten, you allege?" he asked, wiping the corners of his mouth with his gloved thumb and index finger.

Allege? People from Blois must speak a different language, Petite thought.

"My daughter, you mean? Yes—she's ten now. My son Jean is two and a half years older. He knows many noblemen's sons, even princes. He's a good-looking boy, and excellent at sword fighting. It's cold now in Paris, but he's allowed a fire in his room for a half-hour after a meal."

"Can your girl mend?"

"All girls mend," Françoise said, frowning. "In the school common, my son speaks Latin with princes."

"And does she intone? I am partial to hear singing whilst attending to epistolary matters and ledger books."

"In fact, she sings rather well."

"Command her to intone at present."

Françoise looked over at Petite, who shook her head: no!

"I'm afraid my daughter is suffering an attack of . . . an engorgement of her throat."

Petite breathed a sigh of relief. She would *not* sing for this awful little man who was soon to take her father's place.

"Conceivably, it then follows, she should be quiescent in her chamber," the Marquis said, attempting to pull Petite's mother onto his lap.

The time dragged by. Petite lowered herself onto the occasional chair as the

Marquis droned on about the staff at the Blois château: the blackguard boy who had broken three earthen drinking vessels, the marketman who took all day to buy a dram of cream, the butler who insisted that *it was not he* who had written on the ceiling with the smoke of a candle. With his fourth glass of vin sec, the Marquis began to reveal more intimate concerns: the state of his bowels (unforthcoming), the enema and purge he took once a week to balance his humors, his hippo-tusk false teeth. "*Far* enhanced to elephant ivory," he said proudly, slipping them out of his mouth so that Petite's mother might admire them.

"The workmanship is excellent," Petite's mother said with ill-concealed repugnance.

At two of the clock, the Marquis cleared his throat. "I abundantly regret forsaking your society, Madame de la Vallière," he said, rising.

"So soon?" Françoise hid a yawn behind her chicken-feather fan.

At last the Marquis departed, strutting out the door like a bantam cock.

Françoise collapsed into a chair. "I thought he would never leave," she said, closing her eyes and rubbing her forehead. "Don't you ever forget what I do for your sake," she added, her voice weary and sad.

Honor thy father and thy mother. Petite went to her mother and knelt before her. "Don't, Mother," she said. *Don't be bitter, don't be harsh*, she thought, resting her head on her mother's lap.

"Don't what, Louise?" her mother asked, running her fingers through Petite's hair.

Don't marry that old man. "Don't be sad." Her mother's gentle touch felt strange to her.

Outside, a cow was lowing plaintively. "You have such fine hair," Françoise said. "Our little angel, your father used to call you—did you know that?"

Petite sat back on her heels.

Her mother collected her features. "But then I'd tell him not to be fooled, that there was a devil in you," she said with a smile, pinching Petite's cheek.

IT COULD HAVE BEEN worse: it could have been a Great Wedding, a traditional two-day fete, but because both the bride and groom were widowed, and because their families were distant and the groom had responsibilities to attend to in Blois, it was felt that a simpler ceremony would be more appropriate. To Petite's relief there was to be no wedding feast—no hogsheads of wine opened, no pigs slaughtered, no swans, cranes or herons roasted, no toasts called out, no singing "Veni, Creator Spiritus" or dancing to fiddlers.

The Marquis's carriage pulled up the hill to the little church in Reugny as the bells rang ten of the clock. It wasn't customary for a bride and groom to arrive in the same vehicle, but the wagon had already been loaded with trunks and furnishings in preparation for the journey to Blois that afternoon.

A few neighboring families were already at the church, among them Monsieur Bosse with his wife and nine bedraggled children, including Petite's childhood friend Charlotte, whom she'd not seen since her father's funeral. In a worn gown far too big for her, Charlotte grinned a gap-toothed smile.

"Don't speak to them," her mother warned.

Petite recognized the mayor and the owner of the apothecary, both of whom had been her father's pallbearers.

A clerk ushered them into the church. Her mother knelt at the altar rail and the Marquis did the same on the other side of the aisle. Behind them, in the pews, were a few whispering strangers.

Curé Barouche entered, his long cassock trailing. He'd grayed since Petite had last seen him. She wondered if his donkey, Têtu, was still alive. The Curé used to ride the sorry thing out to the manor to teach Petite and her brother the catechism.

The mumbled service was thankfully short. Petite knew it was over when Curé Barouche intoned, "In the name of the Father, the Son and the Holy Ghost," and placed a gold ring on her mother's finger. Then her mother and the Marquis kissed the altar and returned to their places for the Mass, which was offered in their name. At the offering, Petite presented the bridal candle, lowering her eyes as her mother and the Marquis kissed it. Then her mother and the Marquis knelt as Curé Barouche recited a series of long marriage prayers. "O Lord, omnipotent and eternal God, You created man and woman in Your image and blessed their union . . ."

On leaving the church, the Marquis discovered that the church doors had been tied shut with ribbons. Children could be heard giggling outside. The Marquis promised a coin, and the wedding party was released.

Children were leaping about. They'd put up two additional ribbon "barricades" around the coach. The Marquis once again obliged them with coins, the way was cleared, and he helped his bride into the coach.

Petite climbed in and sat facing the newlyweds.

The driver cracked his whip and the carriage lurched down the hill.

Chapter Seven

THE FIRST NIGHT Petite, her mother and stepfather were forced to lodge opposite Amboise. The rain made the bridge crossing precarious and they had been advised to wait until morning. The inn had only one room to offer, but fortunately two beds, so Françoise and Petite shared one, while the Marquis de Saint-Rémy slept in the other. The staff, including an indignant Clorine, were lodged in the stables.

By the light of a single lantern, the Marquis ceremoniously said his prayers and removed his wig and hippo-tusk teeth before propping himself up in the bed to sleep upright. "For only the dead recline," he said. Throughout the night, he belched and farted and snored.

"I will never sleep again," Petite's mother said wretchedly.

HEAVY HORSES TOWED the passenger barge from Amboise to Blois. The servants, trunks and furnishings followed behind on another. The distance was less than fifteen leagues, yet due to the rain the journey took two days. Petite and her mother stayed in the ladies' cabin with three nuns from Bordeaux and a milliner, all of them sharing a washbowl, a towel and a comb. Meals were served in a stateroom, first the men and then the women. Françoise turned ill, so during the day Petite was content to sit and read in the stateroom, now and again looking out at the sandstone cliff, the plantations of sisal and oak, the villages and vineyards. Three times she saw a White—but one was a pony, one was spotted and the last was the stocky sort of horse bred for armor.

Petite stood at the rail of the barge as they approached the ancient city of Blois. She had never seen so many houses in one place, so many gables and turrets. Tours was a grand city, and Amboise even grander, but neither could compare to Blois, where, the Marquis had informed them (several times over), there was a stone bridge of many arches, thirty-two racket courts, an aqueduct from antiquity, a clock and even an academy of riding ("a conservatory of traverse"). At Blois, he claimed, the language was spoken to perfection ("uttered to excellence"). Petite looked for the castle, but it could not be seen from the water.

The boatman let them off at the busy river landing. The Marquis hired a coach to pull them through the narrow streets and up a steep hill to the château, which appeared to have been built on a cliff. They wound around and up until they were on a high terrace overlooking the great river Loire, the clustered houses below and the castle before them.

"We have arrived," the Marquis announced with an air of grandeur as they entered a courtyard. The château was irregular in shape, and each of its many sides had been built in a different style. There appeared to be no symmetry or order. Heaps of construction stone and timber edged one of the wings, which seemed to be under construction.

"Do up your bonnet ties," Petite's mother told her, clutching her casket of jewelry.

The carriage rolled to a stop and a footman with few teeth appeared with a ladder. Petite was the first to climb down. *This* was where King Louis XII was born, where King Francis I and Charles IX had lived. Queen Catherine de Médicis shad brewed poisons in this castle, and it was here that the Duc de Guise had been stabbed to death, assassinated by King Henry III, whose ghost was known to wander the dark passages with a parrot on his shoulder.

Petite followed her mother and the Marquis around the piles of stone and across a manure-covered courtyard to a small house on the château grounds, a humble wood and plaster cottage with a slate roof. "It is not extensive, but the rental is barely two hundred per annum," the Marquis said, pushing open the plank door.

"Two hundred *livres?*" Petite's mother ducked as a bat flew out. "But it's so small." Outside, the servants could be heard unloading their trunks and furniture.

"The bedstead can go at this juncture, by the flue," the Marquis said. "Your daughter and the servants may avail themselves of the upper compartment."

Petite climbed the narrow stairs to the loft, a dark, low space. Pushing away cobwebs, she pried open the shutter. Far below she could see the silver ribbon of the river and, in the distance, the towers of what appeared to be another castle. To the right were the château stables. She stood for a time looking out over the high and low gardens, the paddocks of horses, searching out of habit for a White.

CLORINE PUT THE curling tongs down beside the charcoal brazier and stepped back, appraising her creation. Petite stood sullenly before her, her hair in wax-stiffened ringlets, silk ribbons at the roots, heavy false pearl ear pendants pulling at her earlobes.

"You look highborn," the maid said proudly. "Truly ladified."

Petite heard pounding on the door below. "I feel like a circus monkey," she said.

"Petite!" her mother called up, her voice tremulous. "The Duke and Duchess will receive us now."

"Zut!" Clorine whispered.

The north-facing room below was frigid in spite of the season. Warming herself in front of the smoking chimney, Petite's mother fussed with her side curls, which dangled from wire frames secured to her ears.

The Marquis coughed into his white-gloved hand. "Ready?"

Petite followed her mother and the Marquis as they traced their way across the cobbled yard to a spiral staircase, the grand entrance into the King François wing. "Proceed this way," the Marquis said, already out of breath.

They wound up and up, emerging into a room that smelled of tobacco—the guard room. Four men in uniform were sitting at a table playing cards. The fire in the ornate fireplace at one end was blazing, the room overly warm. Windows of fine horn let in a milky light. Every surface had been ornamented with design, but was blackened by smoke.

"This way," the Marquis said, leading them into an enormous bedchamber, empty of furnishings but for a curtained bed and a wooden prie-dieu set into an alcove. Three terriers jumped off the bed and growled at the Marquis, who kicked them away with his boot. A chambermaid and a footman emerged from behind brocade curtains and stood at attention.

"This way," the Marquis repeated, leading Petite and her mother into a narrow oratory that smelled of incense. A guard in uniform stood at attention by a great double door (which had, Petite noticed, a horseshoe nailed over it, to keep out witches and evil spirits). "We have arrived," the Marquis announced. He smoothed the white towel he had folded lengthwise over his right shoulder and rearranged his cape over his left so that it draped in the manner of nobles.

"Remember, Louise, never turn your back to royalty," Françoise whispered, fussing over Petite's ribbons with trembling hands. "When dismissed, walk backwards while curtsying."

"Yes, Mother."

"Arranged, Madame?" the Marquis asked.

The doors opened onto yet another ornate jewel box of a room, this one smoky from a smoldering fire. Though it was daylight, the room was dark, the drapes drawn. It took a moment for Petite to make out the large mound of a woman lying on a wide chaise in front of the fire. An equally round man, his face bright as a red Holland tulip, sat blowing smoke rings. His bucket-top boots were such as a country magistrate might wear. Petite thought perhaps this room was an antechamber, and that these were neighboring nobility, awaiting an audience with the royal family.

"Your Highness, Your Highness," the Marquis said in a low voice.

These were the Duke and Duchess? Petite was astounded that this man in a sagging ruff was the son of King Henry the Great.

The Marquis made an extravagantly subservient bow. Petite and her mother, likewise, made deep reverences. When Petite looked up, she saw that the Marquis was still bowing. How did his wig stay on? Finally, he straightened and cleared his throat.

"I understand that congratulations are in order, Saint-Rémy," Monsieur le Duc d'Orléans said, admiring a smoke ring that emerged from his lips. "This must be your wife and . . . her daughter? Very well. Your wife will work with you, I presume? As for the girl—" The Duke looked Petite up and down. "How old is she?"

"Ten, my Lord. Unsoiled in her routine and trained at a convent in Tours."

"The Ursuline convent?"

The Marquis glanced at Françoise, who indicated that it was so.

"I was once summoned there," the Duke said, fussing with his pipe, "to dispel an infestation of demons."

"A prodigious quantity of time ago, my Lord," the Marquis said. "The girl had not even been birthed—in Tours, I might add, to the august la Vallière family, renowned throughout the land for religiosity."

"What sign was she born under?" the Duke asked, inhaling sharply, trying to get the tobacco to relight. "Is she Scorpio? She has that look about her, something . . . *irregular*."

Françoise glanced at Petite in alarm. "Your Highness." Her trembling hands causing her skirts to rustle. "I beg you, permit me to speak."

The Duke nodded his assent.

"My daughter was born under the sign of Leo. She is devout as well as dutiful."

"Our Marguerite is Leo," the Duke noted, blowing a smoke ring and watching it float, disintegrate, disappear.

"*Exactly*, my Lord: an auspicious auspice," the Marquis said with a stutter. "A most portentous indication. And—in that Princess Marguerite necessitates an auxiliary chamber attendant—I thought *perchance* that the girl might . . . furnish attendance on Her Highness."

"How many attendants does Little Queen have now?" the Duc d'Orléans asked.

"Ten and one," the Marquis stuttered, "together with the two pages, but barely one waiting maid, the girl Mademoiselle Nicole de Montalais, my Lord."

"The noisy one," the Duchesse d'Orléans said dreamily, selecting a sweetmeat from the china platter beside her..

"And nosy," the Duke added, knocking his pipe embers into a bowl. "Well, perhaps you have a point. Marguerite is six now—one waiting maid is insufficient."

"Marguerite is ten," came the ghostlike voice of the Duchess as a footman stepped forward to usher them out.

"Back out," Petite's mother whispered as they exited, then collapsed onto an upholstered bench. "Mon Dieu!" she gasped, pulling her fur-trimmed tippet close around her shoulders.

"You are not to relinquish your senses, Madame. I shall revisit you presently," the Marquis informed his wife, handing her a sweat-cloth and signaling Petite to follow.

Petite shadowed her stepfather back down the circular stairwell and across the courtyard, climbing yet another stairwell and going down a vast gallery before coming to a halt before a vaulted door. A guard with a rusty halberd snapped to attention.

The Marquis, perspiring, turned to face his stepdaughter. "The Duke and Duchess are graced with three daughters," he said, clearing his throat. "Princesses."

Petite nodded. She'd never seen a princess.

"Princess Marguerite is the eldest. She has attained the epoch of nine."

"I thought the Duchess said she was ten," Petite said, puzzled. She'd noted it because she was ten herself.

"You're not to discourse if not discoursed to."

"Are you not discoursing with me?"

"Discoursing *with* and discoursing *to* are not an identical identity." The Marquis cleared his throat again. "Princess Elisabeth is fifteen months younger, followed by Princess Madeleine at an additional span of two years."

"Isn't there an older princess as well?" Petite asked. Not long ago, during the Age of Conflict, this warlike princess was said to have climbed the wall of the palace at Orléans *all by herself* and even to have fired cannon from the tower of the Bastille prison in Paris.

"Yes, la Grande Mademoiselle. However, the Duke's offspring by his original mate is a celebratory and lives away."

"The warrior one."

The Marquis raised a warning finger. "It is deeply erroneous, Mademoiselle, to reference la Grande Mademoiselle in this mode. I will have Abbé Patin edify you on the theme of titles and accurate appellation." He frowned, doubling his chins. "Endeavor to be perpetually cognizant that Monsieur le Duc and his progeny are the *descendants* of King Henry the Great."

Petite nodded, fingering the tangle of ribbons at her waist. Often her father had told her tales of the brave and honorable King Henry, a great horseman. Bucephalus was the name of his favorite stallion, a White like Diablo.

"All of his daughters, even the girls, are King Henry the Great's granddaughters. The princesses hold the most uppermost grade in France," the Marquis went on, making his eyes wide for effect, "an echelon bestowed by the supreme Almighty."

Petite put her hand to her cheek pretending a gesture of awe, but in fact surreptitiously to swipe at the spots of spittle the Marquis had showered upon her.

"Subsequently, Mademoiselle, they are *under no circumstances* flawed." With a shaky sigh, he raised his head, made the sign of the cross and commanded the guard to open the door.

It was not yet nightfall, yet the room was ablaze with candles and lanterns. The air smelled of smoke, candle grease, and—regrettably—urine. Three girls were stooped over a game table, silhouetted in front of a blazing fire. The eldest had a long face and prominent chin. Her plump lips were dark, her lower lip drooping. Her hair was curly, to judge from the strands poking out from under her nightcap. The middle girl had a wandering eye, and the youngest unsuccessfully disguised an enormous nose under a hooded linen night rail. All three of them were hunchbacked.

"No!" the youngest screamed.

A buxom maid in a window alcove and an older woman sitting to one side of the fire took no notice.

"Spin it," the eldest commanded, tossing a bone top onto the felt-covered table. "Ha, ha, you lose," she said, scooping up coins.

Put-and-Take? Petite wondered. They were playing with real coins. In the convent, no games had been permitted, and certainly not this gambling game played by ruffians on the street.

"Your Highnesses," the Marquis stuttered.

The girls turned to stare.

"Princess Marguerite, Princess Elisabeth, Princess Madeleine," the Marquis intoned, "may I have the honor of introducing Mademoiselle Louise-Françoise La Baume Le Blanc de la Vallière . . . my wife's daughter."

"Your turn now," Princess Marguerite said, pushing the bone top over to the middle sister.

The Marquis turned to the elderly woman knitting by the fire. "Madame de Raré, it is the aspiration of the esteemed Duke and Duchess that Mademoiselle de la Vallière adhere to Princess Marguerite in the function of waiting maid."

"The Princess already has a waiting maid," the woman said, her chin buried in an old-fashioned figure-of-eight ruff.

"The esteemed Duke and Duchess deem that the Princess is of an epoch to necessitate further than one, Madame."

The buxom maid stepped forward. "Then perhaps I should be introduced, Monsieur le Marquis?" She was a tall girl with thick black braids, each tied with a wide scarlet ribbon. "I am that *other* waiting maid, Mademoiselle Nicole de Montalais." She made a pert curtsy.

Marguerite, the eldest princess, jumped up and grabbed hold of Nicole's braids. "Go, horsey," she commanded, as if holding reins.

Nicole yanked away and drove the Princess off using one of her braids as a whip.

"Oh, stop. Please stop," the woman by the fire said faintly.

"Stop, stop, stop," the princesses sang out in chorus as the Marquis bowed out, abandoning Petite to the chaos.

Chapter Eight

PETITE GAVE WAY to tears in her garret room that night. Her introduction to the princesses had been raucous, and she was filled with confusion. She had expected a castle not to stink and nobility to act . . . well, noble. She had a new father, a new home, *responsibilities*: it was all too much. She longed for the convent, Sister Angélique, the silence. What did a waiting maid even do?

"Well, first, you must be well turned-out," Clorine said, looking around their tiny room, her hands on her hips. She pushed Petite's trunk into one corner. "I'll do you up in ringlets every day."

"I *hate* ringlets," Petite said. Plus, she was ravenous. Clearly, from the extraordinary size of both the Duke and Duchess, there was food in the château—but where? She threw herself down on her bed—a crackling sound startled her. The mattress was straw? She could hear her mother and the Marquis talking downstairs, something about the fireplace smoking. She didn't like that the floor was so thin. She didn't want to hear them talking . . . or worse. "I'm starving."

"I found out that the last sitting for the higher staff was about an hour ago," Clorine said, digging around in her basket and handing Petite a length of jerky. "In the morning it's at prime—they'll ring a bell when the table is laid. That will give you plenty of time because the Princess doesn't rise until terce, just before Mass."

"But then what am I supposed to do? Do I put her fire on?"

"No, the butler does that."

"Do I take out her chamber pot?"

"No, there will be a chambermaid for that."

"Do I wake her?"

"I believe her nurse will be the one to do that."

"Does her nurse help her dress as well?"

"That's the job of the mistress of the wardrobe, but you or the other waiting maid may be asked to tie a ribbon, or comb out the Princess's hair, for example."

"I can do that," Petite said, reassured. "Do princesses ever eat?"

"Of course. You're to stand behind her commodité de la conversation when she's at table."

"A commodité de la . . . what?"

"Conversation. That's what they call a chair here." Clorine rolled her eyes in exasperation. "You may eat what's left on the Princess's plate after she's finished."

"And then what?"

Clorine shrugged. "And then you just stand around waiting. You are, after all, a *waiting* maid."

Chewing on the jerky, Petite gave this some thought. She could do a lot of things passably well, but waiting was not one of them.

"You are to call me Little Queen," Princess Marguerite informed Petite the next morning. The Princess lifted her skirts and sat down on a necessary, a padded open seat over a tin chamber pot. "Everyone does." Broken strands of gold thread glinted on her underskirt.

"Yes, Little Queen," Petite said, clasping her white-gloved hands behind her back. She shifted her hands to the front, and then let them hang down by her sides. There was a correct posture, no doubt.

"Aren't you going to ask why?"

"Why, Little Queen?" The Princess was wearing ear-rings made of bone buttons. Petite had known only a few girls of her own age, and certainly none of them ornamented. A foul smell filled the room.

"Because I'm going to marry the King."

Petite took in this astonishing news. "I didn't know that." Was it permissible to admit such a thing? "Little Queen," she added.

"I'll be ten on July twenty-eighth, so when the King and I marry in four years, I'll be fourteen and he will be twenty. How old are you?"

"I'm ten. Little Queen." Petite calculated that she was one year and eleven days older than the Princess.

"I was born with the sun in Leo." Marguerite put out her hand.

Unsure, Petite placed her hand in the Princess's.

"No, fishhead—a *cloth*."

Petite looked around, then handed the Princess a cloth from a stack on a side table. The Princess cleaned herself and stood, handing Petite the soiled linen. Petite took it by one corner.

"The astrologer said I'll make a good queen because I'm proud, dignified, commanding and powerful," Marguerite said. "The King is a Virgo, but his moon is in Leo. What sign are you?"

"I'm Leo as well," Petite said, tucking the soiled cloth into the waistband of her apron. "Little Queen. But with a Cancer ascendant." The astrologer present at Petite's birth had written out a full report. According to his calculations she was sensitive to others—attuned, even, to mystic vibrations—and although rational by nature, he'd written that her "affective sensibility tended to overheat," concluding with the warning that her mild manner veiled a voraginous passion. Petite had yet to discover what *voraginous* meant, but because of a line in the *Aeneid* ("Neptune came upon them, with all his vorages and his waves full of scum"), she thought it might have something to do with a whirlpool.

"Cancer ascendant? Tant pis! We shall never get along," Princess Marguerite said cheerily.

Nicole, the other waiting maid, jumped into the room.

"Where have you been?" Princess Marguerite demanded.

"Out spying." Nicole gave a sly look. "That harlot from Tours is here."

"Mademoiselle de la Marbelière?"

"*And* she's got her son with her. *Your* half-brother."

"The bastard." Marguerite sounded horrified.

Petite flushed, understanding. Once, in Tours, on the way to the surgeon, Sister Angélique had shielded her from seeing a woman in a passing carriage—this same Mademoiselle de la Marbelière.

The Princess sank down to the floor, her skirts wafting out around her. "She's not here to see my father, is she?"

"I'll find out," Nicole said, leaping back out the door.

A maid of the wardrobe entered with a wicker basket containing a sable snug and a blue velvet cape trimmed with swan's down. As the maid secured the enormous cape to the Princess by means of an ivory button at the neck, Petite tucked the soiled cloth under the pale green carpet of uncut pile.

The Princess took a handful of sweetmeats from a bowl and stuffed them into the snug. "You have to carry my train," she told Petite, pulling toward the door.

Petite scooped up the train as best she could. Holding it high, she hurried after the Princess, down the stone stairs and along the chilly arcades, sidestepping the piles of feces left by dogs.

The chapel abutted the unfinished wing. It looked as if part of it had been destroyed and then patched back together. The Princess entered a small door and climbed a narrow circular stair, emerging onto a balcony that overlooked the chancel and nave. The little chapel had stained-glass windows and a vaulted ceiling, and the altar was covered with a dark velvet cloth trimmed with silver lace. Pews in the front by the railing were already full, a crowd standing behind—shopkeepers and townsfolk, Petite guessed by their attire. Incense failed to cover the scent of sheepskin and damp wool.

"We're early," Marguerite said with disgust, dipping her fingers into a baptismal font set into the wall. She crossed herself, bent a knee to the altar and climbed up into the single chair.

Petite wasn't sure what to do. The Princess would likely be offended if she were to dip her fingers into *her* holy water—but wouldn't God be offended if she didn't?

"My cape," the Princess said, swinging her feet. Petite arranged the fabric so that it wasn't wadded in a lump behind the Princess's back.

The balcony beside theirs was crowded. Petite recognized the two younger princesses, sitting at the balustrade. The youngest stuck her tongue out, then collapsed into a giggle.

"My mother the Duchess says that you're not to smile in the chapel," Marguerite said. "Nor are you to frown. You must maintain a beatific expression."

Petite tried to look beatific, but it was difficult with her teeth chattering. She wished she had brought a wrap.

"I get my own balcony because I'm Little Queen," Marguerite said, making a face back at her sisters—the bratchets, she called them.

"That's good, Little Queen," Petite said, as a tall comely priest in a patched surplice strode up the aisle. Under his thick wool cassock, he was wearing riding boots with spurs, which kept catching on the hem.

Those in the pews below stood, but Princess Marguerite remained seated. "That's Abbé Patin, our tutor," she said.

The Abbé crossed himself, his voice booming out, "The Lord be with you."

"And also with you," Petite intoned. The familiar ritual of the Mass was a comfort.

The Abbé began to read from the Bible in Latin, his voice commanding.

"We call him the Thunderer," the Princess said. "He had a wench in Paris," she went on as the congregation began to sing "Gloria," "but she died of the Plague. Her servants had to cut off her head so that they could fit her into the coffin. When I am queen, there will be no Plague."

Abbé Patin glanced up after the choir finished singing.

"Uh-oh, I'm in trouble: three Hail Marys," Marguerite said, as he began the silent prayer.

A bell sounded and people pressed into the small chapel.

"Peasants." Princess Marguerite pinched her nose. "They come to see the Host. Oh, *there's* Nicole."

Petite recognized the other waiting maid's blue hooded cloak below.

Soon Nicole emerged through the balcony door. "She talked to your father," she reported breathlessly. "Something about money, I think. Oh, speak of the Devil, there she is."

The three of them leaned over the balustrade.

"The one with the straw hat?" Marguerite looked incredulous. "In winter?"

Mademoiselle de la Marbelière was a plump little woman, wearing a traveling suit in an ancient style. She was holding a little boy's hand. Petite thought she looked like any woman, any mother. How was one to tell a harlot? What were the clues?

"She should be put in stocks in the square," Marguerite said indignantly. "That's what they do to sinners."

The crowd murmured appreciatively as Abbé Patin lifted the Host.

"The Duchess pays him extra to hold it up for three minutes," the Princess said. "Watch, his arms will start to shake."

IT WAS A MISFORTUNE that Easter Week was so continuously hectic, the Marquis reflected. The days were still fleeting, the sun both dawning and setting at six of the clock, more or less, leaving deficient light at the end of the day to attend to his private accounts, much in decline due to the commotion of acquiring a wife.

A wife, and a daughter now too. He had hoped for more in the way of attendance. Was it too much to require a girl to sing from time to time? Musical accompaniment would be soothing to work to; it might help obscure his wife's perpetual babble.

He took off his spectacles and turned toward Françoise, who was standing by the smoking fire. Had he heard rightly just now?

"This coming Easter would be an ideal time," she told her daughter.

The girl looked up from the book she was reading by the light of a lantern. (Terrible for the eyes. She would be blind before her time.)

"But I've not been confirmed, Mother," she said.

The Marquis closed his journal of accounts. Not *confirmed?*

"Of course not. You weren't talking then," his wife said, positioning a recent letter from her son next to the candles on the fireplace mantel.

The Marquis cleared his throat. Not *talking?* "Madame, do I comprehend you exactly? Your daughter is not confirmed?" Was she even baptized? He was afraid to ask. In a matter of weeks he had learned 1) that his wife did not find his jokes amusing, 2) that she permitted conjugal liberties only on Thursday nights at eleven of the clock, long past his hour of retiring, 3) that her daughter had no dowry and was malformed, the left leg shorter than the right, and now, 4) that the girl was unconfessed. It was egregiously upsetting.

"No need to get into a hurly-burly over this, Monsieur le Marquis. I have already sent for Abbé Patin in order to make arrangements." The bell sounded. "In fact, that must be him now," Françoise said, settling into a chair and arranging her skirts. "Petite, put that book away. Stand behind me," she said as their chambermaid opened the door.

Abbé Patin strode into the room holding a torchlight. He wedged it into a tin chandler, then made a dignified bow.

The smell of horse manure filled the room. The Marquis frowned down at the Abbé's boots, but refrained from complaining. This unexpected situation was, in fact, delicate. Were it to be discovered that he had placed a heathen as waiting maid to Princess Marguerite, he could be dismissed.

"Madame sent for me," the Abbé said, accepting a stool that the Marquis nudged forward.

"Indeed." The Marquis tightened his cravat. "Madame, perchance you would care to delineate your . . . *quandary?*"

"It regards my daughter, Abbé Patin."

The Abbé glanced over at the girl. "I have been wishing to talk to you about her schooling. Her mind is unusually active."

"It's a problem I have long been aware of," Françoise said. "I've even forbidden her from reading—"

"However, Abbé Patin," the Marquis cut in, "my wife has an even greater postulatum in need of discourse." He nodded at his wife: continue.

"Yes, Abbé Patin. You see, my daughter didn't speak for a period of time," Françoise began.

"The significant point is that the girl was *unable* to make Confession," the Marquis said, "and thus to receive her First Communion, the consequence therefore being that she has yet to be confirmed."

Abbé Patin sat forward. "You stopped speaking, Mademoiselle Petite?"

"Yes, Abbé Patin." The girl bowed her head.

"My wife is in no way accountable," the Marquis said with emphasis. The girl herself was no doubt to blame! She was moon-eyed, somewhat strange. She liked animals—even cats. Two times now, on a Friday night, he'd heard an eerie sound coming from the château gardens, and just the day before, a snake had come into their cottage and then mysteriously disappeared.

"When did this begin?" Abbé Patin asked.

"About four years ago," Françoise said, "in the summer—or perhaps it was the fall? Yes, it was early in the fall . . . the day of the King's majority, I recall."

"The fifth of September," Abbé Patin said, sitting informally with his hands on his knees. "In 1651."

"The day her father passed away," Françoise recalled with a frown.

"No doubt you can ameliorate this unintentional delinquency, Abbé Patin?" the Marquis asked. No need for hysterics. "In hugger-mugger, need one declare?"

"Do you wish to make Confession?" Abbé Patin asked the girl.

"I don't know," she said.

Abbé Patin put up his hand. "That's a beginning," he said, before the Marquis could object.

THE SATURDAY OF the Easter Vigil, Petite entered the confessional. She brushed off the bench before sitting down. She heard movement behind the grille and the scent of a stable filled the small chamber.

"May the Lord be with you," Abbé Patin said.

"And with you," Petite said. And then she remembered to add, "Bless me, Father, for I have sinned." What came next? A sin. "I read when I'm supposed to be doing needlework."

"What do you read?"

"Right now I'm reading Xenophon's book on Socrates."

"*The Conversations.* Are you reading it in translation?"

"Yes, but into Latin. It was my father's book. It's in the library here." She had been shocked to discover the familiar texts in a pile by the door—*Consolation of Philosophy, Poetae Latini Rei Venaticae Scriptores, Histoire naturelle des quadrupèdes*—her father's comments neatly printed at the back, cross-referenced to the page. There was even the leather-bound copy of Saint Teresa's *Life.* She'd been relieved to see that *The Horseman* was not in the collection—covered in pasteboard, it would not have been considered worthy of the Duke's library.

"Have you read Xenophon's *The Art of Horsemanship*?" the Abbé asked.

"Yes. It was one of my father's favorite books."

"It's my favorite as well," he said kindly. "You're going to have to come up with more sinful sins, Mademoiselle. You may kneel, if you wish."

Petite knelt on the padded prayer bench.

"Let's begin again: make the sign of the Cross. This is the Rite of Reconciliation. Remember that God loves you and wants you to be clean for Him. Imagine that I am Christ."

Petite closed her eyes and imagined Christ, but it was her father's face she saw—his gentle smile—and her eyes began to water.

"Then you make your Confession. 'Bless me, Father' and so forth."

"Bless me, Father, for—" Petite's voice broke. "For I have sinned," she whispered, blinking back tears.

The Abbé was silent for a long moment. "Do not fear, child," he said softly. "We will take this step by step."

Petite nodded but did not speak, wiping her cheeks on her sleeve. "Yes, Father," she said finally, sniffing.

"And then . . . then people usually say how long it has been since their last Confession, but today, you will simply say that this is your first."

"Yes, Father. This is my first Confession."

"That's right. And then you list your sins. Some people like to say, 'I accuse myself of such-and-such,' but that's a little dramatic, I think. If you just say the sin and then state how many times you did it, that would be perfectly acceptable. Remember that whatever you say will be kept private, so you don't have to worry about that. You may begin."

Petite clenched her hands together in prayer. Her heart was pounding. "I killed my father," she blurted out with a sob. The words burned! "One time."

The Abbé shifted in his seat. "Perhaps you should explain."

"Just that," Petite said, her breath coming in jags. *O Lord!* She squeezed her eyes shut.

"Don't be afraid. Now . . . just explain what happened."

"The Romas sold my father a wild horse, a White."

"Unbacked, you mean?"

"Yes, but mean. Some said he was cursed."

"We have rituals for such things."

"I know, Father. The village priest tried, but nothing changed. My father was going to kill him, but . . ." Petite paused, her mouth dry and her palms damp. The Abbé was wrong: there was cause to fear. She would not, could not, say the words bone magic. She knew the Devil's power, knew what the Devil could do. "But after the horse was gentled, my father agreed not to—and then he died," she said, choking at the memory of her father stretched out on the stable floor, the stall gate gaping open.

"I'm afraid I still don't understand. The horse died?"

"No," Petite whispered. "My father."

"But the horse was wild, and then he was broken."

"Yes, I backed him."

"How many years ago was this?"

"I was six, Father, and I'll be eleven this summer, so . . . five years ago."

"You were six years old, and you backed an unbroken horse?"

"Yes, Father, a stallion of about four years."

"Do you understand the difference between a falsehood and a truth?"

"I do, Father." Petite knew she was telling the truth, but she also knew that there was more to it, that she alone had not gentled Diablo, that the Devil had had a hand in it.

The Abbé shifted on his bench. "And this had something to do with the death of your father?"

Petite did not answer. She didn't want to lie; nor could she bear to tell the truth.

"You said you felt you had . . . that you were responsible somehow," the Abbé said.

"Yes," Petite said finally. "When my father first saw me riding this horse, he fell over as if dead."

"Did he die then?"

"No, but he was sick for a time after. And then the ploughman found him, dead on the stable floor." Her voice was unsteady.

"Very well," Abbé Patin said finally, after a long silence. "Say five Our Fathers before you leave. In the morning, you may take Communion."

"Is that all, Father?" Outside the tiny confessional, Petite could hear a woman humming tunelessly.

"No . . . there *is* more," the Abbé said with a smile in his voice. "You're to help me out in the stable, exercising some of the horses."

"But—I don't ride horses anymore."

"Yes, I sensed that. Nonetheless, you're to be there tomorrow afternoon, at four of the clock."

"Father, I can't," Petite said, a feeling of panic rising in her.

"Don't fear, child."

THAT NIGHT, PETITE COULD not sleep. When the village church rang for compline, she tiptoed to the window and eased open the wood shutter. Looking out, she saw the gardens bathed in moonlight, the silver ribbon of the river below, the fields beyond the stone stables. The moon hung full in the sky, illuminating horses standing in groups, nose to head, head to nose. In the distance was a glow—marsh gas, or possibly night spirits. She was startled by a screech owl's cry. Chilled and shivering, she slipped back under her quilts, feeling with her toes for the warming pan.

THE CHÂTEAU STABLES were a sprawling stone and wood structure on the far side of the kitchen gardens. Petite stood at the big double doors. The air was fragrant, sweet with the scent of straw and horse dung. Slowly, she went from stall to stall, looking at the noble horses, their muscles hard and gleaming, their coats smooth and shiny. Their standings were dry, their racks and mangers recently freshened with hay.

"Are you the girl they call Petite?"

Petite turned to face the head groom, who was picking his teeth with a penknife.

"Abbé Patin said I'm to saddle up one of the gallopers for you," he said, "but I think there must have been a mistake. You don't look big enough to ride a donkey."

Galloper or donkey, Petite didn't wish to ride at all. She hadn't been on a horse since her father's death.

"Good, you're here." Abbé Patin came striding down the aisle, a milk-colored cloak over one shoulder. He was dressed for riding in a brown doublet and hose. His military-style jackboots reached above his knees. "The horses are ready, Hugo?"

The groom brought out the Abbé's big charger, Eclypse, a handsome black hunter over fifteen hands tall. Following behind, a stable hand led a young stallion, an unsaddled bay.

The horse looked about uneasily. Petite ran her hand over his shoulder, which was deep and oblique: he would be fast. She breathed into his nose, took in his sweet breath. He turned his head to her, an invitation. He was about five years, she thought, feeling his teeth. Her father always said that a colt must be a full five before his wildness could be claimed. (Diablo had been only four.) "What's his name?"

"Hannibal," Abbé Patin said. "But he's not the horse for you. Go saddle one of the older, more settled ones," he told the groom.

"Easy, boy," Petite said in a soothing voice, observing the horse's eyes and ears for signs of fear. His uneasiness helped her forget her own. "Has he ever been shod?"

"Just last week," the groom said.

"He's been backed as well," Abbé Patin said, "but he bucks at a saddle, even with a straw pad."

"I could ride him without," Petite said, stroking his neck, calming the youngster. "Ho, boy," she whispered. "Don't be afraid."

Abbé Patin studied Petite. "Very well. We'll start off in the paddock—where I can keep an eye on things."

PETITE SELECTED A GENTLE bit and insisted on putting it on the colt herself. She took it slowly, letting him sniff the bit before slipping it into his mouth. She led him through droves of chicks and ducklings out to the paddock, the colt lifting his feet so as not to step on one. "Good boy," she said.

Abbé Patin held the reins as Petite mounted, the groom standing by.

She let out a long breath. "Ho, boy," she whispered. She arranged herself so that she was sitting on her petticoat, her skirt falling freely to her ankles.

"Hugo, lead her around. I want to observe how he goes," Abbé Patin said with concern in his voice.

"I'm fine, Father," Petite said, taking up the reins and nudging the colt forward into a walk.

Slowly, she took him through the paces. One ear forward, the other back, he began to relax, responding obediently: no prancing and hopping sideways, no twirling and throwing up his head, no rolling his eyes, pawing or snorting, not even so much as one little buck. Soon she had him cantering, then pulling up short, his head bowed, ears cocked back, awaiting her command.

"I think we're ready to head out, Abbé Patin," she announced. Truth was, riding felt good, like finding her voice again.

They set out into the hills, Abbé Patin on Eclipse, Petite on Hannibal, and the groom and two outriders following behind. The feel of the warm horse under her brought tears to Petite's eyes, conjured memories of riding Diablo.

Turning in his saddle, the Abbé asked, "Would you be all right with an easy hand-canter?"

"Could we gallop?"

"Call out if you get in trouble." He spurred his big charger.

Their horses surged up the trail. Petite's colt flew into the lead. "Whoop!" she cried out, jumping two hedges and a three-barred gate. Abbé Patin, following, kept his saddle, but the groom, in the last attempt, tumbled, falling behind with the straggling outriders.

An hour later, as the cows were being brought in to milk, Petite and a mud-splattered Abbé Patin emerged out of a belt of woodland. Petite, in the lead, slowed her horse to an amble. He was nicely lathered and breathing heavily. She stroked his damp shoulder.

"Splendid," Abbé Patin said with a sheepish grin, pulling up alongside. "There is nothing quite so thrilling as riding in fear for one's life."

Chapter Nine

THE FOLLOWING SUMMER Princess Marguerite turned eleven and Petite twelve. "In three years I shall be queen," Princess Marguerite informed all and sundry, impatient for her glorious future.

Weekly there was news of the King. It was reported that he was comely, that he refused to wear a wig, that he loved hunting, music and theater and danced the lead parts in ballets. Before and after a ball he went riding or did exercises with a lance. He did not eat waterfowl, but had a great appetite for everything else, even salads of green herbs. He and his friends were known as les Endormis—the sleepyheads—because they stayed out all night and slept all day.

"When I am queen, I shall not permit that," Marguerite said.

Two years later, the King almost died of a fever. He was only nineteen! For weeks unending, in every church, in every village and hamlet, citizens fell to their knees and prayed. Daily, the town crier called out alarming news: the King has been given Last Rites at midnight; a detachment of soldiers has been sent from Paris to carry his body back; the King has been given antimony in wine. And then, miraculously: the King's fever has broken! Church bells pealed throughout the night, and towns set aglow with candles and torches.

"He has been saved for *me*," Princess Marguerite said fervently on the eve of her thirteenth birthday. "And soon we shall marry." She had flowered only the month before, but was already big-breasted. Petite, a year older, looked yet a girl, thin, gangly and somewhat mystified over this obsessive interest in what was called *love*, an interest well fueled by the romances Nicole found hidden in the Duke's library.

Late that winter, Petite did flower, at last, and was even courted by the bucktoothed son of a second steward. One of his letters was intercepted by her mother, and the budding courtship put to a halt, somewhat to Petite's relief.

The spring was lush and warm; buttercups and forget-me-nots came early. Petite continued to ride daily, schooling the young horses, exercising them, training them for the hunts. Her mother objected, but Abbé Patin insisted; who else could gentle a horse so well? Petite still had her schoolwork and waited in attendance on the Princess as well. She managed it all by riding out into the dewy meadows at sunrise, revelling in the sounds of larks singing, jackdaws chattering, dragonflies and bees humming in the early light.

As the days lengthened, the princesses and their attendants became impatient to abandon their daily lessons, but it wasn't until the first week in July that they got their wish. Petite was quizzing Nicole on basic Latin grammar in the Duke's library when the panting footman arrived.

"It's something about going to see the Duchess," Nicole said under her breath.

"The princesses see their mother every day from eleven to eleven-twenty," Madame de Raré, the governess, could be heard to object. "Taking them now will throw off the entire day's schedule."

"Her Highness insists," the footman answered.

"Race you." Princess Marguerite jumped up from the study table and took off at a run, chased by her two younger sisters.

"As well as their attendants," the footman added, wiping the sweat from his brow with a grimy lace cuff.

The governess sighed and took up her silver-tipped cane. "Come along, girls. It's one hundred fifty-seven steps to Her Highness's bedchamber, and my old bones ache with every one of them."

PETITE FOLLOWED THE governess and Nicole down to the courtyard and across to the stone stairs. It had been almost a year since she had been in the King François wing of the château. She recalled arriving her first day, remembered being over-whelmed by luxury, intimidated by royalty. Now she saw the shoddy economies, the extravagant waste—bottles stopped up with tow instead of cork, priceless tulip bulbs left to rot in standing water.

Indeed, she'd even come to suspect that the members of the royal family were not a race apart, that they were human like everyone else. Nobility was said to be innate, an intrinsic quality carried in the blood—but was it possible for it to become corrupted? Princess Marguerite and her sisters had the blood of Henry the Great in their veins, but also the blood of a Médicis.

Was it possible that nobility of heart had little to do with high birth? Petite wondered. Her father had not had a title, had not qualified for tax exemptions and civic privileges, had not been entitled to own a coach draped with an impériale, much less the right to wear high red-heeled shoes, but he did have "nobility of heart," she thought, approaching the entrance to the Duchess's suite.

"Are the princesses already in with their mother?" the governess asked the guard, leaning on her cane. "Ah, there they are," she said as Princess Marguerite emerged from the guard room, sweaty and disheveled, followed by her two sisters. Princess Elisabeth's laces had come loose and the lace edge of Princess Madeleine's petticoat train was torn, dragging on the stone floor.

The governess wiped Princess Madeleine's face with her apron, and gave the sign to the footman to open the doors to the Duchess's bedchamber.

The enormous room was empty but for a bed at one end—much as Petite remembered it—although now the walls were covered with bright tapestries depicting scenes from the Bible: Jesus eating a roast guinea pig at the last supper, Jesus eating in the house of Lazarus, Jesus eating with sinners, Jesus eating fish with the disciples, Jesus multiplying loaves and fishes.

The Duchess was sitting up in bed eating a fowl, watched by her three terriers. The princesses dutifully lined up at the foot of the massive bed according to age: Marguerite, almost fourteen, Elisabeth, twelve, and Madeleine, ten.

"Time already?" the Duchess asked, throwing a bone into a porcelain bowl on the floor and holding out her fingers to be washed. "They're early."

"You sent for them, Your Highness," the governess said. "As well as the attendants."

"You remember, Your Highness?" a maid of honor said, spooning laudanum into a glass of spirits and handing it to the Duchess. "It's because the King is coming. We discussed this earlier."

The Duchess downed the spirits and lay back.

"The King?"

"Yes, Your Highness," the maid said. "His Majesty intends to stop at Blois on his way south—something to do with making peace with Spain. It is said that His Majesty is ready to take a bride—"

Marguerite clapped her hands.

"The King of Spain's daughter," the maid of honor said.

Marguerite's face turned red. "But *I'm* the one who is to marry the King. Everyone says so, even the astrologer."

The Duchess wiped her mouth on the bed linen. "The astrologer is here?" she asked.

"Your Highness, permit me to explain," the maid of honor said.

"I wish somebody would," the Duchess said dreamily.

"Princess Marguerite, your mother believes that the King must be made to see that there is no reason for him to marry a Spanish princess when there is a perfect French princess for him right here."

"Yes." Marguerite sounded tearful.

"Therefore, it has been suggested that you put on a performance—you and your sisters and even your attendants. Something that will display your charms and convince His Majesty that you are the perfect bride for him."

Petite glanced at Nicole in alarm. They were to perform for the King?

"It's to be a magnificent show in which Princess Marguerite will star. It has already been discussed with Monsieur de Gautier, who will be your dance master. You have three weeks to prepare."

"Why is the astrologer here?" Petite heard the Duchess ask as they bowed out of the room.

Monsieur de Gautier, dance master, was over sixty, but fancied that nobody noticed. He watched his diet, not even glancing at the tarts the cooks made. He did fencing exercises every morning and sported a short doublet with his linen undershirt showing, the latest in the fashion. He could not bring himself to give up wearing fusty wigs, however, even sleeping in one. It protected him from vermin and drafts, but most of all it prevented him from viewing his bald cranium in the looking glass each morning. Demoralization was not youthful.

He was thrilled about the coming Royal Visitation. As dance master for the Duc d'Orléans, his talents were going to ruin. He aspired to join the Court of the King, who was only twenty and a splendid specimen of male virility. This would be Gautier's chance to demonstrate his skill at set design and theatrical effects—not to mention dance sequences.

Well, perhaps not the dance part, he thought, facing the three hunchbacked princesses lined up before him, as well as the two attendants: Mademoiselle Nicole, a buxom gill-flirt, and the graceful but slightly lame one called Petite. He began with the basics, explaining that the walk employed the movements of the hip, the knee and, last but not least, the instep, and that from these three movements, all steps were formed.

He raised his cane as if it were a baton. "We begin."

He gloomed as the princesses lurched across the floor. "Stop! Princess Marguerite, everyone, please, watch now as . . ." He gestured to the thin girl to come forward. "Demonstrate a walk, Mademoiselle."

Petite's skirts made a swishing sound as her leather-soled slippers slid across the wooden floor.

Monsieur de Gautier cleared his throat. Even with a slight limp, the girl walked with remarkable grace. Her stepping foot touched the ground first, her legs turned slightly outward. She moved neither too fast (which showed folly), nor too slow (indolence).

"Observe: her head is upright, her waist steady, her arms well managed," he said, taking up a pochette to keep time. "As her right foot advances, the left arm moves forward, but only slightly." There was hope.

After a breakfast of beer and mutton, Petite was in the habit of meeting Nicole in a north stairwell, not far from the Princess's chamber. The rarely used landing had a stone bench to sit on and a horn-paned window that could be closed against inclement weather. They had taken to meeting thus most mornings before reporting for duty, sharing confidences regarding their mistress as well as such vital matters as how to increase the size of one's bust, what to do when the monthly courses came unexpectedly, and facts in general regarding the mysteries of the privy part: that redheads were the product of uncontrollable lust during the flowers, for example; that an owl hooting meant that someone was with child. But mostly, of late, they talked of Princess Marguerite's great challenge.

"Marguerite can't even make a curtsy without looking like a mule in a petticoat," Nicole said. "She's never going to capture the King this way."

"Poor Marguerite," Petite said sympathetically. She herself would never want to be queen, but it was different for a princess.

"She must conquer the King, and her only weapon is her bosom. Men like that, especially kings."

Sadly, this was a fact. Petite herself remained stubbornly flat-chested in spite of herbs and growing-chants.

"But the Duke insists that Princess Marguerite wear a tucker," Nicole persisted. "If I were Marguerite, I would kill myself. Then maybe the King would fall in love with her."

"But then she'd be dead," Petite said.

A FLURRY OF preparation preceded the King's arrival. The château swarmed with butlers, pageboys and maids hired specially for the grand occasion.

"I've observed the kitchen, the dairy, the food cupboard, the laundry," the Marquis complained to Françoise, shuffling to and fro with his hands behind his back, "and in every region there is a crisis. In the antechamber, a damaged candle was fixed into a powder-horn. In the cabinet neuf, some idiot has used the extremity of the Duke's ivory staff to awaken the embers, and in the salle de conseil, a magpie was unleashed. There are leavings everywhere!"

It was decided that the King, the Queen Mother and the rest of the royal family (including la Grande Mademoiselle) and their hundred and twenty-six attendants would stay at Chambord, the royal hunt château not far from Blois on the other side of the river. But then, of course, additional staff (including four rat-catchers) had to be found to ready *that* château. The four hundred unfurnished rooms were not a problem; the royal entourage would be arriving with its own beds, bed curtains, pillows and linens. But then it was decided, rather late, that the Duke and Duchess and their three daughters would formally greet the King upon his arrival *there*—and so the best coaches were repaired and harnessed, and an escort of fifty guards called up. The royal party departed, the Duke and Duchess in the lead, followed by Marguerite and her two sisters with Nicole in an ancient, but gilded, closed carriage. The servants, overseen by the Marquis and Madame Françoise, followed behind.

Petite, at Abbé Patin's request, rode horseback on one of the younger stallions. Every horse in the stable had had to be saddled. For some, it would be their first journey across the bridge, their first journey away from the security of the stable, and Abbé Patin, as equerry, needed Petite's help.

Petite's horse, Arion, was a young bay hunter. He was uneasy crossing the mighty Loire, but relaxed into a trot once on the other side. It was only his third ride out in the world and he was keeping his head.

As they entered a flat and sandy region, the horizon opened. They rode by vineyards, scattered peasant cottages and orchards, the trees netted to protect the fruit from birds. Women in white caps and clunky sabots waved to them from the fields.

After over an hour, they passed through a gap in a stone wall—the modest gateway to the château—then down a long, straight avenue, the woods on either side a tangle of brush. At last, the enormous round towers of Chambord appeared as if out of nowhere, its numerous turrets, spires and chimneys giving it the appearance of a small city.

It was a monstrous structure, Petite couldn't help but think as she rode across the wide, fetid moat into the courtyard, her horse shying at the shadow of a gargoyle falling across the stones.

Stable boys ran out to take the horses. Petite dismounted, stretched and shook out the wide-skirted safeguard that protected her skirts from mud.

The Duke helped the Duchess down out of the carriage. Her Highness had not been out of her chambers for two years and was under nerval strain, no doubt, for she slipped on a cobble and had to be carried into the château on a litter. The princesses followed, their voices echoing in the vast entry. Immediately, Elisabeth and Madeleine ran noisily up and down the famous double staircase—demonstrating how they could do so without meeting—until, finally, word was sent that they were to be silent or go outside.

The weather was sultry, damp and cloudy. The bored girls sat on the edge of the moat. All was perfectly still but for the buzzing of gnatlike insects, which began to swarm. Slapping at her cheeks, Princess Marguerite ran back into the château, but soon itchy red welts appeared all over her face and neck.

"The sweet itch," Petite said. She knew it well in horses.

"I want to die," Princess Marguerite said, spotting her gown with tears.

"Stop bawling." Nicole slathered the Princess's face with white lead paste.

"What is this infernal squalling?" the Marquis de Saint-Rémy demanded, entering the chamber with Abbé Patin. "Your Highness," he said, on realizing that the offender was a princess.

"Princess Marguerite?" Abbé Patin looked horrified. The paste covering Marguerite's face was now streaked with blood.

"Gnats," Nicole explained.

"Send for my carriage," Marguerite commanded, with a brave attempt at dignity.

"Yes, it would be wise for the Princess to return to Blois," Petite suggested to her stepfather. She and Nicole would draw a cool lavender-scented bath for her, to calm her.

"But the King," the Marquis stuttered. "He's anticipated."

"Exactly," Nicole said.

The coaches had yet to be unharnessed, so they were able to set out quickly—the three princesses and Nicole in the six-horse coach, Abbé Patin and Petite on horseback, accompanied by an armed four-guard escort, two ahead and two behind.

The journey back did not seem to take as long as the one there. The horses, knowing that they were heading home, trotted briskly through the undulating hills and uplands lined with vine trees, the forests of oak, chestnut and walnut trees. A wind had picked up, pushing them along.

Petite was relieved, at last, to see the Blois docks on the other side of the Loire; soon they would be back at the château. The sun came out, briefly, lighting the bright houses at the water's edge, their reflections rippled by wind on the water. Lupin seeds helped soothe itchy inflammations, she recalled. Lupins would not yet be in seed, but the Duke's head gardener might have some saved from last year.

No sooner had they started over the bridge than the mast of a barge crashed into an arch. The stone bridge held steady, but the sound of splintering wood and the sudden appearance of the ship's flag and rigging caused some of the horses to rear up. The princesses screamed. A guard's horse whinnied, threw his rider and bolted.

"It's Helios," Petite called out to Abbé Patin. The colt was only four years old and subject to affrights. "He's been cut." She saw spots of blood on the cobbles.

"Oh, no—he's heading *back*," Abbé Patin said as the colt raced past him, reins flying.

Nicole stuck her head out the carriage window, wide-eyed. "What happened?"

"A barge didn't get its sail down in time," Abbé Patin said. "The horses are steady now, but I have to catch a runaway—Mademoiselle Petite is to come with me."

"He's taking the river road," Petite said, her eyes on the spotted colt.

With that, Abbé Patin turned, spurred his horse and took off, Petite doing her best to keep up (in spite of riding sidesaddle).

Nearing Saint-Dyé, they halted. The Abbé's heavyset stallion, lathered and panting, pranced in place, tossing his head.

"The colt might have cut off here." Abbé Patin pointed his whip at a dirt path through hay fields, half mown. "Or he might have gone on ahead, along the road."

Petite examined the roadway for tracks, signs of blood. There were hoofprints everywhere. "Does the path lead to the castle?"

"It goes to one of the park gates. There's a forester's cottage there."

Petite tried to imagine which way the panicked colt might have taken. He was unfamiliar with this terrain, and although scent was a strong compass, horses didn't always take the shortest path. "He could have gone either way."

"I'll follow the road, and you take the path."

Petite nodded, unsure. She was to ride out alone?

"Meet me back here," he said, and burst off down the road, clots of soil flying.

Petite headed down the dirt track, trotting her horse on the grassed-over flat between the ruts. Not far on, she saw fresh hoofprints. She picked up a hand-canter, ducking under low-hanging tree branches. The wall surrounding the park was made of stone. A gate of peeled logs hung open. Just inside was a cottage with an antlered stag's head over the door: the forester's hut. A man emerged wearing a thick woolen shooting jacket in spite of the heat.

"Monsieur, one of the Duc d'Orléans's horses got loose," Petite said. "He's likely heading to the château." Over the treetops, she could just see the castle's turrets and towers.

The man yawned, scratching his big belly. "I didn't see it."

Didn't hear it even? "Was the gate open?"

"It's open, yes," he said, picking his teeth.

Petite heard a raucous chorus of jays. "I must go after the colt. He's injured, and saddled. He could do himself harm."

"The King is coming today."

"I know." It was possible he'd already arrived. Petite could just imagine the consternation at a colt running loose, causing havoc. "Are the trails marked?"

"There's only one clear."

Petite headed into the park. Stands of fine old oaks had been infested with worms. She stayed on the one trail that had been cleared: the colt would have as well. It was a sandy terrain, without marsh or bogs.

She came upon a woodland meadow. She could see the colt's path through the long grass. Her horse whinnied . . . and a horse answered. *The colt.*

Petite allowed her horse his head. He pushed his way through a dense copse and over a rocky stream into yet another clearing. There, in the distance, she spotted the colt. A man was holding his reins. *Thanks be to Mary!*

Petite approached at a trot, then slowed. "Is he hurt?" she called out. The man was young, not much older than she was—in his twenties, she guessed. He was humbly dressed, but comely. Unhatted, his long hair hung about his shoulders. He was carrying a gun and a game bag—full, it appeared.

"He bucked his rider at the Blois bridge," Petite said. She feared she looked a fright. Her hair had blown free during that long, hard gallop.

The man gazed up at her. "He has a cut on his right haunch," he said.

Petite nodded. His eyes were hazel, and his skin was dark, much rudded by the sun. There was something of the Latin in him, something almost Moorish. He had a commanding figure—strong and athletic. "He was bleeding," she said, her mouth dry.

"The cut's not deep. I found some wild burnet and was able to stanch it. He should be fine."

Petite tried to speak, but could not. She wanted to say that she knew all about burnet, that she had many a time gathered it with her father. She well remembered its large winged leaves, nicked at the edges, gray on the underside. In June, its small purple flowers made it easy to find, but now, late in July, it would have been difficult to see in the long meadow grass.

"Good," she finally managed to say. He must think her an idiot.

"Mainly he's just frightened," he said, stroking the horse's neck.

"His name is Helios," Petite blurted out. She felt dangerously light-headed. She hoped he wasn't a poacher. She admired the gentle way he was handling the skittish colt.

"Tireless Helios, the Greek sun god," he said, glancing up at her again, smiling. "A fine name for a horse."

Petite was surprised and pleased that he knew ancient mythology. Perhaps he was gentry. She wanted to tell him that she knew the Greek myths well herself, that she had named the colt after poring over the ancient texts in the Duke's library. "How did you catch him?"

"Oh, in the usual way: I let him come to me. He was curious—like any youngster." He handed her the reins.

"Thank you." His fingers—which felt soft, not calloused at all—lightly brushed her wrist, sending a jolt through her. She thought of a line from the romance Nicole had been reading to the Princess: *Adieu, my beloved. I know you not, and yet I know you.* It did not seem like such nonsense to her now.

"My pleasure, Mademoiselle," he said. "You ride exceptionally well," he added, giving a salute.

"Thank you," Petite repeated, moving away, pulling the colt after her. *Adieu, adieu*—would she ever see him again? "The King is coming," she told him, as a warning.

"I know," he said. "He arrived a while ago."

"Oh!" she exclaimed, spurring her mount.

At the edge of the woods, she looked back. He was watching her.

Chapter Ten

CHURCH BELLS BEGAN to ring and then cheering was heard.

"It must be the King," Petite said, fastening the Princess's veil with silver gilt pins. The inflammations from the bites were still visible, in spite of healing ointments.

The palace was a madhouse, and Petite was exhausted. She had been up late the night before, attending to the stricken Princess, and then she hadn't slept. She'd put a pillow over her head to muffle the hourly cry of the night watchman. Finally, in the early hours, she'd dropped off to sleep, wrapped in reverie and sweet longing dreams—only to be woken by the return of the Marquis and her mother from Chambord.

Everyone, it seemed, was vexed: the Marquis had panicked on learning that the delivery of fish for the banquet was delayed, and her mother had an attack of nerves on discovering that her only ball gown no longer fit. At terce, the Duke and the still-hobbling Duchess had returned from Chambord, causing yet more commotion. All the while Monsieur de Gautier, the dance master, had been running to and fro, trying to get the stage effects to work properly.

Trumpets sounded. "It *is* him," Nicole said.

Princess Marguerite popped an anise pastille into her mouth to sweeten her breath. "How do I look?"

"Lovely, Your Highness," Petite lied. She felt on edge herself, jittery as a colt in a storm. She couldn't believe that she was actually going to see the King.

They headed for the grand staircase, where Monsieur de Gautier was positioning everyone to create the best effect. Princess Marguerite was put in the front, on the first step, her sisters on the step behind, flanked by the Duke and Duchess.

Most of the attendants were placed within the château, out of sight. Nicole and Petite were told to stay in the deserted guard room (where at least they had the advantage of a window enclosure).

A gilded, domed carriage with scarlet wheels entered the courtyard, the coachman, footmen and pages all clothed in matching scarlet livery. A footman opened the carriage door and let down the stepping board, bowing deeply. A young man emerged in a brown justacorps and breeches, a cloak flung over one shoulder. All they could see was the top of his tricorn hat with its red cockade.

"That must be the King," Petite said. "Everyone is bowing."

"Be still my heart," Nicole breathed.

GASTON, THE DUC D'ORLÉANS, showed his nephews, Louis and Philippe, and the Queen Mother to the three upholstered armchairs in the vast salle des états. Anyone else with the right to sit had to make do with stools—even *he* . . . yet another annoyance. It irked him to have to sit on a stool in his own château in front of all these guests, over a thousand of the local gentry, dressed in outdated finery. That it wasn't even really *his* château made him even crosser. That God had not graced him with a legitimate male heir meant that everything—*everything*—would be reclaimed by the Crown upon his death—which, given his temper of late, was no doubt rapidly approaching. *Perhaps I should die now*, he thought, *before the performance.*

Ah yes, the performance. His overwrought daughters had been practicing for weeks. At least he wouldn't have to sit through any more tedious rehearsals, endure their tantrums and tears.

The violinists gathered up their instruments. Gaston braced himself. Finding good musicians in the province had been impossible. Romas with pipes and tabors could be had for a sou—but no, his guest was his nephew the King, and Romas simply would not do, even for a festival that (he hoped) was to have a charming air of the Middle Ages.

The expense of all this! Economies were causing him no end of grief. It was simply too much to have to keep track of all the candles and foodstuffs, to count each bale of hay, each bushel of oats, to track the pennies spent shoeing and nailing, to chart the expense of keeping sixteen running dogs and five greyhounds. Where was he to trim costs? The stabling alone required by his nephew the King was costing him a small fortune.

"We should begin, Your Highness?" Monsieur de Gautier gave him a look. "You know: the *performance*."

Gaston groaned as a footman in shabby livery helped pull him to his feet. His eldest daughter by his first marriage (la Grande Mademoiselle—the old, bossy and rich one) insisted it was the damp air at Blois that made his bones ache. She'd persuaded him to take powdered St. John's wort, which did help, he had to admit, but it made him fart, so he'd refrained for the purpose of the Visitation.

The Visitation. Mon Dieu, you would think it was the Lord Jesus himself the way everyone was carrying on. Louis was King, true, but he was also Gaston's twenty-year-old nephew, the one who had bagged *all* the pheasants the Duke had been cultivating for two and a half years, the twenty-year-old over whom his daughters swooned. Was the boy so good-looking as all that? He was fit, certainly, but what twenty-year-old wasn't? A bit of a bumpkin, in Gaston's view—not unlike the dolt his father had been, always on about horses and hounds.

It irked him—it did! Gaston himself might have been king several times over. Were it not for the smallest turn of fate—his hapless brother finally getting his wife with child (after twenty-three years: was that not suspicious?)—he, Gaston, would have been the one in the armchair, everyone bowing and scraping, turning themselves inside-out to please. But no, he was merely the old uncle on the stool, pulled to his feet by a perspiring footman in worn-out livery. His life was coming to an end—he was sure of it—and what had it all amounted to? *Daughters.*

"Where's my tucker?" Princess Marguerite asked through clenched teeth, unable to move her jaw lest the white lead paste covering her face flake.

"I couldn't find it," Nicole told her, adjusting the Princess's lace petticoat. The kitchen boys' ballet was coming to an end; the girls would go on next.

"But I must have a dozen," the Princess said, brushing white flecks off her exposed bosom.

"It's a mystery," Nicole said cheerfully.

Petite peeked out from between the makeshift curtains. The vast room was crowded. She spotted her mother standing off to one side beside the Marquis. Where was the royal family? If only she could see better through the swarms of servants.

Mercy! The Queen Mother was sitting directly in front with the Duke's eldest daughter, la Grande Mademoiselle. As the big princess talked, the Queen Mother frowned down at her hands. (Petite wondered if it was true that she wore pigskin gloves at night to keep them soft.)

Where was the King? Petite thought he might be the man standing behind the Queen Mother with Philippe. With all the people moving to and fro, all she could get were glimpses. She thought it must be the King because of the brown justacorps he was wearing.

"Do you think the King's brother paints his face?" Nicole whispered, looking over Petite's shoulder.

Petite nodded. Philippe—known by the title "Monsieur"—was stylishly adorned in a beribboned periwig and ruffled petticoat breeches. "He's powdered," she said, watching as he turned to address the Duke. She wondered if he used powder of ground-up pearls, which, although dear, was said to be best for the skin.

"I didn't expect the Queen Mother to be so old," Nicole said. "Or the King so well made. Oh là là, his legs."

So that was the King. He stooped down to say something to his mother. "His demeanor is so—"

"So manful," Nicole said with a sigh.

"So noble," Petite said. He looked up, and she gasped. It was *him*.

"What's wrong?"

Petite put her hands over her heart. Her poacher was the King.

LA GRANDE MADEMOISELLE could not believe what she was seeing. True, the set was magnificent. The river waves were convincing (cleverly created by two men waving a painted cloth), and the sound of thunder (cannon balls rolled down tin-covered stairs) was so frightening it made the hounds bark. True, the kitchen boys' ballet was vigorous and charming. Her half-sisters, however, simply could not dance. They stepped all over themselves performing a simple branle. Marguerite, who was supposed to be the star, was the worst. Why was her face covered in white paste? And where was her tucker? She looked like a harlot. And those maids of hers: one brawling and brazen and the other one, the thin one with a limp, stumbling around as if in a dream. What had come over them all?

She had been relieved when the performance finally came to an end and the platters of food carried in . . . or so she had thought at the time, for nothing could have been as shocking as her half-sisters' comportment at the table—or rather, their lack of it. Marguerite, the eldest, wiped her nose with the tablecloth, then gobbled down five raw oysters with loud smacking sounds. The two younger princesses were even worse, fidgeting as they ate, poking at their teeth and sticking fingers in their ears. Hadn't her stepmother taught them anything?

There was a clump of hardened something on her knife and her lap cloth was frayed. And where had the staff come from? Every single walleyed one of them had some sort of twitch, serving up platters with their thumbs in the soup. Was *this* her father's idea of a royal banquet? La Grande Mademoiselle wished she could disappear.

MONSIEUR GASTON, THE DUC D'ORLÉANS, looked down at his plate. Was that even fish under the heavy sauce? It was a Friday, a fast-day, and the King's maître d'hôtel had insisted that he send to the ocean ports for sole, sturgeon, turbot . . . limandes even. As if river fish weren't good enough! Gaston cautiously took a bite. It was chewy, so perhaps it was cuttlefish. He couldn't be sure. The light from the tapers was too dim to see by. Perhaps he should have allowed his bumbling chief steward to order more candles.

Years ago they had lived in light. Now things had changed; now he had "economies"—and all because of his nephew the King. The minute Louis was born, the minute it was known that he—Gaston, the Duc d'Orléans, son of Henry the Great—was no longer first in line for the throne, the laborers building his new wing had quit. They knew there would no longer be sufficient funds for their pay.

The silence at the tables was deafening. All that could be heard was the sound of the guests pushing food around their metal plates. Perhaps, Gaston thought . . . perhaps he should not have dismissed the violinists. A little music—even bad music—might have helped, despite the expense.

The Queen Mother, seated in the place of honor on his right, seemed to be studiously avoiding him.

Well. Gaston sighed: could he blame her? Likely it hadn't been wise to doubt the King's paternity so publicly all those twenty years ago—but having witnessed the baby emerging and seeing in the infant's genitalia his own downfall, was it not understandable that he'd had something of a lapse in judgment?

He'd meant only to make a witticism, after all, say something clever to amuse the few who had dared to join him that evening. Of *course* he'd ordered his cellarer to bore his final cask of Italian white Trebbiano—the costly muscatel would be his last, after all. He could not, in fact, remember saying the offending words, but the next morning he was being quoted everywhere: *I can vouch that the Dauphin came out of the Queen, but I cannot vouch for who put him in there.*

It *was* a clever remark, was it not? Pity that the Queen Mother took it personally. In truth he had always loved his brother's Spanish wife. Indeed, they had once mildly flirted. Her intoxicating beauty—sensual and yet virtuous, an irresistible mix—was wasted on his effeminate dolt of a brother, God rest his soul. No, there was to be no justice in this life. After that comment, the Queen Mother, his sweet Señora Anne, no longer blessed him with her lovely smiles. Even now . . .

Gaston glanced again at the Queen Mother. She'd taken a bite and seemed to be chewing for a long time. Perhaps she'd partaken of the same cuttlefish. Gaston wondered if she had problems with her teeth. She was still a beauty, in spite of her girth, her sober demeanor. Once she had been slender, and oh, *so* gay.

"Your Highness," he said finally, addressing her, "tomorrow evening I have arranged to have a troupe of actors perform a comedy."

"I'm afraid that we won't be here," the Queen Mother said evenly.

Everyone stared. Gaston's wife at the far end of the table stopped chewing.

"We must depart for the south," the Queen Mother announced to them all, placing her serviette on her plate.

"But . . . but we were told you would stay at Chambord for three nights," Gaston protested, stuttering. "I've planned entertainments for you every afternoon, and—"

"There has been a change of plans," said the Queen Mother, rising.

Gaston leapt to his feet. There was a loud scraping of chairs and hurried bows as the royal party rapidly took their leave.

"No dessert?" the Duchess asked, bewildered.

"I will see to their coaches, Your Highness," the dance master told Gaston, rushing after the royal guests.

"What a muddle," Nicole told Petite, her pewter plate heaped with desserts. Indeed, there was food in abundance. The basement table for the upper staff was covered with dishes, but already the fish smelled off, in spite of the richly spiced sauce. The sweets, on the other hand, were tempting: bowls of melting crème glacée, platters of biscuits au chocolat, a vast compote de prunes grillées.

Nicole started to say more, but was drowned out by the parade of servants filing by, en route to the basement kitchens balancing trays of dirty dishes. "I told Princess Marguerite that it's not too late," she continued when it was quieter. "She could run away to Chambord, join the King's entourage as a maid, and then, when he tries to deflourish her, reveal herself as a princess and demand he make an honest woman of her."

"You must stop reading those romances," Petite said. She was too elated and confused to care about the Princess, frankly. All she could think of, with a dizzying pang, was her last glimpse of the King. As the royal party had prepared to depart, she and Nicole emerged from the service entrance. The King had turned. His eyes—she was sure of it—had lingered, for a long moment, on *her*. Did he recognize her? Did he remember?

Chapter Eleven

THE CHÂTEAU FELL into gloom after the King's departure, as if a spell had been cast. Even the announcement that a treaty had been signed with Spain was met with indifference. For the first time in more than twenty years there would be peace—but likely to be sealed by the King's marriage to the Spanish Infanta.

The Duke's humors went out of balance after the abrupt departure of the royal party, and on the twenty-seventh of January he came down with a fever. Two celebrated doctors from Paris were sent for, but after only one week the priests were called in.

"We're going to need mourning gowns," Princess Marguerite informed her waiting maids. "A seamstress is coming this afternoon."

Petite's eyes filled: the Duke was *dying?* She felt she had come to know him personally, albeit indirectly. She had been spending time in the château library, and on a number of occasions she had come across the Duke's notations in the margins: *Ha ha! Preposterous! The fool!* "I'm so sorry. That's . . ." The words *sad* or *terrible* or even *awful* seemed too pedestrian for a man like the Duke, the son of King Henry the Great. "Tragic," she said with feeling, recalling the devastation of her own father's death.

"I know," Princess Marguerite agreed. "Once he dies, we won't be able to live here anymore—because we're only *girls*," she added with disdain. Without a male heir, all the Duke's property reverted to the Crown.

THE DUC D'ORLÉANS's bedchamber smelled of incense, pigeon feathers and caudle, a warm sickbed gruel mixed with ale. The shutters had been fastened, the drapes drawn, and the fire and candles lit. To prevent his soul from escaping, five dead pigeons—messengers to the spirit world—had been placed at the foot of his bed, a massive piece of furniture hung with faded embroidered cloth.

Squeezed between a curio cabinet and trunk, Petite and Nicole stood behind the three princesses at the periphery of the room, watching as Abbé Patin approached the bed. "Your Highness, your devoted daughters have come to see you." Abbé Patin gestured to Princess Marguerite to come forward.

"What should I say?" Princess Marguerite looked stricken.

"Tell him that you will pray for him," Petite whispered, her eyes tearing.

Marguerite stepped to the foot of the bed. "I will pray for you, Sire," she said.

"Your Highness, give your daughter your blessing." Abbé Patin leaned over the bed. "Repeat after me: 'I bless you.'"

"I bless you," the Duke said feebly, his eyes closed.

Marguerite kept her head down, her eyes fixed to the floor. Petite handed her a nose cloth, sensing that she was about to cry. The Princess pressed it to her eyes.

On Candlemas, after all the beeswax candles in the château had been carted to the chapel to be blessed, after every brittle sprig of holly, ivy and mistletoe had been taken down, the princesses and their attendants gathered in the château library to read from their breviaries. Shortly after eleven of the clock, a funereal bell signaled that the soul of the Duke had departed.

The girls fell to their knees and made the sign of the Cross, as Madame de Raré led them in prayer. "O gentlest heart of Jesus, have mercy on the soul of thy servant . . ."

Petite silently counted the solemn tolls of the bell. *One. Two. Three* . . . Outside she could hear the faint lowing of the cattle being brought in from the hay meadows. The scent of freshly baked bread filled the air. *Four. Five. Six* . . .

Then other bells joined in and the pealing turned raucous, joyful even.

"The soul of His Highness your father is ascending," Madame de Raré said uneasily. "Let us rejoice."

"What a racket," the youngest princess said, covering her ears. It sounded as if pots and pans were being hit with metal objects.

And then they heard wagon wheels in the courtyard.

"Why is the furniture being removed?" Princess Marguerite asked, looking out.

Things were being handed out the windows to carters: chairs, candlesticks, even bed curtains.

"We're being robbed," whispered Madame de Raré, and the youngest princess burst into tears.

"By the servants," Petite said, recognizing a water boy.

"We must alert the guards." Madame de Raré grabbed her cane.

"The guards *are* the robbers," Nicole noted as four husky men in uniform loaded an ormolu mirror onto a cart.

"Your Highnesses?"

Petite's stepfather stood in the doorway, looking bewildered and uncharacteristically undone, his ruff askew.

"Your esteemed father, the Duke—"

"We're being robbed," the governess said.

"I comprehend," the Marquis answered with a shaky sigh. There was nothing anyone could do, he explained. Everything had, in fact, been ransacked, stolen the moment the Duke breathed his last. Even the sheet that covered his body had been stripped from him. "It is your mother the Duchess who appeals for you currently, Your Highnesses," he said, bowing with grave formality.

Petite and Nicole stood behind the princesses as they paid their condolences to the Duchess, who was reclining on her bed in a heavy black gown, her head draped with a lace-edged veil of black crêpe. Already the room had been hung in black and the one mirror covered. Two attendants, also in black, were sitting by the fire, making what appeared to be mourning jewelry from the Duke's hair.

The Duchess's maid of honor stood beside her reading a prayer out loud: "O God Almighty, I pray Thee, by the Precious Blood which Thy Divine Son Jesus shed, deliver the soul in Purgatory that is destitute of spiritual aid. Amen."

"Amen," the princesses said, their heads bowed.

"Amen," Petite and Nicole said.

"Eternal rest give unto him, O Lord, and let perpetual light shine upon him. Amen."

"Amen," they all echoed.

"Amen," Abbé Patin said, entering with a document in his hand.

"Where is my Duke?" the Duchess demanded.

Abbé Patin glanced over at the princesses with a look of dismay. "With the Lord Almighty, Your Highness."

"Tell him to come home."

"I would if I could, Your Highness," Abbé Patin said gently, "but I'm afraid that the good Lord wishes to keep him."

"Amen," the Duchess said with a sigh.

"Forgive me, Your Highness, but at present the law requires that I read you the Duke's last wishes." The Abbé held up the document.

The Duchess fell back against the pillows and closed her eyes.

Solemnly, Abbé Patin read the Duke's will, informing the Duchess that her husband had left everything to the Crown: his library of ancient texts, his collections of stamps, medals and engraved stones, even his cabinets of curiosities. His tulip bulbs, however, he had bequeathed to the Queen Mother. What remained was to go to charitable foundations.

"Send for my lawyer," the Duchess said, as if waking from a long sleep.

"WE'RE MOVING TO Paris," Princess Marguerite announced to Petite and Nicole. "*Immediately.* The Duchess says we must take possession of my father's palace in Paris before la Grande Mademoiselle claims it. She has countless castles, and we don't even have one."

Petite set aside the book she was reading (Ovid's *Metamorphoses*). They were moving—to Paris? The city was dangerous; there were murderers there.

"Alleluia," Nicole said.

But then, the King lives in Paris, Petite thought—*as well as my brother.* "Even the Duchess?" she asked. What about the sacred observances? A widow was to stay in a darkened room for forty days after the death of a husband.

"She's leaving day after tomorrow with the chief steward and his wife."

Petite was astonished. Everything was happening so quickly. "But what about the Duke?" His body was on display in the Church of Saint-Sauveur. His heart was to be embalmed and then donated to the Jesuit convent that afternoon.

"She's taking him with her . . . and we're to follow in a week or two." Princess Marguerite twirled, revealing a forbidden red flannel petticoat.

THE PRINCESSES SET OUT for Orléans on the twentieth of February. They were a party of forty-seven: the princesses and their attendants (Petite, Nicole and four others); the governess; the attendants' attendants (Clorine and six others);

a cook and her three helpers; the grooms, equerries and all the guards.

The river, normally placid, was swollen and somewhat treacherous due to ill weather. Teams of oxen pulled the boats upriver against a wind. Carp were caught and cooked over charcoal burners on the blustery deck.

Petite stood against the rail, watching the passing woods and undulating meadows. Horses cantered and kicked in a field, tossing their heads. There was a white horse among them (but it was dappled). She'd never been so far from home.

From Orléans they traveled north by coach, reaching the ancient hunting château of Fontaine Beleau on the sixth day. From there it would be only one long day's journey by barge to the city.

They left before sunrise, in the dark. Wolves could be heard howling in the distant woods. The sky lightened in brilliant hues. The girls played Put-and-Take (Petite winning ten sous) as their governess read out loud to them from *The Book of Vices and Virtues*. Gradually, the river opened onto a vast plain dotted with windmills, and suddenly, there it was before them on the distant horizon: *Paris*, its spires and towers rising up through a haze of smoke.

Part III

THE ENCHANTER

Chapter Twelve

THE RIVER BECAME congested, the water murky, the air scented with refuse. Windmills stood motionless against an ominous gray sky. Boats loaded with grain, livestock, bricks or lumber seemed barely able to float. Madeleine, the youngest princess, waved gaily to them all, even to some chickens bound at the feet, hanging woefully from a pole.

Sprawling monasteries and cloisters gave way to a patchwork of homesteads with gardens, vineyards, pastures of animals picking at weeds. Pigs wandered dirt roads lined with sod huts. A pack of snarling dogs circled an overturned baker's cart. Four children ran barefoot along the shore, chasing after a man driving a high gig, a thin cow tied behind. Laundry boats hugged the shore, patched linens hanging from the riggings like sails.

And then, beyond the towpath, they saw vast gardens and two enormous edifices, the royal palaces of the King—the ancient Tuileries and the newer Louvre, both empty now because the Court was still in the south. They passed under a footbridge and pulled up in front of a tower.

As the barge jolted against a crowded dock, their captain yelled instructions to the workers. The governess grabbed Princess Madeleine's apron strings before she could climb out.

"Smells like a chamber pot," Princess Marguerite said, pressing a nose cloth to her face.

"Why are we stopping here?" Nicole asked. The city proper was farther up the river.

"The Palais d'Orléans is on the other side, outside the city walls, in the countryside," the captain said, throwing a rope to a laborer on the dock. "We have to take boats across."

They had to wait as their papers were checked, the toll taxes paid, the barge-owner, cook and tow-boys tipped, and their trunks reloaded onto passage boats. At last they set off, the eleven laden vessels perilously winding through the busy river traffic, dodging the flyboats darting in and out. A church bell was ringing for vespers by the time they pulled up near a massive stone structure. The city wall was as wide as a horse from nose to tail, and so high Petite had to crane her neck to see the ramparts above. A tree was growing out of a tower.

They were required to wait as their trunks were once again unloaded.

"Ready?" the captain said finally, opening the door of a conveyance with one hand and fending off vendors, tradesmen and beggars with the other.

Princess Marguerite frowned at the shabby hackney.

"It's not a team of six, I know," the captain said, "but it will be nightfall soon and you'll be safer in disguise." The rest of the entourage had long ago set out.

The three princesses, Petite, Nicole and the governess squeezed into the dirty interior, the captain climbing up beside the driver, his sword unsheathed. Clorine and the other servants perched on top of the trunks piled onto the wagons following behind.

They took a muddy road along the outside of the city wall, a stone construction punctuated by peaked turrets. On their left was open country, on their right the tall city wall. Every three, four or five turrets there was a gated entrance: porte Saint-Victor, porte Saint-Marcel, and then porte Saint-Jacques—a large and busy entry crowded with vendors and beggars, full of ragged children.

"This is where Jeanne d'Arc entered the city," Petite said. "I think." *With my great-great-great-great-grandfather.* She craned her head to glimpse the city within. She could see all manner of carts, carrying-chairs and coaches surrounded by swarms of foot passengers: a chimney sweep, two women with their ankles showing, a peg-legged beggar. She looked out for the wanton women, the petty thieves and bandits Paris had in great numbers. The Devil resided in Paris; that was known. She wondered if Jean's school was nearby.

Shortly after porte Saint-Michel, the carriage turned away from the wall onto a muddy rutted road, bouncing perilously over slop-filled potholes as it passed a two-wheeled cart loaded with barrels of wine. The driver stopped as a mangy dog crossed the road. Beyond, to the left, were open fields and woods dotted with clusters of buildings—a number of them monasteries with large gardens, Petite guessed, reassured by the peace of that landscape.

"Up ahead is the Saint-Germain Fair," the captain yelled down.

Princesses Marguerite and Elisabeth hung out one window. The vast covered market teemed with people—commoners, but also some elite in furs and feathers. A beggar in velveteen breeches knelt by the entrance with two lit candles before him. Beside him a boy played a flute. The scent of fried oysters hung on the air.

"I'm hungry," Princess Elisabeth said.

"We're almost there," the captain shouted as a stately palace came into view.

"I thought it would have a moat," Princess Marguerite said.

The palace was a square edifice enclosing a simple flagged courtyard, symmetrical and well proportioned. Petite was surprised that it was so elegant. It had been built only a half century earlier by Marie de Médicis, yet another evil Italian queen, and Petite had expected something sinister. The vast gardens edged with groves of chestnut trees gave the setting a monastic gloom that appealed to her.

"It's out in the middle of nowhere," Nicole said.

The riding will be good, Petite thought.

An attendant in livery ran to meet them, shooing away a goat in order to open the massive iron gates, which were inscribed, in gold, PALAIS D'ORLÉANS.

"I have to pluck a rose," the youngest princess said, taken by an urgent need as their carriage slowed to a stop.

It was dark in the regal entry. The tapers set in candelabra had not been lit. A butler with a torch led them into a vast, empty room—a guard room, to judge by the spears propped in one corner.

"The steward will be with you shortly," the butler said, lighting three tapers before disappearing.

Petite and Nicole held their skirts wide as Princess Madeleine relieved herself in the fireplace behind them. The cavernous room had been draped in black in honor of the Duke's death.

"It's Saint-Rémy," Petite hissed to Princess Madeleine, recognizing her stepfather's shuffling step.

The youngest princess stepped out of the fireplace, arranging her skirts just as the Marquis and a page holding a wax-light entered.

"Welcome, Your Highnesses," the Marquis announced. "The Duchess has been praying day and night for your safe arrival. In consequence, she has fallen asleep, but she will receive you in the morning at the usual time. I'm to show you to your chambers."

He moved aside for a porter carrying a trunk on his shoulders. "Stack them in the gallery," he instructed as the servants trailed by. Clorine came in hefting two haversacks.

The three princesses and their attendants followed the Marquis through a series of grand, empty rooms, the cavalcade of boots on bare wood floors sounding like an army on the march. The Marquis pushed open a tall door onto a bedchamber where a maid was stooped in front of a small fireplace, stirring the embers with the muzzle of a bellows.

"This will be where Princess Marguerite sleeps," the Marquis said, taking the bellows from the maid and pumping it, sending ashes flying.

Princess Marguerite frowned, turning. But for a bed, there appeared to be no furnishings.

"It's the grandest of the rooms." The Marquis stomped on an ember.

It was almost midnight by the time the princesses were settled and the Marquis was free to show Petite to their own lodgings. Clorine and two footmen followed behind carrying the leather haversacks and trunks. They went down a long gallery lined with enormous paintings. Petite held her taper up the better to see a portrait of Marie de Médicis riding a magnificent White, its mane long and wavy. The painting next to it showed the face of a lusty Devil in the corner, about to jump out. Petite quickly moved on, following the Marquis and Clorine up winding stairs into the peak of a turret.

"This leads to your chamber," the Marquis told Petite, directing the footmen and Clorine through a plank door on the left. "But your mother will receive you now in ours." He opened the door on the right.

The musty room was simply furnished with a curtained poster bed, a table and two ladder-back chairs. A chambermaid stirred under a comforter on a pallet. The high bed creaked as Françoise got up to embrace Petite.

"I prayed for your safe arrival, Louise," she said, tucking her hair under her nightcap. "And Jean did, as well. He's coming to see us tomorrow after Mass."

"How is he?" Petite's brother had just turned eighteen. He'd been only nine when she last saw him—nearly ten years ago.

"He's a proper nobleman," Françoise said, her eyes glinting in the candlelight, "always at his exercises, his fencing, dancing and riding. A galant homme through and through, and with all the best connections. Come, Louise, your room is next to ours. It's a bit shoddy," she warned, her hand on the latch, "but at least we don't have to pay rent."

Petite's room under the eaves was tiny as well as shoddy, and smelled strongly of smoke—but it was warm, at the least (unlike the majestic rooms below). A night candle threw a dim light over the furnishings: a bed with patched linen curtains, a bench, a pallet for a maid, two wooden chairs and a small table, a close-stool and a trunk. Hung on the pale blue walls were a cracked mirror, a crucifix and a moth-eaten tapestry of the Last Supper. A shuttered window opened onto the street, to judge by the sound of squeaking carriage wheels and the clip-clop of horses going by.

Françoise straightened the mirror and bid her daughter good night. "I had my girl smoke out the bugs," she told Clorine before closing the door.

Clorine took a gown out of Petite's trunk and sniffed it. "I'll lay everything out in the sun tomorrow," she said, and then checked to make sure that the door to the passage was double-bolted, safe for the night.

Petite took out her wooden keepsake box, which she set on the wobbly table. Hidden within, wrapped in a lace mantilla made by her aunt Angélique, was the worn leather-covered book *Life* by Saint Teresa. She'd stolen it from the Duke's library before leaving—*saved* it, she told herself.

Petite woke to the sound of a rooster crowing and horses' hooves on cobblestones. She parted her bed curtains.

Clorine was lying on her back, staring at the ceiling. "We're in Paris and we haven't yet been murdered," she said, struggling to her feet.

"We're not actually *in* Paris," Petite said. It pleased her to be in the countryside. She wondered where the palace stables were. She would miss riding with Abbé Patin, who had stayed behind in Blois.

Petite and Clorine joined the Marquis, Françoise and their pimpled chambermaid for morning prayers. At the peal of Sunday church bells, Petite and her mother left for Mass.

"O Heavenly Father," Petite heard her mother pray in the vast marbled palace church, "I commend my children to Thy care. Strengthen them to overcome the corruptions of the world and deliver them from the snares of the enemy. Amen."

"Amen," Petite said to herself.

"There he is," Françoise said, emerging from the chapel.

A young man was leaning against a marble column, one gloved hand on the hilt of a low-slung sword. He was wearing a green velvet doublet and tight knee-britches. With his many sword knots, topknots and rosettes, he looked for all the world like a young man of birth and quality.

Is it truly Jean? Petite wondered. A comely young man, he had their mother's pretty round cheeks, her pouty mouth, her curls.

Jean grinned, tipping his extravagantly feathered hat. "Madame," he said, taking his mother's gloved hand and kissing it, "is it possible that this lovely young lady is my sister?" He flourished his hat, then pressed it against his body, under his left arm.

Petite made a shy curtsy. She felt she was meeting a stranger, yet there was so much that was wonderfully familiar—Jean's two dimples, the way his forelock fell into his face, his teasing manner.

"I see I'm going to have a job on my hands keeping the young bucks away." He touched the hilt of his sword and winked.

Yes, it was her brother, a brother now grown, yet a boy still to judge by the playful twinkle in his eyes.

"You may be a man of quality, son, but you're all askew," Françoise said with pride, reaching to straighten his ruff.

Jean jumped back (a tidy jeté, Petite thought, impressed).

"This little neck rag happens to be from Perdrigeon, the best linen-draper in Paris," he said, straightening it. He repositioned himself into a standing pose—head upright, shoulders back, legs extended with the feet turned outward.

"I hope it didn't cost you," Françoise said, brushing off a stone bench with her muff and taking a seat.

"I won it at cards off my friend Michel de Tellier, son of the minister of state."

"Truly? But then, of course, you sit down with princes."

Jean made an offhand gesture. "Michel tells me what's going on. He grew up with the King, so he knows him well."

The King, Petite thought: her poacher. The way they had met seemed a mythical tale to her now, like a fable from some faraway time.

"In fact, the last time I saw Michel, he told me the King is getting married to his cousin, the Spanish Infanta."

"Ah," Françoise said, catching Petite's eye. "So it's official, then."

"It's soon to be announced. The King told Michel he's none too happy about it, but it's part of the treaty with Spain, so—" Jean shrugged. "The price of peace, I guess." He put on his hat and adjusted the tilt. "So, Mademoiselle Petite—I have to be back at the college for a fencing lesson this afternoon, but I've time until then. How about a tour of the city?"

"You'll take care, son?" Françoise said.

Jean took up a pose, then lunged, thrusting high and low, as his mother and sister laughed. "You should have seen the fights during the festivals before Lent."

Jean and Petite walked their mother back to the palace, and then set out. Petite felt shy taking a young man's arm, even if he was her brother.

"Do you mind a walk?" Jean glanced down.

"I bet I can outwalk you," she said.

It was but a short distance to the porte Saint-Michel, where they joined a line of foot passengers. An official with a huge mustache examined their papers. "You're with the Palais d'Orléans?" he asked Petite.

"She's with me," Jean said, showing his student identification papers. They were waved through.

Inside the city walls they were assaulted by a tumult of sound: coachmen cracking whips, church bells tolling, dogs barking, vendors yelling—one selling herbs, another figs, yet another oranges from Portugal. A girl sat on a stool milking a goat, splashing streams of steaming white into a tin pail. Gangs of beggar children swarmed until Jean threatened them off.

A wide avenue stretched before them, congested with people and all manner of conveyances. Jean squeezed Petite's gloved hand.

"Don't be afraid."

"I'm not," Petite lied, for there were beggars everywhere—cutthroats, no doubt— as well as women of a certain type, although many were young, not women at all, just girls with pleading looks and soiled petticoats. A blind man with a copper cup sang at one corner as people hurrying to Lenten sermons tossed in coins. The streets were mucky; many wore patens. At every corner, porters clamored to offer chairs. Two pigs roamed free, their snouts in garbage piled up beside the market stalls.

They headed south, Jean talking of his skill at backsword and single-rapier; of a recent adventure he'd had when the report of a pistol caused his school horse to jump a fence and gallop away at breakneck speed; of a chestnut hunter he longed to buy, with its short back and broad forehead, its long, thin tail; of hunting boar with princes in the forests of Saint-Germain-en-Laye.

"Speaking of boar," Jean said as an old woman pushed past, bent under a pole supporting buckets of water, "I'll never forget your returning on that White, draped over his back like a sack of grain."

"All I can remember is getting on him," Petite said. What she would never forget was the searing pain in her leg, the fear she'd felt looking into the boar's beady eyes. "I don't remember anything after that."

"We thought you dead." Jean patted Petite's hand with affection. "Strange the way that horse just disappeared."

"For a long time, I kept looking for him," she confided, stepping over a stream of stinking sewage. *And now?* she wondered. Had she given up?

They passed through the peaceful, tree-lined courtyard of a convent and came to another road. After a time they entered an arched tunnel, emerging onto a bright cobbled road lined with shops and houses of roughcast stone and wood. A butcher displayed a CLOSED FOR LENT sign. Three boys crouched by the door, playing with tops. Petite could smell the river, but she couldn't see it.

Around a corner the street opened onto a broad pavement, and suddenly there it was—a congested gray expanse of water crowded with houseboats, barges, sailing ships.

"You always knew your way with horses," Jean said, throwing a pebble at a gull—but missing it. "Do you still ride?"

"I backed horses for the Duc d'Orléans." Light sparked on the murky water.

"Fie! Really? You should have been born a boy," he said, leaning on the stone balustrade. "Mother wants me to find a husband for you. She says it's time you settled. I think she expected the Marquis to be more of a help." He thumbed his nose. "What a simpleton! He can't even get his teeth to sit right. He had them in upside down the other day." Jean found another stone and threw it, this time striking a gull in flight.

"I don't have a dowry, Jean." Petite cringed, thinking of the marrowless spinsters in their baglike hairnets. Was she destined to be one? She dreamt of being loved by a good man—a man rather like the poacher—but that was a fantasy, she feared. Many men treated their wives like beasts of burden, even beating them. To be a spinster was a terrible fate, but how much better was it to be a wife, attending to mindless spinning and mending? She dared not voice such doubts: a Christian woman submitted without complaint.

"You're pretty, even if thin." Jean chucked her chin. "We need to fatten you up. Men like something to hold onto."

Petite flushed.

"And you'll have to give up your romping ways. Saint Paul said that a girl must not be boisterous."

"Since when did you listen in church?" Petite hadn't expected her brother to take his role as head of the family quite so seriously.

"Since the priests started talking about matters of importance—like women. And since I had to pass exams," he confessed with a grimace. "I can get a post in Amboise as a lieutenant, but the pay is only six hundred livres a year, hardly enough to cover the cost of a good sword. I'm hoping to get a better position here in Paris."

Great bells sounded. "Those must be the bells of Notre-Dame," Petite yelled over the din. They were louder than any she had ever heard.

They came to a clearing in front of the great cathedral, the square teeming with coaches and carts, horses, mules and little dogs everywhere. Two men had falcons on their shoulders. A grandly dressed woman carried a poodle in her basket, her train held by two boys in rose velvet livery. Another lady had a monkey on a ribbon and was wearing a full face mask of black velvet to protect her skin from the sun's darkening rays. Petite felt she was at a masquerade ball. In Paris, it seemed, the festival days before Lent never ended.

There were three massive portals at the entrance of the church, the one in the center depicting the Last Judgment, with the good filing off to the left, and the sinners to the right, headlong into Hell.

"Not yet," Jean said, guiding Petite toward a narrow entrance at the side.

Petite followed her brother up steep winding stone stairs that became increasingly narrow. Four hundred and twenty-two steps later (Petite counted), they emerged breathless at the top.

"Behold," Jean said, his arms stretched wide. There, below them, was the city. Church spires glittered in the spring sunlight.

Over the shoulders of glowering stone gargoyles, Petite looked down upon the houses pressed together, the carriages and boats, the little people moving about like ants. In the distance was a mountain, and all around the crowded city she could trace the line of the great wall and the open fields beyond. She crossed herself and grabbed hold of her brother's arm. It seemed a monstrous and unnatural thing to see the world from such a height.

Chapter Thirteen

As Jean predicted (and Princess Marguerite feared), it was proclaimed: the King was to marry his cousin, the eldest daughter of the King of Spain. The long-prayed-for peace between France and Spain was to be sealed in the marriage bed. Fire rockets flared and bonfires were lit and citizens danced wildly around them.

Princess Marguerite burst into tears anew.

"He has to marry her," Nicole said, trying to comfort her. "It's part of the peace treaty."

But the Princess was inconsolable, tearing at her laces and howling piteously, refusing all food but calf's heels.

In the melting days of August, Paris swelled with visitors. The city bustled with activity, everyone preparing to welcome the King and his bride, their new Queen. He'd been gone from the city for over one year. At five intersections triumphal arches had been erected, festooned with foliage, banners and tapestries. During the Court's absence, shopkeepers had suffered, as had fan wrights and milliners, blade smiths and falconers, actors and singers. When the Court was away, the city was dead; the moment the Court returned, business thrived.

On August twenty-fifth, la Grande Mademoiselle and the two youngest princesses departed for Vincennes in order to be part of the King and Queen's entry into the city the next day. Princess Marguerite was not taking part in the triumphal procession, of course, but had at least consented to watch it.

The morning of the grand entry, the courtyard of the Palais d'Orléans was crowded with conveyances, still draped in black mourning. The coaches made their regal progress down the wall road to the porte de Bussy.

Crossing the river at the Pont Neuf took almost one hour. Once across, they moved slowly downriver along the right bank to the Place de Grève. No executions were scheduled that day, but the square was crowded nonetheless. Already fountains were spurting wine, and people were staggering. Banners and tapestries had been hung from every window and flowers set upon every sill.

"It's cruel to have to wear mourning on a day like today," Princess Marguerite said, fussing with her hairnet of black beads. "I will never forgive my father for dying."

Their coach turned into a narrow sideroad. A footman yelled at people to clear the way. "It's a princess," he yelled, and bystanders cheered.

They entered the small courtyard of the Hôtel de Beauvais.

"That's my father's sister, Henrietta Maria, Queen of England," Princess Marguerite said, pointing to the woman about to enter the hôtel, surrounded by attendants.

La Reine Malheureuse, Petite thought. She was dressed entirely in black, still in mourning for her husband, King Charles of England, beheaded by his own people years before. His head had been severed with one stroke—perhaps that was a consolation. That and the fact that her son King Charles II had finally regained his father's crown, and justice had been restored.

"That's her daughter in the purple cloak, my cousin Henriette," Marguerite said, indicating a tall, thin girl with flaming red hair.

Petite tried not to stare, but hair of such a hue was a curiosity, evidence that her parents had had congress during the mother's courses. She flushed to consider the Queen of England in such a light.

Princess Henriette looked back over her shoulder. Recognizing her cousin Marguerite, she smiled and fluttered her lace fan. Her teeth were white and fine.

"How old is she?" Petite asked. The Princess's eyes were bright.

"My age, ten and six, but she has no chest."

Like me, Petite thought with sympathy.

"She looks younger," Nicole said as the royal party disappeared through the doors.

"She's going to marry the King's brother, Philippe," Princess Marguerite added with chagrin. She'd been passed over yet again.

A footman opened their carriage door. "Mother," Princess Marguerite cursed, very nearly stepping into manure. "Of pearl," she added quickly, holding up her skirts.

"Your Highness?" A butler, beribboned in red, led them up a wide circular staircase to an enclosure overlooking rue Saint-Antoine.

"No balcony?" the Princess objected, but on learning that the Queen Mother was seated in the window alcove immediately to the right, she was appeased. A crowd milled below them. Children in rags scrambled for the coins, sweetmeats and sausages flung into the street.

"Isn't that your brother?" Nicole asked Petite, pointing to a group of young men perched on a rooftop. One was waving his red cap—the cap of the students of the Collège de Navarre.

"It is Jean." Petite waved back. Soon he would be graduating and moving south to Amboise. His marks had not been good enough for him to get a position in Paris, as he had wished.

"Alleluia!" Nicole exclaimed as a fire rocket flared close by and a cannon boomed.

Petite looked up the crowded avenue, aflutter at the thought of seeing the King again.

"This could go on for days," Nicole said as caparisoned mules and horses passed by, followed by the officials of the Queen Mother's household, soldiers, the Hundred Swiss and the marshals of France.

"Here comes Her Virginship," said the Princess, referring to her half-sister, la Grande Mademoiselle, famously adorned in a masculine hat. "And the bratchets," she added as her two sisters appeared, the youngest waving as if she were queen.

At last, a glittering chariot came into view. "The happy bride," Marguerite said sourly.

The new Queen of France was riding in a Roman-style chariot drawn by six Danish horses. She was draped in a black robe decorated with golden thread and pearls. She sparkled in the hot August sun.

"Thanks be to Mary, they finally got her out of a farthingale," said Nicole.

"Vive la reine!" people cried. Queen Marie-Thérèse smiled as they showered her with rose petals, cornflowers, jasmine and carnations.

"She's tiny," Petite said. The Queen looked like a child in her ornamental chariot embellished with cupids.

"Ah—and here *he* comes," Nicole said, pointing her fan.

The King. Petite cheered along with all the others. *How splendid he looked,* she thought. A glittering diamond brooch held a bouquet of white ostrich feathers to his hat. His horse, caparisoned in silver brocade, was a handsome Spanish bay. Even its harness was studded with gems.

"Be still my heart," Nicole sighed.

"He's grown a mustache," Petite said, smiling. She liked that he didn't wear face paint or a wig.

He halted directly in front to solemnly salute his mother. "Vive le roi!" the crowd cried out. He untangled a rose that had caught on his wide lace collar and held it to his nose. Then he stroked his horse's neck and moved on.

He's good with horses, Petite thought, recalling how he'd calmed the frightened colt at Chambord. Her poacher: her secret.

Days later, Princess Marguerite returned from her daily twenty-minute interview with the Duchess incensed to the highest degree. "I've just been informed, by On High," she announced, lifting her eyes to the ceiling, "that I'm to marry." The Princess threw her fur muff to Petite and tore into the arduous task of unfastening the six buttons on one of her leather gloves.

"That's wonderful," Petite said, emptying the sweetmeat wrappers and junky trinkets out of the Princess's muff and handing it to the maid of the wardrobe.

"To the Duc de Lorraine?" Nicole asked hopefully, taking over the task of the glove buttons. The Duke and his nephew Charles were visiting, and it was rumored that the old Duke had lusty intentions . . . on Nicole.

"No, Cosimo de Médicis."

"The *third?*" Nicole glanced at Petite, one eyebrow raised. Cosimo de Médicis was heir to the Grand Duke of Tuscany.

"You will be a grand duchess," she said with awe. "That's almost as good as being a queen."

"I'll have to live in Florence."

"It will be an adventure," Petite said. Perhaps she would be going as well. She would learn Italian; she would read Dante.

"Florentines have unnatural habits and never bathe."

"We don't bathe either," Nicole said.

"Plus they lie and cheat."

Nicole frowned. "Don't we?"

"I want to die." Princess Marguerite covered her face with her gold-embroidered nose cloth.

"Can you refuse?" Petite asked. She suspected that the princess fancied Young Prince Charles, who was often in their company of late.

"Refuse to be a grand duchess?" Nicole said. "Are you crackbrained?"

Princess Marguerite burst into tears. "I have *no* say in this. The King wishes to bind Tuscany to France. I have no more freedom than a galley slave."

Petite and Nicole did their best to soothe her. With tender words they removed the Princess's tucker, her bodice and skirts, and helped her into a silk-lined morning gown. Settling her on a mountain of soft pillows, Nicole massaged the Princess's feet as Petite read aloud from *The Treasure of the City of Ladies*. At last, with tearstained cheeks, Marguerite fell asleep.

Night had fallen. By the light of a long taper set in a silver candlestick, Petite headed down the long gallery to her room in the turret, her thoughts troubled. Marguerite might be a princess, the granddaughter of Henry the Great, yet she had no more freedom than any other girl controlled by a father or husband.

Petite paused, as was her custom, to admire the painting of Queen Marie de Médicis riding the White, its long mane reaching down below its belly. She hurried on, avoiding the image of the Devil in the next painting about to jump out at her.

Petite found her mother in her dressing gown, being prepared for bed by her maid. The Marquis was already propped up on his pillows, sleeping upright, his toothless mouth agape.

"Ah, there you are," her mother whispered, following Petite into her small chamber. She sat on the spindle chair, clutching a folded piece of paper.

"The Princess needed me," Petite explained, putting down the candlestick. "She is unhappy."

"Why? It's a prestigious alliance," Françoise said. The spindle chair creaked, broken in the joints. "Although—"

Petite waited, puzzled. Her mother's face in the candlelight looked severe.

"We have a problem. After the Princess is married," Françoise said finally, "the Duchess intends to make economies."

Petite wasn't sure what that meant. The Duchess was always making economies.

"She's going to cut staff, Louise. The Marquis, thankfully, will still have a position, but all of Princess Marguerite's help is to be let go. You won't have a position here any longer."

"Maybe Princess Marguerite will want me to go with her," Petite said. Both her and Nicole.

"That won't be possible. Once married, all her staff must be Florentine and chosen by her husband."

"But who will she talk to?" Petite wondered out loud. Marguerite had no talent for languages—she didn't even speak Latin. How would her maids know that she could not sleep without her rabbit's foot charm under her pillow, that three candles must be left burning during a thunderstorm to prevent evil from happening while spirits were at war?

"This is the way it is."

A night watchman outside called out, "Ten of the clock, sleep in peace. I am watching."

"I understand," Petite said, but with a tone of defeat.

"The problem is, where will you go? You can't stay on here, and . . ." Françoise sighed wearily. "We've yet to find a husband for you."

The eternal problem. Petite couldn't remember a time when her mother had not been distressed over the impossibility of getting her married. She didn't mind that bleak prospect as much as she supposed she should. "Perhaps I could join a convent," she suggested.

"You'd need an even greater dowry for that," Françoise said, rolling her eyes. "No, we must persevere. I've recently had the good fortune to find a matchmaker whose fees are reasonable. She has one client, an elderly widower, who might be a possibility." She unfolded the sheet of rag paper. "He's in trade," she said, handing it to Petite, "so the Vallière name might interest him, she said."

Dumbfounded, Petite held the paper to the candlelight.

"It's not an ideal match—but what can we do? He's not a young man, so at least he wouldn't live long." Françoise stood to leave. "That would be a consolation, believe me," she said, pressing her dry, powdered cheek to Petite's.

Petite closed the door after her mother. She felt despair through and through. Abruptly, she took up the candlestick and headed out into the corridor. Her candle aloft, she felt her way down the steep, winding stairs. The passages were forbidding in the dark. The moon was new, a dark moon, and no light shone through the small openings. She thought of the Devil, his leering eyes. The Dark Lord, Prince of Darkness. She dared not whistle, for that was how he was summoned. Instead she made a low hissing sound to scare off rodents. *O rats and other crawling creatures, in the name of God, leave this place and go outside to a field. Amen.*

With relief, she knocked on the door to Nicole's dormitory. "It's Louise—to see Nicole," she said through the planks. She heard bolts sliding and the door opened a crack.

"My God. I prayed to see you, and here you are." Nicole's face was covered in a mud plaster and her hair done up in curl-papers.

There were six trundle beds in the narrow room. One girl was sitting up having her hair combed out by a maid, two were under their covers and two more were playing cards by the light of a lantern. A maid was preparing her pallet on the floor near the fire grate. It was not a time to come calling.

"In here," Nicole said in a low voice, opening a door to a small trunk room under the eaves.

Petite set her candle into a wall sconce, dripping candle grease onto the stone floor. "We're going to be let go," she said.

Nicole shrugged. "I've decided to leave in any case," she said, settling herself on a trunk.

"What do you mean?"

"I'm going to tell the Duchess that my mother and father are dying and that I have to return home immediately."

"Both your parents are dying?"

"It makes a good story, don't you think? If I don't disappear, I'll be trapped into marrying the Duc de Lorraine, I just know it."

Petite made a face. The disgusting old man had been grabbing every maid within arm's reach. "My mother thinks she has found someone to marry *me*," she confessed.

"That's a relief."

"But he's in trade, and he's—"

Nicole made a sputtering noise. "A merchant?"

Petite didn't mind the trade part so much, but the letter her mother had shown her revealed that the man was practically illiterate. "He's seventy-six years old," she said, revolted.

"Maybe the Duke would marry you," Nicole suggested. "The addled frack is desperate, and at least he's noble."

"I'd rather die," Petite said.

NICOLE WAS GONE the very next day, leaving Petite to look after the stricken Princess.

"I have a favor to ask of you," Marguerite whispered to Petite after Mass, pulling her into a window alcove.

"I'm always at your service, Your Highness," Petite said, taken aback by the Princess's deferential tone.

"I need to have a talk with Prince Charles this evening." Marguerite's lips were shiny with the lip salve they'd made out of egg whites, pig lard and sheep feet. "A private talk." She arched her eyebrows. "The prince will call at seven. Before that, I'd like you to leave—by the window, so that it will be assumed that you're with me. You can climb down the tree."

"I'm to climb out?" *In the dark?*

PETITE LEANED AGAINST the wall and looked out over the great woods, and the gardens rich with scent. The moon cast an eerie light. All was silent but for the occasional hooting of an owl. She loved the stillness, in truth, the feeling that she was alone in the world, the chance to be with her thoughts.

Soon the Princess would be married by proxy and go to Florence to meet her husband. He would embrace her and then she would have babies. Petite thought of Nicole, who had lied in order to flee an old man's lusty interest. She thought of her own dilemma, her awful future. What choices did they have? They were all of them ensnared. She recalled a fox she had seen as a child, caught in a trap: it had tried to chew off its leg to get free.

Petite recited Latin conjugations to distract herself from such thoughts: nolo, *I am unwilling;* nolebam, *I was unwilling;* nolam, *I will be unwilling.*

Nolo, nolebam, nolam.

Nolo, nolebam—

She started at the sound of footsteps on the cobblestones, and saw the shadowy figure of a night watchman. She crouched down, holding her breath, and heard him making water into the bushes. Then she saw something that made her heart stop: the dark figure of a dog, ambling along the path. It raised its head, sniffing the air. Then she heard it growl.

"What is it, Bruno?" she heard the man say.

"It's just me." Petite stepped forward. In a second, the dog would be upon her. "Mademoiselle de la Vallière."

"The chief steward's girl?" The guard took hold of the mastiff's collar.

"Her Highness thought she heard something in the bushes outside her window," Petite said, raising her voice so that the Princess might be warned.

Marguerite stuck her head out the open window, her hair disordered.

"Your Highness, you may rest safely," Petite called out.

PETITE WAS IN THE Commons eating pigeon and chine of suckling calf with two of the Duchess's waiting maids when Clorine appeared, her long face flushed.

"The Marquis de Saint-Rémy and your mother wish to speak with you—now, in their chamber."

Petite stood and excused herself. "Do you know why?" she asked Clorine as they rushed down the gallery.

"I think it's something to do with a letter they just got," Clorine said. "It had a royal insignia on it."

Petite paused at the first stair landing. Had she been found out? There had been blood on the Princess's underskirt, even though it was not her time of the month.

"Entrez," she heard her mother say in a tired voice.

Petite stepped into the room, alone.

The Marquis was sitting in his cracked leather armchair by an unlit fire. "You may procure a stool," he informed Petite, signaling his wife to join him and the maid to depart.

Petite lowered herself onto a footstool beside her mother.

The Marquis adjusted his hippo-tusk teeth. "This has to do by way of the matured widower."

Françoise sat forward. "The matchmaker has finally contacted us."

Petite's initial reaction was relief (her collusion in the Princess's sin had not been discovered), only to be overtaken by a deeper despair.

"The candidate of whom we discussed previously—" The Marquis took his teeth out and frowned at them.

Petite waited with silent dread. *Nolo, nolebam, nolam.*

The Marquis put his teeth back in and sucked to position them. "He has," he began, swallowing, "regretfully, begged to be excused from further negotiations."

Petite glanced at her mother. What did that mean? "The widower has . . . declined?"

Both the Marquis and her mother nodded.

Sing ye! Petite did her best to appear crestfallen.

The Marquis cleared his throat. "The matchmaker proposes to persevere—she projects that the widower would annul his decision were he to see you in the flesh, but providentially we have had a more advantageous alternative."

"Oh?" Petite said, confused, as usual, by her stepfather's odd way of speaking.

"Yes," her mother said, "it seems that you've been awarded a position as—"

"Maid of admiration to the imminent Madame," the Marquis said.

"Maid of honor," Françoise corrected. "And she's not 'Madame' yet."

"Madame who?" Petite asked, incredulous. Maid of honor was a step above a waiting maid.

"The English Princess who is to unite with the King's brother," the Marquis said.

"Henriette?" Petite asked. Surely she had misunderstood. Henriette, daughter of the Queen of England, the beautiful princess with the flaming red hair?

"Yes," her mother said.

"Are you sure?" Petite was stupefied. To be maid of honor to this Princess was impossible to imagine; such positions went to the daughters of the highest sword nobility. Her own father had been merely a knight, the lowest status of nobility in France.

"You'll have to live with the Court, of course," Françoise said, as if dazed herself. "They summer in Fontaine Beleau."

So far away! Petite recalled staying at that hunting château the year before, on the long journey to Paris with the princesses. It had been dark when they had arrived, and dark when they left. Their room was vast and unfurnished and had smelled of burnt sealing wax. They'd had to sleep on pallets on the floor.

"The disbursement is a mere one hundred livres per annum," the Marquis said.

"But if you're clever," Françoise said, raising a finger, "and save toward a dowry, you should be able to make a more suitable match."

"ARE YOU NOT over-happy, Mademoiselle?" Princess Marguerite asked the next morning, her smile teasing.

"You know, Your Highness?" Petite took up a silver tray of half-eaten black pudding and artichoke pie. She was, in fact, tingly with excitement. She'd not slept at all, thinking of her good fortune, dreaming of the wonders that lay ahead. She would be living at Court—with the *King*.

"Who do you think got you the position?"

Petite put the tray aside and clasped the Princess's hands. "Your Highness, I owe you my life." She bowed to the floor and considered kissing the Princess's feet—as was done, she knew—but decided against it. The Princess was still in her stockings.

"Come, come," Marguerite said, tapping Petite on her head with her fan. "I command you to rise." She'd been practicing being regal. "It's your numeration."

"Remuneration?"

"For being helpful about my *adorer*."

Petite felt chagrined.

"I want you to have this, as well." Marguerite handed Petite a cambric nose cloth embroidered in gold. "Blessed with my own tears."

"Your Highness, I don't deserve this." Petite stared at the crumpled square of fabric. "How can I ever repay you?"

The Princess fluttered her fan. "By going out the window again—tonight."

MARGUERITE WAS MARRIED by proxy to Cosimo de Médicis on the nineteenth day in April. The solemn, unhappy ceremony took place in the chapel at the Louvre.

Petite made a profound reverence before the future Grand Duchess of Tuscany. That evening, Florentine attendants would prepare the Princess for bed, turn back her sheets. "I must take my leave of you, Your Highness," Petite said, a catch in her throat. The royal coach would come in the morning to take her away to Fontaine Beleau.

"Beware the pleasures of Court, my friend," Marguerite said in a tragic tone, her eyes red-rimmed.

Petite kissed the Princess's hands. "I have something for you, Your Highness," she said, presenting her with a small stoppered vial. "It's for your wedding night," she whispered.

The Princess held it to the light. "Face paint?" she asked, for the contents were crimson.

Petite, her face growing hot, explained in a low voice that it was blood of a pig for the Princess to spill on her marriage bed. "To save you from your husband's wrath, Your Highness." Then she embraced the Princess, blinking back tears. *Little Queen.*

THE NEXT MORNING, Petite paced in her room. Her new boots (with one raised heel) pinched, but she didn't give it a thought. Her trunk was packed and ready to go. Clorine was in the basement, saying farewell to her friends on staff. She would alert Petite as soon as the coach arrived.

Her mother entered and Petite curtsied.

"We must talk," Françoise said.

Petite offered her mother the chair.

"No, you sit there." Françoise sat on the edge of the bed. "The matchmaker agrees that your having a position at Court will improve your chances, but she warned that you must be exceedingly careful of your reputation. Court society is known to be riggish."

Petite nodded, amused by her mother's use of the word *riggish* in this context. Sheep were said to be riggish when they broke through fences.

"The appearance of sin is as damaging as the sin itself. You must never allow yourself to be seen alone with a man. This would reduce your value in the marriage market."

"Yes, Mother," Petite said, dissembling her impatience. She was eager to go out into the great world (eager to be free of lectures).

"If a man ever tries to press his way with you—to kiss you, for example—you must turn away with all your strength and give him a slap. That is the proper response of a virtuous woman."

"I *know*, Mother."

"You will be seventeen this summer, and you must marry as soon as possible. After eighteen—" Françoise threw up her hands. "Do at least try to be pleasing. Don't let men know that you can read. Eat as much as you can bear: you are far too thin. Refrain from riding, but if you must, ride like a lady on a quiet palfrey. You will not have much money to spare, but whatever coins you can manage to put aside for a dowry will help. The Marquis and I are saving as well, as is your brother."

"Thank you," Petite said with a confusion of sentiment. Separation was truly at hand. The thought filled her with both apprehension and joy.

Clorine appeared at the door, her hair uncharacteristically done up in ringlets. "The royal coach is here for you," she announced. She had applied something red to her lips, and it had stained her tongue. She looked ghoulish when she smiled.

Both Petite and her mother stood up. "I won't go down," Françoise said, reaching into her skirts and withdrawing a string of beads. She thrust them into Petite's hand.

The wooden beads were worn. "Father's rosary?" Touched by Saint Teresa of Avila.

"May God go with you, little one," Françoise said with unexpected tenderness.

"And with you, Mother," Petite replied, her eyes stinging.

Chapter Fourteen

"Mademoiselle de la Vallière?" A footman in mismatched livery opened the door of an ancient berlin studded with gilt nails. Petite put her gloved hand lightly on his and climbed in. Her new left boot, with the raised sole, was hard to get used to, and she felt strange in her new gown—one of Marguerite's castoffs of heavy yellow brocade.

An elegant young woman had taken the best seat, the middle one facing forward. "Good morning," she said. Her blue eyes were startling, reflecting her iridescent cape, an elegant confection lushly trimmed with point-de-Venice lace. "Why—you could be my sister," she said with a smile. Her accent was southwestern, but cultivated.

Petite bowed her head, perplexed. They were both fair, true, with blonde curls and blue eyes, but there the resemblance ended. Although only a few years older than she was—nineteen or perhaps even twenty, Petite guessed—this young woman had a worldly air.

"How do you do?" Petite said uncertainly.

"I am the Marquise de Rochechouart," the young woman said, snapping open a painted fan. Her laced gloves were embroidered at the wrist with gold thread. "But I prefer to be called Athénaïs."

The carriage jolted forward. Petite glanced back. She thought she saw the figure of her mother in the window.

"After the Goddess of Virginity," Athénaïs said, toying with a pearl-encrusted cross that hung from a pendant attached to her bodice.

Her companion's skin was delicate, alabaster pale. Petite felt like a rustic by comparison. "Mademoiselle Louise de la Vallière," she introduced herself in turn, stuttering over her own name. "But people call me Petite," she said, foolishly adding, "although I'm not." Perhaps now she would go by her Christian name. Perhaps now she would be Louise.

"Well, I'm not exactly a goddess either." Athénaïs laughed, a musical sound. "You have a position at Court?"

"I'm going to be one of Madame's maids of honor." Petite found it hard to believe, even now.

"Ah, Henriette," Athénaïs said, raising her arched brows. "You will find her amusing, at least."

"Are you with Madame, as well?" It would be comforting to know someone.

"Alas, no, I serve the Queen. I've been with her household for almost six months."

"Then you must often see *him*," Petite said, flushing like a convent schoolgirl. "The King, that is." She took a deep breath and sat up straight, clasping her gloved hands in her lap.

"Our enchanter?" Athénaïs's teeth were small, straight and pearly white.

Enchanter? Yes.

"Certainly—although I dare say you'll likely see more of him than I do, for he's more often in Madame Henriette's chambers than in those of his wife."

Petite was uncertain what Athénaïs meant, but assumed that it could not be what was implied.

THE COACH STOPPED to pick up two other young women—newcomers to the Court like Petite—before heading south out of the city. Petite was happy to sit by the window, in spite of the grime. She was intrigued by all that she saw: the pilgrims on foot, the pack-mules laden with sacks and sticks, the barefoot man leading a donkey, an old woman in a horse litter. Once she noticed four covered wagons, and she looked to see if it might be the Romany troupe of her childhood (it wasn't, of course).

The coach darkened as they entered a deep green shade. Labyrinths of broad alleys wound through groves of majestic oak, beech and poplar.

The driver yelled out to the footmen to take up their swords.

"Perhaps we'll have some excitement," Athénaïs said lightheartedly, but clasping her cross. The forest and rock cuts surrounding Fontaine Beleau were a known haven for bandits.

One of the girls took out a rosary and began to pray, but at the first decade there was such a stink that she was forced to stop and hold her nose. Hanging from the limbs of an oak were the bodies of three men.

"Finally," Athénaïs said, coughing. "The King has been after those rogues for months."

Petite closed her eyes until they were well past.

Gradually, the road leveled. They entered a silent village through a long avenue of trees, pulling finally—and safely—through an ivy-covered arcade into the outer courtyard of the ancient hunting château.

Petite took in the vast quadrangle punctuated by high-roofed pavilions, the long facades with many windows. The want of uniformity, the weeds coming up through the cobblestones, the ornate if crumbling grandeur gave her an impression of melancholy, of wanton neglect. An evil Médicis queen had lived in this palace as well, Petite knew, and here, only four years before, Queen Christina of Sweden had commanded one of her footmen—her amoroso, according to Nicole—stabbed to death. It was said his ghost was here, as well as that of Diane de Poitiers and Mary, Queen of Scots. The château's history was long, tragic and very romantic.

From somewhere came the sound of a violin and a woman singing an aria. "Welcome to Paradise, fair maidens," Athénaïs said as the coach lurched to a stop. "And may maidens you remain," she added with a wry smile, adjusting her hood.

"Where does the King sleep?" the plump girl sitting next to Petite asked, then giggled.

"You can't see His Majesty's bedchamber from here," Athénaïs said. "It faces east, onto the gardens, but his cabinet is over there." She pointed through the inner courtyard grillwork to a bank of windows.

Awed, they craned their heads to look.

A horse caparisoned in blue and gold came cantering through the gates, stopped smartly beside their carriage and reared. The boy riding the black courser waved a feathered hat.

"Lauzun," Athénaïs called out, "stop showing off. We're not impressed." But her smile told another story.

The rider vaulted off the horse, throwing the reins to a page who came sprinting across the cobblestones.

"He's a good rider," Petite said, "for a boy."

"He's not a boy, I assure you," Athénaïs said.

A masked woman with gray hair and a nose cloth in her hand appeared at the top of the staircase. She looked in their direction.

"It's the Duchesse de Navailles—superintendent of the novices—come to meet you." Athénaïs gathered up her cashmere shawl as a footman opened the coach door. "Madame Jailer, we call her," she said in a low voice, for Petite's benefit. "I will see you tonight?" She planted a breathy kiss on Petite's cheek before climbing down.

"Oh, yes," Petite said with warmth, both proud and pleased to have made such an acquaintance.

"Welcome," the Duchesse de Navailles said, removing her black velvet mask. "I am your supervisor." She looked over the three newcomers standing before her in the courtyard: a short, plump girl with acne, a thin one with wispy golden curls, a stout brunette. How long would they last at Court? How long before a protective parent recalled them in a panic? How long before one of them was required to "disappear" mysteriously for six months?

At thirty-five, the Duchesse de Navailles had already gone gray, in large part due to the magnitude of her responsibility. As superintendent of the maid-attendants, her job was to protect the chastity of thirty-two young women: eleven serving the Queen Mother, twelve serving the Queen, and nine serving Henriette, the King's brother's new wife. It was not an easy task. Most of the girls had only recently been released from the protective custody of a home or convent school, and the warm breezes mingled with the exotic perfumes of the handsome and ever-so-charming courtiers were intoxicating indeed.

It didn't help that Madame Henriette was only sixteen herself, a madcap young woman with flaming hair and an unpredictable imagination. It was already known throughout Court that her husband was jealous, not so much because his flirtatious wife smiled brightly upon lusty young men, but because the lusty young men preferred his wife to *him*.

Nor did it help that the King was of an extraordinary virile beauty and restless, it appeared. Not even a year had passed since he married, and already His Majesty showed signs of being weary of his devout Spanish wife.

Not that he could be faulted, the Duchesse de Navailles thought disloyally. The Queen was, after all, newly with child, and required to abstain from the royal biweekly coupling—but it wasn't just that. If only the Queen would learn a few words of French. If only she didn't consume quite so much garlic and spend *all* her time at devotions. If only she weren't so dumpy, and—yes, the Duchesse de Navailles had to admit—somewhat dim.

Ah well, such was the way with royal marriages. Soon, no doubt, the King would crown some seductive beauty with his favor and all would be well—so long as that beauty wasn't one of her girls . . . or, for that matter, his brother's wife.

"Follow me." The Duchesse de Navailles led her newest charges through an entrance to the right of the inner gate and up a spiral staircase to a vaulted gallery with rows of trestle tables and benches set at one end. The flagstone floor was sticky, flies hovered and the air smelled strongly of mutton and onion.

A lackey came running with a chair. The Duchess sat and addressed the girls, fanning herself. "This is the common room, where you will take your meals and, more importantly, where you will receive instruction—which will be *continuous* so long as you remain at Court." She fixed them with a glare. It took time to teach girls how make their toilette, how the fan should be carried when walking, and how to curtsy and bow. With the precision of a military drill, she would require them to practice the basics—the passing incline, the cold bow, the slight bow, the acknowledging bow, the bobbing curtsy, the full curtsy, as well as the ceremonious kneeling and groveling bows. Devotion and obedience must be evident even in their fingertips!

"Your rooms are above. You will rise at daybreak," she intoned as the servants trailed in, hefting the trunks. She raised her voice. "On waking, your maid will say 'Jesus,' and you will respond 'Deo gratias.' You will get out of bed without lingering, fall to your knees and say a prayer."

The girls nodded.

"You will be required to wear a fresh shift every day." She would address the details of personal cleanliness later in the week. Immersion was not healthy, but that didn't mean that certain parts of the body could not be washed—with the exception of the face, of course, which developed wrinkles, it had been proved.

The Duchess patted her neck with her prized cambric nose cloth and examined it for signs of grime. She feared that they were in for a hot summer. How would she ever be able to enforce the rule that the girls keep their shutters locked? "An open window at night will be counted as a full transgression. Three transgressions and you will be required to leave Court."

The girls murmured.

Good: they were paying attention. "Your rooms must be kept tidy and free of fleas. Alder leaves will be provided to scatter on the floor. A candle set into a trencher of bread covered with bird lime will work overnight if the leaves prove insufficient."

She would spare them the rat lecture. That would come later. "Warm chocolate and rolls are available here each morning at six. The day's schedule will be posted on the door." She held out a sample so that they could see. "One thing is invariable: you must attend Mass every morning at ten of the clock along with the King."

"Cock-a-hoop!" The brunette slapped her hands over her mouth, mortified by her outburst.

The Duchess sighed. The girl would not last one month; she should begin looking for a replacement immediately. "Your trunks have been taken to your rooms, where you may freshen. You will find necessaries at each end of the passages and in the courtyards. Meet me back here at six of the clock to be shown to your respective courts. There is an outdoor entertainment tonight, so be sure to bring a wrap."

A PAGE SHOWED Petite to an east-facing attic room, where Clorine was already busy checking the lock and key to make sure that they worked.

"Do you know who that was you were sitting across from in the coach?" Clorine asked, yanking on a leather strap and pulling the trunk lid open. The ceiling was so low she had to stoop.

"Mademoiselle la Marquise de something-or-other," Petite said, staring at the ceiling. There was a spiderweb in one corner. The room was conveniently close to a necessary, but consequently somewhat smelly. "She calls herself Athénaïs." Petite smiled. Athénaïs had called her *sister*. "After the goddess," she explained.

"The Marquise de Rochechouart, by chance?"

"That's it," Petite said, feeling the blankets, bolster and pillow to see if they were dry. She checked under the bed for creatures.

"Did she happen to mention that she's a Mortemart—from Poitou?"

"Really?" Petite stood up, astonished. Her father had talked of the Mortemarts.

The family was of old nobility and had held important positions at Court for generations. Whenever a Mortemart had come through Amboise, her father had had to put on a royal welcome.

"That's as highborn as you get," Clorine said, shaking out a dark blue brocade skirt, one of the ones Princess Marguerite had passed on. "Higher even than the King, some say."

"No wonder she's so pretty," Petite said. Her little window overlooked a moat edged with dirty suds. Beyond, she could glimpse parterres, overgrown gardens and a mossy grotto. A group of stable boys was sitting in the shade of a grove of trees, one holding the reins of a mouse-colored pacer with a bushy mane. Petite wondered where the stables were—not far, to judge by the smell. She wondered if Athénaïs liked to ride.

At six of the clock Petite and the two other new maids waited in the common room as instructed. The Duchesse de Navailles entered, attended by a footman and two pageboys—one carrying her train, and the other fanning her with ostrich plumes.

"Ready, girls?" she said after a quick demonstration on how to melt into a reverence with dutiful subservience. She instructed the footman to show the plump girl to the Queen's apartment and the brunette to the Queen Mother's suite.

Leaving Petite.

"I'll take you to Madame Henriette myself," the Duchess said, looking over Petite's bodice. "It fits you ill." She frowned.

"It was given to me," Petite said. The gown, a heavy winter-weight brocade, was all she had suitable for the evening, adorned as it was with ribbon rosettes and full sleeves bunched with matching rosettes down the arms. She was sweltering in it.

"The corset must come to more of a point." The Duchess fluffed Petite's curls to hang onto her shoulders. "Madame Henriette insists that her attendants be 'in the fashion,' as the young people say. She has a creative sensibility, an imbalance of yellow bile that should soon be remedied by motherhood. Your job will be to please her, but at the same time to exert a calming influence. One reason that the Queen Mother, in her great wisdom, approved your appointment is that you have a reputation for virtue."

Petite was surprised that she had any reputation at all.

The Duchess smiled, but not kindly. "Never forget, child, that at Court, everything you do and everything you say is observed and recorded." She tapped her head. "Here."

"Yes, Madame la Duchesse," Petite said.

Petite followed the superintendent through a dark passage into a galley, which opened onto yet another courtyard. At the far end they climbed a wide stairway, emerging into an elegant antechamber richly decorated with tapestries and paintings.

"We are expected," the Duchess informed the two guards, who threw open the doors.

The room was Oriental in its opulence, every peeling surface ornamented, the walls hung with dark pagan art: Venus reclining nude, the rape of Europa. The air was perfumed with the sweet rosemary scent of Hungary water. Servants in red livery stood like sentinels in the shadows.

In the center of the room, with her back to them, was the Princess. Her red hair was pulled into a bun at the nape of her long neck and embellished with pale green ribbons that matched her gown.

"Do you know a pavane by Aisne?" she called up to the quartet of musicians standing in a balcony above.

The men gathered up their instruments—two violins, a theorbo and a violo.

"A little faster," she said, making a circling motion with one hand. "That's it." She made a graceful glissade to the left and then one to the right. "Like that, Mimi?" she crooned to a spaniel she held tucked in one arm like a baby. "Ah!" she exclaimed glancing up, finally noticing her visitors.

"Your Highness," the Duchesse de Navailles said, bowing.

"Your Highness," Petite echoed, making the melting reverence she'd just been taught.

"I bring you another maid of honor," the Duchess said. "Mademoiselle Louise-Françoise La Baume Le Blanc de la Vallière," she said all in one breath.

Petite looked down. She well understood that the Duchess had listed all her family names in order to compensate for the fact that her pedigree was inferior, going back only a few hundred years, and certainly not to the Crusades.

The musicians sounded the last bar of the pavane and without pause began it again. The Princess hummed the melody, then opened her eyes. A fringe of bright corkscrew curls across her forehead gave her an endearingly frazzled look. "Forgive me if I seem somewhat distracted. I love this piece passionately, and the King's musicians are the best in the world. De la Vallière, did you say? Where is that?"

"Near Reugny, Your Highness," the Duchess answered. "It's a town in the south, not far from Amboise. Mademoiselle de la Vallière's father was governor of the castle there."

"La Vallière is a Duchy?" the Princess asked, one hand moving slowly to the music. The dog in her arms watched her hand expectantly.

"No, Madame."

The Princess set the dog down on a tasseled cushion and stroked its head. "A Marquisate?" she asked, standing, turning her full attention to the matter at hand.

"Not yet," the Duchess said nervously, examining the papers. "It has been applied for, but the letters patent has yet to be issued. One of Mademoiselle de la Vallière's ancestors rode beside Jeanne d'Arc."

"And one of my ancestors condemned her to death," the Princess said with a laugh, toying with one of the side curls that hung loose to her shoulders.

"Your Highness," the Duchesse de Navailles persisted, her voice betraying uneasiness, "Princess Marguerite d'Orléans, the future Grand Duchess of Tuscany, highly recommended Mademoiselle de la Vallière, who served her for . . ." She looked down at the papers. "For over six years."

"My cousin Marguerite?" Henriette touched one finger to a heart-shaped patch of fabric stuck to her chin. "She's something of a romp, don't you think?" she asked Petite, her look mischievous.

"She is a high-spirited princess, Your Majesty."

Henriette laughed. "Some might describe me in this way, so perhaps we shall get along. Come closer."

Nervously, Petite advanced ahead of the Duchess, holding out her skirts.

"You walk with a slight limp, I notice."

Petite felt chagrined. She'd changed out of her new corrective boots into evening slippers.

"From a riding accident, Your Highness," the Duchesse de Navailles interjected.

"But you do ride, Mademoiselle?"

"Oh, yes, Your Highness."

"I am given to understand that she is an accomplished horsewoman," the Duchess said.

"Good, because the King insists we go out riding with him constantly," Henriette said with an arch grimace.

"Mademoiselle de la Vallière's needlework is delicate," the Duchesse de Navailles went on, still reading from the documents, "she's a pitch-perfect soprano and she reads well, in French, of course, but also Latin and . . . Greek?"

Petite nodded. "But only little Greek. I am studying it now."

"What? No Spanish or Italian?" Henriette put her hands on her hips in mock horror. "Do you dance, Mademoiselle de la Vallière?"

"I love to dance," Petite confessed.

"Show us." Henriette motioned to two young ladies to watch, one in a powdered wig, the other in ribboned ringlets (the other maids of honor, Petite surmised). Henriette held her hand up to the musicians. "A gigue—just one movement."

The gigue—a lively dance comprising fast, springing steps—was one of Petite's favorites. Concentrating to compensate for her short leg, she performed four pas de bourrée, finishing with a contretemps de gavotte.

"Very nice," the Princess said. "Didn't you think?"

The maids—introduced as Yeyette and Claude-Marie—nodded begrudging assent.

"His Majesty has entrusted me with the creation of the Court entertainments this summer, Mademoiselle, and I am in need of girls who can dance well. Speaking of which, Madame de Navailles, am I not to have one more maid of honor?"

The Duchess was silenced as pages flung open the double doors and a butler announced Monsieur, the King's brother. Everyone in the room made a reverence as he entered the room.

Petite had seen Monsieur Philippe at that disastrous fete at Blois, two years before. She remembered him as a short man, even in high red heels. Now, with his wife towering over him, he seemed even shorter. He was wearing a yellow justacorps with gold facings and ribbons, the long lace ruffle of his petticoat breeches showing at the knees.

"What's that on your chin, my sweet?" he asked his wife, his gloved right hand on the hilt of a gold-crested sword. He was wearing a periwig in the new, natural style, topped by a three-cornered red hat with white plumes hanging down. He was not that comely, but he made up for his looks in his dress.

"A mouche, darling," Henriette answered her husband, touching the spot. "They are the fashion in London."

"And this is a new attendant?" he asked, turning to Petite. Night was falling, and servants began to light candles.

"Yes, Your Highness," the Duchess said. "Mademoiselle Louise Françoise la Baume le Blanc de la Vallière."

Petite made a gracious bow, her toes well turned out. Under her skirts, her bent knees were trembling, and she hoped no one could tell.

"Am I not to have four maids of honor?" Henriette asked her husband, picking up her little dog and caressing him.

"Yes, Your Highness," the Duchesse de Navailles said over the sound of trumpets outside. She squinted at her papers. "Another maid will be arriving in a week or so."

"We must not keep my brother waiting," Philippe said, seeming anxious to set out.

"Mademoiselle de Montalais," the Duchesse de Navailles read as Philippe ushered his wife out the doors.

Nicole! Petite could hardly refrain from exclaiming.

"You take this," the maid in the wig told Petite, pushing Henriette's fur wrap into Petite's arms.

In a daze, Petite followed the royal couple's entourage out the big double doors and through a succession of rooms, eventually emerging into a dark oval courtyard. Henriette, concerned about the horse leavings on the cobbles, called for two litters. One was not sufficiently ornate for Monsieur, so they called for a third. Once the couple was settled, the hefty bearers took off at a run across the courtyard and through an arched portal under a grand stone staircase. Petite raced to keep up, following the party through a guard room and a series of cabinets before coming to an abrupt halt in a long colonnade that opened onto a terrace.

Outside, courtiers in all manner of exquisite dress strolled about in the torch-light. Beyond a low balustrade was a dark expanse of water, reflecting lights. Off to one side, chairs appeared to have been set in front of a raised platform at the water's edge—for a theatrical performance, Petite guessed, to judge by the props. Candles were being lit all around the platform.

"We were supposed to make our entrance from the top of the stairs," Monsieur said with annoyance, adjusting his hat so that the plumes did not fall into his eyes.

A page was sent running for the musicians, who arrived shortly, lugging their instruments. They formed two lines, and at a signal, the arrival of the couple was announced. The crowds parted, and courtiers bowed as Monsieur and Madame proceeded to the water's edge.

"I'll put Madame's wrap by her chair," Yeyette explained, taking the furs from Petite.

"Meet us by the steps after the King and Queen arrive," Claude-Marie said over her shoulder before disappearing into the crowd.

For the first time that day, Petite was alone—albeit in the midst of a mingling throng. She walked down to the water, where three ornate gondolas and a gilded barge were being tended by boatmen in red and blue silk. The smoke of perfume braziers misted the air.

Musicians began to play a minuet—but from where? The music was faint, coming from a distance. Petite didn't recognize the piece, but it was magical, filling the air with mystic sweetness. It took a moment before she could make out the lights of a barge on the dark water. She felt enraptured, as if under a spell.

"The Comédie-Française is performing again tonight?" Petite heard a woman behind her say. "The Queen won't be pleased."

Petite turned to see Athénaïs, the elegant Marquise de Rochechouart who had sat across from her on the trip down from Paris. Petite smiled, relieved to see a familiar face, then felt herself flush (aware now of Athénaïs's high station).

"At least they make the King laugh," said a little man. He had an ugly face and was shorter than Athénaïs by at least a head.

From his dress, Petite realized that he was the man she had seen on horseback earlier, the one she'd taken for a boy.

"He could use a little gaiety," he said, jumping to see over the heads of the courtiers. "Where is he?"

"The Queen insisted on two hours of prayer this afternoon, so they're running late." Athénaïs's tapered bodice was cut daringly low. "Ah! It's my sister," she said, recognizing Petite. "Look, Lauzun." Athénaïs put her gloved hand on Petite's arm. "Do we not look alike?" She pressed her cheek against Petite's.

The little man twisted his face into a skeptical expression, his brow furrowed like a field in spring. He looked Petite over and let out a sound remarkably like that of a donkey braying.

"Stop that, Lauzun. You'll unnerve the girl. Come on: don't you think we look like sisters?"

"Well, yes, perhaps, but with the exception of . . ." He stared unabashedly at Athénaïs's bosom.

Athénaïs burst out laughing. "Mademoiselle de la Vallière, meet His Clownship, Monsieur Lauzun—the King's fool . . . and my folly."

"My pleasure," Petite said with a curtsy. He was the smallest man she had ever seen—no taller than a sword.

"Mademoiselle de la Vallière is fortunate to be serving Madame," Athénaïs said, "who is a bit more lively than—"

Athénaïs was interrupted by a blare of trumpets.

"Jingo! It appears Their Majesties have finally arrived," Lauzun said, disappearing into the crowd.

As the King, Queen and Queen Mother came down the stairs, everyone fell into a reverence, and then a second, and then a third, as if the courtiers were one great exotic flower blowing in a gentle breeze.

Petite felt breathless watching the King approach, the Queen and Queen Mother a few steps behind. He was wearing a rhinegrave, its hooped skirt and full breeches adorned with brightly colored ribbons. He was even more comely than she remembered. He walked like the king that he was, but something in his expression—a shy glance to one side—hinted at the rustic she'd met that day in the meadow: a kind man who had a way with horses.

Aunt and niece by blood, the two queens looked very alike. Dressed in dour black silk, the Queen meekly followed behind her formidable aunt, her eyes cast to the ground.

"We frighten her," Athénaïs whispered. "Poor thing."

"Is she in mourning?"

"She likes to dress as a nun," she said with upcast eyes. "Especially now that she's finally been *made*."

Ah, Petite thought, so the rumors were true: the Queen was with child. She gasped to see a tiny face peek out from under the Queen's train.

"It's just José," Athénaïs said, "Her Majesty's favorite dwarf—her Holy Fool. He's harmless, but watch out for the blond one." Athénaïs slipped off a glove and held up her index finger, wrapped in a plaster. "The little beast bites."

At the water's edge, the King removed his plumed hat and bowed to his brother's wife. "Madame," Petite heard him say, "it's my wish that this evening's entertainment will be pleasing to you."

"Your Majesty," Henriette answered, making a graceful reverence, "*all* that you do enchants us."

Athénaïs caught Petite's eye. *What did I tell you?* she mouthed behind her fan.

Chapter Fifteen

My FIRST MORNING *at Court,* Petite thought, rising before the sun was up. *My first morning prayer, my first breakfast* (a roll, dried venison, a bowl of cow's milk). *My first nervous stomach,* rushing to be at Madame's before eight of the clock.

Petite joined a crowd of attendants in the antechamber to Madame Henriette's bedchamber.

"Monsieur Philippe just left for the King's levee," Claude-Marie told her with a condescending smile. The ringlets around her face were tied up in blue and white striped ribbons, matching her gown.

Petite liked her only a little better than the first maid of honor, Yeyette, whose eyes had a calculating cast.

Men in periwigs and women in brilliant silks stood quietly conversing, looking expectantly toward the white and gold doors. Petite stood beside Claude-Marie, wondering what was going to happen. Men turned to stare, as if appraising her. There was a statue in an alcove of a woman with uncovered breasts. Petite looked away, but the ceiling and walls were likewise adorned with erotic images.

A garçon in gray livery made his way through the crowd, followed by an officer with an armload of wood. A valet opened one of the double doors for them and then immediately closed it, only to open it again for two other garçons coming out, one carrying a servant's camp-bed and the other a night lamp.

Yeyette appeared at the door, a frilly bonnet set high on her wig. "Summon Madame's breakfast," she commanded a valet.

"That's the signal that Madame Henriette is awake," Claude-Marie said in a low voice. "We can go in now."

Petite followed her and a number of others into a grand chamber. The massive four-poster bed was hung with richly wrought curtains. The Princess was sitting up in bed, wearing a frilly nightcap. A nurse bent to kiss her. "Good morning, my child."

Henriette mumbled "Morning" and held out her hands. Yeyette poured wine over them, catching the drops in a basin. A chamberlain stepped forward with a vase of holy water. Henriette dipped a finger in it and made the sign of the cross as the chamberlain read from a prayer book, Henriette repeating the phrases, her eyes clenched shut. A hairdresser came forward with two hats. Henriette frowned at them both, then indicated the one trimmed with a wide forest-green ribbon. She slipped her feet over the edge of the bed.

"Get her slippers," Claude-Marie told Petite under her breath.

Petite took the silk embroidered mules by the bed and offered them to the Princess. "Your Highness," she said, bowing. The cloth-of-gold bed curtains were dirty, she noticed, closer in color to copper.

"You've got them turned around," Henriette said with a giggle.

Flushing, Petite backed away for the chamberlain, who handed the Princess a dressing gown. The Princess slipped it on, crossed herself again with holy water and sat in an armchair that had been placed in the middle of the room. The chamberlain took away her nightcap and handed it to a maid of the wardrobe.

"You hold the mirror," Yeyette whispered to Petite, passing her a tin mirror.

The frame of the looking glass was plated with silver, but it was dull as lead, in need of a polish. Petite stood a few feet in front of the Princess, holding it up.

"Closer," the Princess said, and Petite took a step forward. "I won't bite," she said, and laughed.

The two other maids of honor came up beside the Princess holding lit candles in silver holders. "I'm ready," the Princess told a valet as the hairdresser combed out her frizzy curls. A man in livery repeated the words to the garçon at the door, and two of the men who had been milling outside in the antechamber came in: a doctor and a surgeon.

After the Princess's hair was coiffed—"You may put down the mirror," she told Petite kindly—and after the doctor and the surgeon were content that her health was good, a maid of the wardrobe presented an embroidered girdle and two skirts. The Princess chose the one of yellow silk, and another maid of the wardrobe handed her under-stockings and garters, which the Princess daintily put on herself. The maid of the wardrobe then knelt to put on the Princess's shoes, which were ornamented with a gold buckle.

"Breakfast now," the Princess said as a page took away her slippers.

Yeyette went to the door and asked the garçon if the officers of the goblet and bouche had arrived. He opened one door, and four men entered: two with a porcelain service, one with a folding table and one with the linens. The table was set up, and a flagon of wine emptied into a glass and cup. One of the men stepped forward, testing the wine in the cup. He nodded and handed the Princess her glass, which she downed thirstily.

"Sour," she said with a playful grimace, and Petite smiled with all the others. The Princess was so charming.

Henriette slipped off her dressing gown herself. Her nightdress under it was white and embroidered at the edges, pretty in spite of a few patches. She took off a ruby cross on a ribbon and handed it to the first valet, who placed it in a little velvet sack.

"You hold up this end," Claude-Marie whispered, handing Petite a corner of the Princess's dressing gown. They held it high to give the Princess privacy.

A maid of the wardrobe helped the Princess off with her nightdress—holding it by the right sleeve while Yeyette held it by the left—and handed it to another maid of the wardrobe. A third maid of the wardrobe stepped forward with a chemise, the embroidered girdle, two petticoats and the yellow skirt. Petite averted her eyes from the naked Princess (red hair *everywhere*), but at the same time watching carefully, trying to memorize what was done and who did what.

Yet another maid of the wardrobe was let in with a tray of pearl necklaces and earrings. The Princess picked out the strand she wanted. The maid attached the necklace at the back of her slender neck, but the Princess put on her ear-rings herself. A valet of the wardrobe presented three lace nose cloths on a silver-gilt tray and another a tray of gloves and fans.

"How do I look?" the Princess asked, adjusting her camlet partlet with its matching hood.

"Beautiful," the maids said in chorus.

Henriette waited as a valet placed two cushions on the floor beside the bed. The valet stood watching as she and the chamberlain knelt and prayed.

"*Quaesumus, omnipotens Deus,*" everyone chanted as she signed herself with holy water.

The Princess clapped her hands. "Now to Mass, my good ladies."

They joined an enormous crowd of courtiers gathered in a long gallery. Two guards stood beside double doors. "The King's cabinet," Claude-Marie explained to Petite.

Petite and the other two maids stood behind the Princess as she conversed with three women—two duchesses (to judge by the length of their trains) and Athénaïs, who caught Petite's eye.

There was a murmur in the crowd as the doors opened. Everyone sank into a deep reverence when the King appeared, followed by a crowd of men: his brother, the ministers of state, princes of the blood, foreign ambassadors, valets. Petite barely noticed the others; it was the King she watched. As he scanned the crowd, guards cleared a path. A man stepped forward and pressed a paper into the King's hand. A secretary stepped forward to take it. Another man followed with a bow and a few words. The King nodded with a backward glance at his secretary and proceeded toward the chapel, raising his hat to the ladies. A woman swooned and was helped into the privacy of a window enclosure.

Henriette sank into a graceful reverence. The King took her gloved hand and kissed it. Petite, directly behind the Princess, touched the wall to steady herself. He was so close she could smell his cinnamon-scented breath. His eyes caught hers: paused.

Petite's heart jumped. He nodded and passed on.

With trembling knees, Petite followed the King and his entourage into the chapel. She sat with the other maids behind Princess Henriette, clasping her hands tightly as they joined the King in prayer.

THE BALL THAT NIGHT was held in the François I gallery, yet another enormous room of fading opulence, its ceiling, walls and floor carved and painted like a jewel box. Grand windows overlooked the terrace and what Petite now under-stood was a large carp pond. Silver candelabra were placed on gilded tables set along one side. Great crystal chandeliers of at least twenty branches hung from the high ceiling.

Petite stood with Madame Henriette's maids, watching as a parade of noble men and women circled the room in richly embellished satin and velvet. Prince de Condé was easy to identify because of his big nose. An elegant older gentleman with a lively manner was Nicolas Fouquet, the minister of finance. Petite spotted Athénaïs on the far side of the room and waved her fan. Their journey in the carriage the day before seemed a lifetime ago now.

Henriette was, Petite thought, one of the most beautiful women present, in spite of her freckles and red hair. In a gown of shimmering gold brocade—hurriedly hemmed only an hour ago—the vivacious Princess fidgeted excitedly, using her fan violently and calling out to people like a child at a fair. Monsieur, wearing face paint and three red silk patches in the shape of diamonds on his cheeks, hushed her. "Be still."

At seven of the clock, trumpets sounded and the musicians took up their instruments. The courtiers all stood at attention and then fell into a reverence as the King, Queen and Queen Mother entered.

The King scanned the room with his eyes, his expression masklike. With calm dignity, he received the passionate adulation. A woman at the back slumped to the floor and was efficiently whisked out of the room. (Petite gathered that swooning happened rather often.)

The King sat, followed by the Queen Mother and the Queen, in that order. Then Philippe and Henriette sat down, and after them, the princes and princesses of the blood and all the dukes and duchesses, taking their places according to the seniority of their title. And then the King stood, and everyone did likewise, the sound of scraping chair legs drowning out the music.

Solemnly, the King bowed to his wife. The Queen put her tiny hand on his arm and followed him out onto the dance floor. Petite could see the swelling of her belly, confirming what had been whispered. Monsieur and Henriette proceeded to the center as well, Henriette towering over her husband. Couple by couple, men and women of the inner circle positioned themselves, gentlemen on the left, ladies on the right. The musicians struck the opening chords and the dancers bowed to one another. The ball began.

Frowning in concentration, the Queen danced the branle. Her moves were mechanical—left, right, left, right—while those of the King infused the simple swaying motion with graceful solemnity.

A man whispered in Petite's ear, "I think you will agree that His Majesty dances exquisitely."

"Monsieur de Gautier!" Petite gasped. Her former dance master from Blois looked dapper in a felt wide-awake hat and white satin doublet.

He smiled, held his index finger to his painted lips and slipped away through the crowd.

A courante in triple time was announced, and men and women moved forward. The crowd murmured as the King bowed before Henriette and led her to the center.

"Now for the *real* performance," a woman beside Petite said. It was Athénaïs, lushly adorned in crimson silk.

"You don't dance?" Petite asked as the musicians took up their instruments.

"I prefer more sedentary amusements," she said, watching the dancers make a deep reverence.

"Oh là là!" Petite whispered as the King took a springing step forward, then jumped back into fourth position with both arms raised.

Henriette answered his moves delicately and with precision.

"His Majesty and Madame Henriette seem made for each other, do they not?" Athénaïs asked behind her fan. "Pity." She rolled her eyes toward Philippe, who was sitting out the dance with a frown.

Petite wasn't sure how to respond to the comment. "They dance well," she said, intent on the dancers.

The King advanced, balanced, turned and then made a deep bow to Henriette, his arms just so. Petite gasped as he sprang forward, performing one flawless pas de bourrée after another. As the cadence of the music came alive, he made a quick series of pirouettes with such graceful vivacity that it took her breath away. At the finale, he sprang into the air, beating his legs together in a vigorous cabriole.

"Bravo!" Petite cried out as the crowd burst into cheers. *Bravo!*

PETITE AND THE OTHER maids stayed late at the ball, not returning to their rooms until two of the clock. The next morning, Clorine had to shake Petite awake, but she was quickly revived by the thrilling prospect of a hunt—her first with the Court.

The courtyard opposite the chapel was already crowded with riders by the time Petite arrived. The King, at the gate, sat his horse with both reins in his right hand, his left hand resting on his thigh. Over a leather jerkin, he was wearing a brocade long coat with cuffs turned back to reveal billows of fine lace. A cloak was slung carelessly over his shoulder. The howling of the tufters could be heard in the distance.

Gentlemen riders were assisting the ladies of the palace onto stalking horses—old, steady, half-blind geldings that would never shy or bolt. "Don't worry, he's quiet," a rider assured Petite, leading a bay pony to a mounting block. The black leather sidesaddle was finely tooled. Even the bridle was embossed, its headband ringed with ostrich plumes. The rider gave Petite a leg up into the saddle.

With the cry "Halloo!" the King spurred his powerful mount and set off into the deer park, followed by the master of the hounds with a circular horn on his shoulder. Varlets with leashed running hounds chased after them on foot. The Queen and Henriette followed in a light open carriage, two of the Queen's dwarves hanging over the sides, making faces. Petite's pony reluctantly ambled into the park after the others. At a sharp tap from her riding stick he picked up his pace, but only for a step or two.

Inside the pale, at a bend in the path, a woman awaited on a small black horse. "I thought it was you."

Petite was pleased to see Athénaïs, the elegant marquise.

"You sit a horse nicely, I see," Athénaïs said with a smile. "Have you been on hunts before?"

"I used to hunt with my father," Petite said. "As well as at Blois."

"Hawking?"

"Most everything, but hart mainly, and hare." A tree branch cracked above them, but Petite's stale didn't even twitch an ear. "It was not at all like this." Not nearly so grand . . . so boring. Confined within the limits of a park, her father would have called it "hunting at force."

Athénaïs slapped at an insect. "I hate being out in May," she said, examining her glove for blood.

"It's early to be hunting hart." Petite's father had preferred to wait until August. By then the bucks had lost their antler velvet and begun to put on rutting weight. *Not so good for the chase, but better for the larder,* he used to say. Clearly, the King was more interested in the chase.

"Frankly, I hate being out at all, but His Majesty insists on hunting at least three times a week. I think he would live outdoors if he could." Athénaïs gave a rueful sigh. "And of course we all go along cheerfully . . . at least long enough to make an appearance," she said with a sly smile, bidding adieu and turning her horse onto a return path.

With a sharp tap of her whip, Petite managed to get her palfrey to gallop on a loose rein. Guided by the sound of the horns, she came to a great carrefour with alleys stretching off in every direction, long straight lines of trees on each side and a thick undergrowth of ferns. She heard the faint sound of the horn, enough for her to distinguish the vue, which meant that the hounds were still running. Then suddenly she heard the great burst of the hallali, the horses, dogs and riders all joining in. Pushing through thick brushwood, she found herself on the edge of a sizable pond.

In the center, a fine stag was swimming about, his eyes bulging and his breast heaving. The dogs were swimming after him, followed in a small boat by the master of the hounds. The King and his men were on horseback on the far bank. Petite spotted the Queen and Henriette in their open carriage at the edge of the wood, people in carts and gigs behind them. The sound of the horns had brought out a crowd.

The stag finally attempted to get up on the bank, and the master of the hounds, close at hand, gave it the coup de grâce, the death blow delivered with a hunting knife.

Petite watched from the woods as the stag soiled itself and was half-eaten by the dogs before the master of the hounds succeeded in calling them off. She circled her horse around to join the Court as the bloody mass was hauled to the shore. There, with an attempt at dignified ritual, the King cut into the breast of the stag and presented the heart to the Queen. One of her maids put it into a leather hunt pouch, which the Queen hung from her neck, displaying her trophy proudly. The heart of a buck contained a bone that kept the animal from dying of fright; it would serve as a protective amulet when her time came.

Petite rode back with the others, following Henriette and the Queen's caroche. The King rode at the head, his shoulders slightly slumped. A stag at bay was a fine sight indeed, but this kill had not been clean.

By THE TIME PETITE got back to the château there was time for only a quick change of clothes before she was expected back at Madame's.

"You'll never guess who came by looking for you—your old dance master from Blois," Clorine said as she combed out Petite's fine hair, which tended to tangle. "Monsieur le Duc de Gautier."

"He's been made a duke?" Petite winced as Clorine pulled out a knot.

"Indeed! He's director of festivities and gentleman of the King's bedchamber—one of the King's most trusted aides, according to the head pastry-cook. He wanted to make sure that you knew about the change in the day's schedule. There's going to be a gathering this afternoon to decide who dances the parts in a ballet. Now, now," Clorine said, in response to Petite's look of fright. "I assured him that you would go since—"

"Clorine, you didn't." Petite was aghast. She couldn't.

"—since Madame will be there."

Petite groaned, allowing Clorine to dress her in a plain linen bodice and skirt. Biting her lips and slapping her cheeks for color, she rushed through the arcades to the antler gallery, finally slipping in behind the crowd of chattering courtiers.

Monsieur le Duc de Gautier, at the front, rang a silver bell and everyone quieted. "The *Ballet of the Seasons* will open on July twenty-third, a Saturday," he began. "It is, as most of you already know, to be a Madame creation."

Henriette stood, made a charming curtsy, and everyone cheered. Lauzun made a donkey bray. Petite, standing at the back, laughed with the others.

"We have six weeks to prepare," Gautier said, "which should be sufficient. Monsieur Benserade has already composed verses." He motioned the poet to stand. "And Monsieur de Lully the music." A handsome young man with Italian features made a bow. "As to the performers, the King will play two roles—" Gautier paused until everyone stopped applauding. "Initially that of Ceres—"

A murmur of amused surprise went through the crowd. The King was to dance the part of a goddess?

"—and then as Spring. Madame Henriette will dance the part of Diana, queen and huntress. It's to be a ballet and opera in nine acts."

Gautier reviewed all the acts, concluding, "The fifth act is Autumn, with vintagers, four female and four male—one of whom will be Monsieur."

The King's brother Philippe stood and was heartily applauded.

"I could be a vintager." Lauzun staggered drunkenly.

Gautier waited for the room to quiet. "Thank you, Monsieur Lauzun. I will let you know. The sixth act is a brief interlude of six country gallants. The seventh, masques playing cards . . . or rather, losing."

"I know that part well," Lauzun called out, provoking laughter yet again.

"Thank you, Monsieur Lauzun," Gautier said, raising his voice to be heard, "but I believe there are a number present who are qualified."

Prince de Condé made a look of despair and everyone laughed knowingly.

"The eighth scene," Gautier went on, "representing winter, sees the return of the King in the part of Spring, attended by Game, Laughter, Joy and Abundance. We'll conclude with the ninth and final scene, which will feature Apollo in the company of Love and a number of muses.

"And so . . . to work." The dance master opened his arms. "I will begin by casting Diana's ten attendants, the nymphs. Who among you could perform a solo bourée?" Gautier surveyed the silent room. A lively dance in double time, the bourée had to be performed at staccato speed, with a playful, almost elated fervor. "Mademoiselle de la Vallière?"

Petite sent him a pleading look. *No.*

"Step forward, Mademoiselle," Gautier said—kindly, but with a tone of command.

Petite shook her head.

He smiled with paternal suavity. "Ready?"

The musicians took up their instruments.

O Lord. The music swelled, reviving her courage. Petite took a step, and then leapt into the dance.

"Congratulations, little sister," Athénaïs said, touching the heart-shaped mouche stuck to her cheek. Following Henriette's example, all the ladies had taken to wearing spots. "I understand that you got one of the principal parts in Madame's production."

"Yes," Petite said grimly. The gondola skimmed across the surface of the mirror-smooth carp pond, the reflection of the moon and stars shimmering on the water like a carpet of diamonds. Musicians were playing on a barge not far behind.

Athénaïs laughed. "Don't look so apprehensive. You have, whether you like it or not, been propelled onto the main stage of this life of fantasy." She waved her jeweled hand out over the water.

"Monsieur le Duc de Gautier was my dance master at Blois," Petite explained, "so of course I knew the steps he requires."

"You appear to have been a good pupil," Athénaïs said with a slow and languorous wink.

PETITE HAD NOT BEEN able to sleep the night before the first rehearsal. "I won't be able to go," she told Clorine on rising. "My courses have started." Or were going to at any moment. She was sure of it.

"Courage, Mademoiselle," Clorine said. "Didn't your ancestor ride alongside Jeanne d'Arc?"

"But he didn't have to think about ordinaries." Petite groaned, clasping her belly. "Please, Clorine. The King will be there, and I know I'll fall on my face. I can't even remember my name when he's around. Tell them I can't come. Tell them I've got the Black Plague or something."

"Come, come. You'll be fine. I'll make you plantain juice. We wouldn't want to disappoint the dear old Duc de Gautier, now, would we?"

A bowl of clarified plantain juice—generously laced with laudanum—and Petite was fine, as her maid had predicted. A little dreamy, perhaps, but pain-free. And thankfully, there was a reprieve. "His Majesty is held up in a council meeting," Gautier informed everyone. There was a murmur of disappointment.

"But he will join us later, he said." Henriette looked up from a pile of fabric scraps on a table in the corner of the great room. "At three of the clock."

"Excellent. That should give us time to go through the entire sequence," Gautier said. "We will begin with the overture."

There was a great shuffling about as members of the choir moved into position. Monsieur de Lully raised his baton. The deep male voices reverberated in the cavernous room: "Who, in the night—"

Monsieur de Lully made a sour face and covered his ears, shaking his head. "Autre fois."

"Who, in the night—"

There was laughter this time. "Une plus de fois, questa volta con energia," Monsieur de Lully said, mixing French and Italian, but his meaning clear.

He raised his little baton and the men's deep voices boomed: "Who, in the night, brought back the sun? Such beautiful stars have never been seen."

"Magnifico! Quello era bello!"

The rehearsal went on all afternoon, Monsieur de Lully working with the choir and musicians, Monsieur Benserade making changes to the lines, Gautier directing the dancers through their steps.

Petite worked through her sequence nine times, yet even so it eluded her. She was concentrating so hard trying to master it that she didn't notice when the King entered. Belatedly, she fell into a reverence.

"Don't stop on my account, Mademoiselle," the King said, tipping his hat.

Petite looked behind her.

"No, *you*," he said. "Show me that sequence."

Petite froze. She doubted that she could take even three steps without stumblings and slidings.

Gautier caught Petite's eye. "Your Majesty, Mademoiselle de la Vallière will be delighted, I'm sure, to perform for you." He made a twirling motion with his index finger as if to say, *Mademoiselle, wake up, the King has spoken.*

"Your Majesty," Petite said with a curtsy, her heart pounding so violently she feared she might faint, "I am honored, but . . ." She raised her eyes, not sure what to say. She saw then not the King, but the young man she'd encountered in the wilderness at Chambord, calming a skittery horse with gentle authority. "But it's a challenging sequence, and I've yet to master it."

"I understand, yet you danced it beautifully just now."

"Thank you, Your Majesty," Petite said, her voice tremulous.

"Perhaps if I danced it with you?" He signaled the musicians and held out his hand.

Petite put her hand on his. Pulse racing, and conscious of her feet, she stepped crossways over her left leg and made a sharp quarter-turn to the right.

Smiling with his eyes, the King led her through the fast, intricate steps: forward, behind and before; to the right, to the left, open. "*Now*," he said, rising on his toes, and she gave herself up to the delirium of the quick, shuffling and stamping steps. *Sing ye!*

The room burst into applause.

IN THE DAYS THAT followed, everyone accorded Petite a noticeable respect. Even the Duchesse de Navailles nodded to her in passing. Petite told herself that it was insignificant, that it meant nothing, yet even so, she walked in a reverie. She had yet to wash her right hand, the hand he had touched.

Chapter Sixteen

NICOLE ARRIVED IN THE MIDDLE of June, the day Henriette turned seventeen. Petite didn't recognize her at first; she was wearing face paint and she'd wired her dark hair so that it stood up high over her brow. She made a clumsy curtsy before the Princess, not daring to tip her head lest the construction topple. Petite smiled at her encouragingly.

"You must be my birthday gift, Mademoiselle de Montalais," the Princess said in that ebullient way that everyone found delightful. "What are your unique abilities?"

"I can hear what people are saying from a distance," Nicole said after a moment's reflection.

Henriette laughed. "That's a dangerous talent at Court."

"And I keep secrets," Nicole added.

"I shall make use of you," the Princess said.

"I have so much to tell you," Petite whispered at the first opportunity.

Nicole stared over Petite's shoulder. "That man with the big nose must be the Prince de Condé. And isn't that Maréchal d'Albret talking to the Comte de Guiche, and . . . Oh là là, that's surely Nicolas Fouquet, the Marquis de Belle-Île."

"How do you know all these people?" Petite asked, turning to look behind her. Impeccably dressed Nicolas Fouquet was standing close by in the company of an older woman. Fouquet was only a marquis, but as minister of finance he was one of the most powerful men at Court. "I've been here over three weeks—" Three weeks, five days, two hours. "—and I'm only beginning to sort out who's who."

"Monsieur Fouquet's saying his château is almost finished," Nicole told Petite in a low voice. "And the woman he's talking to wants to know how his wife is doing." She paused, concentrating, then added, "He said she's uncomfortable in this heat. Is his wife with child?"

"I didn't even know he was married," Petite said as the musicians began to play. Certainly, he didn't behave as if he was.

After an outdoor excursion, followed by a feast, a theatrical performance and yet more food and drink, Petite showed tipsy Nicole back to their rooms, leading the way by the light of a taper. The moon was a sliver; here and there candles could be seen flickering in the château windows.

"This place is a gossip's paradise," Nicole said, making herself comfortable on her rumpled trundle bed.

"Not everything you hear is true," Petite cautioned, checking the stability of a stool before sitting down on it.

"For sure the King covetises his brother's wife—and that's understandable: the Queen is with child, so he can't swive her, and if his seminal backs up, he'll die."

"Nicole, it would be wrong, and you know it." Petite sounded more sure of her convictions than she was, in fact. Everything she'd been taught about right and wrong seemed to be different at Court. "And in any case, I don't believe it." She *had* been at Court long enough to know that much was not as it appeared.

"Didn't you see Monsieur Philippe go stomping off into the woods?"

"People go into the woods for lots of reasons."

"According to the Marquise de Plessis-Bellièvre, he was in a jealous fury."

"The Marquise du . . . ?"

"You know—the woman with bad breath, Fouquet's spy."

"Monsieur Fouquet has a spy?"

"Practically everyone is in his pay. That ugly, short little guy . . . what's his name?"

"Monsieur Lauzun?"

"Yes, the funny one. He intimated that Monsieur Fouquet is angling to take over—wear the crown."

"And to think that you've only just arrived." Nicole's wild stories were at least amusing.

"But what I've yet to figure out is who *you're* sweet on."

"No one," Petite said evenly. It wasn't going to be easy hiding her heart's passion from her friend.

AT BENEDICTION EACH evening, Nicole held the candle as Petite read the Psalms out loud. Afterward, Henriette and Philippe walked out into the fragrant gardens, followed, at a distance, by their whispering attendants.

"Henriette and Philippe had congress last night," Yeyette confided. There had been evidence in the sheets.

"Philippe touches a rosary to his privates before the act," Claude-Marie said. His valet had told her himself.

And then everyone started talking at once.

"The Queen is complaining—she doesn't like that the King is always at Henriette's."

"The Queen Mother is suspicious as well."

"She's always watching."

"Yesterday she told Madame that night excursions will harm her health." They laughed at such a notion.

Petite walked on, only half listening to the chatter. She had had two letters and a parcel in the post that morning: one letter was from Jean in Amboise (complaining of boredom), the other from her mother in Paris (with advice on how to cover blemishes). The parcel was from her aunt Angélique in Tours (with laces she'd made and prayers for her safety).

"But then, the Queen Mother is sixty," Petite heard Nicole say behind her, "impossibly old. Don't you agree, oh sage one?"

Petite turned and smiled—although, in truth, she thought the Queen Mother wise to be watchful.

The following day, the first Monday in July, Petite was in the château library, looking for a book to read aloud to the Princess, when Nicole entered, flushed and out of breath.

"Guess who just arrived," she said, panting. She'd run all the way from the carp pond.

"Who?" Petite asked absently, deciding on *Cléopâtre* by La Calprenède to read to the Princess, and Cicero's *On the Good Life* for herself. She wanted to improve her Latin, and his essays "On Duties"—providing a moral code for the Roman aristocracy—were of interest.

"Henriette's *mother*."

The Queen of England?

"I think the Princess is in for a scolding," Nicole said in sing-song.

That night, the gathering at Henriette's was gay, but in a careful, deliberate way. Henriette deferred to her mother, and was unusually gracious to the Queen Mother and the Queen. As for the King, she gave him the respect he was due, but beyond that, not a glance. For most of the evening Henriette sat beside her husband and even laughed at his jokes.

"So, she *was* scolded," Nicole said.

Petite closed her fan, reflecting on a line from Cicero: that if one adopted moral goodness as a guide, understanding practical duties followed automatically.

"Mademoiselle?" A man's voice interrupted her thoughts.

Petite looked up. "Your Majesty!" Had she done something wrong?

"May I request the pleasure of hearing you sing?"

"Of course," Petite stuttered.

"Oh, yes," Henriette said from across the room. "Mademoiselle Petite has the loveliest voice of all my maids."

Petite got to her feet and went to the harpsichord, where Claude-Marie was seated. She stood frozen for a moment, both terrified and perplexed. She loved to sing, but only when alone. Had Henriette ever even heard her?

"Well?" Claude-Marie asked in a miffed tone, pulling on a ringlet.

"'Enfin la Beauté'?" Petite suggested. It was a lovely air de cour.

Claude-Marie screwed up her face. "Enfin what?"

"I can sing it without accompaniment," Petite told her and turned to face the room. *Mercy.* The King was sitting directly in front of her, flanked by the Queen Mother, the Queen *and* the Queen of England. Behind them were Henriette and Philippe and several princes of the blood, ministers of state, the dukes and duchesses. Standing in the alcoves and against the walls were all the lesser nobles and their attendants.

Petite looked up at the ceiling, not daring to meet anyone's eyes until a moment of dizziness passed. What was it her aunt Angélique used to say? That song was God's language. She took a deep breath.

PETITE WAS AWAKE for a long time that night, going over what had happened in her mind. The King had asked her to sing, he'd listened to her intently and, after, he'd applauded vigorously. At two of the clock, she finally fell into sleep, giving way to a blissful dream: that the King was not married, that he was not even King, that he loved her to sing for him. She woke the next morning, her covering sheets in a knot, her heart aching. She slipped out of bed and onto her knees, praying for a guide to moral goodness.

That morning, Henriette greeted her warmly. "Our angelic singer," she said brightly, tossing back her hair. "You please the King, Mademoiselle Louise, and that pleases me." She gave a simpering smile.

Claude-Marie and Yeyette glared. Nicole threw Petite a look of consternation. *What does it all mean?* Petite wondered. Clearly, she had done something wrong—but what?

In the days that followed, Petite's confusion increased. On the Friday, instead of joining Madame Henriette's table for cards, the King joined hers. The night following, when it was her turn to dance as Henriette played the virginal, he pointedly turned to watch. The next afternoon, he commanded Yeyette and Claude-Marie to be silent as she read out loud from *Don Quixote*.

The King seemed to be favoring her—but why?

It means nothing, Petite told herself, her heart quickening. She knew he couldn't be serious. Coquetting was an innocent diversion at Court—but even so, why would the King coquette *her*? (And why not Henriette?) For that matter, why would he pay court to her at all?

"TODAY: A REVIEW of the impolite actions," the Duchesse de Navailles announced in their usual place of instruction in the common room. "Mademoiselle Louise de la Vallière, perhaps you can begin."

"Cutting nails in company. Laughing loudly," Petite offered. They'd been through this lesson several times already.

"Especially at the mistakes of others." The Duchess nodded with approval. "And?"

"No yawning," Petite went on. Not only was it rude, it was how the Devil got in.

"But what of reading?" the Duchess asked, noting the girdle book Petite had hanging at her waist.

"One is not to read while others are talking," Petite said, distracted by Yeyette and Claude-Marie snickering behind her. "Nor the reverse." No reading while others were talking, and no talking while others were reading. Between the two, it was hard to know what to do.

"And no reading aloud in company without being asked," Nicole offered.

"By the person of the highest station," corrected the Duchess.

They all nodded. That was the one clear rule: every move, every glance and breath, was determined by station.

"I should not have to remind you that there is to be no talking while someone is reading, or singing, or playing an instrument," the Duchess said, pointedly addressing Yeyette.

Nicole nudged Petite. The evening before, the King had commanded Yeyette to be silent while Petite sang.

"Tomorrow, we'll review the etiquette of the stools," the Duchess said as her footmen helped her to her feet.

"No mocking others," Claude-Marie whispered after the Duchess had left, limping out the door in an imitation of Petite.

"No gazing rudely," Yeyette said, turning to make bug-eyes.

Nicole linked Petite's arm in hers. "And above all, no spitting," she said, aiming neatly at Yeyette's cheek.

"You shouldn't have done that!" Petite hissed, pulling Nicole away.

"It was just a spray," Nicole said, shaking free. "The wenches," she added, making a monkey face at them over her shoulder. "Simpering giglets. They're just jealous because the King shows you favor."

"That's what I don't understand, Nicole," Petite said as she headed to the pond. "Why me?" She picked up a flat stone and skipped it hard over the water's smooth surface.

"Maybe because he likes you?" Nicole suggested, but with doubt in her voice.

"You know that's not possible."

"I know. You're right—but he makes as though he does."

Petite kicked up the blossoms that carpeted the ground. She was bewildered by the way Henriette seemed to be encouraging the King's attentions to her, and dismayed over Claude-Marie's and Yeyette's jealousy. She couldn't help but be honored by the King's apparent regard—but what about the Queen? He was married and he shouldn't be acting this way, to Henriette or to her.

"Maybe that's what it is—an act," Nicole said, lowering herself onto a wide stone bench. "Maybe he's trying to make Henriette jealous. That happens in books."

"But that's just it." Petite sat beside her friend. "Madame doesn't seem jealous in the least."

Nicole leaned forward, elbows on her knees. "Something's not right."

"Nicole, could you find out?" Petite asked, desperate now.

"You mean spy?" Nicole grinned.

"I solved it," Nicole whispered to Petite the next morning, joining her at the breakfast table. "I had to bribe one of the pastry-cooks." She bit into a roll. "You owe me six sous." She looked around to make sure no one was near. "It's just as I thought," she said, moving close. "He's *pretending* to court you."

"Like in a play, you mean?"

"Yes, like acting a part."

Petite thought of the King's applause, his approving smile. Had it meant nothing? "But why?"

"To fool his mother. That way, the Queen Mother won't think he's in love with Henriette. If he pretends to be courting one of her maids—you, as it happens—he can visit Henriette without suspicion. It was even Henriette's idea. So that's why she's not been jealous."

Petite started to speak, but could not. She was angry and heartbroken, both.

"I knew it was Henriette he loved," Nicole went on, gloating. "I knew it all along."

Petite had an urge to leave, to get out in the open air, to be with horses—creatures she could trust. That the King was not, in fact, interested in her did not surprise her. It hurt, yes—that she was shamed to admit—but her disillusion went deeper than that. The King, a married man, courted his sister-in-law. Worse, he and Henriette had contrived for him to pretend interest in her in order to fool his mother. That was not noble. That was not even gentlemanly. It was a base thing for any man to do—the more so for a king.

"I'll have the money for you tonight," she told Nicole, standing abruptly. She rushed from the room before bursting into irate tears.

THE ROYAL STABLE at Fontaine Beleau was a long, low structure constructed of stone and thick beams. A man in a frayed straw hat was filling pails from a well near the entrance. He turned to stare as Petite stomped by. On one side of the muddy courtyard was a shed for storing hay and beside it an enormous mound of soiled litter. A two-wheeled cart was piled high with horse dung. A man relieving himself against a wall turned away. Three horses, one a docked curtail, were tied to iron rings set into a stone wall beside a covered sand-bath. From somewhere, an ass brayed.

Pretending authority, Petite entered an open door. She stopped within, her eyes adjusting to the dark. Horses of all sizes and colors peered over the gates of the lay-stalls that lined the walls. Had she ever seen so many? The stables at Blois seemed small by comparison. She listened to the horses' rhythmic munching, the rustling in the straw, inhaled their familiar scent. *Home.* There was even a switch on the wall to keep witches from riding the horses at night.

Petite felt rather than heard the steady beat of a horse's hooves. She stepped through an arch into a circular arena. In the center, a black man—a Moor, she gathered, from his headdress—was working a dappled stallion, which cantered the perimeter. It was a young gray: it would turn white as it aged, but it was not a true White.

The Moor slumped and the horse turned to face him, its ears up-pricked. The Moor took three steps toward the horse with one arm extended, and the horse twirled and cantered on. He put his other hand out, and the horse stopped.

The horse ambled up to the Moor, its head low, a submissive grazing posture. The Moor stroked the horse's neck and slipped a halter over its ears, then turned toward the gate with the horse at his shoulder. He was a slender man. His collarless tunic and britches were of the same cloth, the color of a summer sky. A fringed carpetbag was tied to his waist. Had Petite seen him somewhere before? There was something familiar in his manner.

"Can I help you, Mademoiselle?" he asked, bowing his head in the Moorish manner, with his hands crossed over his chest.

A small gold cross hung from a chain around his neck. The cross stirred up faint recollections of a Moor, Romas, *Diablo*. She had been with her father. "Are you a gentler?" she asked hesitantly. "Did you ever travel with the Romas?"

"I am Azeem. Do I know you?" he asked, his teeth white and straight.

"Years ago, north of Tours, my father bought a white stallion."

His eyes widened. "Are you . . . ?" He held out his hand, palm down, to indicate a child's height.

Petite nodded.

"That horse was crazed," he said, touching the cross.

Petite started to say something about bone magic, but dared not. "He settled . . . over time."

"Truly?" he asked, sounding incredulous.

"He was a wonderful horse, but after my father died, he—" *Disappeared.* Petite took a careful breath. "He ran off."

"I thought I saw him once," the Moor said, tying the gray to an iron ring. "But I was mistaken."

"I know." Diablo would be about fifteen years old by now. Some horses lived to be older, but that was rare. "It's unlikely he's still alive," she said sadly, turning at the sound of spurs on the cobblestones.

The master of the hunt entered the arena. "Do you require assistance, Mademoiselle?" he asked, taken aback by her presence.

"No, Monsieur," Petite said with a reverence.

"Have thirty-two mounts ready for one of the clock, seven for ladies," he commanded the Moor, snapping his riding whip against the gate and disappearing.

"Do you ready the horses for the hunt?" Petite asked Azeem.

"Generally, yes. Will you be riding this afternoon with Madame and the King?"

Henriette and the King—their names alone rekindled Petite's anger. "I'd hardly call it riding," she said. Yet another boring walk on some old stale. "I would love to ride this horse," she said, stroking the stallion's neck. He had a raw energy, matching her mood.

"He's not a suitable mount for a lady."

"I rode Diablo."

"*You* rode Diablo?" He regarded her with astonishment.

"He was my horse." It seemed a fable to her now.

THE HUNT WAS rigorous. Chasing down a hart, the King and his men rode through bogs and fields, thickets and vines. Petite's skirts got well splattered with mud.

After the last kill, the party headed back to the château, the King in the lead. Coming upon a meadow, he raised his left hand, signaling a race. His horse leapt into a hard gallop and the whooping men thundered after him, hats flying.

Petite held the gray in check. She was riding sidesaddle, and in any case, it wasn't befitting for women to race against men—and especially against the King. "Easy, boy," she said, burning with annoyance. Why should she care about what was befitting? The King certainly didn't. Anger filled her yet again, thinking of his base deception.

"Get out of the way," a man called out behind her and thundered past, dirt clots flying.

The gray pranced in place, tossing his head. Petite longed for the wind in her face, that heady surge of power—but most of all she wanted to prove that she was not to be toyed with. She loosened the reins and leaned into her horse's neck. "Go!"

The gray surged across the meadow, pounding down a long, straight alley and jumping wide over a creek. Three men by a stone wall yelled warning: a rider was down. Petite picked her spot and her horse flew over. She could see the men galloping in a clump ahead, three stragglers trailing out behind. She kicked her stallion into a hard gallop. He raced across the field, passing one rider after another. Petite gave herself up to the joyous sound of pounding hoofbeats, the muscular strength of a racing horse. Mort Dieu, she was flying! She let out an unladylike whoop. *Sing ye!*

The King on his black hunter was lengths ahead. She passed him in a blur, galloping into the lead—into unknown territory.

She sat back, slowing her horse to a hand-canter. She was in the lead, but she did not know the way. She glanced back over her shoulder. The King and his men had slowed their horses and were turning into the woods. Lauzun stared at her. Frowning, he shook his head.

Petite waited until the men had passed, then turned to follow, the glory of her triumph turned sour.

THE COURTIERS CROWDED into Henriette's chamber fell silent when Petite entered.

"There she is," the Princess informed a tall man in the King's livery.

He sauntered across the room to meet her. "Mademoiselle de la Vallière, the King has summoned you," he announced in a deliberately loud voice.

A soft murmur was heard throughout the room. Nicole, standing behind Henriette, gave Petite a look: *uh-oh.*

"What is this about?" Petite asked, following the servant out.

He turned at the stair landing and grasped her rudely by the elbow. "You have humiliated the King: men have been beheaded for less."

Petite shook free. "Just tell me what's expected, Monsieur."

"An apology—to begin with," he said with a mocking smile.

The antechamber to the King's cabinet was small—a dark, unfurnished room smelling strongly of dogs. Two hounds curled by the fireplace got up and stretched. One sniffed at Petite's mules. The King's attendant shooed it away with his boot, rhyming off instructions. "If you have any sense—which you clearly do not—you will grovel," he concluded, turning on his heel.

Petite stood for a time, watched by the hounds. *So.* She would be banished. Her mother would be less than sympathetic, she knew. She didn't relish the thought of having to live once again with her stepfather, listening to him go on (and on) about his hippo-tusk teeth.

The door to the inner chamber opened. Petite was comforted to see that it was kindly Gautier, her former dance master.

"The King will see you now, Mademoiselle de la Vallière," he said with a worried look.

Petite stepped inside. The King was sitting by the chimney, in the circle of light from the fire, a milk-colored dog curled on a cushion at his feet. He was dressed in dark silks and velvets, an ornamental sword propped against the arm of his chair.

Petite made the obligatory reverence. "Your Majesty, I owe you an apology," she said as she had been instructed, dropping her eyes.

"Come forward, Mademoiselle."

Petite took five hesitant steps. She was reassured to see two Swiss guards standing in the shadows: she and the King were not alone.

"I remember you," the King said.

Petite met his eyes. Did he? Was it possible he recalled meeting her in the meadow at Chambord two years before? She'd grown. Her hair was braided and coiled now and covered with a cap.

"Aren't you the girl who danced the bourée?" he asked, contracting his brow.

"I am, Your Majesty," Petite said, both disappointed and relieved. She noticed that he had a blemish on his chin, like any young man of two-and-twenty.

"You ride well," he said with a smile. The lean hound got up, her belly drooping with teats. She put her chin on the King's knee and wagged her tail. "Women don't usually ride with such authority," the King said, stroking the hound's ears. "Where did you learn?"

"From my father, Your Majesty. He liked a good race." Petite didn't know how to interpret the King's tone. He did not sound angry—if anything, there was admiration in his voice.

"Did your father teach you to dance, as well?"

"No, Your Majesty. I was taught at Blois, under the direction of Monsieur le Duc de Gautier."

"*My* Gautier?" he asked, surprised.

"Yes, Your Majesty." The hound sniffed Petite's hand. Petite stroked the silky head, felt the moist nose in her palm.

"Her name is Mitte," the King said with affection.

"She's a good-looking hound, Your Majesty." Her eyes were large, intelligent.

"I can hardly see you there in the shadows." The King held out his hand, but Petite stepped back. "Do I frighten you?" He sounded puzzled. "Have I not shown you favor?"

There was a long silence.

"You must answer me," he said.

"Forgive me, Your Majesty, but I would have to speak truthfully." Petite felt blood rushing into her cheeks. "And I am reluctant to do so."

He shifted in his chair, his eyes fixed upon the fire. "Truth might be amusing," he said finally, looking up, meeting her gaze. "For a change," he added with an ironic smile, his left eyebrow raised.

Petite sensed something sad in him. "Your Majesty, with respect, I have reason to believe that although you have, as you put it, shown me favor, you have done so with . . ." She summoned her courage, reminding herself that she was the descendant of a man who had ridden beside Jeanne d'Arc. "With false intentions," she said.

The King sat back. "And why, pray, would I do that?"

Petite stepped forward, into the circle of light. She didn't want the guards to hear. "In order to deceive the Queen Mother, Your Majesty," she said, her voice low. "Because it is your brother's wife you court, and that makes the Queen Mother unhappy. It's better for her to think you court me." She put a hand on the back of a chair to steady herself. Her heart was pounding! "That way you can call on Madame Henriette as often as you like without your mother suspecting."

Petite waited uneasily for the King's response. She had spoken, and now she would be banished . . . or worse.

"You are as fearless in speaking your mind as you are on the back of a horse," the King said finally. "And frankly, I commend you."

Petite looked up. She was not to be banished?

"And I regret to say that you are not mistaken," he went on. "I love my brother's wife—but as a dear friend and sister. My mother . . . she's of an age when men and women did not have friendships, and she would not understand. It is true that Henriette and I contrived this ruse so that we might continue to enjoy each other's company unfettered. It was something of a prank, but in retrospect, I see that it was not an honorable thing to do. Please accept my apology."

Petite stared at her slippers, worn at the toe. She had had the impudence to accuse the King. It seemed an unnatural, unholy thing. "Your Majesty," she said, "I am a Vallière. My family is humble but loyal. Our family motto is *Ad principem ut ad ignem amor indissolubilis.*"

The King grimaced. "My Latin is not as good as it should be, I confess."

"For the King, love like an altar fire," Petite recited, her cheeks heated. "Eternal." She glanced up and met his eyes.

He sat rapt, stroking his mustache. "Will you be riding with us tomorrow, Mademoiselle?" he asked, tilting his head.

"If you wish," Petite stuttered.

"You see," said the King, reaching for the bell rope, "I enjoy a good race too."

Chapter Seventeen

PETITE RODE WITH the King and his men the next afternoon, a small party of twenty-three. The King gave a signal and they set out, ambling, then trotting and cantering down the wide allées, across blooming meadows, jumping streams, fences and bogs.

The dogs almost immediately scented the leavings of a hart, a deer of good size. The varlets set off into the bush, the braying running-hounds pulling at their leashes, following the scent, the King and his men thrashing after them through the woods. The splendid buck was finally put to bay, and the King gave it a clean coup de grâce.

I'm the only woman present, Petite realized. The stag had drawn them into a thicketed corner of the park, and the ladies of the palace had chosen not to follow for fear of scratches and mud.

At the unmaking that followed, the veneur who had flayed the hart got the shoulder and the head varlet the hide. Mitte, the King's best hound, was ceremoniously awarded the stag's head. Growling, her long tail wagging, she worried her prize as the other running-hounds got their share.

The King watched his dogs with pleasure.

"Award Mademoiselle de la Vallière a foot," he told the veneur, who hacked off a hoof and handed it up to Petite.

"Thank you, Your Majesty," Petite said, hanging the bloody trophy from her waist.

IN THE WEEKS that followed, Petite rode with the King and his men almost every afternoon. She astonished them, riding in close behind the hounds and proving to be steady, fearless and strong, as good with a spear as any man. In a race, it was sometimes Petite who pulled into the lead, and sometimes the King. The courtiers could not keep up.

Petite returned from the hunts smelling of horses, her boots muddy, her curls in disorder. Yeyette and Claude-Marie regarded her uneasily. What sort of girl was she?

Evenings, in Henriette's sitting room (the "withdrawing room" it was called at Court), the King often had a word for Petite. She was allowed to join in as the men discussed the day's kill, the strengths and weaknesses of the various horses, the King's dogs. Henriette watched with a puzzled reserve.

The weather turned gloriously balmy: clearly, the gods were smiling. When there wasn't a hunt, there was a rehearsal, and every evening feasts and festivities, followed by moonlight carriage rides through the park. Even when the moon was a sliver, Henriette and her revellers would set out into the park for an excursion. Much amusement could be had under cover of night.

"I think we have a visitor," Nicole told Petite as their carriage headed back to the château after a midnight ride.

Petite looked out the coach window. A tall bay horse was keeping pace. Its rider tipped his hat, his face illuminated by the coach's torchlight. "Your Majesty?" Petite asked, surprised.

"How are you this evening, Mademoiselle de la Vallière?" the King asked.

"I am well," Petite answered self-consciously. "And you, Your Majesty?"

He nodded. "I thought the rehearsal went well today."

"Yes. Your solos especially." The performance was to be held in six days.

"I wish I could agree. I thought yours was remarkable."

"Thank you!"

"What did you think of the hunt yesterday?"

"In all honesty?"

"That's what I've come to expect from you." There was a smile in his voice.

"My falcon was excellent, and my palfrey obedient, but in truth, hawking . . . It isn't my favorite."

"It was requested by the ladies."

"Yes. They were pleased with it, especially Madame."

"But you prefer something more vigorous, I take it."

"I admit I do."

"I'm planning a boar hunt after the Feast of Saint Michel. My dogs should be well trained by then."

"I saw evidence of a solitary yesterday, Your Majesty, down by the first marsh. There were fairly large tracks by a wallow."

"That must be the boar my hunt master is keeping an eye on. He's in his fifth year. Perhaps you could show me where you saw the tracks. We're hunting stag tomorrow."

"I'd be happy to."

The King tipped his hat, spurred his horse and cantered off, causing the coach horses to surge.

"Well, now," Nicole said, unfurling her fan. "*That* was interesting."

"I didn't think you found hunt-talk all that engrossing."

"So that's what you call it? Hunt-talk?"

THE MORNING OF THE performance dawned cloud-free thanks to the daily Masses commissioned by Henriette in favor of good weather. Everyone was in a flurry of last-minute preparation, rehearsing lines, going over steps, making adjustments to their costumes. Henriette broke into tears at the least provocation, and her chamber was a riot of fabric scraps and ribbons.

Outside, everything was just as chaotic. The gardens swarmed with workers installing torches to light the avenues. Carpenters hammered and sawed, putting the finishing touches to the outdoor stage by the carp pond, decorating it with tree branches to create the illusion of a wilderness. Gautier ran from place to place, frantically attending to the problems that inevitably arose immediately before an important event, special Masses or no: the vertical track for the clouds kept jamming, and the great velvet curtain that had just been installed was too short.

Nonetheless, at eight of the clock, trumpeters announced the Queen and Queen Mother. The great brass gong was struck and thirty-two pages set thirty-two stage torches alight. The musicians took up their instruments, Monsieur de Lully raised his baton, and the hastily lengthened curtain rose as the chorus of shepherds sang out: "Who, in the night . . ."

Backstage, however, it was bedlam. Gautier, dressed as a fawn, counted heads. "Where's Pierre?"

"Answering the call of nature," Monsieur Philippe, in mask, called out, adjusting his brother's crown of wheat.

Dressed in a toga as the goddess Ceres, His Majesty patiently stood as his makeup was applied.

"My quiver!" Madame Henriette searched through her basket of props.

Nicole, who was helping with makeup, handed her mistress the clutch of silver-tipped feathers.

Petite, standing with the nine other nymphs, all dressed in green tissue spangled with silver, heard Gautier call out, "Première entrée."

"That can't be us." Henriette adjusted the silver crescent on her brow.

Nicole thumbed through the script. "No, first come the fawns, and then Diana and the nymphs."

"Blessed Virgin, watch over me," Henriette said, signing herself. "At least I don't have to descend from the heavens."

"Like *me*," said the King, and everyone laughed.

Petite glanced at him over her shoulder. It was hard not to smile at the image of a muscular goddess with a mustache.

The deep voices of the chorus boomed out—"Who, in the night . . ."—followed by an angelic voice singing of echoes that spoke of love, followed by the chorus's booming refrain, and then applause, more cheers, Lauzun's famous donkey braying and the clumping boots of the fawns crowding back offstage.

"Entrée, second act," Gautier called out, trying to straighten one of the tree branches.

"That's us," Henriette said, taking a place in the wings, her nymphs lining up behind her, each holding a basket of flower blossoms to throw at the feet of their goddess mistress.

"Your bow, Your Highness." Nicole rushed to give Henriette her prop.

Henriette arranged herself prettily on the fern-covered throne on the platform. Then the curtain parted, the music began and Henriette's ten nymphs danced a minuet around her.

By turns, each of the dancers went to the center for a solo. Petite, second to last, grew faint with nerves watching as Madame de Gourdon stumbled and Mademoiselle de Méneuille forgot her steps. Her left leg began to tremble— would it hold?

Hearing someone from the wings whisper her name, she turned to see the King give her an encouraging smile. Heart pounding, Petite stepped to the center of the stage.

THE MORNING AFTER the performance was still and sultry. A midday collation in the woods had been planned, but Henriette, touchy-headed, informed her ladies that they would be leaving early in order to go to the bathing pond before joining the King and his men. She sent Nicole and Petite down to the courtyard to make sure that everything had been packed.

"Madame's in a glout," Nicole said, handing a hamper of drying cloths to the wagon driver.

"Likely it's because of her condition," Petite said, checking the list of provisions. The Princess's courses had not come, and it was thought that she might finally be with child.

"I think it's because of the performance yesterday."

"But it went so well," Petite said. Hemp line, tapestries, drying cloths, carpets, bathing costumes: it looked as if everything was in order.

"Somewhat too well. Claude-Marie says she's jealous because you got applause for your solo."

"Everyone was applauded," Petite said, folding up the list and tucking it into her waistband.

"Yes, but the King *cheered* you," Nicole persisted.

Petite smiled. He had, and most enthusiastically. She glowed to think of it. "It's not like that." She glanced toward the entrance. There were voices in the stairwell. "I like horses, the King likes horses. That's all."

"He likes dogs, you like dogs. He likes to hunt, you like to hunt. He likes to dance, you like to dance. He likes—"

"Hush!" Petite whispered, as Henriette emerged, followed by Athénaïs, Claude-Marie and several other maids.

Two footmen in gray livery stepped forward to hand Henriette into the head coach along with Athénaïs, Nicole and Claude-Marie. Petite, standing by, was ceremoniously handed into the second coach with two maids-in-waiting from the Queen Mother's household and a chambermaid. Petite took note: Was she being shunned? Usually she rode with the Princess.

At the bathing hole, valets laid carpets over the grass and strung tapestries from the branches for privacy. Nicole helped Henriette out of her gown. Petite held out the long gray bathing costume, but the Princess pointedly turned her back.

I'll take care of it, Nicole mouthed, taking it from Petite.

In the maid's tent, her cheeks burning, Petite stripped down to her shift. Angrily, she stomped past the women sitting by the water's edge and sloshed into the shallow water. Little fishes darted over the stones.

"Little sister?" It was Athénaïs, sitting in a rock hollow.

"Madame la Marquise, I didn't see you."

"I prefer this to sitting on sand-heaps." Athénaïs checked to make sure that her hair was tucked into her blue turban. Gems sparkled on two fingers. "I commend you on your performance last night. Madame Henriette must be pleased."

"Not exactly," Petite said, glancing skyward. There were dark clouds on the horizon to the west. How much should she reveal? "She's annoyed with me." She lowered her voice so that it would not carry.

"Of course. You were applauded."

"Henriette invited me to perform because she likes the way I dance."

"Ah, you are such an innocent." Athénaïs smiled, but with sympathy. "We speak a different language here at Court—*ce pays-ci*, we call it, as if it were another country entirely. And it is. One must learn the fine line between doing something well, and doing something to great applause, which is the exclusive domain of a prince or princess. Why do you think only the son of a prince may be the dealer at Basset? Certainly it's not because he has the talent for it. It's because dealer is the lucrative role. *Lucrative* is the magical word: everything turns on it. It is the cipher that makes all things clear."

"This was only a dance performance."

"Do you not see the connection?" Athénaïs regarded Petite indulgently. "The King's regard is highly coveted. Why? Because it is lucrative. A woman of Court, even a princess, will do anything to get his—" She paused for effect, smiling coquettishly. "His friendship."

"You make it sound dangerous," Petite said.

Trumpets blared as Madame's three carriages pulled up to a forest glade. Horses whinnied and the men cheered. Tables had been set up on the grass under a canopy.

The men had just arrived themselves. They had yet to put a hart to bay, but were nonetheless enlivened. Hounds barked excitedly. Five violinists standing off to one side played a mournful melody at odds with the liveliness of the occasion. The King caught Petite's eye. She made a passing reverence and looked away.

Madame Henriette was shown to the place of honor to the right of the King, her husband Philippe on his left. Then the ladies of the palace were shown to their places. Nicole gave Petite a look of chagrin as Henriette's valet led Petite to a chair at the far end of the table, the lowliest spot—farthest from the King.

Butlers stepped forward with dishes of scented water so that the ladies could clean their hands. Petite, aware of her lowered status, made sure to wait until everyone had placed their serviettes on their shoulders before placing hers.

The food was rich, the wine abundant. Everyone drank to His Majesty's health, and then to the health of the absent queens, who were spending the day at a convent. As the musicians launched into a lively sarabande, they drank to the health of Madame and Monsieur, and then again to that of the King. The King threw a bone to the hound sitting on the grass beside him—the dog named Mitte—and a valet stepped forward to clean his fingers. He dried his hands on the damask napkin and sat back.

The sky darkened and the corners of the canopy flapped. There was a sudden loud crack of lightning. At the ominous roll of thunder, the King stood. Suddenly there was pouring rain and another sharp clap of lightning. Pages ran to check on the horses while varlets gathered their hounds. Women screamed as a gust of wind tipped over the table, splattering wine and scattering bones. Quickly, the King and his brother helped Henriette into her coach and struggled to fasten the leather window coverings against the rising storm.

At yet another flash of lightning and thunderous roll, Mitte ran whimpering into the woods, her tail between her legs. Petite caught the end of the dog's leather lead.

"Easy," she called out as the hound pulled her pell-mell into the brambles. Yanking on the lead, she brought the terrified dog to a halt. The rain was coming down heavily. Pulling the dog close, she pushed through some bushes into a thick clump of trees.

The copse was dry at the center. Petite, soaked through, sank onto the pine needles. The trembling dog licked her chin. "Easy, girl," she said, stroking her head.

"Mitte!"

It was a man's voice—hard to hear over the howling wind.

"Mitte!"

The dog whimpered. "She's in here," Petite called out, but she was silenced by more thunder.

She heard branches breaking, and a man's head appeared. "Your Majesty!" Petite tried to rise, but she was hemmed in.

"Mademoiselle de la Vallière? And my dear Mitte." The King stooped and embraced the terrified creature. "She has always been frightened by thunder," he said, stroking the dog's soft ears. "What a storm." His features were illuminated by a flash of lightning.

Petite untied her neck scarf and handed it to him. "Your Majesty?"

"Thank you," he said, wiping his face and then handing the kerchief back. "It's dry here," he said, feeling the ground.

"Yes," Petite said, shifting to give the King room. It was tight for two, especially with a nervous hound. There was a strong scent of wet dog, rain and something more, a pleasant floral perfume—jasmine, she guessed.

The King held the dog between his knees. His elbow touched Petite's arm, his knee her thigh. She drew her elbows in tight and crossed her arms. All was in violent motion but for this one still refuge. All was still but for the beating of her heart.

The King turned to look at her. "Your hair."

Petite put her hands to her crown. Her scarf had fallen off in the rush into the woods. She felt exposed, her head uncovered, her hair tangled and wet.

"It's golden," he said, his expression one of surprise and dawning recognition. "*Now* I know where I've seen you before."

Petite was confused. He saw her daily: at the hunts, in rehearsals, at Henriette's evening gatherings.

"I can't tell you how many times I've looked at you and wondered why you seemed so familiar—and now I know," he said with a smile of satisfaction. "You were the girl chasing the runaway horse in the park at Chambord."

Petite felt a deep blush spread over her face.

"You're *that* girl—"

Petite bowed her head without reply.

"—the goddess Diana."

Was this a jest?

But the King's voice was ardent. "I've often thought of you since, the way you appeared in the meadow like some young goddess with long golden curls, the proud way you sat your horse."

His eyes were a soft hazel, his lashes long. How well Petite knew his face: his chiseled nose and rounded chin, his broad forehead, full lips.

"Are you chilled?" he asked.

"No." A violent crack of lightning made her jump.

"Yet you tremble." He paused, then reached out his hand, lightly touching her chin.

"I'm fine, Your Majesty," Petite said, briefly meeting his gaze.

They were sprinkled with a sudden shower of rain from the branches above. *Like a baptism*, Petite thought, as he leaned toward her.

The dog licked her hand. Petite pulled back, her heart beating violently.

"I apologize," he said.

The dog whimpered. The King stroked Mitte's long ears gently, first one and then the other. His fingers were long and fine—a musician's hands. He wore no rings.

Petite touched his hand.

He turned toward her. It was so dark now, she could hardly make out his eyes. The rain was coming down harder, the wind howling. They were in their own little world.

Petite felt his breath on her cheeks, fragrant with wine. Her heart stopped, and then raced.

The King's lips touched hers very lightly. Then he put one hand on her shoulder and pressed his forehead against hers.

Again, Petite prayed, holding her breath. She wanted to taste him. "I've never been kissed, Your Majesty," she said, her breath coming now in gasps. "I'm not sure how to go about it."

He ran his fingers through her hair and bent over her, holding the back of her head in one hand. He was strong; Petite felt cradled within him. She felt his lips, his rough chin, and then his tongue, soft against her teeth. She felt flooded with warmth. The dog whimpered again, the storm howled, but there was only this, this one magical touch. A moan of pleasure sounded—her own.

Chapter Eighteen

Never again, Petite vowed, wringing the rainwater out of her hair into a blue glass jar. On leaving their forest nest, she had snapped a small branch off the tree—the one they had leaned against, the one that had sheltered them—and this she stuck into her looking-glass frame. Three leaves, one for each swooning kiss.

Never again. She laid her kerchief out flat on the tabletop—the kerchief he'd used to dry his face—and placed the blue jar of rainwater on top of it. These were her relics, this her reliquary.

Dear Mary, Mother of God, you know how weak I am, give me strength in my frailty.

Clutching her father's rosary, Petite prayed before the statue of the Virgin until her knees ached. She was still chaste, yet she felt entirely undone. *O Mary, give me strength.* Never again kiss him, never again look into his eyes. Never again feel his strong, gentle fingers in her hair. *O Mary!*

Never again. Never again. Never again.

The next morning, Petite did not attend Madame Henriette or join in the Court festivities. "I just don't feel well," she told Clorine. The very thought of facing Her Majesty the Queen made her stomach tighten.

"I'll get the surgeon," Clorine said.

The surgeon, a man with terrible breath and no front teeth, pronounced Petite at death's door. He bled and purged her, charging four deniers. Then Petite had no need to pretend: now she truly was ill and far too weak to rise.

On the third day, Gautier called. He stood outside the door for some time, talking to Clorine.

"He's such a gentleman," Clorine said after he left. "I think he might be just a little stuck on you." She handed Petite a worn leather volume. "He said this is for you. He said he was given to understand—and that's exactly how he put it, *given to understand*—that you liked poetry. Thoughtful, don't you think? It's unlikely, I know, given his status, but maybe he'd forgo a dowry. Such things do happen from time to time."

"Clorine, I'm not going to marry the Duc de Gautier," Petite said, taking the book. If the King wished to send her a personal message, Gautier would be the man he would trust to do so.

"He's highborn."

"Gautier is not going to ask for my hand, I assure you," Petite said. It was a lovely little volume covered in tooled leather: *Idylls*, by Theocritus, in translation. She adored bucolic poetry. Then she saw that a note had been tucked into Idyll four, "The Herdsman." She slipped it under the covers so that Clorine wouldn't see.

When Clorine finally left to get water from the courtyard well, Petite withdrew the folded paper. It wasn't from Louis, as she had feared (and hoped), but from Gautier. *The King wishes to see you*, he wrote in a spidery hand. *Privately.*

O Mary.

On Clorine's return, Petite handed her the book. "I'm too ill to read poetry," she announced. "Return this to Monsieur le Duc, with my regrets."

PETITE HAD THE STRENGTH to refuse the King, but she could not control her thoughts. At night she dreamt of him and woke to thoughts of him, imagining that they were back in the forest. The storm passes, and she and the King emerge into sunlight. The Queen has died—or something—and he's not really King anymore. She calls him Louis, and he calls her Louise. He takes her hand and they walk into the wild, where a wandering priest unites them. They come upon an abandoned forester's hut, and there they make a home. He takes her into his arms . . .

O Mary!

Petite prayed on waking and continued praying throughout the day, all the time worrying about a fluttering in her heart and other inexplicable changes. Her buds ached and her lower place had become maddeningly sensitive. She was concerned about a discharge. At first she'd thought it was her ordinaries come early, but the fluid was clear. She had some frightful disease, no doubt.

"Look at the lovely bouquet the Duke brought you," Clorine said. The scent of carnations filled the room. "He's going to make an offer for you any day," she said. "Mark my words."

ON THE FIFTH DAY, Clorine handed a small parcel to her mistress. "It's another book from Monsieur le Duc—but a romancy, he called it, by that Scudéry woman, easier to read than poetry, he said, especially when one is ailing. He thought it might be *diverting*. I do love the old-fashioned words he uses, don't you? He's a highborn man through and through. He's an older gentleman, true, but he's young at heart. He'd make an excellent husband for you."

Petite nodded distractedly, thumbing through the pages as Clorine chatted on. No note?

She sank back into the pillows, gazing at her relics—the jar of rainwater, the scarf, the branch of three leaves, one for each kiss. *Never again.*

Maybe it was true, what the loathsome surgeon had said: maybe she was at death's door.

IT WAS IN THE margin on the eleventh page that Petite saw it: *Please, I must see you. L.* She pressed the book to her heart. Then, with an effort of will and a prayer to the Virgin, she handed the volume back to Clorine. "Return this to Monsieur le Duc de Gautier, with my regrets."

EVENTUALLY, OF COURSE, Petite had to rise. There was a limit to how many purgings and bleedings a healthy young woman could endure.

"You look like a ghost," Clorine chided, trying to entice her to eat a little of the cake she'd gotten the cook to make in honor of Petite's seventeenth birthday.

"Thank you, Clorine, but I just can't." The linsey-woolsey bed gown hung from her thin shoulders.

There was a knock on the door. Petite turned to see Nicole with four oranges in her hands.

"When are you coming back?" Nicole demanded. "I've had to take over reading *Don Quixote* to Madame and I'm tired of it." She gave Petite the fruit. "I stole them from Henriette's table," she said, pleased with herself. "She's not angry at you anymore, by the way." She turned to see if Clorine could hear. "I suspect the

Princess has *another interest*," she hissed, her black eyebrows arched suggestively. "She even asked after you. Are you dying, or what?"

"I'm ill," Petite said, confused. She was relieved that Henriette was no longer angry, but what did Nicole mean by "another interest"?

Nicole put her hand on Petite's forehead. "You must have caught a chill in that storm. You came back soaked through." She regarded Petite with enquiring eyes. "The King, as well, and both of you rather flushed. Where did you go off to, anyway?"

"Clorine?" Petite got her maid's attention. "See if there's a bowl I could use—something to put these oranges in. Listen," she told Nicole as soon they were alone, "I don't want you saying anything about the King, not in front of my maid."

"So something did happen. Mon Dieu, I don't believe it."

Petite put her hand on her friend's arm. "It was only a kiss, but you can't tell anyone." Well . . . three kisses. Three swooning kisses.

Nicole put her hands over her heart. "The King kissed you?"

"Promise, Nicole. It's never going to happen again. You're not to say a word."

"We need a code. How about Prince Chéri. No, too obvious. How about Ludmilla? I'll say, 'Have you seen Ludmilla?' And you'll know who I really mean."

"Except that there will be no further need to speak of her," Petite said, as Clorine returned with a cracked wooden bowl.

"Alas, my dear friend, I must return to my duties, to tiresome Señor Quixote," Nicole said, rising. "Take care of yourself and get well. There seems to be some sort of ague going around. Ludmilla looks rather unwell herself."

"Ludmilla is no concern of mine," Petite said, seeing Nicole out before she could say more.

"Who is Ludmilla?" Clorine asked as soon as the door slammed shut.

"Nobody you know," Petite said. She startled at yet another tap-tap on the door. She hoped it wasn't Nicole again.

"Zut. Now that must be the Duke." Clorine stepped out, but returned immediately. "Just as I thought," she said. "He desires a word with you, Mademoiselle."

"Tell him no," Petite said weakly.

"You've lost a stone, but I can pad you out."

"That's not the reason."

"Don't you ever want to get a husband?" Clorine grabbed Petite by the shoulder. "Get out there—and be nice."

MONSIEUR LE DUC de Gautier tipped his hat and bowed his head. Mademoiselle de la Vallière had been a mere minikin of a girl when he'd first known her at Blois, four years before. Now she was a young woman, slim and graceful as a flower . . . a delicate wildflower, as he thought of her, out of place amongst the exotic flora of the Court.

He looked up and down the dimly lit hall and leaned in toward her. "His Majesty has asked me to speak to you on his behalf," he whispered. He put up one hand. "Please, Mademoiselle, just hear me out. Will you not agree just to talk to him?"

"*No,* Monsieur."

"Mademoiselle, His Majesty has not slept or eaten in days." The King, whose appetite was legendary! At one meal, it wasn't uncommon for His Majesty to consume three or four bowls of different soups, several platters of spiced, strong meats, plus a plateful of cakes—but now he wouldn't take even a bowl of soup. On retiring, he usually took iced orange-flower water—but even this he had refused. His doctor was worried. "Please, Mademoiselle?" Gautier was prepared to beg if he must.

She shook her head.

"He's wasting away," he persisted. "He hasn't attended Council meetings or gone out hunting. He is suffering, I tell you." Tears came to her beautiful azure eyes. How like an angel she was. Gautier sensed her weakness: she was in love. "He asks only for a few words with you."

"Would you be present?" she asked.

"Trust me."

SEEING THE KING privately was not an easy matter—his was a public life—so it was arranged that he and Petite would meet in Gautier's room. "Today at four of the clock," Gautier told Petite, providing her with a dressmaker's cloak. Dressmakers were often to be seen coming to his quarters due to the theatrical productions he directed. He gave Petite a diagram showing the way. The château was a labyrinth; one could easily get lost.

Petite set out as arranged, in disguise. She'd had to lie to Clorine, had told her that she was going to Henriette's, that all the ladies would be dressed as menials, that it was just another fanciful notion the Princess had come up with, one of her crazy ideas. "You know how she is."

Clorine had frowned, puzzled, but returned to mending Petite's riding overskirt.

"I'll be back soon, to change for the evening," Petite said, pulling her hood on at the door. She listened for footsteps, voices, the rustle of skirts, and slipped out, hurrying down the narrow stone steps. At the first landing she turned left, heading down a passage lit by torches. *I am going to meet the King*, she thought.

She stopped by a narrow window to examine Gautier's drawing. It shook in her gloved hands. No, she was going the wrong way. She reversed her direction, making a passing reverence and lowering her eyes as she met a party of noblemen. At the next stairwell, at the statue of Venus set into an arched alcove, she turned left, and then right, and then . . . there it was: a door with a small brass plate bearing Gautier's name.

She paused before knocking; it was not too late. She could turn back. *"O Mary,"* she whispered, and the door opened before her, as if thrown wide by the Devil himself.

"It's you." Gautier looked relieved.

Petite didn't remove her hood until she was safely inside and the door shut behind her. The shutters had been closed; it was dark in the room, only three candles burning. It took a moment for her eyes to adjust. The chamber was small, but tastefully furnished. A bed hung in pale blue brocade took up most of it. Petite set her wicker basket on the floor and took off her gloves.

"I got lost," she said, unbuttoning the cloak, starting with the big wood button at her neck.

"His Majesty should be here soon," Gautier said. "I'm sorry that I don't have a chair for you to sit on. May I offer you a dish of veal broth?"

Petite shook her head, leaning against a curio cabinet for support.

"It's refreshing, flavored with mint."

"Thank you, but no, Monsieur." She didn't want to have to use the necessary.

There was a light knock at the door. Petite closed her eyes. If she started to feel dizzy, she would lower her head, breathe deeply.

The King entered, disguised as a seller of sheet music, wigged, cloaked and hooded. He'd shaved off his mustache. "What do you think?" he asked, holding out his arms. "I even have some good songs."

"Nobody recognized you, Your Majesty?" Gautier asked, wiping his brow.

"Not even the Duchesse de Navailles," the King said, taking off the wig and shaking out his hair.

Mercy. Superintendent of the maid-attendants? Petite pressed her hands against her pounding heart.

"Your Majesty, by your leave, I will go now." Gautier placed the song sheets on a small escritoire under the window. "Open the shutters when you wish me to return."

Petite looked at Gautier in horror. He'd lied to her. "I'm going with you," she said, reaching for her cloak.

Gautier stepped in front of the door, his hand on the iron latch.

"You promised," Petite said.

"Mademoiselle de la Vallière, please." The King's voice was gentle. He held his hat in his hands like a penitent. "I don't mean to alarm you. Truly, I only wish a moment with you."

Petite shook her head. She remembered her mother's caution, to never be alone with a man. But her mother hadn't said anything about kings.

"Just to talk," the King persevered. "Nothing more: on my honor."

He smiled at Petite and warmth filled her. She nodded consent to Gautier, who quickly slipped out of the room, closing the door behind him.

And then there was silence. Petite didn't know where to look, what to say. She shifted from one foot to the other. She was in a room alone with the King, a man she had kissed—and most willingly.

The King cleared his throat. "Why don't you sit here?" He gestured toward the bed. "I'll stand."

"Thank you, Your Majesty, but I'm more comfortable this way."

There was another long moment of silence.

"Please, Mademoiselle, sit down." He put out his hand. "I insist."

Petite gathered her skirts and perched on the edge of the bed. The King leaned against the dresser in front of her, his arms crossed over his chest. Petite waited, her heart doing strange flips.

"Are you all right?" he asked.

Petite felt her cheeks heat up. "It's nothing, Your Majesty." Outside, there was the rumble of carriage wheels, footmen yelling, the clip-clop of horse hooves on the cobbles. She glanced up at him. *O God.* "You remind me of my father—your smile."

"Is that a good thing?"

"He was a saint."

"He's no longer living?"

"He died just after my seventh birthday," she said. Ten years ago now—on the King's own birthday.

"How old are you?"

"Seventeen, Your Majesty." Seventeen years and three days. "I was born in Tours on the sixth of August—"

"A Leo."

"Yes. In the second year of your reign."

He regarded her thoughtfully.

I know you . . .

"Why do you smile?" he asked.

"I have a confession to make, Your Majesty." Petite knew she should put a guard on her tongue, but she felt agitated, sparkling. An abounding joy was welling within her. There was so much she wanted to tell him. "When I saw you in the meadow at Chambord, I thought you were a poacher."

He laughed. "Really? I like that."

"I've been reading Virgil's *Eclogues*," she blurted out, and then was mortified by her clumsiness. "It's similar to *Idylls* by Theocritus," she persisted. "I usually prefer the Greek poets, but I took up *Eclogues*, thinking to improve my Latin, and now I'm quite enraptured by Virgil."

"'Now that we are . . . seated on the . . . soft grass,'" the King recited slowly, recollecting.

The third Eclogue. Petite knew it well. "'Now that every field and every tree is budding.'"

"'And the woods are . . .'"

"'. . . green, Your Majesty . . . and the year is at its fairest.'" *Sing ye!*

The King smiled. "I'd like you to call me Louis," he said.

"I couldn't, Your Majesty."

"Please," he said with a look of inexpressible sweetness.

"Louis," Petite said softly, and then had to lower her head and breathe.

THEY ONLY EVER talked, but Petite knew it was wrong for them to meet. She yearned for him in a way that frightened her. *O God, have pity on me, remove the longings in my heart, protect me from thoughts of sin.*

"I am enamored of a married man," she told her confessor.

"Have you . . . ?"

"No, Father."

"Yet you desire him."

She answered with a sob.

"This is a sin: you know that."

"Yes, Father."

"Pray for the strength to resist," the priest said.

"I do, Father." But she knew she was weakening.

In the early dawn, the mist still clinging to the lowlands, Petite went out into the fields. She sat at the edge of a meadow, seeking wisdom in the silence. Who was she to resist the King's need? His *love*—for that was the word, finally, that trembled between them. Who was she to make light of such a gift?

PETITE SUCCUMBED IN the first hot week of autumn. She no longer had the strength to say no, no longer the will to deny fate.

"Don't ever let me go," she begged as Louis embraced her. The linens of Gautier's bed had been newly washed and smelled of sunlight.

"I love you, Louise," he whispered with stuttering helplessness. "I *love* you."

Passages from the Bible came to her, inexplicably and unbidden, as from a song that would not leave, the words not quite known: *and the mountain was altogether in smoke, and the mount quaked greatly, and all was thunderings and lightnings, and the noise of trumpets, and Fear not, for the Lord is come to prove you . . .*

Prove you.

"I love you," she wept, for the pain, and for the pleasure, and for the very great sin she was committing. She was ruined now, truly—and yet made whole. She wept, for she had found her one true love, but he was the King, and forbidden to her.

Part IV

MISLOVE

Chapter Nineteen

O GOD, I AM SORRY for having offended Thee. I dread the pains of Hell, and I resolve, with the help of Thy grace, to do penance, and to amend my life.

I am sorry, I am sorry, I am sorry.

If I say it enough times, Petite thought that night as she slipped under her covering sheet, maybe it will be true. For in truth she wasn't sorry in the least. *O God.*

The next morning, she took her place beside the other maids of honor. As usual, she handed Henriette her slippers, held the mirror and read to her out loud. But she was changed entirely, and surely it was visible.

When Louis emerged from his cabinet to go to Mass, he caught Petite's eye. She lowered her gaze. *O God, forgive me.* For feeling so wonderful, for feeling so proud.

Out of the corner of her eye she watched as Henriette kissed Louis on both cheeks—a privilege of the high nobility. Lower nobility were allowed only one royal kiss, one royal cheek. Petite flushed, thinking of their ardent kisses everywhere.

At Mass, Petite prayed for guidance. Did Louis? she wondered. She watched as he knelt before the altar. They were sinners—of that there could be no doubt. She closed her eyes: she must not look at him. She was a fallen woman, no different from a strumpet covered with spittle in the village stocks. Then why did she feel so brilliant, so clear, as if her very soul were alight? Was this the Devil's magic?

That afternoon, after the hunt (she downed a buck with an arrow), Petite took special care with her toilette, choosing to wear one of the gowns Marguerite had passed on to her, recently altered by Clorine so that it fit. The golden bodice fell below her shoulders and laced tightly at the waist. She felt beautiful.

Athénaïs met her at the door of Henriette's salon that evening. "You look lovely this evening, Louise."

"And you," Petite answered, her skirts swishing softly on the wood parquet. (Where was *Louis?*) The room was already crowded. The moon was at its fullest and the Princess had announced that there was to be a midnight excursion.

"Indeed. She has a telltale glow," Nicole said, regarding Petite with enquiring eyes.

It seemed that everyone was watching. The least movement would tell all—a hint of a smile, a blush. "Am I rudded?" Petite asked. "I neglected to ride with a mask."

"I saw you on His Majesty's new Irish charger," Fouquet said, insinuating himself into the conversation. Powder had failed to hide the network of veins on his cheeks.

"Lancelot." Petite nodded. Tall at almost sixteen hands, the stallion had the markings of a good hunter: his feet were tough and he bent his knees nicely over jumps.

"You ride often with the King, I notice," Fouquet said, suppressing a sly smile. Fine linen and lace billowed from under his gold-embroidered doublet.

"We all ride with the King, Monsieur," Petite said. Fouquet was the darling of the Court, a charming, witty and generous man—and cultured, she gathered, patron of playwrights and poets, including Corneille and Scarron. But arrogant, she sensed, and powerful, certainly. She was wary of him. "I and scores of others."

"She most often rides *ahead* of His Majesty," Lauzun piped up, joining the group.

"So I'm told." Fouquet opened the end of his silver walking stick and inhaled an aromatic—as if his aristocratic sensibilities had been offended by lowly Lauzun.

"I understand that you are planning a fete, Monsieur Fouquet," Petite said, changing the subject. The currents were dangerous; it was hard to know what to say.

"A magnificent entertainment, I've heard," Athénaïs said, her eyes surveying the assembly.

"With a ballet and fire rockets," Nicole added as trumpets blared and the doors were thrown open for the King.

For Louis. Petite bowed low as he entered with his wife on his arm.

Engulfed by an absurdly wide ruff, the Queen smiled timidly at the crowd. She was stocky by nature and even more so now that she was heavy with child. Her yellow hair was contained in an old-fashioned hair net and topped by a plain black cap. She frowned back at the three dwarves struggling to carry her train. One, a Pygmy, was only two feet high but perfectly formed. He tumbled and the Queen giggled, her teeth black. The courtiers laughed as well; later, they would ridicule her, Petite knew. Making fun of the Spanish Queen was a popular form of amusement at Court.

Louis scanned the room and found Petite. There was a hint of warm recognition, and then a hint of a frown. (*Why?* Petite wondered, alarmed).

Fortunately, the Queen did not stay long, retiring just before the midnight excursion. The courtiers followed Louis, his brother and Henriette down to the courtyard. The moon was a full circle of light, the stars bright, the air smelling of dung and smoke from all the torches. The men mounted their horses as the women were helped into coaches. Petite joined Nicole in the last, a covered cabriolet for two.

Under cover of night, Petite fell silent as Nicole pattered on. She was exhausted from the day's effort to dissemble, overwhelmed yet enlivened by the enormous change in her life. She was no longer chaste. *Ruined*, her mother would say—yet she did not feel ruined in the least.

A night bird warbled, a breeze picked up. The leaves of a beech tree quivered in the moonlight. How beautiful everything seemed. She had given up her chastity for him. Did he scorn her for it? Did he love her less? No, she could not believe that. His love for her was true.

Nicole touched Petite's arm. A rider was approaching. "I think it's Ludmilla," she said, her eyes wide.

Louis? There was a cloud over the moon, and Petite could not be sure. The rider said something to their driver, turning his horse to keep pace with the carriage.

It *was* Louis. Mercy. Petite stuck her head out the window. "Your Majesty?"

Not Louis. Not Beloved. Not my heart's desire. She had to be careful.

"Your driver's going to stop at the fork ahead," Louis told her, his face shadowed by the brim of his hat. "Go into the woods on the left." He spurred his horse and galloped ahead.

"*Well,*" Nicole said with quiet astonishment, fluttering her lace-edged fan.

"I'll explain later," Petite said as their coach slowed. Her emotions were in disorder. Now she would have to confide in Nicole, but what would she say? She felt caught in a maze. "I won't be long."

"You can't go into the woods at night alone," Nicole said, grabbing Petite's arm.

Petite wrenched free and jumped to the ground. It was dark under cover of the enormous trees. It took a moment for her to make out a narrow footpath through the brush. She felt her way slowly. She could smell wolf. Soon the path opened onto a wider riding track.

She stood, waiting, recovering her breath. She started at the loud, whistling call of a nightingale. She felt the pounding of Louis's horse on the earth, and he emerged around a bend, riding a small bay trotter.

He vaulted off the horse, looped the reins over a branch and approached, faint shafts of moonlight glinting off his sword. He stopped at a distance and tipped his hat—as if they were at Court. An owl hooted.

Petite's eyes filled with tears. She held out her bare hands.

Louis stepped forward and placed his hands in hers, the leather of his gloves soft. *Handfasted.*

"I talked to my confessor, Louise," he said. "I must give you up." There were tears in his voice.

"What do you mean?" Fear filled her. His confessor was right. They would both go to Hell. But Hell, surely, would be here on Earth, should he forsake her.

"This life will ruin you," he said, his tone almost pleading. "I've already ruined you."

Petite started to raise her hand—to slap him, she realized with horror—and then quickly stepped back, frightened by what she might have done. She took a shaky breath. "Never say that you've ruined me, Louis."

He gathered her into his arms. "My love," he said—awkwardly, as if the word was still new to him, an ancient tongue.

Petite's knees buckled as he kissed her, an unholy sweetness filling her veins.

NICOLE SCRAMBLED FOR a kerchief as Petite climbed back into the coach. She wiped Petite's cheeks and put her arm around her friend's heaving shoulders.

"I can't bear it," Petite said, weeping. She felt joyous, euphoric—as well as bewildered. She and Louis had vowed to meet, again and again. It was wrong, but they were helplessly in love. "If you tell, Nicole, I'll kill you," she said with a quiet ferocity that shocked them both.

A WEEK LATER, after Mass, Petite was followed out of the chapel by the Marquise de Plessis-Bellièvre. Lost in thought, Petite didn't notice. Louis had arranged for her to talk to his new confessor a few days earlier. Polygamy was common in the days of the apostles, the priest had explained to her. Holy men such as Moses and David had more than one wife and, historically, the King of France often had a mistress. The King was of God; even Petite was absolved. Petite didn't really believe it, so she was walking along silently praying for clarity, absolution and forgiveness (as well as, in truth, the chance soon to meet with her lover), unaware that her attention was wanted.

Finally, the short, plump widow made an obsequious bow before her, sliding her right foot forward and bending at the waist so low that the two ostrich feathers on her cap touched the stone floor. "Do you have a moment, Mademoiselle de la Vallière?" she asked, rising. In spite of the heat she was wearing a heavy green gown trimmed with spotted brown fur.

"Madame is expecting me," Petite said, resisting an urge to stand back. The woman's breath smelled rotten.

"This won't take much time," the Marquise de Plessis-Bellièvre promised, ushering Petite outside with surprising strength. "Come, here's a shady bench. You know, my dear, you are regarded as one of the beauties of the Court. It wouldn't do to brown your lovely skin."

"Madame la Marquise de Plessis-Bellièvre," Petite said, pulling away, "truly, I must be going."

The Marquise leaned her sunshade against the bench. "How charming to be punctual," she said, sitting and patting the place beside her. "I assure you this won't take long. I have a message from the minister of finance."

Reluctantly, Petite sat. The Marquise de Plessis-Bellièvre organized Nicolas Fouquet's social engagements, she knew, and she suspected that this might have to do with the minister's upcoming fete at his new château at Vaux-le-Vicomte. It was all anyone talked about of late.

"He'd like to make you a gift," the Marquise said, pulling a fan from her bodice. "A token of friendship." She snapped the fan open and fluttered it vigorously.

Petite stiffened. *A gift?* Why? "That wouldn't be right, Madame," she said, flustered. Was this how bribes were made?

"Come, my dear, this is no trifle—twenty thousand pistoles. Half that would make a respectable dowry, set you up nicely, and all you'd have to do is let him know what's going on from time to time." She smiled, covering a broken tooth with her fan. "What could be the harm in that?"

Petite was at a loss for words. Did Fouquet want her to spy for him? Surely not.

"Just imagine what one could do with such a sum," the Marquise went on.

"Madame la Marquise de Plessis-Bellièvre, I believe there has been a mistake," Petite said, standing abruptly.

"My dear girl—"

"I am not in a position to know what's going on—as you put it—and even if I were, I could certainly not be *bought*," Petite said, inflamed now with anger.

At that, she curtsied and headed back to the château, overcome with an inner trembling. Court seemed an unknown world to her. She felt unmoored, afloat.

As she climbed the stairs to Henriette's suite, she tried to compose herself. Courtiers gathered on the landing were watching; there could be talk. She stopped at a window enclosure, her heart palpitating. Fouquet had tried to bribe her to spy . . . on *Louis?* She gasped, realizing that that must be the case. She took a careful breath, leaning against the stone sill. Fouquet must know; he must have found out.

How can that be? she thought, an icy panic filling her. They had been so careful. Petite had had to tell Nicole, true, but only after Nicole had vowed not to breathe word of it to a soul. And other than Nicole, who but Louis's confessor and Gautier knew anything at all? She had to tell Louis—*warn* him.

PETITE LOOKED TO make sure nobody was around before pushing open the heavy door to Gautier's room. The small chamber was empty. Louis wasn't there yet. She put down her basket of linens and leaned against the door, closing her eyes and collecting her breath. She'd passed Athénaïs in the stairwell.

This time, Petite was well disguised as a laundress and thankfully—Dieu merci—she'd not been recognized. Gautier thought it safer for her and Louis to change their costumes each time they met. (*Each time*, he had said, the words implying an indefinite future.)

The drapery had been drawn against the afternoon sun and two night candles lit. The bed curtains were open, the covering sheet pulled back. Petite took off her hemp apron. A rectangular cloth, folded in half and wired at the edges, was pinned to her cap. It scratched. She lifted it off and unpinned her braids, coiled into a bun. Louis liked her hair hanging loose.

Where is he? she thought, sitting down on the bed. A small sponge had been placed on the bedside table, next to a bottle of brandy. Gautier had thought of everything. *O Mary . . . Sin upon sin.*

Louis entered without knocking. "Ha," he said with a grin, throwing off his cloak and diving onto the bed, taking Petite into his arms. "I can't stop thinking of you," he said, his hands roving, fumbling with the back laces of her bodice.

Petite sat up to make it easier for him. She shrugged out of the bodice so that he could loosen her skirt. At last she was down to her chemise (skirt and petticoat ties edged with laces made by her aunt Angélique, she realized with chagrin).

Louis took her hands and pressed her fingertips to his lips. "Your hands are cold." He looked at her face. "What's wrong, Louise?"

He said her name softly, almost in a whisper—as if they were children, playing a secret game. She wanted it always to be thus, the two of them, hidden away. She pressed her cheek against his. She loved the cool feel of his skin, the rasp of his chin, his breath in her ear. Their love was spiritual in its intensity—how could it be a sin?

"I'm frightened," she said, looking into his eyes.

He regarded her with surprise. "Why?" he asked, stroking her hair. "Has something happened?"

"It's Monsieur Fouquet," she said, unfastening the cloth ties of his leather doublet. She longed to feel his skin on hers.

"Nicolas?" His eyes squinted jealously. Fouquet had a reputation as a seducer, in spite of his age. "He didn't—?"

"No, it's not that. He offered me money, through the Marquise de Plessis-Bellièvre . . . to spy—on *you*, I fear."

"How much?" His voice was cold—the voice of a king, not a lover.

"How much has nothing to do with it." She snorted with proud contempt. "I cannot be bought."

Louis tucked a wisp of hair behind her ear. "Unlike the rest of us," he said, smiling with sad irony.

Petite covered his hands with her own and kissed him lightly. "He must know," she said, feeling his lips on her neck. The thought that they were watched chilled her. She ran her fingers through his long hair, felt an edge of teeth in his kisses. "How?" she asked, her breath quickening.

"Fouquet has spies everywhere," Louis said bitterly. "I told you this was a dangerous place. We all wear masks. Nothing is as it seems."

"Some say he's assembling arms, Louis, that he intends to rule." She lay down and he followed her. She laced her hands under his shirt, feeling the long smooth muscles of his back.

"I know," he scoffed. "He's not the only one with spies. I've been watching him. I'm not the dupe he imagines. He thinks I'm young and frivolous, that I'm more interested in hunting than ruling. He assumes I'm not paying attention, that I don't know what he's up to." He regarded Petite for a long moment. "He underestimates me."

Chapter Twenty

NICOLAS FOUQUET WELCOMED his royal guests to his new château with an effusive show of grandeur. "This modest fete is in your honor, Your Majesty." Attired in lace and brocade, he handed the King and the Queen Mother down from their royal coach himself, presenting the Queen Mother with a tiara of diamonds. He expressed regret that the Queen, great in her maternity, had been unable to make the three-hour journey from Fontaine Beleau.

Madame Fouquet, fully with child herself, made a curtsy and was helped to rise by the Marquise de Plessis-Bellièvre.

Petite glanced away when the Marquise—Fouquet's spy, she now knew—looked at her coldly.

"Ah, my dear Fouquet," the Queen Mother said as one of her attendants placed the glittering bauble on her head, "you honor to excess."

"Nothing is too great for Your Majesty," Fouquet said, but glancing over at Louis, who was surveying the grounds. The limestone château was encircled by courtyards and a moat. Vast gardens, defined by clipped hornbeam hedges, extended down to a canal.

"Ah, the beautiful Madame," Fouquet exclaimed as a swarm of footmen unhitched Henriette's litter from the backs of two palfreys. "What a trial for you to have come all this way," he said, bending to kiss her hand.

"I wouldn't have missed it for the world, Monsieur," Henriette said dreamily. She was officially young with child now, and delicate. Her doctor and Philippe had objected, but she had insisted on making the trip. She had had to travel by litter, well dosed with laudanum.

"And in such heat, such dust! Come, Your Majesties, I will show you to your suites so that you might refresh."

Petite followed as footmen hoisted Henriette's litter up the carpeted stairs. The château was exquisite in every detail: frescoes, rare mosaics, porphyry tables, gold-framed mirrors, ancient Greek sculptures everywhere. She noticed an emblem carved into the cupola high above—Fouquet's device. It showed a squirrel climbing a tree, and underneath, the words *Quo non ascendet?*

She puzzled over the translation. Where to not climb? To what not to climb? To what place—what height—would he not climb? That was it, she realized with a chill. To what heights would he not climb?

Does Fouquet seek the crown? Petite wondered. Certainly, he was acting the part. It was said that he had spent over a hundred thousand livres on this fete alone—more than Louis spent in a year. Where had the money come from? Louis suspected that Fouquet was taking money out of the national treasury, that his wealth was embezzled—from *him*, from the people. Such display of luxury would no doubt confirm his suspicions. Where would it lead? Louis was intent on change, intent on rule without corruption—by force if need be.

"Look up," Nicole sang out softly beside her. "Ludmilla's watching."

Louis was standing on the landing. He glanced beyond Petite and then directly at her, his eyes lingering. With the slightest of smiles, he looked away.

Fouquet appeared at the balustrade beside him. He too caught Petite's eye. He lifted his gloved hand to the brim of his green hat in salute.

"What did that mean?" Nicole asked.

"Hush, Nicole," Petite said under her breath. What *did* it mean? She longed to be somewhere else, in a field among silent horses, with creatures she trusted, whose language she knew.

After the royal family refreshed and the hot August day began to cool, Fouquet proposed a promenade in the gardens. Louis and Philippe helped their mother into a light open-topped calèche as Nicole and Yeyette helped Henriette, prettily coiffed and newly attired, into an embroidered litter shaded by a cloth-of-gold canopy and carried by four footmen.

Reclining on the down pillows, the Princess held out her hands so that Petite could arrange the scarlet ribbons at her thin wrists. Her ringlets hung low onto her shoulders and were sprinkled with the same rosettes that adorned her gown.

"Hurry," Henriette said, flushed with excitement. "I don't want to miss a thing."

Guests were arriving in droves—hundreds upon hundreds of them, an endless stream of men and women in silk and satin, glittering with diamonds, and adorned with rare plumes and a profusion of ribbons: on hats, canes, sleeves, swords, shoe buckles—even on walking sticks.

Petite waved her fan at Athénaïs, who was standing with two of the Queen Mother's attendants and Lauzun.

At last the promenade was put in motion, with Louis and Fouquet in the lead. Fouquet waved his arms about, effervescent with excitement, the courtiers following like an infestation of tropical birds. They cried out with delight as hundreds of water jets shot into the air and all the fountains suddenly came to life.

"The garden changes as we move through it," Petite observed as she and Nicole followed after Madame's litter. The pool wasn't rectangular, after all, but square. What appeared to be a grotto, just beyond the pool, was in fact some distance away, separated by a canal. What appeared to be a row of water jets turned out to be a roaring cascade. Everything appeared symmetrical, but teasingly was not.

A garden of illusion, Petite thought: *how apt.* Fouquet played the part of the devoted servant, while plotting to rule. Louis publicly applauded his minister of finance, while planning his demise. *At Court, nothing is as it appears,* Louis had said. *We all wear masks.*

Torchbearers, thousands of them, appeared as the sun began to set, escorting the guests back to the château, where tables had been set with gold—*solid gold*—platters of pheasant, ortolan, quail, partridge, ragouts and bisques. Wine flowed in abundance as musicians played. The buzz of revelry grew as the tables were refreshed six times.

The abundance was shocking, an affront. Could the royal family afford such a display? Louis was taking it all in. Indeed, everyone seemed to be watching. How many present were Fouquet's spies? Petite wondered. Who could be trusted?

Trumpets sounded. "To the outdoor theater," pages announced.

The courtiers surged out into the night, wending their way through fragrant parterres lit by thousands of beeswax candles, and down an avenue of spruce trees to a terrace at the base of a fountain. There, chairs had been set in front of a large platform.

Petite and Nicole took their positions behind Madame's litter, next to the thrones set up for the King and Queen Mother—and Fouquet. Now and again

Petite glanced at Louis. He was jovial with his host: playing a part, she knew—and playing it chillingly well.

After an overture, Monsieur de Molière appeared on the stage in street clothes. With frenetic despair, he apologized, bowing before the King. "Some of my actors have fallen ill, Your Majesty, and I've not had time to prepare a divertissement."

There was a stir of consternation, when suddenly there were grinding mechanical sounds and a pastoral landscape magically appeared. In the midst of water cascades, an enormous rock broke open, revealing a shell within, out of which stepped a long-haired nymph. The audience cheered and applauded.

"The heavens, the earth, all of nature stands ready to bow to the King's command," the nymph proclaimed, as dancing dryads, fauns and satyrs emerged from the trees.

The play—called *The Bores*—soon had everyone howling with laughter as first one and then another of the Court's more notorious fools were lampooned. Lauzun's donkey bray sounded with each roar of recognition. At one point, when the joke was clearly on Gautier, the old man stood and made a dignified bow. Everyone cheered and hooted.

Between each act, they were entertained by light ballets. Petite had never seen such a spectacle, such a brilliant melding of theater, dance, music and song.

After the entertainment, the guests returned to the château for more music and refreshment. In the grand withdrawing room, stalls had been set up like a market. Ladies swarmed as trinkets were handed out: jewel-embellished pocket mirrors, musk-scented pigskin gloves, lace mantillas, fans of carved ivory. Saddle horses and diamonds were awarded to the highest nobility.

Petite excused herself from the party to go to the necessary set up in Henriette's suite. Her courses had started, at last (she'd been worried). She lingered for a moment in the quiet of the library—taking in the extensive collection of manuscripts, treatises, rare books—and then headed for the stairs.

"Ah, there you are, Mademoiselle de la Vallière."

Petite turned to see Monsieur Fouquet rushing to catch up with her.

"May I help you?" He placed his gloved hand lightly on her sleeve. "Is there *anything* you desire?" he asked with the gracious manner of one born to a very old family.

"No, thank you," Petite said evenly. "This is a marvelous fete, Monsieur."

Fouquet pressed his hands to his heart. "I am devoted to His Majesty, Mademoiselle," he said, his voice unctuous. "I *sincerely* wish to please him," he added, his eyes on hers.

"Of course," Petite said, a giveaway tremor in her voice. She dipped her head and turned away, hurrying up the stairs in a panic of confusion. The words had been intended for Louis, she well knew.

After midnight, everyone returned to the gardens, now dim in the weak light of a third-quarter moon. Louis, the Queen Mother and Fouquet mounted the royal carriage and proceeded to the center of the garden, just above the cascades. Musketeers sounded their trumpets and fire rockets were set. The horses of the royal carriage bolted—*mon Dieu!*—as the night sky lit up like day, the landscape showered in blazing images of fleurs-de-lis, stars, the King's name spelled out in fire.

A swarm of footmen quickly quieted the panicked horses. Louis jumped from the carriage, followed by Fouquet. The Queen Mother stuck her head out of the coach and smiled bravely, at which everyone cheered.

"Morbleu!" Nicole exclaimed, grabbing Petite's hand.

A mechanical whale-like shape was moving slowly down the canal, fireworks exploding from its belly, sending streams of fire across the water. Rockets shot up from the dome of the château, a grotto nearby exploded into light and the garden became a vault of fire. Louis stood watching the sky, his face illuminated. Fouquet came up beside him and put his hand on Louis's shoulder, as if he were a familiar.

As if he were his superior, Petite thought.

The two men—the most powerful in the kingdom—were now silhouetted against the light of a carriage lantern. Louis, tall and in the bloom of youth, towered over the distinguished Fouquet. Slowly, Louis removed the minister of finance's hand and put his arm around the aristocrat, giving him a familiar shake. Their laughter resounded.

The display ended in a shower of ash, and the acrid smell of gunpowder filled the air. Petite pulled her shawl around her shoulders, chilled in spite of the heat. *You don't understand*, Louis had told her. Yet she knew her history well: she knew kings were toppled.

RETURNING TO FONTAINE Beleau the next day, everyone saw the royal château in a new light. The vista was hemmed in. Many of the fountains stood dry, and the two that had water were stagnant, covered with green scum. Where was the magic? Where the grandeur? Indeed, the château appeared shabby, a worn remnant of glory long gone.

In Henriette's withdrawing room that night, all anyone could talk about was Fouquet's marvelous fete, the brilliance of the entertainment, the elegance of the architecture. The canals, the cascades, the ornamental gardens. The food, the gifts, the *cost*.

"Twenty million livres is rather a lot to spend on one night," noted Claude-Marie.

"I heard one hundred thousand."

"Either way, it would be a lot to spend in a year," Yeyette said.

"Did you see the purse of gold set on Madame's dressing table?"

"The Queen Mother got one as well."

"With the exact same number of coins," Henriette said, gloating.

With new respect, everyone bowed to the ground as the minister of finance was announced. Even Henriette's spaniel Mimi was attentive, sniffing at Fouquet's boots.

Shortly after, Louis appeared, and even he showed Fouquet marked esteem. *Is it possible he is pleased with him now?* Petite wondered. She knew it could not be. She was beginning to see how skilled Louis was in the theatrical arts. She opened her fan to the side painted with an image of the Apollo. This was their signal. She longed for a private moment—a moment with the real Louis. It unnerved her to see him so false.

But Louis was preoccupied, and private moments were difficult to arrange, so it wasn't until the end of August that at last they were able to meet. Louis seemed distant, tense.

"I must make a trip west," he told Petite after congress—a rather businesslike procedure this time. "To Nantes."

Petite found that curious. Fouquet's island—the fortress of Belle-Île—was not far from Nantes.

"The women are not to come," he said.

WITH A FEELING OF foreboding, Petite watched from a window as Louis departed, surrounded by his men and musketeers—his small flying camp.

The château was ominously silent during the long hours that followed. Without the sound of the men's spurs on stone, their boisterous jests, it seemed a world abandoned. "Only us girls," Henriette said that evening, pouring out a glass of her husband's best brandy.

"THE MINISTER OF finance has been arrested," Henriette announced nine days later, her face pale. Petite helped her to the daybed as Nicole measured out laudanum. "He's in prison," she said, taking the dose and then bursting into tears. "Dear Fouquet."

The news raced through the château. Minute by minute, courtiers arrived, many with questions, and a few with answers.

"Fouquet's house was ransacked and the door sealed," one of the Queen's maids reported.

"A manuscript was found behind a mirror—plotting an uprising against the King."

"That can't be," the Duchesse de Navailles said.

"I heard that *poisons* were found in his house," Claude-Marie said.

"That's doubtful," Athénaïs said.

Petite listened quietly, her thoughts in turmoil. *I'm not the dupe he imagines*, Louis had said. She understood why the minister of finance had been arrested. The senior aristocrat had mistakenly assumed that he could carry on in the corrupt ways of the past. His arrest was just—Petite believed that—yet it was unnerving.

"His wife is under arrest as well. She was sent to Limoges—"

"In her condition?"

"—with only fifteen louis-d'ors in her purse, poor thing."

"Everyone's property was confiscated—Fouquet's wife's, his sister-in-law's. Vaux, of course."

"Even Suzanne du Plessis-Bellièvre was arrested, her correspondence seized."

Petite was horrified to imagine Fouquet's bumbling spy in prison.

"Imagine what His Majesty will do when he reads through *Fouquet's* correspondence," Henriette said weakly, stretched out on her bed as Nicole and Petite fanned her.

At this, a number of women paled, and in the days that followed, several quietly left Court, anxious, no doubt, to destroy all traces of an association with the former minister of finance.

LOUIS RETURNED ON the ninth of September to a different world, his Court no longer gay. Now everyone courted solitude. Devotional prayers and pilgrimages to shrines had taken the place of evenings at the gaming tables.

He was a different king now, in any case. He had shown his strength, punished corruption—yet peace did not reign. With the confiscation of Fouquet's correspondence, a truth had been revealed that shocked even him. It was as if a rock had been lifted, revealing a teeming underground world of trysts and treasonous dealings.

Turbulent weather ruined crops all across the land, and a famine was predicted. Fear tightened purses, and suddenly money was scarce. As the Queen's belly grew, Petite and Louis lay twined, his cries of release drowned by horrendous storms.

THE QUEEN'S LABOR began in the early hours of All Saints' Day, a good omen. The château came alive with torchlight, courtiers rushing to the Queen's chamber to witness the birth.

Clorine, up by candle, helped Petite into her gown, pinning her braids up under her nightcap. Petite poured some water into a china bowl and rinsed her hands, running them wet over her face. She felt sluggish, heavy on her feet. *O Mary, may his baby be well*, she prayed.

Eight days earlier, she had persuaded Louis to forsake their clandestine afternoons in Gautier's chamber until after the birthing. He needed to prepare for Confession, take Communion, commend his soul to God. So much had gone awry, she feared the worst. The fall weather had been stormy, ruining the harvests throughout the land. It was only the first of November, and already peasants were starving, swarming at the gates.

When had the gods stopped smiling on them? Had it been with the arrest of Fouquet—the arrest and ruin of Fouquet's wife, his brothers and sisters, his friends and supporters, his innumerable spies?

Had *that* been the turning point? Or had it been earlier, Petite wondered, taking up a candle—when they had become sinners? Or earlier even still? She'd had a dream of monsters swimming in dark waters. *Gone to the river*. Had a demon put that in her thoughts? Was the Devil following her even now? *O God, I beg you: the Queen is innocent.*

"Pray, Clorine," she said at the door. "Pray for the Queen."

"Wait," Clorine said, taking the simple rosary hung over the betony statue of the Virgin. "You'll need this."

THERE WAS QUITE a congestion in the antechamber to the Queen's rooms. Petite spotted Athénaïs, leaning against a pillar. "Are you all right?" Petite asked, alarmed by how pale Athénaïs looked.

"It's stifling in there." Athénaïs smiled wanly.

The Queen could be heard screaming. *Mercy.*

"Les douleurs de l'enfantement," Athénaïs said, raising her eyes to the ceiling. "It's not going well for her."

Petite followed Athénaïs into the dark and airless birthing chamber, packed with courtiers staggering about in a sleep-deprived state, wigs askew. She scanned the crowd, looking for Louis. She spotted him sitting in an armchair to one side of the Queen's bed. The Queen was writhing in agony as the midwife, a stout woman of middle age with a pockmarked face, applied steaming cloths to her great belly.

"The baby's posterior presented first," Athénaïs whispered, pressing her way through the loudly praying courtiers.

Petite's heart sank. Women died from such a birthing.

"The midwife almost had apoplexy. One of the Queen's maids fainted and Claude-Marie upheaved. Everyone's dropping like flies."

Petite saw Yeyette and Philippe, but where was Henriette? "I should see to Madame."

"She's already retired," Athénaïs said over the Queen's piercing screams. "She couldn't take it."

Petite held back.

"Don't worry—Nicole is with her. Stay: we may need you. You've foaled horses, haven't you?" she asked with a wink.

Petite followed Athénaïs through the crowd to the Queen's bed. Louis looked up, startled to see her. Petite lowered her eyes and made a deep reverence to the Queen, now silent and panting.

She looks like a girl, Petite thought, *like a mere child with a giant belly*. Her face was flushed, her eyes bulging. She clutched her amulet, the dried heart of the deer that had been slayed on a hunt. The midwife, her hands soaked in oil of white lily, was stroking, kneading, pushing and plying her—trying to turn the infant around.

O Mary, I implore you. Petite clasped her rosary.

"The baby has turned, Your Majesty," the midwife announced at last. The welcome news reverberated throughout the crowd.

But even so, challenges remained, Petite knew. The Queen was practically a dwarf and the baby locked within. The midwife gave the Queen an enema, but it failed to widen the birth canal. Eel liver powder failed to alleviate her pain. A sneezing powder only produced convulsions. Even ergot fungus did not give the exhausted Queen sufficient strength to push the baby out.

But strength for yelling? Yes, this the little Queen had aplenty. Petite was in awe of her vocal strength, the violence of her expression. The timid young woman threw herself violently from side to side with amazing vigor, her screams rattling the horn window panes. "No quiero dar parto, quiero morir!" she cried out in Spanish with each contraction. I don't want to give birth, I want to die!

"Hold her down," the midwife barked at Athénaïs, who appeared senseless with fear.

"Santa Virgen!" the Queen cursed in Spanish, shaking free.

"Get her to drink this." The midwife thrust a glass of milky substance into Athénaïs's hands.

Athénaïs spooned some into the Queen's mouth but the Queen spat it back in her face. "Quiero morir!"

Petite placed her hand on the Queen's damp, cold forehead and turned to Louis. He looked terrified. "Your Majesty," she said softly, "perhaps it would help if *you* told her that this fluid will ease her pain."

Louis stared at Petite, dumbfounded. "Esto facilitará tu dolor," he repeated, standing over his wife.

"Touch her," Petite whispered. "It will calm her." The King's holy touch.

Louis placed his hand on the Queen's shoulder and she quieted . . . but dangerously so, her breathing becoming irregular.

As priests approached, droning sonorously, Athénaïs spooned the liquid into the Queen's mouth.

She stopped breathing.

One second, two seconds, three seconds . . .

Everyone stared. Had they lost her?

Then the Queen gasped, as if drowning.

The midwife was checking the Queen's pulse when her assistant called out.

There it was—a slippery, bloody infant emerging from between the Queen's legs. The nobility craned their necks to see the genitals.

Louis lowered his head, praying.

"A prince, Your Majesty," the midwife said, deftly cutting the cord.

"Glory to the Father, to the Son and to the Holy Spirit," Louis prayed out loud, taking his naked and squalling son in his hands.

Petite blinked back tears and joined with all the courtiers as they echoed the King, "As it was in the beginning, is now and ever shall be, world without end."

"Amen," the courtiers said, falling to their knees. "O Lord, let us rejoice."

"Un príncipe sano, Your Highness," Athénaïs whispered to the Queen, who lay weeping in a pool of blood. "A healthy prince."

"Gracias," the Queen whispered, then fainted dead away.

The squalling baby was cleaned, wrapped, blessed yet again and presented to the King. The great balcony doors were opened to a riot of cheering, ringing bells and fire rockets. The courtiers parted, heads bowed, hats pressed over their hearts, as Louis stepped out onto the balcony with the infant in his arms. A prince!

Amen, my love, Petite prayed silently, weak with relief.

Chapter Twenty-One

THE WEATHER THAT CHRISTMAS season in Paris was wet and gray. A chill came off the dank stone walls of the Tuileries Palace that no amount of burning wood could ease. Petite's garret room was so cold, the water in the wash basin froze. Clorine had to jab it with her finger to break the film of ice. She was adding salt rocks to it when there was a familiar tap-tap at the door.

Gautier stood in the dim hallway, a wall sconce candle illuminating his lively eyes. He was wrapped in layers of wool, bringing to mind a swaddled baby. "I must be quick," he said, closing the door behind him to keep out the cold. Under his arm he clasped a cloth-wrapped bundle. "I've come to deliver His Majesty's invitation to Mademoiselle de la Vallière to join a hunting excursion in the country."

Clorine frowned. "In this weather?"

"When?" Petite asked. She'd had little chance to see Louis since the birth of the Dauphin and the Court's return to Paris. Gautier had been assigned a room next to one of the Queen Mother's valets, so meeting there hadn't been a possibility.

"First thing in the morning," Gautier said. "His Majesty will be riding to Val-de-Galie, a village to the southwest. The going is apt to be rough, so only the hardiest riders have been invited." He tipped his hat to Petite, as if to congratulate her. "There is a château there, a rather primitive hunting box, but sufficient for a stay of two days' duration."

Two days with Louis? (*Two nights.*) "But what about my duties here?" Petite asked.

"Madame is to be purged in the morning, and will not require attendants for several days."

Petite glanced at Clorine, then turned away. She didn't want her maid to know about her relationship with Louis. "Thank you, Monsieur, but I'm afraid I couldn't consider it." It made her want to weep. "A ride through rough terrain would be too difficult for my maid."

"There's sure to be a baggage wagon I could go in," Clorine said, protesting.

"The keeper's wife is in residence at the château, Mademoiselle," Gautier pressed. "She could attend you."

"The keeper's wife will do fine. My maid will stay here," Petite announced, avoiding Clorine's eyes.

"Very well." Gautier doffed his hat. "I will await you at dawn in a carriage in the courtyard, at the end of rue de Chartres. A horse will be held for you at the porte Saint-Honoré. From there a small party will set out to meet the King at Saint-Cloud. If I may make one suggestion, Mademoiselle?" Gautier cleared his throat. "Of those going down on horseback, you will be the only female, which might excite public curiosity. Therefore, it would be advisable for you to dress as a man." He held out the parcel, wrapped in linen. "It's a gentleman's riding ensemble. I am informed that you ride astraddle. There's a hat and wig, as well as a pair of jackboots." He bowed and closed the door behind him.

Clorine sniffed the clothes suspiciously and laid them out on the bed. Petite recognized Lauzun's red cloak and his leather doublet with a missing button. She pulled on one of the high boots. "At least they're small enough," she said.

Clorine snorted, her shoulders hunched.

"You heard what Gautier said." Petite pulled on the wig and looked at herself in the clouded looking glass. "It's a primitive hunt camp. It's best this way, really." She took off the wig—it was itchy. She hoped it wasn't lousy.

"I don't mind so much being left behind." Clorine used a corner of her apron to wipe her cheeks. "What I mind is you lying to me!"

Petite was dismayed to see her maid's tears.

"You don't want me there."

Petite sat down, deflated. She'd been entirely taken up with her own concerns. She hadn't considered how Clorine might feel. "I'm sorry, Clorine. It's because . . ." But no—she could not speak the truth.

Clorine sat down opposite, her hands on her thighs. "It's because you're hiding something, Mademoiselle," she said with an accusing glare. "And I know what it is."

"What do you mean?" Petite asked anxiously.

"I can't believe Gautier would be such a cad." Clorine hit her thigh with her fist.

"But he's not."

"Has he bedded you?"

Petite almost laughed.

"He treats you like a lady?"

Petite nodded.

"He's pledged his troth?"

Petite had to find a way out of this treacherous conversation. She could not reveal the truth, but she did not wish to lie, either. "I can't marry, Clorine."

Clorine stood and paced. "Of course a man as noble as Gautier would require a dowered bride."

Petite's silence was a falsehood, she knew, but not as great as a spoken deception.

"The King shows you favor—it would be foolish not to use that to some profit," her maid announced, inspired. "Maybe when you're out riding, for example, you could mention to His Majesty how nice it would be to have a brooch for your hat, maybe a diamond one like Madame Henriette wears. Or a jeweled riding crop, something you could sell or exchange for paste without the King knowing. He's easily fooled, I've noticed. Then, before you know it, you'd have your dowry. You wouldn't need much, just enough so that Gautier could honorably marry you. But *first* you must swear to me . . ."

Petite regarded Clorine apprehensively, unsure where this was leading.

"Swear that you will not allow Gautier to bed you until after you are married."

"I swear," Petite said, relieved, both hands pressed against her heart.

CLORINE INSISTED ON accompanying Petite to the courtyard the next morning, carrying the leather portmanteau. "But I'm a man, remember?" Petite said, trying to take the case from her maid. It felt strange to be wearing breeches and high boots. It reminded her of the times she had helped her father in the barn, dressed in her brother's castoffs.

"There he is," Clorine said, spotting Gautier snoozing in a coach, his mouth hanging open. She turned to Petite with a glowing look. "Your betrothed."

The dance master sat up and feigned to be wakeful as they approached, straightening his wig. Petite handed her portmanteau up to the driver and made a swaggering sort of step onto the running board, climbing into the coach without assistance. She nodded to Gautier, and then looked off into the distance, pretending a masculine indifference. The clouds to the east were a radiant pink.

Clorine wagged a finger. "No shenanigans—"

"Don't worry, Clorine," Petite said, cutting her off before she said more.

"Remember what I said about the King," Clorine called out as they pulled away.

"What did your maid say?" Gautier asked, thick of hearing. "Something about the King?"

Petite nodded, but did not speak. They were heading west along rue Saint-Honoré. They slowed to make their way through a herd of bleating goats, heading to market.

Gautier fussed to open his snuffbox. "Mademoiselle de la Vallière, may I presume to ask you a question?"

"Certainly, Monsieur," Petite said, adjusting the hat. It tended to slip down over her brows.

"Does your maid know about His Majesty?"

Petite stared out the carriage window: one of the goats had fallen behind and was helping itself to apples on a cart. *How much can I tell him?* she wondered. She felt she could trust him. Indeed, Monsieur le Duc de Gautier was the only person she could talk to about Louis. "I don't want her to know," she confessed. "She would not approve; she's a woman of principle."

"Mademoiselle . . ." Gautier's tone was fatherly. "I've had the pleasure of knowing you since you were a girl, and I wish you to know that I consider you to be a woman of principle yourself. Your . . . your situation is complex. His Majesty had to marry for reasons of State—but what of his heart?" He inhaled a pinch of snuff and sneezed. "Just because he is King does not mean he doesn't have yearnings like any other man—perhaps even more so because of his vital spirit, his noble race. It's not healthy for a man to be starved in this way. The sacrifice of your virtue is a worthy act, but not one that many people would understand."

"I do not see it as a sacrifice," Petite said, her voice thickening. "I hold the King dear."

"I know. Unlike other ladies of the Court, you are free of ambitious intent," he said as they approached the porte Saint-Honoré, a fortress-like structure with turrets. "It speaks well of His Majesty that he has chosen you."

The stench of the moat filled the air, in spite of the chill. Pressing a scented cambric cloth to his nose, Gautier addressed the guard, who, seeing the royal insignia on the coach door, Gautier's sword and the gems in his hatband, waved him through without even looking at his papers, much less the forged ones Gautier had had made up for Petite as "Monsieur" de la Vallière.

Their credentials unquestioned, they clattered over the moat into an open area congested with horses, riders, carts and coaches.

Petite recognized Lauzun sitting a bay and Azeem helping two laborers load a wagon. A page in the King's livery was holding a horse's reins—her horse, she guessed. It was Poseidon, a powerful and stubborn barb. He required a strong hand. "Are you riding down with us, Monsieur?" she asked Gautier as their coach pulled into a clearing.

"No, that's for you young ones. I'll be following behind in the baggage wagon— to protect it." Gautier mocked a threatening expression. "Need help down?" He reached for his walking stick.

"No, thank you," Petite said, jumping out as soon as the coach rolled to a stop. The driver handed down her bag.

"I didn't recognize you," Azeem said in a low voice, taking Petite's portmanteau and putting it in the wagon.

"Good." Petite spat into the weeds for effect.

"Well done. That was disgusting." Lauzun grinned down at her from his horse.

"Good morning, Monsieur Lauzun." Petite kept her voice intentionally low-pitched. "I can take him now," she told the page, gathering up the stallion's reins. She pulled the saddle pad smooth and tightened the girth. It was a workmanlike running saddle, well used. She clasped hold of a hunk of mane, put her left foot in the stirrup and threw her right leg over. How much easier it was not to be encumbered by skirts.

"I imagine that type of saddle is new to you," Lauzun said.

"Not entirely," Petite said, checking the length of the stirrups. Lauzun's jackboots came up over her knees. "But as a girl I mostly rode bareback."

"Ah, like a Roman emperor."

"Like a pagan, my mother said." Petite laughed.

Lauzun looked her up and down, his forehead furrowed. "I didn't think my leather doublet looked so good."

With Azeem in the lead, Lauzun and Petite set out to meet up with the King's party at Saint-Cloud. They made their way along the fetid moat and turned east at the river, already busy with boats and barges. The rising sun sparkled on the water. The river looked like a long silver ribbon edging meadows, farms, groves of bare walnut trees. A flock of pigeons perched on the roof of a dovecote.

"Go on ahead," Lauzun commanded Azeem, slowing his horse to a walk. "Tell His Majesty we will be at the pavilion as expected." The gentler's horse broke into a hand-canter and disappeared around a bend.

"That's the village of Chaillot." Lauzun pointed his riding whip at gardens on the hill to their right. "That convent's fairly new—Sainte-Marie, I think it's called, Sisters of the Visitation."

Four nuns were tending the large garden. Petite thought of the stone hovel she had built as a child—her "convent"—remembered the happy moments she had spent there, caring for wounded animals as she hummed hymns to herself, talking to God (her best friend).

A bell rang for morning Mass, and then other bells joined in, a chorus. Petite thought of her aunt Angélique. Right now she would be singing in choir, a lovely way to begin the day. And then Petite thought, cringing, how her aunt would feel were she to see her now, riding to meet her lover, the King.

"The hunting is supposed to be good in the woods there to the west. I've heard talk of boar and hart," Lauzun said, picking up a trot. "Some say they've seen wild horses in the hills behind."

"Runaways, likely," Petite said, surveying the wooded hills. She thought of Diablo. Perhaps he had simply run off. Perhaps her father had opened his stall and then fallen.

After a time, the high road veered away from the river, entering a forest. The footing was good and the horses broke into an easy canter, weaving in and out between the carts and foot passengers, cows and even a flock of sheep. Petite held her horse back behind Lauzun's big bay, reveling in the pleasure of the early-morning ride, the smell of the woods, the birdsong, the steady rhythm of the horses' hooves.

They came upon the river again and stopped to water their horses. Ahead was the arched stone bridge to Saint-Cloud. At the top of the hill, above the winding streets of the village, Petite could see the white walls of the château, one wing covered with scaffolding. Like every royal residence, it was undergoing renovation.

As they crossed the bridge, Petite spotted the gentler on his horse on the opposite bank, near a pavilion.

"His Majesty won't be long," Azeem called out as they neared, pacing his horse back and forth, its hot breath misting.

"Jingo! There he is now," Lauzun said.

Four men on horseback could be seen making their way down the hill, Louis in the lead. He sat his horse proudly, his legs dangling loose out of the stirrups. He was riding Courage, a hunter with a large, round chest.

Following Lauzun's example, Petite made a seated reverence, taking off her hat and pressing it to her heart.

Tipping his cocked hat, Louis smiled at her with his eyes, his right hand holding the reins, his left hand on an embroidered bandolier, the rapier hanging high at his hip. He was wearing a worn green-leather tunic that reached to his knees.

Behind Louis were three trusted companions: the Duc de Chevreuse, the Marquis de Dangeau and the Duc de Beauvillier. In casual dress, they would be taken for a party of noblemen setting out for a day's hunt. They regarded Petite knowingly, but with respect.

Louis set out at the lead. At the château gate they were joined by two armed guards. They followed the post road west, climbing steadily uphill. Petite fell to the back, in front of the gentler and the guard who brought up the rear. Listening to their easy chatter, she kept her eyes on Louis. Twice he turned to catch her eye.

After a few hours, they stopped at an inn on the outskirts of a village. Petite dismounted and tied her horse's reins to a hitching post. Louis, Lauzun and the men circled around to the back of the inn. The gentler and the guards turned their backs, relieving themselves by the road. Petite paused, unsure, then ducked into a thicket of bushes.

Emerging, she saw three of the men going into the inn and followed them inside. The hall was full of trestle tables lined with travelers eating from wooden bowls. The place smelled of sour beer and seared meat. The men of the King's party were standing beside a table in the corner.

Petite heard Lauzun's voice from behind. "Your Majesty, the men have—"

"Criminy, it's the King," a man cried out, and suddenly there was a great scraping of stools and chairs as everyone stood, bowing in a chaotic fashion. An old woman beside the fire was helped to her feet.

"Be seated," Petite heard Louis command.

Lauzun cleared a path for the King to the corner table, and people slowly returned to their bowls of mutton and pitchers of slow beer, the buzz of conversation filling the room once again.

Lauzun spotted Petite and gestured to the chair beside the King. Louis held out his hand, palm up, summoning her. Pressing her wide-brimmed hat to her heart, she sidled through the crowd and into the empty place.

"I'm having the stable boy beat the stuffing in my saddle," Lauzun was saying.

"Your horse is galled?" Louis asked.

"Damn nearly," Lauzun said. "His withers are wrung."

"My withers are wrung too," Louis said with a sidelong glance at Petite. He pressed his thigh against hers.

Petite took a slow and careful breath as the serving girl placed a tankard of beer and a bowl of stewed beef in front of her.

THE ROAD CONDITIONS were passable until they left the high road, circling back onto a rutted laneway heading east. The terrain turned scrubby, marshy in the valleys, the road washed out in two places. The first flooded stretch was shallow, posing no difficulty, but at the second, the horses balked.

Louis studied the torrent of water, then spoke to Lauzun, who nodded and turned his horse. "His Majesty suggests you lead the way across," he told Petite. "He thinks you might be able to get Poseidon to go over."

Petite walked her horse to the water's edge. It was December; the water was cold, but not icy. She pressed her horse forward, but he reared up. She turned him in circles, stung him sharply on the flank with her crop and spurred him on again. He flattened his ears but surged into the water. "Good fellow," she said, stroking his neck. Midway, the ground fell off. She was relieved when at last he gained purchase and struggled up onto the bank.

"There's only the one deep spot in the middle," she called back, but Louis was already across, his horse scrambling up behind her onto the bank.

"Ride beside me," he told her once everyone was safely across. The men fell respectfully behind, at a distance.

They entered a wood, crossed a valley and climbed a hill.

"A boar bog," Petite said, pointing off to the left.

"My father hunted here when he was only six," Louis said. "He bagged a levret, five quail and two partridges."

Petite whistled.

Louis regarded her with astonishment. "I didn't think women could do that."

Petite whistled again, then laughed. "Race?" Her horse surged ahead, galloping as if the Devil was at his heels.

Breathless, with their horses lathered, they crested a hill. Below, in a marshland clearing, was a château. Close by was a church and a huddle of poor houses: a small village. Smoke rose from one of the château chimneys.

"It's so isolated," Petite said, gazing out across the low forested hills.

"Does that disturb you?"

"I love it."

"I thought you would." He reached for her hand.

THE HUNT CHÂTEAU was like a fairy tale house: slate roof, wrought-iron balconies, marble courtyard and a little dry moat. Made of red bricks and white stone, it reminded Petite of the château at Blois, but in miniature, and all of a piece.

"Welcome, Your Majesty!" A stout, red-faced man with a drooping mustache cried out greetings, waving his hat about in a confusion of etiquette. "We were told that the road was washed out." He held the reins of Louis's horse as the King dismounted. "We feared you might not get across."

"Nothing stops this rider," Louis said, indicating Petite.

"Get this young man's horse," the stout man called out to a boy sprinting across the cobblestones.

"I think he's a girl," the boy said, studying Petite as she dismounted.

"I think so too," Louis said with a laugh. "Messieurs, please pay your respects to Mademoiselle de la Vallière," he announced, swiping off Petite's hat and wig, allowing her golden curls to fall to her shoulders. "Mistress of *this* château."

THE CHÂTEAU WAS more than a simple hunting box, as Gautier had described it, but small nonetheless. Petite was surprised, in fact, when the keeper's wife—Madame Menage, a hunched-over woman—informed her that there were twenty-six habitable rooms.

"Although not much in the way of furnishings," Madame Menage said, "and that suits me fine. I'm the only woman here year-round, not even a chamber-maid." She spread a toilette over a table and set a tin bowl of water on the cloth. "Will you need help dressing?"

"No, thank you." Petite had thought to pack a sensible gown that laced up the front.

"Maybe I should have put finer linens on the bed," Madame Menage said, lighting a candle, "but my instructions are to take you to the King, so I didn't think he would be coming here to do his courting."

"No, I don't think so," Petite said, flushing. "But perhaps you could take me to him now."

LOUIS TOUCHED THE small of Petite's back. "These were my father's rooms," he said, holding a lantern aloft. He was wearing a squirrel-lined green velvet gown—his father's, he told her—which smelled disagreeably of wormwood. "And this was his study."

It was a dark room, taken up largely by a billiard table covered with a patched cloth. Louis held up the lantern the better to show her the leather-topped writing desk at the far end. Along the near wall were two trunks, with a smaller chest stacked on top.

Near the door was a four-pillared game table, bone chess pieces arranged on a chequered board, ready for play. The knight was the head of a unicorn, Petite noticed, intricately carved. She had the urge to pick it up, feel its weight.

"Your father must have liked to play," she said, glancing over the games stacked on a shelf: backgammon, trou-madame, chess, tourniquet, renarde, moine, spillikins.

"I don't think of him as a playful man," Louis said, leading her into the next room, the bedchamber, "but how would I know?" A fire burning in the grate threw off little heat. He placed his hand on the back of her neck, his fingers lightly caressing.

The moon cast a cold light through the leaded windows. Petite looked up at Louis, his high cheekbones outlined by shadow. She longed for the familiar security of his arms.

"He died when I was four."

"That's young to lose a father," Petite said with sympathy, leaning into him.

"He wanted to die here, in this bed," he said, nodding toward the massive four-poster structure, draped in green damask curtains. "But he breathed his last at Saint-Germain-en-Laye."

Petite was relieved. She didn't like the thought of sleeping in a deathbed, especially a historic one.

"So he didn't get his wish," Louis added, his tone sad now, "although he did manage to hold on until the fourteenth of May, the day his own father died."

Louis's grandfather, Henry the Great. How often had her father told her stories of "the gallant Green"? It awed Petite to think that Louis had this celebrated king's blood. There was much of Henry the Great in him, she thought: his forthright manner, his courage, his *goodness*.

"It's best to die in a bed," Petite said, thinking of her father, lifeless on the stable floor. She wanted to ask Louis how he felt on May fourteenth, whether he feared Death on that day, but she wasn't sure how he might take it. "Are there any ghosts here at Versaie?" Every village had its ghost, every château.

"You'll have to ask Madame," Louis said with a laugh. "Although I doubt it. Nobody but a member of the royal family is allowed to die here."

How comforting, Petite thought, to be able to rule such things, to be so . . . so godlike. She recalled the stories she'd been told, of Louis curing the Evil with a touch. How wonderful (and scary) it must be to have such power, the power to heal suffering.

"Have you ever seen one?" she asked.

"Only once. My father's ghost, at Saint-Germain-en-Laye, but in the new château by the river." He smiled, recollecting. "In the room in which I was born, in fact. It was long past nightfall. My brother and I were having a fight with pillows, feathers everywhere. Our father appeared and told us to go to sleep."

"How like a father," Petite said, laughing with him. She would love to see her father again, even if he scolded her. "Did he look real to you?"

"Yes, strangely—though we could see through him."

"Just as people say."

"And then he vanished—a very proper apparition." He threw up his hands. "But then, of course, we couldn't sleep at all," he said, closing the shutters and pulling the drapes against the night spirits. "This thing stinks." His voice was muffled as he pulled the green gown up over his head. He threw it into a chest and shut the lid.

"You don't feel the chill?" Petite asked, her voice thick with love-longing. He was down to his under-linens and already in a manly state.

"I rarely do," Louis said, opening the bed curtains and sitting down, testing the stacked fustian mattresses. He held out his hand. "Hot-blooded, I guess," he said with a teasing smile.

Petite kicked off her mules and sat beside him. She wondered if she would be staying the night.

"May I undo your laces, Mademoiselle?" he asked, gently tugging on the silken cord. It knotted, and they groaned.

"Here," she said, untangling it, her bodice falling open.

He pulled her to him, into the bed.

PETITE WOKE IN the dark room, curled naked around Louis, her cheek on his chest. She listened to his slow breathing and nuzzled into him. He moaned and turned, pressing against her, one hand cupping her breast. She felt him harden against her buttocks. She was wet still, slick with seed. They fell into a slow rhythm..

"I love you, Louise," he rasped, clasping her breathlessly. They fell into sleep enjoined, and woke twined in each other's arms.

PETITE RODE WITH Louis and his men the next morning. He smiled to see her sitting Poseidon so proudly. The stallion arched his neck.

Louis motioned Petite to come forward, to ride at the front with him. The men backed up their horses to give her room. He gave a signal and they all set out, ambling at first, then trotting and cantering.

Entering an open plain, Louis's horse lengthened into a hard gallop. Petite crouched over Poseidon's neck, pressed him forward. Soon they had outdistanced the others. Racing back to the château, Petite won by a length.

"She's a devil," Louis said, handing his reins to the gentler.

"He's not even damp, Mademoiselle," Azeem said, feeling the horse's chest. "If you wish, we could—" He nodded toward the fenced-in arena.

"I've asked Azeem to teach me how to stand on a horse's back—while it's moving," Petite told Louis. "He used to train trick riders."

"This I'd like to see," Louis said, leaning on a fence rail.

"So far I can only do it at a walk." Petite opened the gate and led the stallion in.

"First I just lunge him, Your Majesty," Azeem explained, fitting the horse with a snaffle bridle and cavesson, and then a surcingle around his chest with leather loops sticking up—something Petite could hold onto if needed. "To get him going smoothly," he explained, removing the reins. He raised his hand and the horse moved to the perimeter. "Walk." Azeem raised his right hand and Poseidon circled. Azeem sent a wave through the lunge line and the horse stopped.

"You've got him listening nicely," Petite said, studying the gentler's method.

"He's strong-willed," Azeem said. "One must assert authority."

"Like with my kingdom," Louis said, and they laughed.

Azeem signaled the stallion to come to him. "Ready, Mademoiselle?" he asked, tightening the surcingle, checking to see that it wasn't rubbing the horse's withers. "It's best without boots and stockings."

Petite glanced down at her feet. Her corset stays prevented her from bending over.

"Allow me," Louis said, kneeling to unfasten her buckles and slipping off each boot and stocking. He held one naked heel and looked up at her—teasing. His hands were warm on her skin. Desire inflamed her; they hadn't coupled since morning. Petite smiled and poked him with her toe, but he was strong; she couldn't topple him.

"Azeem, how does one gentle such a woman?" Louis made a playful swipe for Petite, but she dodged him.

"Your Majesty, I believe you know that very well," Azeem said, leading the horse to the rail.

Petite started out at a walk, kneeling on Poseidon's back and holding onto the leather loops on the surcingle. The stallion's pace was steady and his back broad, so that soon she could stand without holding on.

"Isn't this boring to you?" she asked Louis, but a sideways glance made her lose her balance. She grabbed mane, and he laughed.

"Stand on the rail this time, Mademoiselle," Azeem said. "As the horse comes by, step on."

Petite landed steadily. "Well done." Louis applauded.

"This is the easy part," she said.

She progressed quickly through the walk and trot.

"Mademoiselle, I believe you are ready for the canter," Azeem announced.

"I don't think so," Petite protested, yet climbed back onto the rail. Poseidon's gaits were vigorous.

The first time Poseidon went by, she held back and missed.

"You have to jump sooner," the gentler said. "I'll tell you when."

Louis nodded: *You can do it.*

This time, Petite got on as the horse cantered by.

"Bravo!" Louis called out.

Petite clutched the handles for balance. The trees were a blur. She tried to straighten, but she kept losing her footing. Twice she nearly fell off. "I can't," she called out to Azeem, lowering herself onto the horse's back, her legs encircling his chest. "Ho, boy," she said, slowing him to a trot, and then a walk. "It's hard," she said, discouraged, thinking of the Romany woman of her youth. She'd made it look like the most natural thing in the world—and the most wondrous.

"It takes time," Azeem said. "You did well."

"I've never seen anyone even try to do that," Louis said.

THEY DID NOT SLEEP very much that night, so great was their pleasure. Even so, they rose shortly after dawn, mounting their horses and riding into the untamed wasteland. Midday, over a repast—and love, always love—Louis asked Petite question upon question: Did you and your father hunt wolf? bear? unicorn? He was astonished that a boar could be taken on foot, amazed that one good dog could put a hart to bay, that a hare or woodcock could be felled with a well-aimed stick. He wanted to know how her childhood home had been organized, how many cooks they'd had (only one?), how many equerries (none!), how many horses (only five?), what they ate, and when. Petite felt she was an exotic foreign country, and he her explorer.

As their horses grazed, she told him about her family, her father and her aunt, Sister Angélique. And then she told him about Diablo.

Louis sat up. "He was truly wild?"

"He was more than wild," Petite said. *He was possessed.*

"A horse in the wild is a beautiful thing," Louis said reflectively.

Yes, Petite thought. She loved nothing better than to watch a horse galloping across an open field, tossing its head and bucking, its long tail flowing in the wind. "He taught me the language of horses." She felt she could tell Louis anything—anything but bone magic. She didn't want to tempt the Devil near.

They set off yet again, exploring marshes, swampy meadows, pits of sand. Petite pointed out the wildlife, the birds especially, for she knew most everything by its call. The place was teeming with game. "It's a hunter's paradise," she said, dreading the thought of returning to the city the next day.

"Our paradise," he said, clasping her hand.

Here, they could roam free.

Chapter Twenty-Two

"WE'RE GOING TO SEE my mother," Petite informed Clorine on New Year's Day. It was about time. She had not been to see her since the Court had returned to Paris. Madame Henriette had been sick with child, so Petite had been busy—but today, the first of the new year, all the attendants had been given the afternoon off. "I'll hire a hackney for us," she said, counting out coins. They could walk, but it was bitter, and the lanes would be icy. As well, after fall storms had ruined the harvest, starving peasants had been flocking into the city; one had to be careful.

Clorine tugged on her earlobe. "Do you have a gift for her?"

Petite looked over the items she had laid out on her trunk: six brass hairpins, a trinket box, a scent bottle of eau de Chypre—items to be given to Nicole, Athénaïs and Henriette later that evening. In a book stall by the river, she'd found a translation of Xenophon's *The Art of Horsemanship* to give to Louis. It would have to wait until they had a moment alone—which seemed impossible in Paris, where people were always watching (the queens especially, and their minions).

"I'll give her my gauze shawl," Petite said, "the green one." It had been part of her nymph costume for the ballet at Fontaine Beleau that summer.

They wrapped warmly and set out, well muffed, to a stand of cabriolets. After close inspection, Petite engaged a one-horse open carriage, settling with the driver on a price. The cab was without a head, and not many would venture out in such cold without a cover, so he reluctantly agreed to half the usual rate. The nag looked more like a sumpter mule than a carriage horse, but the driver swore she was sound, so Petite and Clorine climbed in. Yelling out to people to clear the way, he cracked his whip. The old mare took fright, very nearly running over a man in a long matted wig before settling back to a reluctant walk.

"Here we go," Clorine said excitedly, holding onto her hood.

It took forever to cross over the river; the bridge was congested with coaches and dog carts. Once on the other side, the clanging of the iron and wood cart-wheels was deafening. On all sides, hawkers reached out to them, selling their wares: caps, songs, shawls, pies . . . Beggar children were everywhere, swarming for a coin.

"I have a knife in my basket," Clorine confided, looking about uneasily.

At long last, they joined the line at the city gate. Clorine handed Petite a bit of cheese and bread, but Petite tossed it to a child in rags, who bit into it hungrily.

Petite was relieved when they finally gained entrance to the Palais d'Orléans. It was much as she remembered it: new (as palaces went) and stately. She found it hard to believe that she'd left for Court only seven months before. Much had happened in that time. She had much to be proud of—and much to hide.

The driver yelled out "whoa, whoa" as the nag headed for the horse trough at a distance from the entrance. As soon as the wheels stopped rolling, Clorine climbed down. Petite handed her their basket, but did not alight. She was apprehensive, suddenly, of seeing her mother. *Chastity, humility, piety:* these words had been drummed into her as a child.

"Need a hand?" the driver asked, picking at his teeth with a dirty nail.

"No, Monsieur," Petite said, resolutely jumping down.

The butler at the entrance sent a torch boy to see if Petite's mother was receiving. The boy returned huffing and puffing—"Yes! she said"—and they headed down the long gallery and up the winding stone stairs into the turret.

At the door, Petite paused. Inevitably, there would be a discussion about finding a husband for her. "Clorine, don't say anything to my mother about Monsieur le Duc de Gautier," she whispered. "It's privity for now—and you know how my mother talks." The secrecy and subterfuge seemed never-ending, one falsehood leading to another, and another.

Clorine nodded conspiratorially.

Françoise opened the door herself and gave Petite a vigorous embrace. She'd become rounder since Petite last saw her. "What a surprise," she exclaimed, fussing with her coif anf tucker.

Petite kissed her mother's powdery cheek, inhaled her vanilla scent, unexpectedly moved. Her mother's face was lined with wrinkles.

"Pity the Marquis isn't in," Françoise fussed, but noting with interest the mouche on Petite's chin, the fashionable details of her gown (the wide chemise sleeves runched with ribbons, the long, pointed stomacher).

"Yes," Petite said, but relieved. She'd not brought her stepfather a gift.

Françoise sent her maid for posset and sweetmeats and they settled in the chairs by the fire, exchanging news: Petite's duties at Court (not too demanding), the weather that summer (hot and stormy), the Marquis's health (dropsical), a letter from Jean (bored in Amboise and short of money).

"I almost forgot." Petite glanced back at Clorine, standing by the shuttered window. "The basket?" She reached in for the shawl. "For you—for the new year."

"I love it," Françoise said, holding the thin tissue to the light, "but where will I wear it?"

"Wear it now," Petite said, arranging the fabric around her mother's shoulders. "It looks pretty on you."

Françoise stilled Petite's hand with her own. "You should not be spending money on fripperies, Louise. How much have you saved toward your dowry?"

"A little," she lied, feeling the blood rush to her cheeks. Surely her mother could see right through her, could sense, with a mother's instinct, the momentous change that had taken place in her daughter, know that she was no longer a girl, but a woman—and a fallen woman at that, a woman who knew what it meant to swoon in her lover's arms.

"Your brother has been looking out for a husband for you."

"How is Jean?" Petite asked, changing the subject. She didn't trust Clorine to hold her tongue.

"He guarded that minister of finance, I forget his name."

"Monsieur Fouquet?" The former minister of finance was being brought to Paris to be tried. It had never occurred to Petite that he might be held at Amboise on the way.

"Jean guarded him for almost two weeks, but as for finding a husband for you, he thinks you should—"

Petite stood abruptly. "I'm afraid I must be leaving, Mother," she announced. "Our driver is expecting us, and I've duties to attend to."

It was late afternoon by the time Petite and Clorine arrived back at their attic room in the Tuileries Palace. "I'm going riding," Petite told her maid. The emotions provoked by the visit with her mother had unnerved her and she needed to settle.

She had just put on her overskirt when there was a tap-tap at the door.

"I believe that must be your suitor," Clorine said cheerily. She stopped at the cracked mirror to adjust her frilly cap before unlatching the bolt. "It *is* you."

"I'm the bearer of heathenish New Year's tidings," Gautier announced. He was wearing a jaunty beaver top hat, and his cape was short, showing off petticoat breeches like those the young men wore.

"Happy New Year, Monsieur," Petite said, wondering if he had a message from Louis.

"Mademoiselle, for you, with best wishes for an excellent New Year, a bowl of fruit—note the enclosure within—as well as a smaller parcel," Gautier said, ceremoniously plucking a beribboned box out of the bowl, "for your ever-so-capable maid."

"For me, Monsieur?" Clorine wiped her hands on her apron before unraveling the knotted ribbon.

"I wrapped it myself," he said proudly.

"And most securely," Clorine said, using the point of a letter-opener to pry the knot loose.

Petite set the bowl on the table. It was filled with fresh pears, oranges and figs. Such luxury in winter. She spied a rolled paper tied with a white ribbon tucked under the fruit. She took advantage of Clorine's distraction to slip behind the cloth partition.

My love, I am desperate to see you. Feign to be ill tomorrow. I will come to your room at three of the clock. You may entrust Gautier with your answer. I impatiently await the moment when I can hold you again in my arms. L.

Petite pressed the note to her heart. Since the trip to Versaie, she'd hardly had a chance to even talk to Louis—but to meet him *here*, in her own room?

She stepped out from behind the screen. Gautier was demonstrating how to operate a mechanical device.

"Zut!" Clorine exclaimed, lifting her skirts as the object clattered across the floor like a rodent possessed.

"I thought you'd enjoy it," Gautier said, chuckling.

"Monsieur?" Petite's solemn demeanor broke the general levity. "My answer is yes."

It took a moment for Gautier to comprehend.

"I will be here tomorrow, at three."

"Oh?" he said, as if he'd forgotten the purpose of his excursion. "*Excellent*," he said, clearly remembering, then tipped his plumed hat and took his leave.

"Step back." Clorine wound up the toy. "It jumps." She squealed with laughter as it leapt across the room.

Petite sat down on the chair by the table. She took a pear out of the bowl and held it. Such beautiful fruit. Louis took a personal interest in his gardens. Were he not king, he would happily have been a gentleman farmer.

"Clorine, we must talk."

Clorine picked up the contraption, waited for it to run quiet and then placed it on top of her trunk.

"I believe you should sit down," Petite said, steeling herself.

Apprehensively, Clorine lowered herself onto the wooden bench by the door.

"First: you must vow *never* to reveal what I'm about to tell you."

Clorine nodded solemnly.

Petite took a deep breath. She would give her life for Louis, but this seemed so much harder. "In the morning, I'm going to send you to inform Madame Henriette that I'm ill and that I won't be able to be in attendance."

"You're ill?"

"I'm not."

"You're not ill, but you will be tomorrow?" Clorine frowned. "How do you know?"

"Because it won't be true." *O God, please forgive me*. "It will be a story, a cover. I've agreed to . . . to receive someone."

"Here?"

"Yes, but—" Petite closed her eyes. She didn't want to see Clorine's face. "But privately," she said finally, taking a deep breath. For a loveday. *Mercy*. She opened her eyes and added, in a matter-of-fact way, "It would be a good time for you to go to the market."

Clorine squinted. "Has this to do with the Duke?"

"No, Clorine, it has nothing to do with him." Petite pressed her fingertips to her eyes, then looked up, blinking away stars. "It's time I told you the truth." She felt her heart sink. "I am not betrothed to Monsieur le Duc de Gautier."

Clorine started. Petite held up her hand. She had to see this through. "I do have a . . ." She thought of all the words women used: *love-lad, galant, swain, amoroso, squire*. None of these were right. Her sweeting, her beloved . . . her life. "A gallant," she said finally. It was the most refined. "But he is not the Duke." *Dear Mary, Mother of God, give me the strength to tell the truth, even if it is a sin.* "It's the King."

Clorine sat still as a wax figure, her heavy eyes fixed, and then slumped to the floor in a faint.

That, Petite had expected. What she hadn't anticipated was the torrent of tears that burst from her maid once she'd revived.

"The King's mistress? You'll spend eternity in Hell! Oh, your poor old mother. This will be the death of her—"

"My mother must never know, Clorine." *Never.*

"—the death of *me*. How could you? You're so much more sensible than other girls. You were raised in a convent! Just imagine what your aunt will think—your aunt Angélique who sends you such lovely laces."

I know, Petite thought, tears streaming.

"Oh, the shame of it! You're ruined."

I know.

"Who would marry you now? Not even that old merchant who couldn't read would have you. All my life, I've wanted only one thing," she ranted on, sobbing as if her heart would break, "and that was to serve the wife of a highborn man. I had such hopes that you would marry dear old Gautier. He's highborn, a titled gentleman, and a good, *good* man—but now . . . Now you can't even become a nun. Oh, my girl—how could you?"

THE COURTIERS GATHERED in Madame Henriette's bedchamber that evening to celebrate the new year. Henriette's pregnancy had rendered her dangerously ill and her doctor had confined her to bed, so the courtiers had come to her, in sympathy. The room was abuzz with talk and laughter, warm from the heat of blazing Yule logs, the smoky air sweetly scented by the Hungary water Henriette sprinkled over the carpets.

"What's wrong?" Nicole asked, embracing Petite, very nearly tipping her goblet of mulled wine. "You look like a death mask in a procession."

Petite felt drained, in truth. Her conversation with Clorine had been unsettling. "I told my maid," she whispered. It was a relief to have it over, but she felt shattered. No matter how sacred her love for Louis, she was, after all, a married man's mistress.

"About Ludmilla?"

"She fainted."

"She's always fainting. I should think she'd be pleased. I have good news—but first, my new year's gift for you." She handed Petite a small packet. "Not fancy, but . . . well, amusing?"

Petite read the label. "Passion powder?"

Nicole glanced around the crowded salon. "It's from that woman all the ladies go to," she whispered. "Madame la Voisin—out in Villeneuve-Beauregard."

"You went?" The district was known to be rough, a haven for criminals.

"It's to make a man crazy for you . . . although I don't think you need it." She smiled.

"What's the good news?" Petite asked, giving Nicole her gift of brass hairpins.

"It has to do with our Goddess of Virginity." Nicole pinned her black ringlets back behind her ears and checked her reflection in the window.

"Athénaïs?" Petite had sat beside the lovely Marquise at Mass the day before.

"And Alexandre, the Marquis de Noirmoutiers—" Nicole pulled one curl loose so that it would fall at her cheek.

"He's perfect for her." The Marquis de Noirmoutiers was rich, well-born as well as comely.

"I know! I've been taking their notes back and forth, and—" Nicole turned to the door. "And speak of the Devil."

Athénaïs stood in the door, waiting to be announced.

"She's always so lovely," Petite said. Athénaïs was wearing a russet gown of flowing silk, the neck cut daringly low. Her hair was parted in the center, her long blonde curls touching her bare shoulders.

"And look who's behind her," Nicole said. "The comely beau himself."

"Are they betrothed?" Petite asked, noticing the way Athénaïs looked up into the young man's eyes, the way she placed her hand on his. *Love:* she knew the signs well.

"Just tonight." Nicole made a swooning gesture.

ALL THE NEXT morning Clorine lectured Petite about what a woman had to do to prevent "swelling of the stomach": stick a sponge soaked in vinegar "up there," or have the man put pig gut over his engine. "Or both," Clorine said, "to be safe."

Petite patiently listened to her maid's lectures, not letting on that she already knew "all that." From the beginning, she and Louis had been using a sponge soaked in vinegar (or brandy). As well, Louis had been informed by his doctor that conception could only happen if they spent at the same time, so he usually managed to hold back until Petite was ready to discharge. Common knowledge advised a woman not to clench her buttocks—but this Petite found impossible. Alternatively, lascivious movements were believed to scatter the man's pleasure-fluid: *that* was much easier for Petite to manage.

"Don't worry," Petite told Clorine, relieved to see that her maid was finally putting on her cloak. Louis would arrive in a half-hour, and she planned to let down her hair, entwine it with ribbons. She opened a book of bucolic poetry and feigned to read it. She didn't want to appear the harlot, but her thoughts were indeed inflamed. If only Clorine would leave!

"I'm going to church to pray for you," Clorine informed her. "I'll be back at five. I should imagine that will give you enough time," she added with pointed disdain.

"Thank you," Petite said, but thought, *Go! Go!*

"Zut!" Clorine exclaimed, opening the door.

Petite looked up: it was a chandler with his wares.

"We have no need of candles," Clorine informed the man curtly.

"May I speak to your mistress, Madame?"

Petite put her book down and stood. *Mercy*, Louis was early.

"Absolutely not," Clorine said, laying a hand on his shoulder as he stepped into the room.

"Clorine, it's *him*."

Louis fell against the closed door, laughing.

"Uh-oh, Louis," Petite said. "Catch her: she's going to faint."

"Nonsense," Clorine said, but clasping the back of a wooden chair. "I'd curtsy, Your Majesty, but I don't think I can manage."

"You must be Madame Clorine," Louis said kindly. "My dear Monsieur le Duc de Gautier has talked often of you."

Clorine could not refrain from smiling.

"Are you sure you're all right, Clorine?" Petite asked.

"Perfectly fine." The maid pulled up her hood. "I'll be leaving now."

Louis opened the door and bowed her out, as if he were a footman.

Clorine paused at the door. "You look after my lady," she said with a scolding air.

"I assure you," he said in all seriousness, his hand to his heart as if making a vow.

Chapter Twenty-Three

HENRIETTE WAS LOSING her sparkle. She didn't like having a big belly, and she detested having to stay in bed. But most of all she was weary of her wretchedly cramped quarters in the Tuileries, and positively sullen-sick of being under the critical eye of the two queens. She and Philippe were supposed to have moved into the Palais Royale months earlier, but the work on it—predictably—continued to move slowly. After considerable yelling and a few fits, she had finally accomplished her mission: the Palais—*her* palace—was ready.

The January weather was chill, but sunny. The cobbles were not icy, and the move was accomplished more easily than Petite could have predicted. Hundreds of workers loaded hampers, furnishings and trunks onto wagons to travel the few blocks from the Tuileries to the Palais Royale, where hundreds more directed each of the seven hundred staff to their various chambers.

Petite carried her treasures herself: her father's rosary wrapped around the statue of the Virgin and the wooden keepsake box. Her books (*Life*, by Saint Teresa, *Wisdom's Watch upon the Hours*, a prayer book, three volumes of bucolic poetry, Ovid's *Metamorphoses*) she had entrusted to Clorine to bring later with the rest of their meagre belongings.

Nicole met her at the top of the stairs. "We're sharing a room."

The stairwell was musty, with a hint of the sweet, sickening scent of a dead mouse.

"That's . . . wonderful," Petite said uncertainly, following Nicole down the narrow hall to their room, a chamber under the eaves. How would she manage to meet with Louis? Since Clorine had been let in on the secret, they had been meeting almost every afternoon.

"Both beds are uncomfortable," Nicole said. Her maid, Annabelle, was on her knees scrubbing the tiles. "Take whichever one you want."

Petite chose the bed next to the window, overlooking the stables. The bed curtains were musty; she would have Clorine set them out in the sun. She positioned the figure of the Virgin on a side table, arranging the rosary around her neck. Then she opened the keepsake box and took out the brittle tree branch (the three dry leaves still on it), the moth-eaten scarf she'd given Louis to dry his face during that fateful storm, and the blue jar of rainwater.

She peered back into the box. Tucked in with the packet of "passion powder" Nicole had given her, and Princess Marguerite's gold embroidered nose cloth (too scratchy to use), was a locket on a frayed lilac ribbon. She withdrew the locket and held it to the light. It was a simple brass piece such as a girl would wear, now tarnished and spotted. In packing for the move, she'd discovered it in the hidden drawer of her trunk. She'd forgotten all about it.

She pried it open: inside was a coil of white hair. She touched it: it was springy, coarse. Horsehair.

Mercy. Petite sat down on the edge of her bed.

She had no recollection of putting it in the locket . . . and *then* she remembered: after her father's funeral she'd gone to the barn to place cornflowers on the spot where her father died. Then she had sat for a time in the empty stall, praying for an answer, a sign.

"What do you think?" Nicole asked, interrupting her reverie. She held up a pink satin bodice and skirt, much frilled with lace and ribbons.

"It's beautiful," Petite said faintly, recalling that moment when she had seen the strand of hair caught in the metal bolt on the gate. He was real.

"It's for the inaugural ball next week," Nicole said, twirling.

Petite closed the locket and clasped it in her hands: she hadn't imagined him. "Henriette is actually going ahead with the fete?" she asked distractedly.

"She plans to be carried in on a feathered litter, reclining like Cleopatra," Nicole said, hanging the gown on a coat hook and standing back to admire it. "Very romantic."

THE GRAND EVENT came . . . and went. It wasn't romantic in the least. Petite and the other maids of honor were required to sit beside Henriette all evening, watching from a podium as everyone else enjoyed themselves: Athénaïs dancing with her beloved, Lauzun entertaining every woman on the floor with his droll antics; la Grande Mademoiselle laughing with a group of ladies ("the spinster club"). Armand de Guiche and Philippe stopped by now and again to keep Henriette entertained, but Petite didn't listen. Her courses had started, and there was no opportunity to dance, much less to even have a word with Louis. He made only a brief appearance with the Queen, in any case, so Petite was relieved when, at last, Henriette retired and she could return to her room. Hours later, she heard Nicole stumble in.

"You missed all the excitement," Nicole said, waking her maid to prepare her for bed. "There was a fight on the stairs: Prince de Chalais slapped Monsieur de la Frette," she said as Annabelle fumbled with her laces.

Petite heard a night watchman call out two of the clock. "Frette is often into scraps," she said. The young galant was hotheaded.

"Particularly when in drink," Nicole said, stepping out of her petticoats and slipping under the covers. Soon she was snoring.

Petite was woken the next morning by a knock at their door. She parted her bed curtains. Light was streaming in through a gap in the shutters. The two maids were already up and folding their bedding.

"Get the door," Petite heard Clorine command Annabelle, but Nicole's maid turned a deaf ear.

"I'll get it," Petite said, pulling her comforter with her. Unbolting the door, she was taken aback to see Athénaïs before her, wrapped in furs, her face paint streaked. "What's happened?" she whispered, ushering her in out of the cold.

"What hour is it?" Nicole asked groggily, sticking her head out of her bed curtains.

"There's been a duel," Athénaïs told them in a low voice, sitting down in the chair beside Nicole's narrow bed. The hem of her ball gown was edged with mud.

Mon Dieu—a duel. Duels had been outlawed and were punishable by death. Petite glanced back at the maids. They were arguing over how to fold up the bedding and appeared not to have heard.

"Because of that fight on the stairs?" Nicole asked.

Athénaïs nodded. "There were eight of them. They met out on some field in Chaillot. The Marquis de Noirmoutiers was one." At the mention of her fiancé's name, Athénaïs's voice quavered.

"Was anyone hurt?" Petite asked fearfully.

"They all were—but the Marquis d'Antin was killed." One of Athénaïs's eyes began to twitch.

"The kid with the big ears?" Nicole put her hands over her mouth.

"He was stabbed—I was there. I saw it. I saw him die."

Oh no. "What about the Marquis de Noirmoutiers?" Petite asked, reaching for her rosary.

"He's—" Athénaïs took a shaky breath. "He's wounded in one leg . . . badly." She looked at Petite and then Nicole. "He needs help," she whispered. "He needs a doctor who won't talk. I thought you might know of someone. He needs to get out of the country, and quickly."

"Of course," Nicole said—but tentatively. She glanced uneasily at Petite.

"I'll stand outside," Petite offered, understanding Nicole's discomfort. Athénaïs's fiancé would have to flee the country, hide from the law—from *Louis.* She slipped out the door, wrapped in her comforter.

She felt like an exile, shivering in the dark corridor. Soon, the door creaked open and Athénaïs appeared.

"You'll not say a word?" She pressed a ring into Petite's hand.

"I don't need that, Athénaïs," Petite said, handing the gem back. "You can trust me."

"Forgive me. I'm not myself." Athénaïs bit down on her knuckle, a high little cry escaping. "Everything's ruined."

"I'm so sorry," Petite said, wishing she could comfort the Marquise, so elegant and regal—and yet so broken.

THE DUEL WAS all anyone could talk of at Henriette's salon the next evening.

"Frette was drunk when he came down the stairs," Yeyette said.

"I heard him yell at the Prince de Chalais to get out of his way," Claude-Marie said.

"Frette's rude," Henriette said weakly, reclined on her daybed with her little dog Mimi curled up beside her.

"So of course the Prince slapped him," Yeyette concluded.

Then blows had ensued. Athénaïs's fiancé and others had joined Prince de Chalais, and others had joined Frette, and soon there were a dozen. The melee was stopped, but later, outside, a duel had been called.

"It's tragic." Petite was careful not to say too much.

Court was awash with gossip that week. All that Petite could discern with any certainty was that eight young men had gathered at dawn in an isolated field behind a monastery in the faubourg Saint-Germain, and that the Marquis d'Antin had been killed by the Chevalier d'Omale's sword. They had all been wounded, Athénaïs's fiancé the most seriously. After hiding Antin's body in some bushes, they had fled the country—some to England and some to Spain, it was whispered.

"They'll be tried anyway—*in absentia*," Yeyette said.

"Condemned to death: the law is clear."

"They'll never return," Henriette said sadly, stroking Mimi's long ears.

"That's punishment enough."

"Their poor families!" Claude-Marie exclaimed.

"The law is too harsh. They're *boys*."

"Yet duels must be stopped," the Duchesse de Navailles said.

"But to ruin so many lives?"

"His Majesty will pardon them, surely," Nicole said, joining the group.

"Surely," Petite echoed, but without conviction.

Everyone hushed when Louis entered. He looked about the room solemnly.

"Resume your diversions," he said, stone-faced and drawn.

What was he feeling? Petite wondered. He'd grown up with these eight young men, hunted and gambled with them. One or two of them had been members of Les Endormis, party to boyish pranks and mischief. Petite signaled to Louis with her fan, but he didn't notice.

"I must see His Majesty," she whispered to Gautier under her breath. Louis's trusted attendant had finally managed to secure a room in the Louvre at a discreet distance from the queens.

"Four of the clock, tomorrow afternoon."

EVEN WITH A fire blazing it was too cold to undress. Louis and Petite shivered under the fur covers fully clothed. "This weather," Louis said. He seemed drained of energy.

The winter had been brutal. There had been stories of starvation in the south, of peasants living on cabbage stalks and roots. It was whispered that seventeen thousand families had perished in Burgundy, some eating human flesh in order to survive.

"I'm sorry, my love—I just can't," he said, chagrined by his want of passion.

"I understand," Petite said, trying not to sound disappointed. Soon would begin the season of want, the forty days of Lent in which they would be abstaining. "Just hold me." She sensed he needed refuge, comfort. He'd been working hard: on financial reform, on providing food for the starving. Halls of the Louvre had been turned into storehouses for grain for the poor. In the courtyard of the Tuileries, bread was baked in huge ovens, and thousands of loaves given away every day.

And on top of all this, the tragedy of the duel. The eight young men—all from fine families—would be tried and condemned. They had found the means to flee (such was their privilege), but upon sentence of death they would never be able to set foot in the country again.

"It must be hard, Louis. They were your compatriots."

"The law must be upheld," he said. He clenched one fist, opening and closing his fingers.

"I know," Petite said. He was remote in a way she'd not seen before—this was King Louis, the man behind a mask. She put her hand on his arm, but he shook free.

On Mardi Gras, Petite was wakened by Clorine, dressed in one of Petite's gowns and fake pearls.

"You look beautiful," Petite said—although in truth the ensemble looked grotesque on Clorine's stocky form. "I should be serving you," she added, dipping into the earthen cup of bread dunked in wine. On this, the last carnival day before Lent, everything was supposed to be topsy-turvy. On this day, everyone went mad.

"I'll finish hemming your costume this afternoon," Clorine said.

Petite planned to go to the masquerade ball as Pierrot in a white tunic and pantaloons with red edging. A red velvet mask would complete the disguise.

"His Majesty sent the mask over yesterday—rimmed with little diamonds. *Real* diamonds, I think," Clorine added, rolling her eyes.

"That, I doubt," Petite said with a smile. It had taken time for Clorine to be at ease with her liaison with the King—time, the persuasive intercession of Gautier, as well as a long consultation with the King's confessor—but having at last resigned herself to the relationship, she'd taken on the roles of guardian, parent as well as spiritual adviser: plying Louis for favors, lecturing Petite on caution and insisting on rigorous prayers. After each visit, it was Clorine who insisted that Petite wash her privates with vinegar and then pray on her knees before the wood figure of the Virgin. (Petite might be a fallen woman in this world, but Clorine was resolved to do everything she could to ensure that she would not be damned in the next.)

"Listen." Clorine went to the window. A man outside was calling out the route of the fattened ox: the procession would reach the gates of the Louvre between two and three of the clock.

FROM THE PALACE balconies, members of the Court gathered to watch the parade of butchers—their wives and daughters laughably adorned in noble dress—followed by Druids leading the ox garlanded with flowers and mounted by a child dressed as Cupid. In former times, the bull would have been slaughtered right there, its blood flowing onto the courtyard cobbles. Now, in their more civilized times, the animal would be led to the slaughterhouse to be butchered and eaten by courtiers at the Mardi Gras ball later that night.

Bonbons were thrown onto the cobbles. The courtiers laughed as men, women and children in rags frantically scrambled to get them. Someone opened a bag of flour onto the crowd below and a great shout went up, followed by mirth.

Louis, standing with his mother and wife, glanced Petite's way. Petite put a gloved finger to her chin, meaning. *Later, my love.* That night, in disguise, they would be free to meet. It would be their last encounter before the long sacrifices of Lent.

That evening, Petite (dressed as Pierrot) and Nicole (as a milkmaid) helped Henriette into her costume as Claude-Marie and Yeyette sat by entertaining them with stories of pagan revelries of times past—the illicit trysts, the secret groping and meddling. The evening inevitably gave way to madness, they warned, an orgy of eating meat and sating fleshly desires, for on the morrow everyone began a regime of fasting, chastity and prayer.

The two pious queens would not be attending (of course), and had cautioned Henriette, who was close to eight months along. Philippe had even forbidden his wife from going, but Henriette could not bear the thought of missing the best ball of the year. She'd been feeling much better, she claimed, "thanks to laudanum," so her plan was to sneak in disguised in the voluminous black hooded cloak of a Domino, a common costume worn by both men and women. "My husband will never know," she said, instructing her attendants not to hover lest her entourage betray her.

Petite pulled on her mask and hung back from the others before entering the thronged ballroom, slipping in behind a party of hussars. The assembly was already a riot of loose manners, men and women gorging at a table littered with bones as footmen in velvet gowns carted in heaped platters and maids dressed as hussars ran about filling mugs of wine. Off to one side, a butcher was carving a black-roasted sheep and a heifer. The night was young, but the musicians were already playing the vigorous risqué dance called "Shaking of the Sheets," the dancers twirling like tops.

Petite made her way to one side, the better to watch—the better to look out for Louis. She saw a Domino—Henriette? she wondered. It was hard to be sure, for there were many. She was mistaken, she realized, when the figure disappeared into the shadows with a man dressed as a sultan. Taking their pleasure? It was not a night to be venturing into dark corners unannounced.

She felt someone grip her elbow.

Alarmed, Petite turned to see a tall man dressed as a master falconer. A feathered half-mask covered his eyes. "You were supposed to be a Trojan." She smiled, faint with relief.

Louis led her into a narrow passageway and pulled her into a dark chamber. She heard the sound of the bolt. "Wait," she laughed as he pulled at her clothes, found skin. She suspected he'd been drinking.

"Help me with this." He tugged at the sash that held up her costume bloomers.

"Are you sure, Louis?" If only there were a candle, a hint of light. She ran her finger down his face to his mouth, and reached for a kiss.

He thrust his tongue into her. He tasted of spirits. "Quick."

With difficulty, Petite pulled the cord free and, holding onto Louis for balance, managed to step out of the wide costume pantalons. It was cold, and the room smelled of urine. She had been longing to see him, but had not imagined it like this.

She stood in the dark, the skin on her bare arms rising up in goose bumps. She couldn't see Louis, but he was close: she could hear him breathing, hear fabric rustling. Such dark frightened her; she imagined the Devil lurking, imagined him pinching her ankles, her neck. She startled when Louis tugged on her arm.

"I put my cloak down," he whispered.

Holding onto his hand, she knelt, feeling for the cloth. "I found it," she said, lying down. Her buttocks were on the cape, but her head was on the stone floor. *This is miserable*, she thought.

Someone was trying the door, but the bolt held. "Don't worry," Louis said, lying down over her.

She wound her legs around his back. The stones cut into her spine in spite of the cape. *If I moan and thrash*, she thought, *it will be over sooner* . . . but then her moans were real.

"Mon Dieu," Louis said with a gasp as Petite convulsed. He collapsed and rolled off her. "You're a devil."

A devil. Petite lay on the floor, staring into the dark. Waves of pleasure surged through her still. A tear tickled down her cheek into her ear. She reached for Louis's hand, for reassurance. Mislove, it was called. Sinful love.

PETITE SLIPPED BACK into the ballroom alone. Still weak, she leaned against a stone pillar, watching the revelry. She recognized Nicole dancing with a big man dressed as Henry the Great.

She felt dizzy, as if she'd just emerged from a dark cave—a cave of licentious desire.

They had performed unnatural acts. He'd held her down as he spent, called her his whore. She had imagined that it was not Louis but the Devil himself . . . and yet even this had inflamed her.

La petite mort, it was called. Indeed. She had died several times over, shortening her life by a minute each time.

In the morning I will repent, pray and fast, Petite thought. *In the morning I will go to Confession*, she decided as Nicole approached. Confess to insatiable desire.

"Where have you been?" Nicole demanded gaily, slurring slightly. "It's a little early in the evening to be disappearing."

"I've been here," Petite lied, refraining from saying that it was a little early in the evening for Nicole to be so tipsy. "Have you seen Henriette?"

Nicole made mysterious wide eyes. "Well . . . Philippe is over there." She pointed to a couple dancing. "Pretty, isn't he?"

Philippe often dressed as a woman, but this ensemble was exquisite, the bodice of black silk set low at the shoulders and adorned with parchment lace. "Is that Armand de Guiche he's with?" Petite asked.

"Not exactly." Nicole pointed her fan at the Domino and sultan Petite had seen earlier. "That's Henriette . . . and that's Armand de Guiche she's with," she whispered behind her fan. "He's the sultan."

Petite was shocked—although she realized she shouldn't have been. Armand de Guiche was a regular attendee of Henriette's evening entertainments, his kohl-lined eyes following her every move.

"I've been taking their letters back and forth," Nicole confessed.

"Nicole, you already have two transgressions," Petite said with alarm. One for being drunk at Mass and the other for sneaking out after curfew. "You must stop intriguing. You're going to end up banished."

"Promise not to tell Ludmilla," Nicole said, suddenly sober.

Two DAYS LATER, Louis lay beside Petite in Gautier's chamber. It was the second day of Lent, and they had made a vow to abstain. It wasn't easy being together thus, but for Petite it was better than being apart. They chastely embraced as they talked of his son, of his horses and dogs, of the financial reforms he was attempting to make, the duel trial, Henriette's health (his concern about the quantity of laudanum she took, her high and low spirits).

"She's cheerful when Armand's around, I've noticed," he said. "Sometimes I wonder . . ."

Petite held her breath. Armand de Guiche was being dangerously open in his passion for Henriette.

"Why are you flushing?" he asked, studying her face.

"No reason." Petite smiled—falsely, she feared. She had no talent for dissembling.

"Do you know something?" he asked teasingly. "You're red as a pulpit cushion."

Petite faced the wall.

"Louise, you must tell me if you know." He turned her toward him. "Do you?" He was not teasing now.

"Louis, I can't."

"You know something—and you're not going to tell me?" He sat up. "Are you serious?"

She did not answer.

"Henriette is the King of England's sister," he said evenly. "What she does is not a private matter. It's of national concern."

"Louis, I promised I wouldn't," Petite said, not meeting his gaze.

"And this promise—to who-knows-who—is more important?" he demanded, his voice rising and his jaw muscles clenched.

Petite was dismayed. Didn't he understand?

"If you loved me, you'd tell," he said, standing, his hands on his hips.

Petite smiled, hoping to soften the mood. His voice was cold and commanding, his tone imperious—threatening even. "Of course I love you," she said, sitting on the edge of the high bed, "but I made a promise."

"You defy me?"

"I'm not defying you."

"Yet you refuse to tell me." He stood before her, his arms crossed, staring down at her. "I *command* you to tell me."

"Louis, don't be like that."

"I am *King*, Louise." He stood for a long moment staring at her, his face muscles quivering. Then—with an expletive—he banged the wall with his fist. Two framed prints fell to the floor. He kicked one, sending it flying. It shattered against the wall.

"Louis, don't!" She had never seen him give way to rage. He was always so contained, so controlled—so masked. But now, suddenly, he looked like the Devil himself. She fell to her knees and began to pray, her eyes clenched shut. *O Mary.*

"Damn you!"

She watched Louis in horror as he took up a silver candlestick and raised it—as if to strike her. "In the name of God," she whispered, instinctively cowering. The blow could kill her.

Louis threw the candlestick against the curio cabinet with all his might. Artifacts and curios fell to the floor: shells, stones, bones. He stood in the wreckage, breathing heavily. "Whore," he said under his breath, then rushed from the room, slamming the door behind him.

Petite curled up on Gautier's bed, sobbing. She didn't know what to do. Soon Gautier would return. *Mercy—the room.* Shakily, she got to her feet and began picking things up, but she was too stunned to think. How could Louis have said what he said? He might have struck her. She closed her eyes, but his angry face was always before her. He did not love her. There was no love in him. She wept again as she reached for her clothes, her silly hat-maker disguise hanging on a wooden peg next to Louis's butler cloak. He'd stormed out without a thought to caution.

The meal bell ran. Soon Gautier would come back. She put on her cloak. Thank God for the veil, the mask. She'd leave the costume—she wouldn't be needing disguises anymore.

Anymore.

Petite pressed her forehead against Louis's cloak. It smelled of cinnamon comfits. What would become of her now?

She gathered her courage and left Gautier's room, wending her way back to her chamber under the eaves, lowering her head as she passed others. At last, she arrived at her door.

"Zut!" Clorine exclaimed when Petite removed her mask. "What's wrong?"

"I'm ill," Petite said, thankful that Nicole was not there. She headed for the safety of her bed.

"You look white as curd," Clorine said worriedly.

"I just need to rest." Petite's voice broke. "I'll be fine." She flung her bed curtains closed and pressed her face into her pillow. Whore, he had called her. Dream images flooded her, one upon another: of a death mask, a swampy room, a masked figure holding a cross. She *was* a whore. The Devil was within her.

It was not yet dawn when Petite sat up in bed. She'd heard the night watchman call out six of the clock. She had not slept at all. In an hour or so the sun would rise, and the world with it.

She sat on the edge of her bed for a moment, waiting for her eyes to adjust, waiting until she could make out the three sleeping forms, dimly illuminated by the light of the night candle. The night before, she'd heard the maids making up their beds, heard Nicole stumbling in from the gaming tables, heard Clorine setting the door and shutter locks, then parting Petite's curtains to look in at her, heard her worried sigh.

Outside, a dog was barking and a rooster crowed. Shivering, clenching her jaw to keep her teeth from chattering, she put on the clothes Clorine had set out: a chemise, a bodice, two petticoats, a skirt, thick wool stockings. As quietly as she could, she took her hooded cloak down off the peg. She grabbed her boots and tucked them under one arm. She felt for a taper in the basket on the shelf and knelt to flame it on the embers. Nicole snorted in her sleep and turned, mumbling. Silently, Petite unbolted the door and crept out.

In the dark passage, Petite set the taper in the tin wall sconce and put on her boots, fumbling with the buckles, her fingers numb with cold. She felt for her wool mitts in the sleeve of her cloak and, after a few poor attempts, managed to get them on properly. Clasping the candle first with one hand and then the other, blowing on her mitts to warm her fingers with her breath, she headed down the passage to a stairwell that opened onto the garden. It was bolted, but from within, and unguarded.

There was a guard at the garden gate, however. She'd not thought to bring her identification papers, her pass, so she lied, telling the sleepy attendant that she served Madame Henriette and that the Princess had a sudden hunger for the gingerbread and liquorice-water sold by a vendor in the market. "You know how it is when a woman nears childbed."

"But it's not yet dawn," he said, holding a torch to her face.

"The Princess never sleeps," she said with a sigh. He was young, just a boy.

"You should have a footman with you. It isn't safe."

"It's not far," Petite assured him. "Let me through. I must hurry."

"Take my dog with you." He whistled, and a mastiff appeared, yawning.

"If you insist," Petite said uncertainly.

She took the dog's lead, and the guard opened the gate. "Thank you," she said, and headed down the narrow cobbled street, still littered from the Mardi Gras revelries. At the first corner, she let the dog go free, shooing him back to the palace. Then, holding her candle before her, tipping it so that it did not drip candle grease onto her mitt, she headed for the river.

As she neared the water, she stopped, overcome with sobs. She stumbled, unable to see. *Whore.*

The sky was lightening; the surface of the river shimmered pink, flecked by the rising sun. She blew out the candle. There weren't many boats out yet. Charred bits of wood floated on the surface. Gulls cried, circling above.

Chapter Twenty-Four

THE PRIORESS HURRIED into the convent courtyard, nearly slipping on the icy cobblestones. Who could be ringing at such an hour? She prayed it was not a drunken reveler. It was annoying to tend the gate, but the lay nun charged with the task was ill, yet again, with an ague. The ring of keys shook like a tambourine in her hand as she opened the first lock and then a second. She paused to pull her veil down over her face and cracked open the heavy gate, taking care—on pain of excommunication—not to touch the threshold.

"Mary," she exclaimed, startled to see a young woman of the nobility before her, splatter-dashed with mud. How old was she? she wondered. Even yet twenty? It was difficult to tell.

"Mother, I beg you, may I enter?"

Her voice was soft, her enunciation refined, but with a hint of the land to the south. Golden curls flew out in wisps around her waiflike face, which was unadorned, without paint or patches. Her red-rimmed eyes were those of an innocent—luminous.

The Prioress opened the gate enough for the young woman to come through, then pushed it closed and double-locked it. "You're chilled," she said, taking her by the elbow lest she fall. The hem of her cloak appeared wet, and her boots—one with a thick raised sole—were covered with mud. "Where have you been?"

"I've come from the city," the young woman said. Her breath was coming in gasps.

"All that way on foot? Glory—you're shaking like a leaf." There was no hint of liquor on her, so it wasn't that.

In moments, the Prioress had her settled on a wood bench in the parlor. "I'll have a trencher and small beer brought to you," she said, stoking the fire.

"No, thank you. I will be fine," the young woman said, then slumped to the floor in a dead faint.

HOURS LATER, THE Prioress made her way through the various chambers and along the inner courtyard to the reception chamber. It was not even prime, and already it had been a busy morning: Ash Wednesday rituals, the girl falling unconscious in the parlor and now—she'd been informed—a man demanding entrance.

The hinges of the shutter covering the grille squeaked as she opened it. "*Adoremus in eternum,*" she intoned to the tall young man wrapped in a gray cloak.

"*Sanctissimum sacramentum,*" he answered, awkwardly sitting on the little cushioned bench in front of the grille, his spurs catching on the fabric. His hazel eyes were dark with emotion.

The Prioress studied his face, his proud hooked nose and high cheekbones. An unusually comely man, tall and broad-shouldered, he was clearly of the noble race. Where had she seen him before? "I understand you demand entry, Monsieur, regarding a young woman in our care." She had fallen into a trance, an insensible swoon, and looked to be more dead than alive. They'd tried giving her syrup of dry roses, an excellent cordial against tremblings of the heart, but without success. If she didn't waken before terce, they would send for the priest. "We don't allow men entry." Especially on Ash Wednesday.

"I am the King."

She tried not to scoff.

"I am the *King*," he repeated with passion, "and if you don't allow me in to see her, I will have this convent destroyed."

Mon Dieu, she thought. *He is the King.* She recognized him now. Years ago she had seen him touch the sick, cure hundreds of the Evil. She crossed herself, bowing her head. "The young woman, Your Majesty, she's—" She paused to catch her breath. "Insensible," she warned, opening the door and leading the way into the visitors' parlor, still bone-chilling cold in spite of a crackling fire.

The young woman was as they had left her, lying stretched out on the floor. The Prioress and two of the nuns had considered moving her onto the bench, but decided it best to make her comfortable where she lay, taking off her wet boots and stockings, and wrapping her in fur and woolen comforters.

The King fell to his knees. "Louise," he whispered, touching her hand.

She opened her eyes.

Thank the Lord, she's alive, the Prioress thought. She looked like a wounded angel, her curls spread out on the wax-greased floor—but she was no angel, the Prioress knew, to judge by the King's treasuring words. Hurriedly, she withdrew behind the grille, chanting the rosary to keep out the sounds.

PETITE FELT RELIEF, then alarm. Louis was with her—but where was she? What had happened?

Something.

She tried to sit up, but she was too weak.

"Don't," Louis said.

Why was he crying?

And then it came back to her in dreamlike fragments: their fight, the *water*. "What happened?" she asked, clasping his warm hand, pressing it to her cheek.

"I'm not sure." Louis looked up at the ceiling. Took a shaky breath. "You don't know?"

"Is this a convent?" she asked, looking around. They were in a small chamber with a stone statue of Christ on the cross at one end and a fireplace at the other. Biblical tapestries hung on the stone walls. There was only one small window, high up and barred. She closed her eyes against tears. "I tried . . . I tried . . ." she stuttered, her breathing coming in gasps.

"Hush," Louis said with tenderness. He took her in his arms.

Slowly, very slowly, she returned to the world. They sat huddled for a time by the fire as her socks and boots dried.

"I would never strike you," Louis said, repentant of his rage. "And I'm sorry . . . about what I called you. I love you."

Petite looked away, her eyes filling. *Whore.* She could forgive him—but could she ever forget? "I made a vow to secrecy, Louis, and I had to honor it. To do otherwise would have been a sin."

"There can be no secrets between us."

Petite thought about this. "I wish you weren't King," she said, her head on his shoulder. The nuns could be heard singing in choir.

"But I am, and I must know what is going on at Court. It can be no other way."

Petite stirred the embers with an iron. She loved Louis with all her heart—but she did not love the King. How could she live with both? "I love you."

Louis placed two small birch logs on the bed of glowing embers. The paper-thin bark flared and sparked. "Then you must choose," he said sadly.

Petite looked into his eyes, his soft hazel eyes so full of feeling. She saw traces of his tears—his love—but she saw his resolve as well. He *was* King. She had to accept that. "I choose you," she said quietly, holding her palms to the flames for warmth.

PETITE'S CARRIAGE JOLTED forward. She leaned back against the hard leather seat. She was still quite weak, overcome with fatigue. Louis had kissed her, promised the Prioress a generous compensation (the price of her silence), ordered a coach to take Petite back to the Palais Royale and then left, spurring his horse into a full-out gallop, his cape billowing out behind him.

Petite pulled her cloak closely around her. She had broken her promise and told Louis what she knew. There was no other way: she saw that now. She'd been naive. He was the King, after all. The security of the realm rested on his shoulders.

The sun was well up, the water congested with boats.

The water . . .

What had happened? She remembered looking down at the river, longing for relief, for sleep. But then . . . ?

And then all that she could recall was lying on the bank in the cold mud, her boots and the hem of her cloak soaked through. She had a faint recollection of a woman singing, and a horse's scream. A chill went through her. She remembered sitting up, dazed. She remembered looking for hoof marks in the mud—but of course there were hoof marks everywhere.

Tears started to come again. *Gone to the river.* What did it mean? And then she recalled: it had been said of a man who had used bone magic, lost his senses. Long ago. Men who used bone magic went lunatic—"gone to the river," it was said.

But what of girls? What of a girl who had used the magic—a child?

Petite lowered the leather covering so that she could not see the water. She closed her eyes, lulled by the rumbling sound of the wagon wheels on the cobbles, the clip-clop of horses' hooves. *O Mary . . .*

IT WAS DRIZZLING rain by the time Petite's coach pulled up in front of the Palais Royale. She gathered the hood of her cloak up over her head and alighted, heading quickly for the stairwell that led to the servants' wing.

Clorine cried out when Petite pushed open the door to her room. "Dieu merci," she exclaimed, then burst into tears. "I've been looking everywhere for you, Mademoiselle," she said angrily.

"I'm sorry," Petite said. "Where's Nicole?" Her trunk wasn't against the wall and her pomade jars, ribbons and pins had been cleared from the little table by the chimney.

"Banished. She even took that useless maid with her," Clorine said, "thanks be to Mary. But she left you this." She handed Petite a rolled-up length of rag paper.

My dear friend, I've been found out. Princess Henriette won't even speak to me—after all I did for her! I think that cow Yeyette snitched. I'm being banished from Court and will be locked away in some musty convent for good measure—in the south, I hope, where at least it will be warm. You were right—I should have listened.

Your friend, Nicole

P.S. Keep an eye on our Goddess of Virginity. Dead Antin's brother has been sniffing at her like a shit-nosed hound.
P.P.S. I overheard la Grande Mademoiselle saying that Princess Marguerite has had a baby (or two?) and that her Tuscan husband is a beast. Poor dear.

Petite sat on a stool as Clorine unbuckled her muddy boots. She felt sick with remorse.

"If you don't mind, I'd like to take her bed," Clorine said.

"I'm going to miss Nicole," Petite said.

"Zut. Are you serious? We haven't had a good night's sleep in months. Let me get you into a clean gown. Madame has summoned you."

HENRIETTE SENT THE servants out of the room as soon as Petite appeared. "Well," she said, lowering herself slowly onto a wide divan. But for her hard, protruding bulge she was stick thin. "You told the King," she said accusingly. "The King who just happens to be your *lover*," she added with contempt. "Quelle surprise." She'd been crying too.

"I'm sorry, Your Highness." Petite lowered her head. So, now Henriette knew. "I had to."

"My husband must never find out," Henriette said, her hands over her belly.

"I know." Pretty Philippe, who would not kill a bird, could be cruel in his jealous contempt for his wife.

"His Majesty has forced my hand. I must give Armand up." Henriette's voice quavered in speaking her lover's name. She took a sharp breath. "Mademoiselle de Montalais has been banished, of course."

"Nicole is innocent of wrong," Petite protested.

"None of us are innocent," Henriette said wearily, her tone that of a much older woman. "And particularly Nicole, as you no doubt know," she added. "The King was none too pleased by her role as . . . matchmaker, shall we say? And certainly she should never have told *you*."

"She vowed me to silence," Petite persisted.

"As I vowed her. She's deceptive by nature, given to schemes and intrigue. Time locked away in a convent may even be for the best. And in any case, the King has spoken and there is nothing more to be done."

Petite's eyes stung with tears. There would be no imploring Louis, she knew, no way to protest. She knew the rules, and she had made her choice.

"Plus," Henriette said sharply, her voice bitter, "in addition to giving up *my* beloved, I must keep *you* on as my attendant"—she stood, walking the length of the room, her arms crossed tightly, her hands gripping her sleeves—"so that His Majesty can have *his* secret pleasure."

She turned to face Petite, her eyes red-rimmed, her neck flushed. "I ask you: do you not find that ironic?" With abrupt passion, she swept the pomade jars off her toilette table. One shattered, filling the air with the aroma of Hungary water. "I hate this stinking world!"

"I'm so sorry, Your Highness," Petite said with feeling, falling to her knees. It was said that Court was a country where the joys were visible but false, and the sorrows hidden but real. "I understand your torment." She shared it.

Petite felt Henriette's finger lightly tap her shoulder. "Rise, Mademoiselle," the Princess said.

Awkwardly, wiping her wet cheeks with her sleeve, Petite got to her feet.

"It won't do, you know, for the King's paramour to grovel." Henriette smiled sadly. "You're going to have to be stronger."

Chapter Twenty-Five

As the leaves of the chestnut trees unfurled, Henriette went into childbed. Her doctors feared she would die. After two days of pain, she gave birth to a weak baby girl. "Throw her in the river," the Princess cried out in her rage. Only a girl, after all that. Two weeks later, she uprised, churched, and was ready to entertain.

It was May now, after all, the old "Joy Month." Court festivities continued unabated in spite of duels and infidelities, tragedies and scandal. Nicole disappeared without a trace into a convent somewhere in the south. The duelists—including Athénaïs's intended—disappeared into foreign realms. And the Court? The King and his courtiers disappeared into the wilds, hunting, hawking and riding.

The Court returned to Paris in June to find preparations underway for the next grand event. In the quadrangle between the Louvre and the Tuileries, where the bread ovens for the hungry had been not long before, stands were being constructed to hold five thousand spectators. The city was now enlivened: the people had survived a famine and escaped the Plague. The weather had turned fine: crops were growing and money was flowing once again. Their Spanish queen had birthed a healthy baby boy: the Dauphin was now six months old and thriving. There was cause for celebration.

Heralds were sent out to announce a tournament in honor of the King's fat son. Foreigners filled the city as news spread that the King himself would compete. In the evenings, men arrived at the salons complaining of sore muscles and smelling of the stable. Everyone was in a state of excitement, talking of armor and horses, anticipating an old-fashioned carousel with tilting at the ring and chariot races, dancing bears and chattering monkeys.

"Just like in days of old," Henriette said in an effervescent rapture. "Just like in the celebrated days of King Henry II," she added (for she'd been studying her French history).

King Henry's tragic death by jousting had spelled the end of the grand tournaments, and Louis was intent on bringing back shows of bravura—safer, of course (jousting contestants would aim their long lances at rings now, not at each other), but every bit as thrilling.

"His Majesty has been practicing with a lance," Henriette said, her dog Mimi under one arm.

"I saw him yesterday morning, Madame," a new maid of honor said. "He missed one ring, but got another."

"And he's taking lessons every day in tumbling," Yeyette said. "Monsieur Lauzun told me."

"So I've heard," Petite said (without flushing), and Henriette nodded approvingly.

When the day finally came, the Queen and Queen Mother took their places under a gold and purple velvet canopy set up in front of the arena on the east side of the Tuileries. Petite sat with Athénaïs in the section reserved for the maids of honor, listening to the excited chatter, women talking of their husbands, fathers, lovers and brothers. The ladies laughed sharing stories of helping out with the men's costumes, the frantic and inevitable search for lost items, the last-minute changes. They talked of special diets, sleepless nights, how best to soothe riding sores. They talked of giving their loved ones a scarf to wear, just like in the days of chivalry.

"And who, might I ask, is carrying your scarf?" Athénaïs whispered to Petite.

"No one," Petite lied, wondering how much Athénaïs knew. At Louis's insistence, Henriette had been careful about keeping silence, but many were suspicious, nonetheless. Fortunately, the Queen was not one of them (it was impossible for her to believe that the King could love a woman of such inferior nobility).

"See that man down there?" Athénaïs pointed her fan at a tall cavalier in ancient armor, riding a stubby mare. "That's the Marquis de Montespan, brother of the young man who was killed in the duel."

Five months had passed since the tragic affair that had spelled the death of Henry d'Antin and the ruin of so many others, including Athénaïs's fiancé, the Marquis de Noirmoutiers.

"And that's *my* scarf he's got tied to his lance," Athénaïs said, "although it's not what you think. He took it from me. He's horribly persistent. Flattering, I suppose, but somewhat disconcerting."

A clang of cymbals and a blast of trumpets announced the opening procession: mounted pages in gold-embroidered tunics and squires in Roman dress were followed by the King's two equerries, one carrying his lance and the other his shield, emblazoned with an image of the sun.

Petite's heart swelled to see Louis appear riding a chestnut stallion at the head of a Roman squadron. Dressed as Emperor of Rome, he looked afire with diamonds (tiny tin mirrors, Petite knew). His spirited horse's gold-embroidered harness threw off sparks of light. Even his leather ankle boots were gilded and the sword at his side covered with "gems."

"The Sun King!" someone called out, and people cheered. Several times that winter Louis had danced the part of the Sun God Apollo, and the nickname had become popular.

"Mon Dieu, it's enough to make a girl faint just to look at him," a young woman exclaimed, violently fanning herself.

Indeed, Petite thought pridefully.

Louis's silver helmet was covered with gold leaves and crested with flowing scarlet plumes. He looked out over the crowd, searching the faces of the ladies under the velvet canopy—searching for her, Petite knew. She waved her lace shawl, hoping he would notice, but everyone, it seemed, was waving something.

Four heralds trumpeted: *may the games begin.*

What a show! The spectators grew hoarse cheering. Their shoulders ached from waving colorful scarves, pennants, flags, inflated pig bladders. One of the best moments was the Course of Heads, a contest rarely seen. Solemnly, a row of paste "heads" was set up along a barrier: several Turks, two Indians and a Medusa and other monsters from antiquity. Louis entered, first galloping at the heads with a lance, and then with a javelin, and then with a sword. The cheers turned to a stunned silence as, one by one, he mowed down all sixteen.

During the tilting at the ring, Petite recognized Jean. "I think that's my brother," she told Athénaïs. "It's my father's suit of armor he's wearing."

The horseman charged the post at full speed, piercing the ring with his lance. A cheer went up. He circled the arena, his visor up. "It is him!" Petite yelled to get

Jean's attention, but she could not make herself heard over the crowd.

She climbed down the crude wood benches and circled round to the back of the arena where a military tent had been set up for the knights. She hovered with the crowd that stood waiting in hopes of seeing the King or some illustrious Court personality emerge. She recognized Lauzun and ran to catch up with him.

"My brother is in there," she said. "Could you go get him for me?"

"Do you know how many men are in there? And all of them dripping with sweat," Lauzun said with mock disgust.

"I haven't seen my brother in over a year. I didn't know he was coming to Paris. He's with Tellier's men, wearing black chain mail and an old-style helmet, but with a visor. No breast plate, just a leather cuirass."

Reluctantly, fingers comically to his nose, Lauzun turned back toward the tent.

Jean emerged shortly after, drenched. "Michel de Tellier dumped a bucket over me," he said with a laugh, wiping his face with his sleeve. "If he weren't son of the war minister, I'd thrash him. Come, I'm dying of thirst. I know a watering hole not far from here."

The "watering hole" was for men only, of course, so Petite waited by the river while Jean downed a mug or two of beer. "That's better," he said, joining her. "Michel and I were in there last night. The stories he tells!" He offered his arm to Petite as they strolled along the river. "He's the one who told me about the tournament—it was his idea, you know—and suggested I come up for it." He picked up a rock and threw it at a duck floating on the water, but missed. The duck dove, surfacing by a laundry boat. "Michel is a friend of the King, so he knows what's going on. He told me the King is putting together a company of light horse for the Dauphin."

Petite nodded. It was no secret: everyone knew about it. "The positions are going to high-ranking veterans," she said.

"But with his pull, Michel thinks I might have a chance," Jean said, throwing another rock, and hitting the duck this time.

"That would be wonderful," Petite said, but knowing that Michel de Tellier had little influence with Louis.

"Speaking of the mighty, did you know Minister Fouquet?" she added.

"Everybody at Court knew him. Mother said you guarded him at Amboise."

Jean laughed. "What a complainer. He expected a feather bed, rose water in his wash basin. Rose water—in a prison?" He paused. "You know, there was the strangest rumor going around: people said that Fouquet tried to bribe you because he'd found out that you were 'close' to the King."

"There are lots of rumors at Court, Jean."

"Of course that's ridiculous. The King can have any woman at Court he wants."

Petite picked up a flat stone and skipped it across, three jumps.

That afternoon, Louis was distant with Petite. He lay beside her on Gautier's bed, staring at the ceiling.

"What's wrong?" Petite finally asked, slipping a hand under his shirt. It was unlike him not to embrace her hungrily. "You usually ravish me," she said teasingly.

He exhaled. "I saw you cheering someone during the tournament."

"I was cheering for you."

"This was at tilting at the ring. You were cheering a man on Tellier's team." He sounded miffed.

"Oh—my brother Jean," Petite said with a smile. "I was surprised to see him here in Paris. You weren't jealous, were you?" she asked, incredulous.

"You were cheering with such passion. I was watching you."

"He got the ring on the first pass," Petite said proudly, laying her head on his broad shoulder. "Don't you know how much I love you?"

He kissed her passionately—but all the while she was thinking, *Why don't I just ask?* It pleased Louis to help, she knew. He was a generous man.

"And?" he said, drawing back, sensing her detachment.

She sighed. "It's to do with the light horse brigade you're putting together—for the Dauphin? My brother is truly a wonderful horseman, Louis, and he'd—"

"Thy will be done," Louis said with a smile, loosening her laces.

It was winter when Jean moved back to Paris to take up his new position. "Imagine, the rank of cornette," Françoise said, fanning herself in spite of the chill.

"Congratu—" the old Marquis sputtered. He'd shrunk over time.

"Congratulations." Petite raised a glass to her brother. He looked splendid in his new uniform, a red coat with silver lace edging and a silver-edged bandolier to match. She had helped Louis with the design.

"I always knew you'd go far, Jean," Françoise said.

"In truth, I owe this to my friend Michel de Tellier," Jean said, "the war minister's son."

"That was kind of him," Petite said, dissembling her surprise. Michel de Tellier had had nothing to do with her brother's promotion

"And imagine: a pension of four thousand livres," Françoise said incredulously. "Now we'll finally be able to save toward your sister's dowry."

"I have a few prospects in mind," Jean said.

"Good," Petite said, fainthearted.

ON EASTER SUNDAY, Jean stopped Petite at the stairwell entrance to Madame's suite. "I have to talk to you," he said, taking her by the elbow and steering her toward the porticoes outside.

"I don't have a wrap," Petite said. Her shawl was summer-weight. "Or boots." The weather was cool still, and wet.

"Why didn't you tell me?" he hissed.

Petite studied his eyes. He knew.

"I finally got around to going to Michel de Tellier to thank him for the promotion, and—what a surprise—he said he had nothing whatsoever to do with it. And then he told me the truth."

Petite looked away, her heart jumping about like a rabbit on the chase. All her childhood, her mother had lectured her on the importance of chastity. "I'm sorry."

Jean laughed.

Petite looked up at him: why was he smiling?

"Have you any idea what position this puts me in?" he asked, cocking his hat.

Petite put her hand on his arm. "Jean, it's not like that."

"Not like what? We're talking about the *King*."

"Be careful what you say," Petite said in a low voice, noticing Athénaïs on the arm of her new husband, the persistent Marquis de Montespan.

"Listen: I'm head of our family. Don't think I don't understand the ramifications. You've been sullied—that doesn't come free."

"I'm serious, Jean," Petite said, offended by his attitude.

"I guess I don't need to find a husband for you now. Mother's constantly onto me about it. She's driving me crazy."

"Jean, if you value your new position, I advise you to listen to what I'm saying," Petite said, taking care not to raise her voice. "*Nobody* must know." She glanced over her shoulder. "Especially Mother. She'd tell the Marquis, and then . . ."

And then the world would know.

ALL THAT HOLY Season, Petite prayed for her courses to come. Despite their abandon, she and Louis had been careful—most of the time.

Perhaps royal seed is different, she thought as days turned to weeks. Then, after the Feast of the Ascension, she upheaved, and at Pentecost, Clorine had to loosen her corset laces.

"You shouldn't be riding," her maid scolded, clucking with concern.

Petite felt a sick despair, but at the same time she could not help but think that it was a most wonderful thing. Their seeds had mingled. She was carrying his child.

LOUIS LOOKED AT Petite in amazement. "Truly?"

Petite nodded, smiling uneasily. She had put off telling him. Everything would change now; nothing would be the same.

He embraced her carefully, as if she might break.

"What are we going to do?" she asked.

He seemed strangely at a loss. "My mother must not find out."

"Or the Queen," Petite said, chagrined that the Queen Mother was more of a concern than his wife.

"Or the Queen," Louis echoed with a wince. He sat Petite down beside him and took her hand.

"I'll talk to Colbert tonight."

Petite was taken aback. Monsieur Colbert was Louis's new minister of finance, a humorless, dutiful man who kept lists.

"His wife is about to have their fifth child. He'll know what to do."

"Louis—" Petite paused, collecting her thoughts. She'd had a daydream—a foolish one, she knew—of living in a little cottage in the woods at Versaie, raising the baby herself. She could be happy with a simple life. "Is there no way that I could . . . keep the child? I'm serious," she said, in response to his look of alarm.

"You know that's not possible, Louise."

"But why?" This was not how she'd imagined the conversation would go.

He opened his hands in frustration. "You don't understand the dangers. This isn't just any child. You'd be found out, and the baby—" He shook his head. "He could be spirited away."

He. Petite smiled. They would have a son; she thought so too.

"Listen to me." Louis took both her hands in his.

Petite watched him solemnly.

He looked up at the ceiling, as if the words he was seeking were there. "The blood of a prince is believed to have magical qualities. It's only a superstition, of course—but that doesn't make it less powerful. People believe what they will."

Petite nodded. She was saddened to hear Louis say that it was only a superstition. She wondered about the other beliefs.

"Even your birth secretions will have to be guarded," he went on. "The afterburthen can be sold for a high price. It's disgusting, but it happens. One learns to be realistic."

Petite recalled the care that had had to be taken with the Queen's placenta.

"So, you see? It's just not possible for you to keep the baby. He must be carefully hidden away." He opened his arms. "You're not to worry: Monsieur Colbert will find a good home for him . . . and a house for you," Petite heard him say as he stroked her hair. A hideaway for her confinement. "I'll see to it that you have everything you need."

Everything you need . . .

Petite listened to the beating of Louis's heart.

She needed *him*—now more than ever. She'd half imagined that Louis was immortal, but now she couldn't afford that luxury. Now there was too much at stake.

She looked up at him. "What would become of me if you were to die?" Or be killed: the common fate of kings. Without Louis, she'd be at the mercy of the queens.

He smiled. "Are you plotting?"

"I'm serious."

He frowned in thought. "Your brother needs a rich wife," he said finally. "That way, you will always be taken care of—no matter what happens to me."

"Nothing's going to happen to you," Petite said with quiet passion, keeping the Devil at bay.

Chapter Twenty-Six

THE WEDDING TOOK PLACE at the Church of the Assumption. Over sixty of the most noble men and women of France were to be present—even the King, even the Queen, even the Queen Mother. The bride's family had insisted.

Petite took her place beside her mother and stepfather in the chairs of crimson velvet set in front of the pews.

"Soon it will be you," Françoise whispered in a consoling tone as Jean and his bride advanced to the high altar.

Petite bowed her head at the sound of the organ. The statue of the Virgin stood before her, glowing in the light of six massive candles. She felt light-headed, fatigued to her core. She was three months along now, and she recalled women saying that it was hardest at the first. The air reeked with the sweet scent of the flowers that had been strewn in the bride's path. *With child.* She would never marry, never wear the bridal wreath.

Jean, well shaved and dressed in military attire, rocked on his heels nervously beside his bride. Gabrielle Glé, a plump brunette with a cupid mouth, stood stiffly encased in white satin, a high ruff extending up to her ears. A wreath of tiny pink roses sat atop her dark curls.

"She is comely," Françoise said, fussing with the gauze shawl Petite had given her the year before.

Petite nodded, watching as Gabrielle Glé bowed her head for the priest's blessing. Privy to the secret—a secret the family had vowed to keep (on pain of exclusion from all material benefits)—they had bargained hard with Louis, demanding that the Vallière property near Reugny be designated a Marquisate (giving Jean the title Marquis), that Jean be named captain-lieutenant of the Dauphin's Light

258

Horse, that Gabrielle herself be made maid of honor to the Queen and given the privilege of sitting at the head table with the royal family as well as the right to ride in the royal coach.

"And so rich," Françoise said with awe. "She has three country manors. Jean is going to take me to visit each one of them."

Petite nodded. She and Jean had thought it wise for their mother to be out of Paris until after Petite's baby was born.

"And each one *furnished*," her mother went on.

Petite put a finger to her lips. She could feel the dagger eyes of the courtiers in the pews behind. Envy was a lethal emotion at Court. Louis had bestowed his royal beneficence on the Vallière family. She knew that the puzzled courtiers would be trying to figure out how this had come about. Why would Gabrielle Glé de la Cotardais—noble, beautiful, young (seventeen), and rich (worth forty thousand livres a year) give her hand to a nobody?

Jean and his bride knelt at the altar as the priest intoned benedictions and prayers.

"But then, Jean is charming and handsome. Who can resist him?"

"Hush, Mother." Petite inclined her head toward the crowd of courtiers behind.

"Why should I care?" Françoise said, tipping up her chin. "We're richer than most of them now—thanks to Jean."

Petite glanced up to see Louis and the Queen taking their seats in the tribune above. She thought with sick apprehension of the baby she was carrying. The sooner she went into hiding, the better.

PETITE WAS QUITE FAR along by the time Monsieur Colbert, the new minister of finance, managed to find her a hideaway. He'd been busy, he explained, preoccupied by the responsibilities of his new position.

Petite sympathized, but it had become increasingly difficult to hide her condition. Clorine laced her painfully tight, and the bone-chilling cold allowed her to wear layers of heavy woolens, but even so she feared discovery. It had helped that Henriette (at Louis's command) provided a cover—enlisting Petite to perform the quieter tasks, not asking her to perform in her ballets, and, ultimately, letting everyone know that she was giving her maid of honor leave for reasons of health—but the time, "her" time, was drawing near. She was greatly relieved when, at last, a house was secured.

"Two floors, twenty-four paces long, eight wide," Monsieur Colbert said, unlocking the door to the Hôtel Brion. "Small, but sufficient."

Petite entered, followed by Clorine. The entry was basic, it pleased her, and the location, looking onto the park of the Palais Royale, was excellent, hidden yet close. Louis would be able to see her often.

"Guard room and kitchen are on the ground floor," Monsieur Colbert said, leading Petite up a circular stair. "There are four chambers for domestics beyond the kitchen, but your personal maid will have a chamber near you, on the floor above."

The sitting room was bright, looking down upon the garden on one side and a small courtyard on the other. The furnishings were opulent, the chairs gilded, the lemon-yellow damask curtains tasseled and fringed. A bookshelf was filled with classics: Aristophanes, Homer, Plutarch.

"Cardinal Richelieu used this little house as his library," Colbert said, breathless from the climb up the stairs. "Hence all the shelves."

The sitting room was lined with books. A handsome white marble figure of a horse was used as a bookend. Petite touched its cool, smooth surface. *Diablo*, she thought with sorrow: for her lost youth.

She ran her hand over the spines of the tooled leather covers. She was not due for two months, so she would have time to read. "There's even a set of Virgil," she said. Abbé Patin would have been pleased, she thought, recalling his lessons at Blois when she was a girl. She wondered where Abbé Patin was now, and then shame filled her, thinking of where she herself was now, and why.

A large rosewood and ivory lute—a theorbo with a long neck—was set on a stand in a corner, a guitar propped beside it. Notation for a duet by Robert de Visée was on a stand. Petite ran a finger over the theorbo's many strings. Later, she would tune it.

"His Majesty thought he would like to practice here with you. The guitar was made by Checchucci of Livorno in the reign of Henry the Great. His Majesty selected it for you himself."

The slender instrument had a vaulted rosewood back with ebony fluted ribs. The peg box, circled in ebony, opened into a layered rosette. Petite strummed the gut strings; the tones were rich, resonating.

"Fit for a king," Colbert said matter-of-factly, opening the door to the bedchamber.

A gold perfume burner, set on a tripod in one corner, scented the air with attar of rose. Petite could see elm trees through the window facing the massive poster bed. *Our child will be born in this room,* Petite thought, feeling the baby stir.

Clorine pushed open the double doors to the dressing room. A small basin on claw-and-ball feet was set on the black and white marble floor.

"For washing feet," Colbert explained, pushing open a door to a small chamber. "And this is your maid's room."

"Zut." Clorine had never had a room of her own.

"It's lovely, Monsieur Colbert," Petite said, following the minister of finance back into the sitting room. She lowered herself onto the chaise longue, her hand on her corseted belly. A fire had been lit to ward off the fall chill. "You've gone to such trouble."

Monsieur Colbert had been nicknamed "The North" by the courtiers because of his cold demeanor, but Petite found his manner refreshingly direct. He was from the mercantile class—his grandfather had been in trade, a cloth merchant— yet she respected him.

"My wife helped me," the finance minister said, pacing, his hands clasped behind his back. "The brocades and linens are of the finest quality."

"His Majesty will be pleased," Petite assured him.

There was a pounding at the door on the ground floor. "It's likely the men with your belongings," Monsieur Colbert said as Clorine headed down the stairs. "I suggest you withdraw from view," he told Petite. "One of the movers might recognize you."

Petite found the necessary closet in the dressing room. She sat perched on the seat, listening to the sound of men grunting. A few minutes later there was silence.

"You can come out now," Clorine said through the slatted door. "Monsieur Colbert left with the movers."

"Did they bring everything?" Petite asked, emerging.

"Even the dirty laundry," Clorine said. She was going through Petite's trunk.

Petite saw, with relief, the statue of the Virgin and her keepsake box. She looped her rosary around the Virgin and set it on the prie-dieu. "I'm famished," she said, opening the keepsake box and taking out the branch (only two leaves on it now). She wedged it into the frame of a mirror.

"Monsieur Colbert said his wife will be back in one hour with a cook. In the morning one of his maids will come with more linens. She's to be our chambermaid."

A staff: Petite now had servants to manage. She would have to make sure that they didn't drink or gamble and that they said their prayers. She winced, realizing that she was hardly in any condition to insist on the religious piety of others.

Madame Colbert arrived promptly. Petite waited upstairs as the finance minister's wife installed the cook in the rooms below. Petite was not to be introduced, she'd been informed. Only Clorine and the chambermaid would ever be allowed to actually see "Mademoiselle du Canard," the consort of a noble who would always arrive masked.

"There now," Madame Colbert exclaimed, as breathless after climbing the stairs as her husband had been. "The cook's nothing to look at, but she appears to know the pots from the pans, so I doubt that she'll poison you." The finance minister's wife was a short, round woman adorned with frivolous gewgaws. The daughter of a wealthy family from the Tours region, she still spoke with a Touraine accent.

"I remember meeting you at Blois," Petite said. "Long ago, during one of la Grande Mademoiselle's visits." It had been quite early on, during Petite's first Easter there.

"Were you the skinny little girl with a limp?" Madame Colbert gave Petite a warm embrace. Her cheek was creamy soft.

"Has Colby explained everything? He can be a bit terse."

Petite couldn't imagine this outgoing woman in the embrace of the stern finance minister, yet they'd produced five children, the eldest thirteen and the youngest only a few months old. "He told me you were a big help."

"I do what I can. He works sixteen hours a day, every day of the week, even feast days."

"The King speaks highly of him." The honest, hardworking and frugal new finance minister was performing miracles—creating a new Rome, it was said, without the corrupt dealings of the past.

"It's a wonder he's had time to give me any children at all." Madame Colbert chortled. "So he leaves the fiddle-faddle to me."

Petite stood at the window. The sky was gray and a cold drizzle was falling.

Louis had gone to Saint-Germain-en-Laye to make the rounds with his keepers in preparation for a fall battue. In Paris, he became restless. She was growing accustomed to his moods.

"You'll be happy to know that Monsieur and Madame Beauchamp, a couple who have been in our employ for some time, have agreed to look after the baby."

Petite, heart heavy, pulled the drapes against the cold and returned to her guest. "Do they know?" That they would be caring for the King's child?

"Of course not! *Nobody* must know. His Majesty made that very clear. Colby told them that his brother's fiancée had found herself in a delicate condition, and that the family was under obligation to look after the child. As soon as your pains begin, a courier will be sent to alert them. They live in the parish of Saint-Leu, out near porte Saint-Denis. Their rooms are not far from the church."

Petite put down her dish of tea, lest it spill. She had come to accept that the child would never be hers, but she hadn't realized that he would be taken from her immediately. She recalled the stories she'd been told of the various mistresses of the kings of times past: Diane de Poitiers, mistress to King Henry II; Agnès Sorel, mistress to Charles VII; Gabrielle d'Estrées, mistress to Henry IV. Perhaps they too had had to hide away, give up their babies. Petite felt a sudden sympathy for these women who were regarded with such contempt.

"They will hire a coach?" she asked finally, her voice unsteady. The nights were bitter; a newborn could die in such weather.

"They will be provided with one. And a charcoal foot-warmer, as well." Madame Colbert appeared to be as gifted in organization as her husband. "You don't need to worry about a thing, my dear. Madame Beauchamp was wet nurse to two of my own babies. She is clean and her milk is excellent."

"Porte Saint-Denis isn't far," Petite said hopefully. "I could walk."

"You'd have to go through the cemetery to get there and the stink of the dead would make you faint—or worse. If you wish, I can make arrangements for you to see the infant, but frankly, it's best not to think of it. I send all my babies out, and look—" She proudly raised her paps with her hands. "It will be difficult for one week, but soon you will feel your normal self again."

Petite smiled grimly, concealing her dismay. Madame Colbert may have sent her children out to a wet nurse, but she got them back after a time and raised them herself. Didn't she understand the difference?

Madame Colbert reached over to pat Petite on the shoulder. "Think of the King, my dear girl, think of his needs. Think of the glorious service you have the honor to provide."

Petite put a rein on her tongue. It appalled her to think of her time with Louis as "service."

"You've met with Monsieur Blucher, the midwife?"

"Yesterday—" Petite faltered. She had not liked talking to a man about such an intimate matter.

"Don't be embarrassed. He attended my last lying-in, and he's very, very good. He has promised the King that you'll stay nice and tight." Madame Colbert grinned, forming three chins.

PETITE WAS BORED, desperate to go outside. "At least to Mass," she told Clorine. "The help go to church at seven. I'll leave shortly after. Notre-Dame de Recouvrance is not far." It was a shabby little church—not even the servants went there. She would not be seen.

"And leave the house empty?" Clorine asked, considering. "What if one of them comes back?"

"I'll go alone, in disguise—in your old clothes. People will take me for a servant."

At last, Clorine relented, though she fretted. "Are you sure about this?" she asked as she tucked Petite's curls under the crown of a bonnet.

"If I feel even a twinge, I will return."

GOING TO MASS regularly greatly improved Petite's spirits and she continued to go out even when the November weather turned icy. On the twenty-fourth, a Friday, she went to Confession ("Forgive me, Father, for I have sinned. I am about to give birth to a bastard"), staying to pray two Hail Marys and three Our Fathers before taking Communion. She had been worried about going into childbed unconfessed. Women sometimes died in childbed, and she couldn't help but fear what lay ahead. She'd begun to recall the whispered stories of her youth, stories of deformed babies, of women torn asunder. She remembered hearing cries of women in terrible pain. The more pleasure a woman experienced during congress, the more pain she suffered giving birth—and Petite had certainly experienced pleasure with Louis.

It was past eight of the clock by the time Petite stepped out of the musty church into the bright winter light. Boys were playing noisily in the church square, kicking an inflated pig bladder filled with pebbles. She kicked it back to them and hurried on, taking care where she stepped: the frozen mud was slippery and she dared not fall.

As she neared the gate into the Palais Royale gardens, she felt a hand touch her shoulder. She turned to see a woman of middle age in a stiff figure-of-eight ruff and powdered wig, tightly frizzled and covered by a net of black beads.

Her mother.

At first Petite was confused. Was Françoise not in the country with Jean and his wife? And was it truly her mother? This woman had paled her face with white lead and painted her cheeks red. A servant girl Petite didn't recognize hovered several feet behind, laden with parcels.

But yes, it *was* her.

"Forgive me, Madame," Françoise said, taking in Petite's condition, which was impossible to hide, even under her felt cloak. "I mistook you for my daughter."

Petite backed away, nearly tumbling into a pit of sewage. She shook her head, not daring to speak for fear of discovery. She was masked as well as veiled—how could she be recognized?

Françoise glanced down at Petite's boot, its thick sole. "Aye," she said slowly, looking Petite up and down with a cynical smile. "You are *not* my daughter—for I have disowned her."

And with that, she turned and walked briskly away, followed by the servant girl, who, smirking, stared back at Petite over her shoulder.

Petite stood watching until they disappeared around a corner. *Disowned.* She fought back angry tears. She thought of running after her mother, rebuking her, throwing herself into her mother's arms. Begging mercy: *demanding* it. She was nineteen, and sinfully with child—yes—but Louis was her only link to the world, and he was so rarely with her. She had chosen her path, but it was not an easy one. Now especially, approaching childbed, she longed for a mother's counsel and protection—but that was never to be.

Church bells rang. A beggar woman hobbled up to her, leaning on a stick. "A sou?" She poked her dirty fingers into Petite's belly. "For a blessing on it."

Petite shook her head, alarmed by the old woman's evil eye.

"A curse, then?" the woman cackled as Petite turned away and hurried back to the safety of her hideaway house.

"You're late," Clorine exclaimed, opening the door. "What happened?" she demanded, helping Petite up the stairs.

The air smelled of jasmine. "I need to lie down," Petite said, faltering. *Disowned.* She could still hear the contempt in her mother's voice.

"Is there a problem?" It was a man speaking.

"Louis?" Petite asked, groping. Why was it so dark? She touched a wall, felt the flock-work design of the wall covering. "Thank God, you're here."

"What's happened?" he asked. "Is it your time?"

"I don't know, Your Majesty," Petite heard Clorine say, from behind her. "She's unsteady."

Petite felt Louis's hand on her arm, his reassuring strength. "Why is it so dark in here?" she asked, shivering. How could her mother have abandoned her?

"Dark?" Louis sounded close.

"I can't see you," Petite said, stumbling.

Louis held her steady. "What do you mean?"

Petite reached out her hand, ran her fingers over his face, felt his nose, his angular cheeks, the stubble on his chin. This was not the dark of night. This dark was deeper.

"It's . . . it's daylight," she heard him say.

There was concern in his voice, and that frightened her. *Saint Michel, I pray to you, help me in this world of darkness, defend me against the spirits of wickedness.*

"Come. Lie down," he said, urging her forward.

Petite took a cautious step, and another, until she felt the bed at her knees. She leaned over, groping for the pillows. Louis's hand at her elbow, she let herself down.

"Louis, I can't see a thing," she said, her voice breaking.

WITH REPEATED BLEEDING and herbal infusions, Petite's vision slowly returned, but she suffered debilitating headaches and dizziness. Louis, alarmed by the episode, made her promise not to leave her hideaway until after the birth of their child. "You should not have been going out at all. Look what you risked."

"Can't you heal me?" Petite asked him in a moment of weakness. His touch alone cured hundreds of the Evil.

He smiled sadly. "My love, that's for the people. I can't really—" He shrugged and threw up his hands. "I'm mortal."

She embraced him, not wanting him to see the disappointment in her eyes, the disillusion of her childlike faith.

He was with her when her labor began, four weeks later. It was the eighteenth of December, a Tuesday, and he was on his way to Saint-Germain-en-Laye for a hunt. As he put on his feathered hat, Petite grasped his arm, lowering herself onto a wooden chair.

The pain passed and Petite took a deep breath. She lifted her face for a kiss, but it happened again. She grasped her belly, muffling a cry.

"Your Majesty?" Clorine was at the door.

"I believe her time has come." Louis knelt, taking Petite's hands, waiting for her contraction to pass. "I have to leave you."

"I know." The hunt had been organized long ago; four foreign ambassadors would be awaiting him.

"I'll send for Blucher," he said, standing.

"Don't worry," she said, and then gasped as another wave of pain came over her.

CLORINE STOOD BY as Monsieur Blucher examined Petite.

"She will be some time yet," he told Clorine, arranging his implements and positioning the birthing chair. "Call me when her pains come one upon the other," he said, then listed all the things Clorine and the chambermaid were to do (stoke the fires, draw, filter and heat water, get vinegar from the cellar, melt unsalted butter, prepare the compresses, bandages and draw sheets, the wax cloths for binding the stomach and breasts). "But not before," he said, plucking Pascal's *Provincial Letters* from a side table and retiring to the sitting room.

Soon Clorine could hear him snoring. She looked over the syringes, the skein of linen thread, two strings of four-ply thread, a long sharp darning needle, a thin silver tube, two bottles—one labeled IPECACUANHA and another KERMES MINERAL—blunt-ended scissors, a number of knives and, most chilling, a large metal hook (to haul the baby out if it died in the womb). There was even a vial of holy water, in case an emergency baptism was called for.

Clorine crossed herself and said a silent prayer: *may the baby be born straight, may my mistress survive.* Infants born on the third day after the new moon rarely lived.

"My rosary," Petite moaned, writhing.

Clorine tucked the strand of worn wooden beads into her mistress's clenched fist. She wished she'd had the gumption to ask the King for a garment he'd been wearing at the moment of conception. The smell would have helped draw the baby out.

PETITE HELD THE NEWBORN to her breast. The labor had been shockingly painful, but as soon as she saw her baby, all was forgotten (and forgiven). A big and hungry boy, he latched on eagerly. Although the pains, mercifully, had not gone on long—only eighteen hours—it had been a difficult delivery.

"He's handsome, just like his father," Clorine said, checking to make sure that the pillow under Petite's knees was keeping her legs well up.

Petite marveled, cupping the infant's soft head. "Charles," she whispered. Louis's son. A ferocious love filled her . . . love, and fear. *Heavenly Father, protect this precious little one.*

"Mademoiselle?" It was the surgeon, drying his hands on a cloth. "My instructions are to send the infant away before sunrise."

Petite nodded, but clasped the baby to her, close against her breast. *My little prince*, she thought. He would be baptized in the morning, by his new "parents." She thought to baptize him herself, with a spoon of wine and some garlic, as Henry the Great had been baptized—Henry the Great, her son's great-grandfather . . . and the grandson of her own dear father, as well. How proud he might have been—or shamed? Yes, *shamed.*

Clorine went to the window facing onto the garden and parted the heavy damask drapes. "The sky is beginning to lighten now," she said, turning to Petite with tears in her eyes.

This is too great a sacrifice, Petite thought, caressing the baby's fine hair with her lips and inhaling his sweet scent. The baby made a little chirping sound. Her heart would surely break.

Part V

BELOVED

Chapter Twenty-Seven

THAT SPRING, LOUIS PLANNED a weeklong festival at Versaie—"Pleasures of the Enchanted Island," he named it. Ballets, comedies, tournaments and concerts would all unfold as part of an enchantment, a sorceress's seductive allure. The evil witch would be vanquished in the end, of course—but only after everyone had fully enjoyed her temptations. Publicly, the event was to be in honor of the King's wife and mother, the two queens—but secretly, "It's all for you," he told Petite. All for the mother of a fine son.

Charles had grown into a stalwart baby much given to smiles. He looked the image of his father, in truth. Petite had seen the infant only three times—twice during carnival, and then again during Lent—the clandestine meetings arranged through Madame Colbert. The last time Petite had seen him was the Saturday before Easter. That morning, Louis had confessed and communicated before going to the Tuileries gardens to touch those infected with the Evil. The hundreds of desperate souls with grotesquely swollen necks had begun lining up the night before, anxious to be cured by the miracle of the King's touch. Tickets had been sold in order to restrict the numbers, but even so the gathering had threatened to get out of control.

Petite watched from a distance, saddened by the knowledge that it was only a show. She was touched to tears by the innocence of the people, their faith in Louis's godlike powers. The crowds made it easy for her to steal away unnoticed and wend her way hooded to the back entrance of the Colbert household, where, in an attic nursery, Madame Colbert and the nurse awaited, the baby in the nurse's arms. It was never a long encounter—they had to be so cautious—and Petite suffered long after each time. She took care to appear cheerful while attending

Henriette (which was required only occasionally now). Concealing her melancholy from Louis was harder, but tears distressed him, she knew.

In any case, Louis was preoccupied. Thanks to good harvests and the industrious work of Monsieur Colbert, the economy was healthy now, money flowing. Indeed, there was sufficient for grand fetes and ambitious building projects: the Louvre was being rebuilt and grand plans made for Versaie. "The Little Palace," Louis was calling his hunting lodge now. "Soon to become an enchanted palace," he added, unrolling a drawing of the Versaie grounds. He relished building projects, poring over plans, considering every detail of design and construction.

Their wilderness paradise was rapidly changing. A menagerie had already been built to house rare species of birds and animals—not the fighting beasts kings of the past had kept for amusement (and which were still kept at the fortress of Vincennes), but exotic creatures such as ostriches, pelicans, Arabian ducks and Indian geese, hogs from the East Indies. As well, the road approaching the château had been leveled, the avenues lined with trees. Two new buildings were almost completed, forming an outer court—one for coaches and the other for kitchens. On the south side an orangery had been built to house the thousands of orange trees confiscated from Fouquet's château at Vaux. Its roof formed a terrace overlooking the gardens, which now extended to the horizon. Louis loved nothing better than to sit among the orange trees, inhaling the sweet aroma. He often played his theorbo there.

Our Versaie, Petite thought, one hand on Louis's shoulder, looking at the drawings. It had been their secret for so long—the one place they could be free of prying eyes—and now the entire Court was invited. The new developments were dramatic, innovative, aesthetic, yet she could not banish a tinge of regret. She did not voice such thoughts: Louis took pride in the work. He was doing it for her, he said.

The festival in her honor was to be the finest ever experienced. Louis had recruited the greatest artists of the age—Périgny and Benserade to write the madrigals, Lully the music, Molière to take charge of all the theatrical events, and Vigarani the spectacular effects. As they set to work to fulfil his vision, he himself saw to the buildings and grounds. Le Nôtre, designer of Fouquet's gardens at Vaux, had been hard at work for some time supervising massive earth-moving machines called Devils.

Gautier, who was overseeing the festival, was beside himself with anxiety. "His Majesty is inviting six hundred, but everyone will arrive with at least one servant. Where am I to put them all? Where will they sleep? And what about the seventy-four actors and musicians, the clowns and stagehands? They will be bringing their servants as well," he fretted, wringing his hat in his hands.

"There should be more room in the château once the stables and kitchens are completed," Petite suggested, trying to calm him. "And you can put some people in the menagerie." Modeled on Fouquet's château at Vaux, the palace for animals was elegant.

"With the elephant?"

"Elephant?"

"And a bear. And a camel." Gautier shook out his hat, punched it into shape and pressed it back onto his head. "His Majesty's imaginings appear to have no limit."

PETITE AND GABRIELLE rode down to Versaie in the gilded carriage and four that Jean had recently purchased. Clorine, along with Gabrielle's chambermaid, footman and valet, had set out earlier, at dawn, with all their trunks and bedding in order to ready their rooms, and Jean had gone down on horseback the day before, with his regiment. Petite looked forward to some time alone with her sister-in-law, who was so amiable.

"Is this your first time to Versaie?" she asked Gabrielle, shifting so that the whalebones in her corset didn't dig into her flesh. She was thickening, her courses were eleven days late, and she was concerned that she might be with child again. Lovemaking had been different since the birth of baby Charles. She and Louis had had to abstain for long periods of time—for three months before the birth and for forty long days after, and then, in the days before Lent (yet another long period of abstinence), Petite had been tender, inflamed. Once Lent had passed and they were at last free of restraint, they'd not been as careful as they should have been.

Gabrielle nodded. "It's rustic, I hear. A little wild." Gabrielle was young, but not adventurous.

"It's wonderful," Petite said. All winter she'd longed for the wilds of Versaie.

Jean's wife was giddy, but trustworthy. For Petite, it was a relief to have someone she could speak to freely. They settled into a long gossip: about Françoise (her heart-breaking refusal to even speak of Petite); baby Charles (now four months old and charmingly jolly); Gabrielle's frustrating and so far futile attempts to have a child (and Petite's attempts to avoid doing so); the change in Petite's duties with Henriette (occasional daily attendance, when needed, but basically she was now expected to appear with the Princess only at official events); various plots on the part of Court ladies to seduce Louis (fortunately unsuccessful); Louis's growing frustration with the need for secrecy; the porcelain and jewelry Gabrielle had bought at the Saint-Germain fair; how lovely Athénaïs looked at Saint-Suplice holding the baptismal font at the conversion of a young Moor to Christianity, and how unfortunate she was in her marriage (her husband in debt again); Petite's repeated attempts to stand a galloping horse ("Are you crazy?").

The road had been vastly improved, but even so it took hours to get to Versaie, the coach pulling off four times to make use of the woods. They were all day on the road. Never had Petite seen such congestion, an entire Court en route, the coaches loaded down with trunks for the weeklong festival.

"It must be a very large château to accommodate all these people," Gabrielle said as the horses slowed yet again to a walk.

"I'm afraid not." It had been all Louis could do to persuade his tightfisted finance minister to furnish the guest rooms, much less provide the courtiers with wood and candles.

By the time they got to Versaie, the roads were too congested with coaches and horses to get close to the château, and Petite and Gabrielle had to walk. Petite got her sister-in-law settled in her chamber and went to find her brother. The château was crowded—and in chaos. Many appeared not to have a place to sleep.

She encountered Athénaïs on a stairwell. "Do you know where my brother might be?" In the foyer she saw Henriette arriving with Philippe.

"No, but do you know where my husband is?" Athénaïs answered with a laugh, toying with the cross and small silver key that hung from a pendant on the stomacher of her bodice. "*Not* that I really want to know."

"How could so many people be lost in such a small château?" Petite mused—then turned at the sound of Louis's voice.

"Your Majesty," Athénaïs said, bowing as he passed.

"Your Majesty," Petite echoed, nearly tripping over her left boot.

"Careful," Louis said, catching her by the arm. He smiled.

"Thank you, Your Majesty."

"Our King is a gentleman, is he not?" Athénaïs said, making teasing eyes at Petite over her fluttering fan.

IN SPITE OF THE new construction, there was not room for everyone—as Gautier had predicted. Petite and her brother and sister-in-law had rooms, but many courtiers had to scramble to make sleeping arrangements in local cottages and stables while others decided to sleep in their carriages. Much grumbling could be heard.

All the actors, musicians, grooms, carpenters and workmen running about in a panic only added to the confusion. Nothing was going according to plan. Monsieur de Molière, rehearsing his actors in a stuffy attic, was frantic because the costumes had not arrived. A large circle of grass—called a circus as in days of old—had been laid down at the entrance of the new Allée Royale for tilting at the ring, but they were one truckload short of sod. Four thousand torches were required to light the evening entertainments, but only three thousand two hundred had been prepared. The camel and elephant had safely arrived—finally—but the bear, heavily sedated, could not be woken from a deep sleep.

By the morning, however, discomfort had become a source of amusement. Most courtiers had found some form of accommodation, and those with the luxury of a dressing room shared with the less fortunate. Life at Court had become an adventure. What would their young King think of next?

Two hours before sunset, the courtiers gathered at the circus for the first of the enchantments—tilting at the ring. Already it seemed a scene from Mardi Gras, servants dressed as demons, fairies and ghouls. Beyond, near the edge of the woods, Louis and ten knights in armor attended to their horses. And beyond that were cages for the beasts.

No sooner had Jean's page fitted him into his armor (new, black and forbidding) than trumpets and drums sounded.

"You'd better mount," Petite said. Louis and three other knights were already in the practice ring.

Jean picked up his helmet and clanked toward his tall Castilian warhorse.

"Good luck," his wife called out after him.

Jean turned and came back, breathless. "Gabrielle, I need your scarf," he said, pulling off a leather gauntlet.

She drew a purple silk one from her ample bodice, kissed it and presented it to her husband. Jean tucked it under his coat of plates.

"Now I'll win for sure," he said, lumbering off.

Petite and Gabrielle headed toward the stands, where the ladies of the Court had gathered. Petite saw a woman wave them over: Athénaïs, indicating two velvet tasseled cushions beside her.

"Gabrielle just told me the good news," Petite said.

Athénaïs regarded her plump belly with disgust. "And the Queen, as well—have you heard?"

"That's wonderful." Louis's twice-monthly "sessions" with the Queen were strictly duty, and once the Queen was impregnated, he did not visit her bed; Petite liked having him to herself at such times. She thought of herself as Louis's true wife, and the Queen as the wife of that other man, the King.

"And Madame, of course," Gabrielle added, regarding Henriette, who was sitting with the two queens. The Princess was well along in a second pregnancy.

"A fruitful Court," Athénaïs said as trumpeters entered through the foliage-covered arches set at the points of the compass.

"Indeed," Petite said, with a worried thought to her own condition.

Louis entered dressed as a Greek warrior, mounted on a handsome Aragonese. Everyone cheered and he raised his hand. The jewels embedded in his ancient silvered breastplate threw off rays of light. He tipped back his visor and saluted the Queen, and another cheer went up. Petite took off her red neckscarf and waved it—this was their sign. He noticed it and put his hand to his heart.

His horse reared up, and the crowd applauded—thinking it intentional—but Petite was concerned. His prize mount was only five years old and skittish still. Steadiness was what mattered at tilting.

The other knight-contestants entered on horseback, their long lances upright, silk flags declaring their rank attached below the tip. They passed around the circumference as the ladies exclaimed over the beauty of their horses, their armor, their plumes.

"There's Jean," Gabrielle exclaimed with an enthusiasm unbecoming her quality.

"Ahead of the dukes?" Athénaïs's brows arched in surprise.

A man in pink satin climbed a ladder to hang the first and largest ring from a cross-beam opposite the judges.

Louis was the first to run at the ring. He circled his horse back to the starting line, a good distance away. The crowd hushed, and at the sound of a bugle, he lowered his lance and spurred his mount, which put down its head and bucked, then raced wildly down the course. Petite watched, her hands over her mouth, and was relieved when Louis finally got the horse under control. He sat back as he approached the post; the horse slowed, but it was fighting the bit. His lance steady, Louis caught the ring—and the crowd roared. Petite cheered along with all the others. She could handle a boar spear with ease, but not a lance. Although the shaft was wood, it was heavy, almost forty hands in length.

Jean followed the princes. His horse was both fast and steady, and he held his lance straight.

"Well done!" Gabrielle cried out as he caught the ring.

The drama intensified as the rings got progressively smaller and contestants were eliminated. Two fell, one having to be carried off. In the end it came down to Louis and Jean. Petite was proud of them both, but especially of Louis, who had done well in spite of his overly spirited mount. No one, not even her brother, carried a lance with more ease.

Louis checked his horse, not allowing him into a full gallop, then caught the tiny ring neatly. A cheer went up. *Vive le roi!*

Jean ran at the ring full bore and caught it as well.

"That's close," Athénaïs said.

The judges deliberated for some time. A stunned silence fell when they announced that the winner was the Marquis de la Vallière: although His Majesty had shown superior mastery, the Marquis's speed had been greater.

"Don't applaud," Petite told Gabrielle behind her fan, her voice low.

The crowd murmured as the Queen awarded Jean a diamond-encrusted gold sword and buckler.

The sky turned golden. Lully's musicians played as "Spring"—a young lady crowned with flowers—entered on a Spanish charger, followed by gardeners carrying preserves. "Summer" trailed in on an elephant, leading a swarm of harvesters, followed by "Autumn" on a camel leading grape-pickers, and, at the last, "Winter" riding a now somewhat-too-awake bear and accompanied by old men carrying bowls of ice. The charger shied on seeing the camel, and the elephant had to be pushed out of the way. Lully raised his baton and fifty costumed servants bearing food danced in unison as a crescent-shaped table was unveiled. Hundreds of pages holding wax torches stepped forward, twirled. Eyeing the bear uneasily, Monsieur de Molière, as Pan, announced the feast to the queens.

The Queen Mother took her place at the head of the table, with Louis on her right and the Queen on her left. Philippe and Henriette joined them, followed by la Grande Mademoiselle and the other princes and princesses of the blood. Thousands of torches were simultaneously lit, casting a magical light over the tableau. Citizens watching from the crowded terrace cheered. Behold: the royal family, in all its glory.

Petite glanced up at the night sky. The moon was nearing fullness, illuminating the château, the fountains and canal. *It's going to be grand*, Louis had told her. It pleased him to see an army of men working with pickaxes and shovels. From somewhere, she heard a horse whinny, and another horse answer. She looked out over the great dark wilderness beyond—their wilderness no longer.

A WIND CAME UP the next day, after the hunt (Petite: one boar, a clean kill). Louis ordered the tapestries from his bedchamber hung on the west side of the outdoor theater. These and an impromptu fabric dome helped keep the torches and candles from blowing out during Monsieur de Molière's comedy.

Petite sat with the ladies of the Court in raked benches to one side. Louis's armchair was positioned directly in front of the stage, his wife and mother on either side. He caught her eye as he scanned the crowd, smiled slightly, then turned to attend to the Queen. The Queen Mother looked over at Petite and frowned, and then the Queen turned, following her gaze.

They know, Petite thought as the curtains parted.

The play, *The Princesse d'Elide*, began innocently: a fairy-tale story of a prince in love with a princess, driven mad with love-longing. However, the princess loved horses with a passion and would not be wooed. She loved the hunt, the music of the deep forest glens.

"Like someone I know?" Athénaïs said from behind, tapping Petite on her shoulder with her fan.

Petite watched the play unfold with trepidation: the play was about Louis . . . and *her*. She sat very still, hardly breathing, overcome with uneasy delight.

On the third night, the Court assembled for a musical performance at the end of the Allée Royale. The royal family sat on a dais facing the basin of Apollo. Opposite them was a castle surrounded by water.

This was the enchanted lake . . . and *this* the enchanted palace.

As Lully raised his baton and the music began, Petite, Jean and Gabrielle were led to their seats four rows back from the royal family (Jean protesting, "*We* are the royal family").

"Here comes the sorceress." Gabrielle pointed to a barge in the form of a marine monster on the dark water.

Jean whistled along with other men as torches were lit and evil Alcina was revealed, attired in scanty gauze. With a wave of her wand, her palace lit up. Demons, dwarves and giants danced out from the shadows, their devil faces ghoulish.

The innocent knight appeared, ready to storm the palace of the enchantress. Music soared as they prepared for the ultimate battle between good and evil. Alcina and her devious subjects were winning, but the knight had a magic ring—a ring with the power to destroy enchantment.

Petite watched, captivated but troubled, knowing the power of magic, its dark side . . . knowing that it was not so easily vanquished. She was startled by a volley of shots. Everyone roared with astonishment as Alcina's palace was destroyed in a thundering blaze of fire rockets.

The enchantment had come to an end, with evil vanquished, yet the fete continued for three more days: jousting in the dry moat, a tour of the menagerie, a lottery, and, every night, a comedy by Molière. On the last night, hooded and cloaked, Louis finally came to Petite's room, making his way through the dark corridors like a thief.

"At last," he said, removing his mask. The festival may have been in Petite's honor—or so he claimed—but they'd hardly even had a chance to speak. The daily hunts had been far too public, and every afternoon he'd been in meetings regarding a new addition, the work on the foundation scheduled to begin as soon as the Court departed. "I feel like an idiot skulking about like this," he said, sitting on the edge of the bed to pull off his boots. "My subjects parade their mistresses alongside their wives and nobody thinks a thing of it."

There had been only one courtier, in fact—a marquis making a show of parading his wife and paramour side by side that morning—and it *had* been noticed, Petite recalled. Nonetheless, there was a measure of truth in what Louis said. No matter what the Church ruled, courtiers rather expected a married man to have a mistress, and would treat her with respect (so long as she was noble—and unmarried).

"Yet because of my mother, *I* have to sneak around," Louis grumbled, climbing into her bed.

IN THE MONTHS that followed—as the Court traipsed from Fontaine Beleau, to Paris, to Villers-Cotterêts, to Vincennes and then back to Paris again—Louis became increasingly annoyed with his mother's rule. In Paris, in the little house overlooking the Palais Royale gardens, Petite and Louis enjoyed a measure of freedom—long afternoons reading, dancing, playing music and making love, and even (once) an enchanting hour with their baby Charles—but even so, he could not place Petite beside him at entertainments. She could walk with him in the gardens along with all the other courtiers, she could ride with him on a hunt, but she could not join him in a dance or sit with him at the gaming tables at night in his mother's withdrawing room.

"Come to the Louvre tonight," he told Petite one afternoon, kicking off the covering sheet. A fire was blazing, the room over-warm. "I'll call for you in my mother's antechamber at ten of the clock."

"But Louis, the queens . . ." Petite objected. It would be an insult for her to appear in the Queen Mother's salon. She was six months along; even corseted, this was difficult to disguise.

"They won't be there. My mother's ill and my wife stays with her."

"They'll know. They'll find out."

"I'm *not* going to hide you any longer!"

"But why now?" Petite protested. "I'll soon be going into confinement in any case."

"King Frances I had an official maîtresse en titre, King Henry II, King Henry the Great," Louis said, his voice no longer gentle. "My wife's father has sixteen, for God's sake. The kings of England, Austria . . ."

"The Queen is with child, Louis—it will distress her."

"I will not be ruled on this! When they dishonor you, they dishonor me," he said angrily, rising from the bed.

Louis appeared at the entry to the Queen Mother's antechamber precisely at ten, accompanied by his usual entourage: Gautier, Lauzun, ten Swiss guards and a quartet of violinists. He was wearing a feathered and jeweled hat. Bows stiffened with wires adorned the toes of his high red-heeled shoes.

Gautier stepped forward into the antechamber. "Mademoiselle de la Vallière?" He bowed, formally, from the waist. "His Majesty requests your company."

Taffeta rustled as the women in the room turned to stare.

Lauzun did a funny little cat hop to one side. "After you," he said, making an extravagant bow.

Careful not to reveal even a hint of a limp, Petite followed Louis into the Queen Mother's winter apartment. He moved slowly, calm and resolute. She felt like a soldier following a commander into battle: a battle for the King's right to be with the woman he loved.

The carved double doors swung open upon a glittering scene. The courtiers rose from the gaming tables and the musicians put down their instruments. Petite glanced over the room, at all the staring, startled eyes. Yeyette, Claude-Marie and Athénaïs were standing with the Duchesse de Navailles. *Mercy.*

"Step," Lauzun murmured, nudging Petite forward.

Everyone bowed before Louis as he approached a gaming table set by the fire.

Philippe motioned to the armchair on his right. He was wearing a wig with a single curl running around the bottom and his rose silk suit was trimmed in lace. "Your Majesty . . . ?" He shifted his right foot forward and bowed.

Louis acknowledged his brother, then tipped his hat to Henriette, who made a curtsy. She had fully recovered from the birth of a son three months earlier, and looked herself once again, enlivened.

Petite wasn't sure what to do. A reverence was called for—but how deep, and how many? She curtsied to the ground. *Does my belly show?* she worried. She prayed not.

Louis pulled out the chair opposite his. "Will you be my partner in a game of Karnöffel, Mademoiselle de la Vallière?" He watched her steadily.

Everyone in the room was ominously silent.

"Yes, Your Majesty." Petite made another reverence and they all sat down: first Louis, then Philippe, Henriette and lastly Petite. Louis signaled the musicians and they took up their instruments. Laughter and conversation slowly resumed.

Solemnly, Philippe dealt out the pack. "Hearts trump," he announced with an ironic smile.

With difficulty, Petite picked up her cards; they were slippery and new, and her hands were clammy. She glanced across at Louis, but he was intent on his hand.

"I have a two and a four trump," Henriette told her husband, who made a face. Karnöffel was a topsy-turvy game; cards were openly discussed between partners.

"I have the six of hearts," Louis told Petite, "the Pope card."

Petite studied her cards. She had the seven of hearts. Seven in the trump suit had special powers, she recalled, but she could not remember what they were. The game had been forbidden in her childhood as anarchistic: the King could be beaten by a low card, the Pope by an under-knave. And then she remembered.

"I have the Devil card," Petite said, a sick feeling coming over her.

THE NEXT DAY, on learning of the affront, the Queen Mother raged and the Queen took to bed with a sudden high fever.

I warned him, Petite thought angrily, shuffling through a carpet of damp yellow leaves. She entered the silent refuge of a little church. The thin tapers at the altar were bowed, as if burdened by an invisible weight. Petite lit a candle for the Queen and placed it in the sand-filled trough in front of a statue of Mary—the one holding the baby Jesus in her arms, a baby Jesus with old, sad eyes. *O Mary,* she prayed, *the Queen must not suffer for my sin.*

The door behind her opened in a burst of damp wind. The candle guttered and went out.

IN SPITE OF vomitives, purges and bleedings, the Queen's fever did not abate. Almost a full month early her labor began. Church bells chimed three times and then there was silence.

"It's a girl," Clorine said sadly.

"Go find one of the Queen's maids," Petite said. "Find out how the Queen is doing."

She paced until Clorine's return.

"She's in a fever still. The baby's hairy and dark—and ugly as a toad," Clorine reported, putting down her basket.

Petite crossed herself. A demon child.

NIGHT HAD FALLEN when Clorine came running into Petite's chamber. "Come to the window," she called out, throwing back the heavy curtains. "Quick," she said, fumbling with the shutter bolt.

There, in the starry night, was a steak of light.

"A comet," Petite said, turning away. She was full with child and should not be looking at such a thing.

"Someone's going to die," Clorine said, falling to her knees.

"IT WAS FOR the Princess," Clorine told Petite five days later. The newborn had died.

"Oh, the poor Queen."

"The poor King. They say he wept."

Somewhere, Louis is grieving, Petite thought. If only she could be with him.

"Imagine shedding tears for an ugly little monster like that."

Petite pressed her hands to her belly, frightened by a stillness within her.

THE DAY AFTER King's Day—the coldest day of a bitter January—Petite went into childbed. This time, Louis was with her. She tore his lace collar to shreds, so violent was her pain. He stayed with her until the infant was born, another son.

Philippe, Louis named him. "We'll call him Filoy," he said with a smile.

"Yes," Petite murmured, her baby pressed to her heart. Little rascal, son of a king.

"Colbert's valet will come for him after nightfall," Louis said, shifting his weight. "He's to be baptized in the morning."

Petite nodded, feeling the infant's soft skull with her lips. The secretive arrangements had once again been carefully made. Colbert would await in a coach at the gate. At the crossway of the Hôtel Bouillon, he would give the baby to Monsieur François Derssy, the husband of Marguerite Bernard, a former servant of the Colbert household. The baby would be baptized as their son.

"I know," she said. The infant had been born whole, straight and strong. For that alone she should be grateful.

After a month of bed rest, Petite could walk again, but with difficulty. Her left leg was weak, and unsteady. "I'm fine," she lied to Louis, who was overwhelmed looking after his ailing mother.

Early in April, Petite was strong enough to begin attending Henriette. The Princess was with child again and had asked Petite to read out loud to her in the long afternoons: Thomas Aquinas, works by Boccaccio. It helped to lighten the melancholy that hung over the Court. The Queen's recovery after the death of the monster baby had been slow; she wore a bed robe night and day. As well, doctors had discovered that the Queen Mother had cankers in one breast—a cancer, they called it. She cried out often, and needed help to walk. A madman dressed in devil horns had taken to following the royal carriage. Courtiers displayed charms to ward off demons.

The news from afar was likewise grim. Thousands died each day of the Plague in London. There had been few such deaths in Paris, yet fear had taken hold—no one embraced, no one dared touch. Henriette's brother, the Duke of York, had been killed in battle—the report proved to be false, but it caused the Princess to go into convulsions.

Early in July, listening to Petite read from Madame Scudéry's novel *Ibrahim*, the Princess began to weep. "I haven't felt movement for two days," she confessed, her hands on her belly. Her eyes looked hollow and her breath was rank.

The midwife was called to examine the Princess, attendants hovering fearfully. The Princess's breasts were slack and her belly was cold at the navel. Her water, which stank, was thick. The midwife wet her hands in warm water and rubbed the Princess's big belly. There was no movement.

"Oh dear God," the Princess moaned. She'd been having dreams of the dead, she said.

"They got the baby out of her," Clorine informed Petite nine days later.

"That took a long time," Petite said.

"Aye. A girl, it was."

"And . . . ?" Petite's eyes were searching. "How did it go?"

Clorine pulled on her earlobe, looked away. "The midwife had her tricks," she said. She didn't want to tell her mistress what she knew, the grisly details shared between maids from whom nothing could be hidden. The midwife had tried everything, in truth: sage and pennyroyal in white wine, hyssop in hot water. Even an eagle-stone held to Madame's privy parts had failed to draw it out. In the end the midwife had had to cut the child asunder and pull it out by pieces, four gagging footmen holding the Princess down. Mercifully, she'd fainted dead away.

"She was even baptized, I'm told," Clorine said, feigning cheer.

Petite frowned. "But the child was not alive."

"Aye," Clorine said, returning to her sweeping. A dead royal baby got baptized no matter what, she guessed—even a cut-up baby so dead it was rotten. Anything so that it could be buried in the regal tombs at Saint-Denis, not with the suicides in the north corner of some desolate graveyard, like all the other unbaptized stillborns.

DEATH DID NOT tire that fall. In September, the King of Spain died—the Queen's father, the Queen Mother's brother. The Court was once again draped in black, the royal family in deepest purple.

Louis turned gaunt, ashen, as if something in him were dying. His mother was not responding to treatments, and he would not accept the inevitable. He embraced and consumed Petite with a fierce hunger, crying out as he spent, as if in pain. He returned to her daily, and daily it was the same. Few words, an explosive release, and then he'd lie staring, cloaked in a tense silence.

Even trips to Versaie failed to soothe him. The grounds were ravaged by the workmen, and rubble was everywhere. Louis hunted indifferently, spearing boar, shooting hart, preoccupied by his mother's suffering. A regime of enemas, weekly bleedings, senna and rhubarb purges had failed to restore the balance of her humors. The doctors had sliced into her diseased breast, sticking in bits of meat to feed the tumor—to stop it from feeding on her—but to no avail.

Let me be, the Queen Mother begged him. *I am ready to die.* But he could not let her go. He'd found out about a village priest from the Orléanais who performed miracles. The cleric vowed on the Bible that his mixture of belladonna and burnt lyme would harden the diseased breast to marble, but it too had failed. Now, a new doctor, this one from Lorraine, offered a cure—an arsenic paste that would kill the diseased tissue so that it could be cut away. For weeks the suffering Queen Mother had been enduring this operation daily, but without result.

"She is rotting alive," Louis told Petite with tears in his eyes, visibly exhausted from sleeping at the foot of his mother's bed.

"Can nothing be done?" Petite asked, wrapping her arms around him.

"I wish I believed in miracles," he said sadly.

THE CHURCH BELLS of Paris were silent as the statue of Saint Geneviève was solemnly paraded through the streets, followed by a press of courtiers and citizens praying for the life of the Queen Mother. Veiled, Petite joined the procession.

The next day, Louis did not call on her at his customary time. "The Queen Mother has had Last Rites," Clorine informed Petite.

At daybreak, funeral bells began to peal: the Queen Mother was dead.

Petite fell to her knees, praying for the Queen Mother's soul. Praying that this would be the end of it, that Death would be sated, the curse lifted.

Chapter Twenty-Eight

THE COURT JOURNEYED to Fontaine Beleau that summer, to its primeval woods. Petite followed the hunts from a carriage—for she was, yet again, in a delicate condition. Louis was pleased: both Charles, now two and a half, and Filoy, a year younger, were healthy, fine-looking boys, the product of love, strong seed.

On this particular afternoon, a hot Saturday in July, the driver stopped at a carrefour and was listening for the horns when a man appeared on horseback from behind.

"Good afternoon, Monsieur Colbert," Petite called out. She'd come to like the humorless man. "I didn't know you enjoyed the hunt."

He was flushed, sitting his horse uncomfortably. His mouse-colored Frisian mare pawed the dirt. "I have a message for the King," he said, looking into the distance. Horns sounded and dogs brayed—a hart had been put to bay. Colbert spurred his horse and took off, holding his hat with one hand.

"Must be urgent," Clorine said.

"Must be confidential," Petite said. It was unusual for the hardworking minister of finance to leave his desk. She suspected it had to do with preparations for a possible war. Spain had yet to pay the Queen's dowry, giving her the right to claim the Spanish territories to the north—by force, if need be. Louis had been holding military reviews since early in the spring.

They headed toward the sound of the horns, the hounds in full cry. Soon they saw a trio of men approaching.

"It's His Majesty," Petite said. Louis was riding at a steady gallop, his big hunter lathered in sweat. He was holding the reins loosely in one hand, his other hand pressing his plumed hat to his heart. "Stop," she commanded her driver.

The driver pulled up the horses, throwing them forward. Petite unlatched the carriage door. Louis's cheeks were wet with tears. Alarmed, she let herself down.

Louis pulled his horse to a stop and jumped off, throwing the reins to Gautier. "I'll meet you back at the château," he told Colbert, and signaled Petite to follow him into the woods. When they were well away from the others, he turned and took her in his arms. Her hat fell to the ground.

"Our baby is dead," he said, his voice thick. "The youngest."

Filoy? Petite saw Louis's mouth moving, but she couldn't make out the words. She removed her kerchief from around her neck and used it to dry her lover's cheeks. "How?" she asked finally, taking his gloved hand. He was trembling, yet she was steady. She felt she was far above, in the leaves of the towering trees, looking down.

Louis took a shaky breath. "He was with his wet nurse at a procession. There was a thunderclap, and he . . . and he just . . ."

Petite felt she was going to be sick. "Lightning hit him?"

"No, it was just the *sound* of it. His heart . . . stopped."

"But he was strong, Louis." Petite felt sobs rising. The last time she had seen the baby he'd been able to sit propped up by pillows, babbling and sucking on his fingers by turns. She hardly knew him—and now he was gone forever. "He can't have . . ."

"Oh my God, my God," Louis said, his hands over his eyes.

Petite began to tremble, imagining the scene, the horror of it.

Louis wiped his cheeks with his sleeve. "Colbert's returning immediately to Paris. He will look after everything."

"I will go with him," Petite said, her teeth starting to chatter. She held her arms tight, lest she fly apart. She would lay Filoy out, surround him with flowers, bless him with her tears.

Louis gazed up at the sky. "You must not, Louise—not in your condition."

Tears burst from her in a torrent. Was she not to see her baby one last time?

He kissed her hand, wet with tears. "My love, for the sake of the child you're carrying—our child, *my* child—you cannot be in the presence of . . ."

Death.

"No," she sobbed, beating his chest. *No!*

BABY FILOY WAS put into the ground, and sixteen days later two-year-old Charles slipped away in a burning fever. Petite took to her bed and did not rise. Monsieur Blucher feared she would lose the child she was carrying, so silent was her grief.

Louis came to see her whenever he could, but he was often busy now, reviewing troops. He sat by her bed talking of regiments, warhorses, armor and weaponry. Petite's indifference to the things of this world made him uneasy. His own grief—for his infant daughter, his mother, the two boys—overwhelmed him, in truth. He could keep it at bay if he kept moving. He would vanquish Death on the battlefield, have his revenge.

"She should go with Your Majesty to Vincennes," Monsieur Blucher advised him. The Court would be at the fortress northeast of Paris for almost two months. "It's not far, and the change will do her good. She won't be going into childbed until the new year, so that's not a concern."

VINCENNES WAS NOT a pleasant castle. The rooms opened one upon the other; there was little privacy. When the winds came from the west, the stench of the fortress prison was strong. Now and then the captive lions could be heard roaring.

The chapel was small, but often empty. Petite spent time there, just sitting, too angry with God to pray. In the afternoons, she sat with the women, poking at her embroidery, pretending to be interested as they talked about the magnificence of His Majesty's troops, the splendor of the military reviews. London had burned down, the King had turned twenty-eight, the leaves were falling early. It was all the same to her.

The last Saturday before they were to leave Vincennes, Petite woke with a backache and a nagging feeling of restlessness. *Should I alert Monsieur Blucher?* she wondered, rubbing her aching thighs. She'd suffered cramps on and off all night.

Clorine drew back the bed curtains and set a small beer and cake on the bedside table. "It's chilly," she said.

"I'll need Court dress for tonight," Petite said, rolling out of the high bed. Every Saturday the courtiers met for médianoche, the midnight collation, and that evening's would be the last at Vincennes. She would be happy to leave. She felt isolated in her grief, like some malevolent wandering spirit. She'd not slept well for months.

"I've already aired it," Clorine said, holding up a boned corset. She fitted it on over Petite's shift, then pulled the laces.

"Tighter," Petite said. She'd not been eating, but even so she was growing. "Use your feet." She clutched a post as Clorine braced against it, pulling the bindings.

"My last mistress died doing this," Clorine warned her, quickly twisting and knotting the cords. "How can you even breathe?" She helped Petite into three flannel petticoats and a voluminous wool gown that helped conceal her condition.

Petite heard a horse's urgent whinny. She went to the window and drew back the drapes. The thick panes were fogged over. She drew the letter *C*, for Charles, who had loved to draw lines in a mist. Why had they *both* died? she demanded angrily. *O Lord, I acknowledge my sin, forgive me*, she prayed, in fear for the child she was carrying—yet another soul conceived in mislove. She grew ill with dread that it might die in her womb.

She heard a horse snort and pushed a window open, the better to see. Louis and a party of men were on horseback in the courtyard below, attended by six guards armed with carbines. She remembered: he was going to Versaie, and would return to Vincennes the next day for yet another military review. She rubbed the small of her back as she watched him mount his horse—Feisty, the small black trotter he preferred for travel—and set out, his men following.

She closed the window against the cold, wiping out her letter *C. Such beautiful boys*, she thought, and tears flowed again. She slipped behind the screen at the end of the room and lowered herself onto the close-stool, pressing her fingers to her eyes, breathing deeply until the convulsive shuddering passed.

If only, if only . . .

If only they were still with her, if only they were alive.

She felt a rush of warmth and stood up. Alarmed, she stepped back. "Clorine," she called out, in the grip of a contraction.

Clorine appeared with a dusting rag in one hand. She frowned down at the puddle.

Petite held onto the edge of the commode to steady herself as another contraction came over her. "Get Blucher," she hissed. Her womb was opening.

By the time Clorine returned with the sleepy surgeon—he'd been up until dawn at the gaming tables—Petite's pains were steady and strong.

"I can't have it here," she told him, panting. Her room was a passage; the Queen's suite was close.

"I'm afraid you have no choice, Mademoiselle," Blucher said, washing his hands at the little stand behind the screen.

Petite heard the door at the far end of the room open, then a woman's voice.

"It's Madame Henriette, on her way to Mass," Clorine whispered.

"Is there a problem?" Petite heard the Princess inquire.

Petite parted the bed curtains. "I have terrible colic," she gasped.

"My sympathy," Henriette said, and passed through, followed by Yeyette and two pages, who turned to stare.

BLUCHER WAS MEANT to be a priest, but found satisfaction, nonetheless, in his vocation as a male midwife—the first in history, he liked to think. He was philosophical, calm by nature, and that helped. He stood in awe of the strength of a woman in labor, in truth. Strength and courage, for with each birthing, a woman risked her life. God had laid that curse upon her, to bring forth in sorrow and pain. Harlots birthed easily, but they suffered pain later, in Hell.

Mademoiselle de la Vallière's throws were coming quick and strong. The upper part of her belly was hollow, and the lower full: the child had sunk down. He greased his hands with almond oil and felt the open neck of the womb. It was coming down headlong, but with one hand thrust out. This alarmed even him.

Quickly, he beat an egg, mixed it with almond oil, and poured it into the privy passage to make it glib. "This will hurt," he warned the King's mistress. The maid clamped her hands over the young woman's mouth to stifle her scream as he pushed the baby back in. Then he lay her thighs and knees wide open, and anointed the passage again, this time with duck grease. At last—with guidance and prayer—the baby slithered out straight, a pale, weak girl.

"You have a daughter, Mademoiselle de la Vallière," he said.

"She's fainted," the maid said.

He severed the navel-string, cutting it shorter than he would for a boy, so that the girl would be modest and her privy passage narrow. He squeezed a few drops of blood out of the cut-off navel-string into the infant's mouth. The baby cried out and Mademoiselle de la Vallière whimpered.

"The baby must be hidden," the maid said, holding a hamper. "Madame Henriette and others will be returning after Mass." There was a limit to what screens and bed curtains could hide.

"Take her to my room in the service quarter," Blucher said, wrapping the baby in toilettes. "My wife is there; she will know what to do." He put the swaddled infant in the basket and covered her over. The maid rushed off.

Mademoiselle de la Vallière was still in a swoon. He shook her to consciousness. "Snuff this," he said, holding a vial of white hellebore powder to her nose. She was a strong, brave girl, but she did not birth easily and the most dangerous part of birthing was yet to come. He would need her help to drive the after-burthen out. If left in, it would bring fevers, convulsions, death.

She sneezed. He pressed down on her belly. She sneezed again, groaned, and out it came, entire. *Praise the Lord.*

The maid returned, breathless. "The service is just ending—you have to go. Madame will be coming through."

"I need only a moment more," he said, hurriedly anointing Mademoiselle de la Vallière's belly with oil of St. John's wort and laying a rabbitskin over it. "Keep it thus for two hours," he instructed. "It's to close up the womb." He swathed her privates with a wide napkin and wrapped a clean linen cloth over her flanks, winding it down over her haunches. "She must lie in for forty days."

"That would cause suspicion," the maid whispered, her eye on the passage door.

"The holy bone parts in birthing. If she does not rest, her womb will wander."

"Monsieur Blucher, my mistress will not lie abed," Clorine hissed, pulling the bed curtains shut. "I know her well."

"Then pray for her," Blucher said, reaching into his vest and withdrawing a folded-up square of bandage. "And give her this."

Clorine unwrapped it, and frowned. It was a short length of the infant's navel-string.

Voices could be heard approaching. "It will defend her from devils," he said, quickly taking his leave.

"Was it a boy or a girl?" Petite asked Clorine listlessly after the ordeal was over. With its first cry, the newborn had disappeared. To where, she did not even know. She tried to sit up. She was woozy yet.

"A girl," Clorine said, taking up a stained covering sheet.

Where will Monsieur Blucher find a wet nurse for her? Petite wondered, pressing her fingers against her nipples. "I need to wash before you wrap me." She gloomed down at the bloody mass in the chamber pot on the floor. "What are you going to do with that?"

"I'm not sure yet," Clorine said, nudging the pot under the bed with her foot.

Petite heard voices on the other side of the bed curtains: Henriette, returning from Mass. She fell back against the pillows. "I should rest. I'll need my strength . . . for tonight."

Clorine glared, her hands on her hips. "You're not going anywhere, Mademoiselle. You're to stay abed—"

"Don't fight me on this, Clorine," Petite said, closing her eyes.

At eleven that evening, Clorine got Petite to drink some barley water. She took away the bloody bandages and bathed her privates with chervil water scented with honey of roses to guard against inflammation. Petite was bleeding still. Clorine padded her with clean cloths and helped her to stand.

"I can walk," Petite said, but she stumbled. Slowly, she lowered herself onto the stool in front of her toilette table, wincing. "I'll need a light."

Clorine set a lantern beside the jars of pomade.

Petite looked at her reflection in the glass. "I'm a fright."

Clorine dipped her head. The year had been hard on her mistress. Women who rose too early from childbed became wrinkled.

Petite reached out her hand, touched the dry branch stuck into the mirror frame. One of the leaves fell, landing on the table. She brushed it to the floor, and took up a pot of Venice White, dipping her fingers into the goop and spreading a layer over her face with a trembling hand. She dyed her lips with Spanish Red, and, with her little finger, applied a slick red gum to her cheeks. The charcoal smudged as she penciled her brows.

"Let me," Clorine said, reminded of the young girl she'd first served—the silent one, the ghostly one. She retraced the brows and placed a black silk patch on each cheek, but nothing could hide the vacant look in Petite's eyes. *Yes: a ghost*, Clorine thought.

At midnight, Petite entered the ballroom for the Court's last médianoche at Vincennes. Many turned to stare. She walked straight and upright as a wooden doll, her face plastered, her hair shellacked into ringlets.

"You are well, now, Mademoiselle de la Vallière?" Henriette inquired. "You seemed in pain this morning. I was concerned."

"Yes, I had a dreadful attack of colic this morning, but I am quite well now," Petite answered. "Thank you for your concern."

"Did anyone hear a baby crying?" Yeyette asked.

"I heard it," Petite said. "It was the strangest thing."

Athénaïs regarded her thoughtfully.

Petite endured, waiting for others to begin retiring before she took her leave. She walked through the echoing rooms, one after another, until she came to her own. She sat listlessly on the edge of the bed as Clorine unlaced her, freed her from the painful bodice and wiped the flaking white lead from her cheeks.

"There's not so much blood as before," Clorine said, changing her bandages. "So that's good."

"So that's good," Petite echoed, sinking back onto the bed.

"Sleep. I said your prayers for you," Clorine said, pulling the curtains.

Petite stared long into the dark, her hands on the slack skin of her empty belly.

ATHÉNAÏS JOINED PETITE after Mass the next morning. "How are you doing?" she asked, taking Petite's elbow as they climbed the marble stairs.

"Thank you," Petite said, stopping at the top landing, taking a breath. Outside, in the courtyard, a military band was practicing.

"I thought you looked a little weak last night," Athénaïs said.

"I get dizzy now and then." Petite made a smile. "It's that time of the month," she lied.

"I know what you mean," Athénaïs said as they reached Petite's chamber. "In fact, I brought you a little something." She reached into her basket and withdrew a small earthen bottle stoppered with wax. "A tonic," she said. "It's a remedy that has worked well for a number of ladies."

Petite read the label: the handwriting was small, delicate.

"I take it with brandy—*lots* of brandy," Athénaïs laughed, showing her pretty teeth. "Do you mind if I sit down for a moment?"

"Forgive me." Petite pulled out a chair for Athénaïs, next to her toilette table. "I neglect my manners."

"Remember when I used to call you little sister?"

"That was long ago."

"*Long*, long ago," Athénaïs said. "Before I married."

And had two children, Petite knew. She longed to talk to Athénaïs about such things, but that part of her life was hidden. The other—the false part—was in the light. "Your husband, how is he?" she inquired.

"Off on some adventure somewhere." Athénaïs waved her hand through the air. "I only know of his doings because of the men who arrive with mémoires—their 'reminders,' as they so delicately put it. Threatening demands for payment of his gambling debts is what they really should be called—but I don't wish to burden you with my woes." She leaned forward and placed a gloved hand lightly on Petite's shoulder. "Louise, I want you to know that you can speak freely to me."

Petite looked into Athénaïs's sapphire-blue eyes. She was one of the Court's great beauties, but it was her wit that Petite liked—as well as her generous heart. She had always been kind. "I don't know what you mean," Petite said, guarded yet.

"Yes, you do," Athénaïs said with a teasing smile. "I'll be honest with you. I think it's cruel what they're making you go through."

They. Petite looked away.

"Most everyone knows what's going on," Athénaïs said in a low voice.

But surely not everything, Petite thought. Many knew about her relationship with the King, but nobody knew about the babies: the two that had died, much less the one she'd just given birth to, practically in the Queen's own room. "Even I don't know what's going on, Athénaïs," she said with an evasive smile.

Athénaïs smiled kindly, her hand on the bottle. "Just drink this and lie down." She peeled off the wax plug, sniffed the contents and handed the bottle to Petite. "Go ahead. It's sweet. You'll like it—you don't *have* to drink brandy with it." She laughed. "But seriously: it helped me recover after I birthed. It's only natural for things to be wobbly for a time."

She does know, Petite thought—with both chagrin and relief. "Thank you," she said, taking a sip.

That night, Petite slept like the dead, dreaming of her father in a field of horses, of Charles and Filoy. She woke weeping to the sound of trumpets, announcing the King's return.

A FEW DAYS LATER the Court set out: bed frames, toilette tables, clothing trunks, kitchen implements, dishware, utensils, bed curtains and linens loaded onto ninety-two carts. Paris held unhappy memories of the Queen Mother's death—and work was being done on the Louvre, in any case—and so Louis had decided to settle the Court in Saint-Germain-en-Laye for the winter. Petite was relieved. It felt like a new beginning.

"You're not to lift a thing," Clorine told her on packing day, taking a basket of hats out of Petite's hands and putting it down. "You're going to kill yourself at this rate," she scolded, wrapping the statue of the Virgin in small linens and tucking it into the basket. "Sit down. Better yet: lie down."

"Don't forget this," Petite told Clorine, prying the brittle branch from the mirror. The continual round of functions at Vincennes had exhausted her—the military review, two theatricals, the never-ending gaming tables. Even her morning and evening prayers were fatiguing.

"Or this," she said, handing Clorine her keepsake box. Her rosary she tucked into her poke. Someday soon she would feel herself again. Someday soon she would see the child she had birthed.

THE COBBLED PATHS of Saint-Germain-en-Laye were carpeted with golden leaves. Petite kicked them up listlessly as she walked to the new château where Monsieur and Madame Colbert were housed, along with their throng of lively children. Along with Petite's baby girl.

Mist rose off the river. Her teeth chattered as she pulled the bell rope at the door. Louis had named their baby Marie-Anne, after his mother, and arranged for her to reside with the Colbert household. She was reported to be small, somewhat frail—she'd birthed early, Blucher said—and Louis had worried that the infant would not have adequate care in a servant's home. Petite was relieved: she didn't think she could survive another infant death.

A maid led her up the stairs to the nursery. The doors opened on a familiar familial scene: Madame Colbert sitting in a rocking chair tatting lace in a large, sunny room bustling with children.

Madame Colbert shooed her noisy brood away and stood smiling as the nursemaid presented Petite with a tightly swaddled infant. The baby's screams were piercing, and her tiny face was red—a monkey face, Petite thought.

"She's fussy," Madame Colbert said, taking the baby and rocking her vigorously. "There there, sweet Marie-Anne," she cooed until the infant quieted. "Hold her now, quick—before she begins again."

"I think I should be going," Petite said, backing away. Her head was hot and her heart cold.

"I don't think you are well, my dear."

"I'm fine," Petite said.

"I'm fine," she repeated to Clorine on her return to her room in the old château.

"You have heat in your head," Clorine said, pressing her hand against Petite's brow. "I'll send for Monsieur Blucher."

"Don't." Petite didn't want to see the surgeon, didn't want to reveal that she suffered pain in her nether region, that spells of inexplicable weakness came over her now and again. "There's a rehearsal this afternoon for the new ballet."

"I'll send word that you have a fever."

"But His Majesty will be there." Petite held onto the bedpost for support.

Clorine banged the candlestick she was polishing down on the side table.

Petite turned. "What was that?"

Clorine clasped her hands. "Mademoiselle, I do not sleep for worry. You don't have a father, your mother has disowned you, and your brother is something of a gay-blade, so it falls to me to say." She took a breath. "This is no way to live, all this secrecy, all the time pretending that you're not with child, that you're not in childbed, that you haven't just given birth."

Petite teared. "I know, but—"

"All the time pretending that everything is perfectly fine," Clorine ranted on, "that your two boys didn't die all of a sudden, like *that*." She snapped her fingers for effect. "A nice young woman like you should have a husband to look after you, children you can boast of. You should marry a highborn man. I'm sure the King could arrange it."

"Stop."

"A man such as Monsieur le Duc de Gautier would be so very—"

"Clorine, I forbid you to say another word on this subject!" Petite said. "I love Louis. You know that."

"But the King?" Clorine pressed her point. "Do you love the *King?*"

PETITE WAS BROUGHT back to her room in a litter. "She collapsed," Gautier told Clorine, wringing his hands. "Right in the middle of blocking. We hadn't even started going through the steps."

"I'm fine," Petite insisted, staggering toward the bed. Dream images were coming into her head, one upon the other in a frightening rush—of a man in a wooden mask, of her two boys riding away on a White, of a ramshackle coach without wheels. She collapsed on her bed, weakened by the memory of so many losses—her father, the two boys, *Diablo*.

Monsieur Blucher ordered Petite bled from the foot and prescribed weekly purging. "You are not to move from this bed without my permission, Mademoiselle."

Petite groaned.

At the door, the surgeon paused to have a word with Clorine. "She births with difficulty. She must abstain from—" He cleared his throat. "I will not mince words: another pregnancy could . . ."

Kill her.

ALL THAT GRAY winter, Petite did everything as prescribed: refrained from congress, endured bleedings, purges and enemas, downed vile teas and medicinal concoctions. Every other afternoon, Louis came dutifully to see her. She asked him about the ballet rehearsals, the hunts, the military preparations. She inquired of the news, their daughter, the Dauphin's health. Louis would answer, and then sit looking out the window, drumming his fingers.

Petite understood. His love could not follow her into grief. He was of the sun, not the moon. Vainly, she tried to entertain him. Sometimes they would lie side by side, listening to the birds, the wind. Aware of his frustration, Petite offered means of giving relief. It wasn't healthy for a man to go without release.

"It's not the same," he said.

"I would understand if you lay with another woman. The Queen is with child, and I . . ." Her spells of weakness baffled her. She had always prided herself on her strength, her prowess. She'd been his wilderness companion, his queen of the hunt, as bold on horseback as any of his men. Now she was one of the fallen— weak, weary and unsteady on her feet.

ATHÉNAÏS CAME OFTEN to visit. As Petite did needlework, her friend filled her in on the Court gossip. The Queen had consulted her astrologer. She was all in favor of a war with Spain—her native country—to claim "her" Netherlands. All the men talked of now was war, complaining that it was impossible to buy a good mount now, much less find canvas suitably heavy for making a tent. They neglected to mention the money they'd had to borrow to outfit themselves, the heirloom silver they'd had to sell. They were even consulting soothsayers, she reported. Thanks to a spell a sorceress had given the Marquis de Louvroy, he had inherited the five hundred livres he needed for a suit of armor.

"One needs to be careful about such things," Petite cautioned. Outside, someone was beating a kettledrum.

"Indeed," Athénaïs said, raising her goblet of mulled wine, as if in toast. A number of ladies had been to see Madame la Voisin, she reported, the sorceress in Villeneuve-Beauregard, outside the Paris walls. The fortune-teller gave Mademoiselle de Nogaret a charm that appeared to have worked, because the Marquis de Santa-Cruz was now madly in love with her. "But it was his *son* she yearned for."

Petite laughed. "Isn't Madame la Voisin the woman Nicole went to?"

"Most everyone goes to her," Athénaïs said, playing with the key that hung from a pendant (her good luck charm, she claimed).

"Nicole got something called 'passion powder' from her, I recall." The packet was still in Petite's keepsake box.

"She'll have no need for such powder now," Athénaïs said with a laugh. It was rumored that Nicole had joined a convent, become a lay nun.

"Nicole said Madame la Voisin practices dark magic."

"Nonsense. She's a dumpy little woman. I went to her myself not long ago," Athénaïs confessed.

"*You* went?"

"But not for passion powder, I regret to say. How dreary married life is, to be reduced to going to a woman like that for help regarding financial matters."

And then came the more personal confidences: Athénaïs's husband was in debt again. She was going to have to sell some of her jewelry to pay off his gambling losses. "Plus, he's convinced that I'm having a tryst with—" Athénaïs stopped, making an arch smile. "No—I want you to guess."

"Lauzun?" The ugly little man was rumored to have pleasured practically every woman at Court.

Athénaïs gave a look of disgust. "No—*Philippe.*"

Petite smiled wanly. "Doesn't your husband know . . . ?" It was obvious that Louis's brother preferred men.

"I told him, but he thought it a ruse I'd fabricated to throw him off the scent."

There was a scuffle of feet in the entry, the sound of spurs clinking on stone.

"His Majesty," Petite said, her heart lifting.

"I'll be off, then," Athénaïs said with a wink.

Petite checked her face in the glass. Because of her fragile health, Louis had refrained, for the most part, but now she was stronger. They'd begun to have relations—in spite of the pain she experienced, and her puzzling want of desire.

Chapter Twenty-Nine

AT THE END OF MARCH, Louis set up a military camp on the Plaine d'Houilles for three days, not far from Saint-Germain-en-Laye. The Court ladies set out, thrilled by the prospect of sleeping in tents and eating like soldiers.

"Glory," Petite's sister-in-law Gabrielle whispered as their carriage crested a hill. There, before them, was a city of linen tents neatly grouped in rectangles with wide turnpiked "streets" running between. A line of horses stood picketed at the edge of a parade ground. The officer tents could be seen beyond, at a distance from the line of kitchen campfires. Still farther was an artillery park surrounded by carts.

Soldiers cheered to kettledrums as the parade of carriages rolled into the camp, coming to a halt in front of a large, colorful tent with flags flying over it—the camp "palace." A carpet was rolled out and two footmen in livery jumped to hand the ladies down.

The tent filled as more women arrived, crowding into the canopied rooms hung with crystal chandeliers. The officers paused to eye the ladies, then turned back to their companions to talk of weapons, armor and horses. Louis paced before his generals, speaking of maneuvers and munitions. He'd acquired a warrior look, his skin bronzed by the sun.

Petite bowed along with all the other courtiers. He glanced her way, but did not see her.

"Turkey carpets, even," Gabrielle said, assessing the rich trappings.

"It may be lined with Chinese satin, ladies, but it's still a tent," Athénaïs said, squashing a beetle with her toe.

The next morning, the richly attired women mounted horses and rode out to the parade ground to witness a review. The colors were unfurled as a military band began to play. A battalion of foot soldiers and volunteers marched onto the parade ground, the sun glinting off pikes and sabres. Eyes straight ahead, they passed in front of Louis, who, astride a black charger, watched intently. He didn't smile or frown, but now and then said something to his secretary, who stood by taking notes.

Hundreds of men on horseback—small scruffy nags, for the most part—charged whooping onto the field, waving flintlock musketoons in the warm spring wind. One horse bolted, one reared and yet another was left behind entirely, refusing to move. The ladies laughed as a groom ran out and whipped it forward. Once the dragoons had their horses (more or less) in formation, Louis gave a signal and cannons discharged. Horses shied and the women screamed, holding their gloved hands over their noses, complaining of the smell of gunpowder.

"A stirring sight, would you not agree?"

Petite turned in her saddle to see Athénaïs, prettily mounted on a pony. "Indeed," she said, although in truth the war fervor concerned her. This was no longer a game, a show. Many of these men—boys, in fact—would not return to their families. And Louis? He longed to be in battle, she knew, to be in the thick of it, prove his worth.

"You're pale, darling—are you unwell again?"

"I'm fine, thank you," Petite said, embarrassed to admit that she'd tried Nicole's passion powder herself the week before. Although the remedy had revived her "interest" (briefly), it had also made her ill. She dared not complain. A want of spirit annoyed Louis, she knew, who didn't care for infirmities. It pleased him to be surrounded by energetic individuals with vigorous spirits—especially now, now that he courted glory.

PETITE WAS RELIEVED to return to Saint-Germain-en-Laye, to the comfort of her room overlooking the river—the comfort of her bed. The canvas walls of the tent had made it difficult to retch without people overhearing. It was just an ague, she concluded, but it persisted, and persisted—and by Good Friday of Holy Week she knew why.

A sharp rap at her door startled her awake. "Come in, Clorine," she called out groggily. The spring sun was bright, dappling the cushions. She'd fallen asleep rereading Saint Teresa's *Life*.

"His Majesty is here to see you."

Petite sat up, feeling for her slippers. Usually Louis didn't call until after his midday meal. She checked her face in the looking glass, slapping her cheeks to give them color. She was resolved to tell him—and her news would not be welcome, she knew.

Now? Petite thought, listening to the steady beat of Louis's heart. *Should I tell him now?*

She was lying chastely by his side, fully clothed. Lent was over, yet Louis continued to abstain. She understood: soon he would be leading his men into battle, and he must refrain from sin, in order to be spiritually pure—in case . . .

In case he was killed.

She stroked his hand. "Louis, I have something to tell you."

He rolled over to look at her.

"I'm going to have another baby."

"Are you sure?"

She nodded, pressing his hand to her cheek. "And I have something to ask you." Other kings had declared their bastard children. "Have you given thought to acknowledging Marie-Anne?" (And the child to come, in time.)

"I have—I've even discussed it with Colbert," Louis told her.

Petite was pleased.

"But do you understand what it would mean, Louise?"

Petite nodded. Although Marie-Anne would no doubt continue to live with the Colberts—they were like family to her, that was her home—Petite would be able to see her daughter often, and without the need for secrecy.

"I do," she said, knowing the price as well. Everything would be out in the open. Marie-Anne would grow up knowing that she was the daughter of the King—but she would also know that her mother was her father's mistress, that she was born of mislove.

"Yet we must." As it was, their daughter was no different from any other bastard, denied the recognition that she was of the King's blood.

The spring came early to Saint-Germain-en-Laye. Drums competed with the strident tattoo of a woodpecker. Petite set her embroidery frame by the window to

303

catch the light. She winced, rubbing her calf. She was four or five months along, Blucher estimated. The period of nausea had mercifully passed, but now she was plagued by cramps, and her left leg had twice given out on her while she was walking. She stuck two needles into the taut fabric and looked through her box of threads for a bobbin of pale green. She heard footsteps, and looked up to see her maid at the door.

"It's been announced that your girl is the King's daughter, a princess," Clorine said elatedly. "So she's legal now."

"Legitimate, you mean."

"Aye—and you've been made a duchess."

Petite sat back. *This* was a surprise.

"So what do I call you now? Madame la Duchesse de la Vallière, or just Madame la Duchesse? I prefer that, I think, for everyday. You're going to need six horses pulling your carriage and a ducal crest on the carriage door, of course, and long trains on your gown—one . . . no two . . . no three yards long."

"Three feet for a duchess, Clorine." That was quite long enough.

Her portly footman came to the door. "Are you receiving, Madame? There is someone here to see you."

"I don't have very much time." Petite had an appointment to see a doctor in town, and would then be going to the Colbert residence to see Marie-Anne (the new Princess, she thought with a smile).

"Well . . . there are several, in fact. They're in the entry below."

Petite looked up at Clorine, disconcerted.

"Have them wait in the sitting room," Clorine commanded.

The footman scratched his ear. "What about the trunks?"

They'd been preparing to leave with the Court on campaign. "Move the trunks in here," Petite said, standing.

She selected a simple bodice and skirt of pale yellow linen and insisted that she be tightly laced. Clorine persuaded her to wear pearls, even if they were made of ground-up fish scales mixed with wax. "You must get the King to give you a proper necklace," she said, clucking her tongue in disapproval.

Everyone made a deep reverence as Petite entered her sitting room. The air was thick with scents: musk, rose, eau de Chypre. Petite was relieved to see Athénaïs, but she was shocked that the Duchesse de Navailles had made the effort along with several other august ladies of the Court—highborn women who had previously shunned her.

"Madame la Duchesse," they murmured, bowing. The Duchesse de Navailles made a melting reverence.

Petite looked out over their lowered heads. For years courtiers had snickered at her behind her back—mocked her rustic ways (too friendly), her tomboy pursuits, her limp, her "unnatural" aptitude for ancient languages and philosophy. Now that she was a duchess, they could not sit, stand or even speak to her without her approval. There was a certain satisfaction in such power. It chilled her.

AFTER THE GUESTS had finally left, Petite, attended by Clorine, took one of the royal litters into town. It was a beautiful spring afternoon and she easily could have walked, but her left leg felt weak again. She had an appointment with a doctor who'd been having some success with nervous complaints, and these "spells" of weakness were one of the things she wished to discuss before leaving on campaign.

The litter carriers let Petite and Clorine down at rue au Pain and rue des Coches. The men in livery, the royal insignia on the ornate litter, drew a crowd. Petite had grown accustomed to being gawked at, but this time children, street urchins in rags, recognized her and let fly hurling insults: *the King's whore, the King's whore, the King's whore.*

Clorine grabbed one of the boys by the collar, shaking him mightily. Two of his companions threw rocks and one of the litter carriers took chase, but the boys—there were four of them—were spry and danced circles around the hefty man, taunting *whore, whore, whore, whore* before disappearing into a maze of back alleys, their laughter echoing off the stone walls.

"You're going to need a guard whenever you go out," Clorine said, steering Petite down a side street. "Now that you're official."

Official what? Petite wondered, the boys' taunts ringing in her ears. Louis had made her a duchess, given her the highest title in the land, but to the world she'd been revealed as his concubine.

PETITE HAD AN imbalance of bile, the doctor pronounced. Her spells of weakness would be healed easily by a program of herbs and purges. She sent Clorine to the apothecary's with a list and hired a litter to take her to the Colbert residence by the river.

Even from outside, Petite could hear the children laughing. In the upstairs nursery the atmosphere was one of celebration, the young Colberts in an uproar over the recent announcement. They had adorned "princess" Marie-Anne with a paper crown and fancy lace collar, which she drooled on.

Madame Colbert chuckled to see her brood dancing about. "At least they aren't jealous," she told Petite, balancing her youngest on one hip. "Silence," she called out, and the three eldest children quieted. "You too, Jules," she told her eight-year-old son. "Do we not have a proper greeting for Madame la Duchesse?"

The girls curtsied and the boys bowed, and they all ran giggling out of the room.

Petite cradled Marie-Anne in her arms and followed Madame Colbert into a sunny sitting room where they made themselves comfortable on soft easy chairs, their babies on their laps.

"Just like two gossiping nursemaids," Madame Colbert said.

Petite touched Marie-Anne's button nose. The baby gave a chortle. *Princess.*

"Mon Dieu! Forgive me for sitting in the presence of a duchess."

"Please, Madame Colbert—sit," Petite said.

"But seriously," Madame Colbert said, settling back in her chair, "this does change things. I'll need to hire staff for your wee princess here—" She made goggle-eyes at Marie-Anne, who was too preoccupied with pulling at her lace collar to notice. "She should be served at her own table, apart from my children." Madame Colbert's tone was solemn.

"There must not be any changes," Petite told Madame Colbert emphatically. "It would be cruel to separate her from your wonderful children. They're her family."

ATHÉNAÏS CALLED THE next day, full of reproaches. "How can this upset you?" she demanded, tapping the back of Petite's hand with her fan. "All my life I've longed to be made a duchess," she said in a theatrically languishing tone. "A fantasy of my childhood, impossible to attain."

"I would give you this title if I could," Petite said. She was stretched out on the daybed with a damp cloth on her brow. She'd been told that the Queen had gone into rages at the news, ordering all taborets removed from her chamber so that she would not have to suffer the indignity of Petite exercising her ducal right to sit in the Queen's presence.

"His Majesty has conferred the highest honor on you. This should make you happy."

"May I tell you something, Athénaïs, in confidence?"

"Have I not told you all my dirty secrets, my sordid embarrassments?"

Petite sat up, trying to control the flood of emotion rising within her: her apprehension that Louis no longer loved her. How much of a companion had she been to him, of late—much less a lover? "I fear it's a farewell gesture," she said. "Isn't this the way it's done? When a king tires of a woman, he gives her a title and sends her away?"

"His Majesty is devoted to you. You know that."

Yes, Petite thought, *but* . . . "He's been remote of late." He'd not been himself. He'd even lost his nature on a number of occasions and that unnerved him, she knew. His doctor had advised a diet of celery, truffles and vanilla to help quicken him—but without success.

"It's this coming war—it has all the men acting like fools. If I hear another word about mortar or Damascus swords, I think I'll scream."

"Madame?" Clorine set glasses of spiced red wine and comfits of orange rind on a side table. "You have a caller." She widened her eyes. "Madame Françoise de la Vallière, the Marquise de Saint-Rémy."

"My mother?"

Athénaïs's look was one of amusement. "I'll see you on the morrow," she said, taking up her rose-scented gloves.

PETITE'S MOTHER HAD gained weight since their last encounter, that fateful day in the marketplace four years earlier. Indeed, she had become rather large. She bowed with some difficulty, and for a moment Petite feared she would need help rising.

"I thank you for the honor of receiving me, Madame la Duchesse," Françoise said, addressing Petite formally, clenching and unclenching her gloved hands. "The Marquis de Saint-Rémy would have come to pay his respects as well, but he has the dropsy."

"Please, Mother," Petite said, "take a chair."

"One must give preference to a duchess," Françoise said, remaining standing.

Petite leaned against the mantel. She longed to sit down herself, but she couldn't, not with her mother standing. The intricacies of parlor etiquette would soon drive her mad.

"If only I had *known*," Françoise said.

Known that her daughter had been debauched by a king, and not some everyday sinner. Petite felt angry confusion. "It wasn't in my power to tell anyone, not even you, Mother."

"I suppose this is how Jean got his promotion, his rich wife. Even your uncle Gilles has been made a bishop."

Mercy. Her father's brother had hardly been able to get through a Mass without stumbling—and now he was a bishop? Was this Louis's doing? It had to be. "Aunt Angélique must know, then," Petite said with a sinking heart. Gentle, devout Sister Angélique: she would be horrified to learn that Petite—her "little angel"—was the country's official fallen woman.

"No doubt, but I wouldn't concern myself. That woman never could add two plus two. And what's this about a daughter?"

"Marie-Anne is eight months old. She has two teeth already and another one coming in." Petite smiled. "His Majesty was born with teeth, so I guess it's not surprising."

"The King's daughter, *my* granddaughter." Françoise shook her head in disbelief. "But eight months old? It was years ago I saw you in the market—and you were far along."

Petite turned away, dismayed by the anger she still felt. *Disowned.* Pregnant with Charles, her first, she'd been young—and very alone. "I had two boys, Mother," Petite said finally, her voice breaking. "They died." One after the other. "This was long ago." Would the grief never end?

Petite felt her mother's hand on her shoulder. She turned, surprised to see her mother's tears. Had she ever seen her mother cry?

"I had two boys once myself," Françoise said. "Jean, of course—but also a little Michel."

How was that possible? "Why didn't I know?"

"He died just before you were born."

Petite was incredulous, and yet . . . would she ever tell Marie-Anne about her two brothers—Petite's own dead babies?

Françoise wiped her cheeks on her sleeves. "It makes one witless. I was . . .

crackbrained, I guess you would say. For a bit. That's when your father learned about healing. And silence. It was best that way."

Petite nodded, taking this all in. She and Jean had often been in her father's care, her mother "ailing." Now she could begin to understand. They had buried a son together. Her father would have seen her mother's heartbreak, shared it. "You will love Marie-Anne," Petite said, embracing her. She smelled familiarly of vanilla. "And I'm soon to have another."

"I can see that," Françoise said, proudly this time.

She left shortly after, anxious to return to the ailing Marquis, anxious to be back in Paris before nightfall.

Petite sat at the window watching children chase hoops in the gardens below. It had been two days of revelations, one upon the other, and the last, her mother's, was surely the greatest. Seeing her mother's tears, understanding and sharing her grief, had given her something she could not name. Forgiveness, she realized, after a time: a blessing.

MONSIEUR COLBERT CALLED that evening. He was in a hurry; there were a million things to attend to with respect to the upcoming campaign. In addition to having to secure financing for the army's provisions, there were the inevitable last-minute details: the King's tent was already in need of repair and his armor breastplate had to be recast, for starters.

"I just wanted you to know that I'm in the process of negotiating a duchy for you—well, technically, for your daughter, you understand, but for your use until you should" he wiped his spectacles clean with his lace cuff—"die."

Petite nodded. "Yes, Monsieur, I understand."

"My wife tells me that you might be familiar with it." He riffled through his leather portfolio of papers. "Ah, here it is, it's in the Touraine," he read out, "in the barony of Saint-Christophe. Château de Vaujours."

Petite tilted her head. "Did you say Vaujours?" *Surely not.*

Colbert frowned, squinting. He was shortsighted without his eyepiece. "So you do know it."

Petite nodded. The Château de Vaujours was the home of the Lady in White, the young woman who had drowned herself to ease a broken heart. Her ghostly apparition called out to weeping maidens. "I've heard of it."

"The purchase will not be official for another year, I expect. It requires a parliamentary decree, and this type of transact is painfully slow, especially when the King is involved."

Petite smiled. It was said that the King could move mountains, but not Parliament.

"But when it does come through," Colbert went on, "you will be mandated to sign over two hundred fifty thousand livres. Don't worry—Tournais livres, not Parisian. I will make all the arrangements. The property is in the care of a steward, but when the time comes, I will advise you on matters pertaining to management."

Petite felt light-headed. She hadn't quite realized that being a duchess entailed looking after a duchy.

"It's of medium size," Monsieur Colbert said, "the rents yielding about a hundred thousand livres a year. That should set you up nicely." Colbert looked at his timepiece and handed a parchment to Petite. "This is for you. It's a copy of what His Majesty wrote Parliament regarding your title," he said. He took up his portfolio.

"Thank you, Monsieur," Petite said, scanning the text: *well-loved, faithful Louise de la Vallière . . . a multitude of rare perfections . . . an affection that had lasted for years.*

"Yes, thank you," she repeated with a sinking heart. *Had lasted.*

A NEW COACH and six was delivered, ornamented with a ducal crown. The horses were Barbs of a matching golden color, with silky manes and tails. "From His Majesty," Gautier told Petite excitedly. The coach was gleaming, the interior lined with the finest scarlet brocade. It employed the newest suspension system, he explained—one could drink a dish of tea in it, if one wished. Any man in the kingdom would sell his soul for such a conveyance.

"It's beautiful," Petite said, wondering why Louis hadn't come himself to present it. She hadn't seen him since her title was announced, since Marie-Anne was acknowledged.

"His Majesty is unable to call right now," Gautier said, sensing her malaise.

"He has meetings, I know."

"Not exactly." Gautier pulled at his lace cravat. "Dr. Vallot has persuaded His Majesty to take a bouillon purgative in preparation for the coming campaign, so—understandably—he is 'tied up.'"

Louis rarely took his doctor's advice. It pleased Petite that he was looking after himself. "I'm happy to hear that."

"He desires you to know that he will be able to come see you tomorrow afternoon at three, in order to bid farewell."

Farewell? "But I'm going on the campaign as well."

"There has been a change." Gautier cleared his throat. "Only the household of the Queen is to accompany His Majesty."

"I'm not to go?" She'd been bled twice in preparation.

"You must understand—your recent elevation has disturbed Her Majesty, in particular with respect to the girl." He shifted his weight from one foot to the other. "In any case, the roads to the north are primitive and the air is impure. It is not a good season to be traveling."

IN THE MORNING Gautier informed Petite that there had, yet again, been a change of plans. His Majesty would *not* be calling on her at three of the clock that afternoon. He would, instead, be there shortly, at ten of the clock, and His Majesty intended to bring his son, the Dauphin de France, and, furthermore, it had been arranged for Madame Colbert to bring Princess Marie-Anne as well.

"His Majesty is bringing the Dauphin?" Petite asked, stunned by this revelation. And Marie-Anne was to be there? *Mercy.*

"He wishes it known that this is a state occasion," Gautier said, meaning full Court dress.

Petite had just come from an early morning ride and was in her chevalier ensemble. It had been a leisurely outing (because of her condition), but a wind had come up and her hair was disordered. She rang for Clorine: "His Majesty will be here in under an hour. We're to welcome him in full Court dress."

"Zut!"

The situation wasn't as dire as Petite initially had thought. Her wig had been curled and dressed only two weeks before and was presentable. Clorine stripped Petite out of her soiled riding habit and brought her a lacy shift, stockings and decency skirt. Petite chose a brocade girdle embroidered in gold thread and embellished with tiny pearls.

"How many petticoats?" Clorine asked, pulling Petite's shift straight before tightening the cord so that the lace border of the shift lay straight at her neckline.

With the long train, the gown and underskirt were heavy. "One silk," Petite told her, putting the wig on and then taking it off. It was hot and she had her face to put on yet.

Her face: her scowling face. The last thing she'd expected, much less prepared for, was an official visit from His Majesty. It was Louis she longed to see—not the King.

Madame Colbert arrived as Clorine was helping Petite into her gown, a pearl-embellished gold and silver confection. The hefty matron was flushed from the exertion of climbing the stairs in a heavy ensemble of green velvet. Even the nursemaid carrying Marie-Anne was wearing brocade, and Marie-Anne herself was adorned in a tiny gown of embroidered silk.

"I'm almost ready," Petite said, shaking out her skirts. She kissed Marie-Anne on the nose. "How is my princess?" She made a funny face at the baby, but Marie-Anne was having none of it. "She looks sleepy."

"We had to wake her from a nap," Madame Colbert said. "Do you know what this is about?"

"All I've been told is that His Majesty is bringing the Dauphin," Petite said.

"Blessed Mary, Mother of God," Madame Colbert said.

Petite sat down at her toilette table and looked into the glass. No, she would not wear paint. She was flushed from her morning ride: Louis had always liked her best that way. (She wondered if that was still the case.) "Just the wig," she told Clorine.

Trumpets announced the royal party as Clorine was putting on Petite's pearls. Marie-Anne began to fuss, spitting up onto her gown. The nursemaid gave her a white candy stick to suck, which quieted her.

How should we arrange ourselves? Petite wondered, standing. She took the baby into her arms and led the way into the sitting room. Marie-Anne dropped the candy stick, fussing as the nursemaid rummaged in her sack for another one. Both Petite and Madame Clorine were trying to appease her when Louis entered with his son. They were followed by the boy's tutor, Gautier, Lauzun and three guards, all in full dress.

The Dauphin was over five years old and had yet to be breeched, in spite of his inordinate size. He was controlled by two traces, held by his tutor.

Petite made a reverence as best she could while holding a squirming Marie-Anne in her arms.

Louis whispered something to Gautier, who came up to Petite. "His Majesty wishes the Princess to be introduced to his son."

"Yes," Petite said, but unsure. "Am I to carry the Princess to His Majesty?" she asked Gautier under her breath. The King and his son were only two sword lengths away, yet it seemed a great distance.

Marie-Anne began to whimper. Petite slipped a finger into the baby's mouth for her to suck on.

"Perhaps it would be best if you did the honors, Madame la Duchesse," Gautier said, bowing and stepping back.

Jollying the baby, Petite stepped forward and curtsied before Louis and his son.

Louis looked down at the boy. "This is your sister," he told him. "Her name is Marie-Anne. And this is your sister's mother, Madame Louise, the Duchesse de Vaujours."

The boy looked up at his father, confused.

I know how he feels, Petite thought, smiling at the child. She tried to catch Louis's eye: there was so much she wanted to say. She felt trapped, as if they were players on a stage and confined to a script.

"We must go now," Louis informed his party. Everyone parted to make room. He looked again at Petite, then strode over to her. His back to his son, his entourage, he said, his voice low, "I'm sorry, Louise. The Queen, she's—" He made an expression of fatigue. "In time . . ."

Petite nodded, her eyes filling. "I understand."

"I promise you: it won't be a long campaign."

Petite watched from a window as the Court prepared to depart, watched as the Queen was handed into her coach, followed by Athénaïs and several other members of the Queen's household. She watched as Louis, on horseback, laughed with Lauzun and two of his musketeers. She closed the shutters, pulled the drapes. When, at last, there was silence—no more sounds of horses, carriage wheels, voices—she rang for Clorine.

"My walking boots," she said. "And my hooded cape."

She walked out into the fields, alone. She stood for a time, leaning against a chestnut tree, gaining solace in the company of the foals and broken-down nags left behind, the horses unsuitable for show or war. *I've been left behind*, she thought, with bitterness in her heart. The curious horses surrounded her, shaking their heads against the flies. A yearling took a nervous step forward. Petite extended her hand.

Chapter Thirty

IT WAS EARLY FALL by the time the King returned to Saint-Germain-en-Laye. He'd been away five months. The people went mad rejoicing. All summer there had been news of battles won, one upon another. Charleroi, Tournai, Courtrai, Douai, Lille—the towns and cities of the Spanish Netherlands had fallen before the King like a house of cards. He was valiant, young and handsome—but most of all he was victorious. The days of glory had arrived.

A hundred trumpets announced His Majesty. Fire rockets flared from the towers of the ancient château, banners were unfurled and mint and chamomile strewn over the cobbles. Louis, his wavy hair long, his bearing regal, entered the central courtyard gambading on an Andalusian great horse of unusual height. The gold and semiprecious stones on its caparison glittered as the horse reared up, then kicked out, performing caprioles and levades. He waved his feathered hat to the cheering crowds. He had the air of a man who had faced battle and emerged the victor, a man who had tested his mettle and found it strong.

Petite watched the welcoming celebrations from a window above. She was big with child now, and preferred to stay out of the public eye. "I'd best be back in my chamber," she told Clorine. "His Majesty will soon be calling."

LOUIS ARRIVED ACCOMPANIED by four pages and two musicians, who immediately took up their lutes and began to play. The pages, wide-eyed boys in red-feathered hats, gawked at Petite.

"You've been well, Louise?" He leaned forward to kiss her cheek—the chaste kiss of a brother or friend. He was wearing a collared red velvet cloak trimmed with gold braid.

There was something different in his manner, Petite thought, something bold—a polished and gallant confidence she'd not seen in him before. "Yes, quite," she said, her hands on her hard, taut belly. "And you?" She longed to be alone with him.

"Splendid," he said, pacing the room, examining it as if he'd never seen it before. He picked up a book, opened it, then put it back.

"Congratulations on your victories," Petite said, watching uneasily as he lifted the blue jar on her toilette table. He took the top off and sniffed it. At the sound of a child's voice, he set it down.

"Our Princess," Petite said with a smile, turning as Clorine came into the room holding Marie-Anne. The ten-month-old plunged four fingers of her right hand into her mouth, her big eyes taking in the strange men in the room—the strange man in the center.

"And who have we here?" Louis said, his hands on his hips. His stance was that of a musketeer, but his voice was tender, charmed.

The girl clung to Clorine's neck.

Petite took her from her maid. "There, now," she said, holding the child close. "She's become shy," she told Louis, dancing gently to soothe her.

Marie-Anne quieted, her head nestled against Petite's heart, sucking her thumb. "King?" She pointed a wet finger.

Louis laughed.

"Your father," Petite whispered, nuzzling the girl and kissing her, cherishing her.

AFTER THE BIRTH of a son, little Louis (affectionately called Tito, the name a Spanish nursemaid had called Louis when he was a baby), Petite was again bedridden, unable to go with the Court for a weeklong festival at Versaie.

"Why don't you go to Madame Voisin?" Athénaïs suggested. "Don't be rolling your eyes. You never know."

"Using enchantments is dangerous, Athénaïs."

"Ah, yes: the Devil and all that," she said with a laugh. "You make it sound so ominous. One would think you were a member of the Holy League. The powder you tried made you sick, certainly, but it hardly killed you."

Petite flushed. She shouldn't have admitted to Athénaïs her foolish (and desperate) experiment with the passion powder Nicole had given her. "I'm serious. One never knows where it will lead."

"I know perfectly well where it leads: to riches. The spell Voisin designed for me worked. It was just some silly ritual to help my husband get a position—and voilà—soon after, His Majesty awarded him the company of light cavalry in the south."

"I'm happy to hear that," Petite said weakly, unable to reveal that Monsieur le Marquis de Montespan's promotion was due to her own intervention, in fact.

IT SEEMED THAT Petite was always looking for something: she'd misplaced a ribbon, her favorite pomade. The Court was so often on the move it was hard to keep track. She was looking through her trunks, trying to gather her things in preparation for the Court's upcoming trip to Chambord, when Clorine burst in.

"Monsieur de Montespan attacked his wife," she said breathlessly, putting down a basket of clean shifts.

"What do you mean, *attacked* her?" Petite had seen Athénaïs that very morning. She reached for the rosary, usually draped around the statue of the Virgin on the prie-dieu, but it wasn't there. (Yet another thing missing, out of place.)

"Just that. He pulled her by the hair and struck her. It took four men to pull him off."

"Get my cloak and boots, Clorine."

"She's gone into hiding—in Paris, her laundress thinks."

Shortly after, Louis called. He was distracted, busy preparing for the Court's long trip to Chambord—and now this.

"Can nothing be done to protect her?" Petite took his sword, his wet hat and cape. Her health had returned—blessedly—and she had begun enjoying their time together.

"The man is mad. I've ordered him arrested," Louis said wearily, kissing her and then sitting down on the bed, "but now it seems he's disappeared—the police can't find him." He fell back against the cushions, staring at the ceiling. "Why do these things always seem to happen just before a trip?"

A few days later, Athénaïs's husband was finally apprehended. "In a whorehouse in Paris," Clorine reported with disgust. "So now he's locked up in Fort l'Évêque—"

"That's a relief."

"—but not for long. There's nothing they can charge him with."

"But he attacked her."

"She's his wife." Clorine shrugged. "That's not a crime."

"It will be good for the Marquise to get away to Chambord," Petite said, going through a basket of herbal remedies, selecting the ones she might need. "What's this?" she asked, picking out a scrap of linen tucked away in the bottom. She unfolded it—it held a shriveled worm. She sniffed it: it was dry, without odor.

"Zut! That's a bit of Marie-Anne's cord. I've been wondering where it went."

Petite wrinkled up her nose.

"You know, during her birthing at Vincennes, when she was cut free of you—Monsieur Blucher said to give it to you. He said it would protect you from the Devil."

Petite folded it back up and slipped it into the pocket under her skirts. She'd had a frightening dream the night before: a dream of the Devil lurking. She could use protection.

THE CHÂTEAU AT Chambord was a hateful thing. Everyone was lost in it, everyone cross. The central staircase twisted upon itself; the person coming down eluded the person going up. The rooms, suites, windows and passageways were all alike. Were it not for hints of the sun, one might not know where one was at all. The seventy-seven different stairways did not help.

Petite was assigned one of the square apartments. Her brother, mother (recently widowed), nursemaid and children—Tito and Marie-Anne—were on the floor above. Athénaïs was in the round tower apartment beside her. It was possible to go from a round apartment into a square one, as Athénaïs discovered, popping through a small door into Petite's suite.

"This place makes me dizzy," she said, casting herself into a chair. She had disguised her bruises under thick white face paint, but nothing could hide the tic in her cheek.

"I got lost finding my children," Petite said with a smile. But then she regretted her words. Athénaïs's crackbrained husband had been banished to his château in the south, and had taken their children with him—a boy and a girl—telling them that their mother was dead. "You need rest," Petite told her sympathetically.

"What I need is some brandy," Athénaïs said.

PETITE SAW TITO and Marie-Anne each morning and hunted with Louis every afternoon. She tried to persuade Athénaïs to join their excursions, but her friend declined; she needed to conserve her strength, she said, for the evening levee. Every night the courtiers gathered in the King's apartment to play cards, billiards or lansquenet, feast and watch a performance by the Comédie before proceeding to the ballroom. It was a vigorous life, dedicated to pleasure, culture and perhaps too much wine.

"I'm concerned about Athénaïs," Petite confided to Louis after intimacy one late afternoon.

Louis sat up. "Oh?"

"She's still not well." Athénaïs's nerval tic was, if anything, even more pronounced.

"It's no wonder. She stays up all night," Louis said with his usual tone of disapproval. He was often critical of Athénaïs—complaining that she didn't sit a horse properly, that her wit was biting and sometimes cruel.

"Perhaps if she went riding with us," Petite suggested. "It would be good for her to get out." Riding daily had greatly improved her own strength and spirit. That afternoon they had ridden through the meadows where Petite and "her poacher" had first met.

"She detests the natural world," Louis said.

Petite smiled. So true. "But if you insisted?"

"That wouldn't make a difference," Louis said, swinging his legs over the edge of the bed. He was lean and muscular, but even so the deep feather mattress was something of a struggle to climb out of. He stood looking out the window at the wooded hills beyond. "Louise—" he began reflectively, but stopped.

Petite pulled the covering sheet up over herself. "Yes?"

He let out his breath. "Madame la Marquise can't go riding," he said, turning to face her.

Petite held his gaze.

"She's . . . delicate: she's carrying a child." He sat back down beside her on the bed.

Petite frowned, taking in this unexpected revelation. That would explain why Athénaïs was ill so much of the time, of late—but why hadn't she said anything to Petite about it? "I gather her husband is not the father," she said slowly. Thus the secrecy.

"No, he's not," Louis said wearily. "Legally he is, of course," he continued, after a pause, "but no, the Marquis de Montespan is not the father, not in the sense that you mean. But according to the law," he went on with emphasis, "the Marquis de Montespan can do whatever he wants with that child."

That child.

The windows had been opened; it was a sunny autumn day. Birds were chirping in the vines. Petite had the sense that her life was tilting, yet again; that nothing would ever be the same, that the birds would sing, but that she would hear them differently. "So who, then, is the father?"

Louis turned to face her. Petite saw the answer in his eyes.

"I love you," he said, reaching for her.

Petite brushed his hand away.

"You said you'd understand."

As if it were a contract *she* had broken. This Petite could not abide. Angry tears burst from her. Why did it have to be Athénaïs? She could list a thousand answers, each of them wounding. Athénaïs was beautiful, witty, of the highest nobility. She was like a fiery hunter, Petite a hardworking cart pony.

"Do you love her?" Petite demanded.

"I wouldn't call it that," he said, almost with derision. Abruptly he got up and pulled on his breeches.

"Then forsake her."

"No—I won't. I *can't*. And in any case," he said, turning to face her, "it wouldn't be right. I didn't want this to happen, but now that it has, I will not abandon her." He pulled on his doublet, his faced flushed in anger. "You need to know that, and decide accordingly," he said coldly, and left.

Petite sat watching the fire as it turned to embers. She felt numb—dazed. What were her choices, in fact? She reached for the rosary Louis had given her to replace the one she had lost. The tiny perfect diamonds were of little comfort.

"Mademoiselle?" Clorine peeked in.

"Yes, dress me now." She could hear Athénaïs in her room, hear the hard click-click of her heels on the bare parquet.

PETITE DIDN'T KNOCK, but opened the door, startling a maid. "I'm here to see Madame," she said.

"Your card?" The maid pushed a silver tray forward.

She was new; Petite didn't recognize her.

"Claude, I need the scissors," Petite heard Athénaïs call out from within.

Petite stepped through the curtains. It was a lofty chamber, but dark. The floor was matted, and the walls hung with tapestries. A gold vase of flowers had been set in a shuttered window.

"Louise!" Athénaïs said, startled. "What can I do for you?" she asked, closing an enamel and gold snuffbox. Belatedly, she made the reverence due to a duchess.

"Scissors, Madame?" The maid was close behind Petite.

"Not now," Athénaïs said, tidying her hair with her hands. She was wearing a beltless gown of yellow silk, tied at the sides with wide black ribbons.

The maid slammed the door shut behind her.

"The daughter of an actress," Athénaïs said with a dramatic sigh. "No manners whatsoever."

Petite did not smile. "He told me," she said evenly.

"Am I supposed to understand?" Athénaïs asked, then smiled, her head to one side.

"You know perfectly well."

Athénaïs stared at Petite for a long moment, then went to a writing desk and reached for a crockery jug on a shelf above. "Care for some?" she asked, pouring a thick amber-colored liquid into two brandy glasses. "It's a sweet Spanish wine the Queen introduced me to, quite nice," she said, holding out a glass.

Petite held the glass, imagining throwing the syrup in Athénaïs's face. Was that not what was done in the theater? Instead, she downed it quickly, coughing.

"Sit down," Athénaïs said. "Please. I imagine you must be upset."

Petite's brave fury turned maudlin. "I thought you were my friend." Pathetic, but true. She took a shaky breath.

"Don't for one minute think I haven't suffered. Imagine what would happen if my husband were to find out." Athénaïs made a fearful expression, her eyes wide.

The lunatic husband. Petite suddenly understood the logic behind his rage. She felt such a fool. "How much does he know?"

"Only suspicions." Athénaïs's face quivered with tics. "He would kill me if he found out about . . . And God only knows what he'd do to the child."

The child. Her own children's half-sibling. Petite felt caught in a web. "I can't forgive you," she said. It was a small thing, yet it was one truth she could hold on to—one truth in a maze of lies.

"Come," Athénaïs said, "I love you both. The Queen is with child and you have been unwell. Would you have preferred that His Majesty go to a common trollop, bring you back some horrible disease?" She smiled charmingly. "I begin to think you should thank me."

Petite stood abruptly and cracked the glass neatly against the mantel. "You mistake me," she said, holding the splinter. She thought of the animals she'd hunted down and killed. She wanted to see that look in Athénaïs's eyes.

She threw down the glass. "I curse you," she said, and stumbled out the door.

Chapter Thirty-One

PETITE HAD TO GET AWAY. She had been talking with her brother about making the journey to Vaujours to see her duchy—and now was the time. Her mother—free now that she was widowed—wanted to come along as well, and bring Marie-Anne, who was now old enough to go on excursions. They could stop at the farmstead in Reugny on the way, make it an outing. Petite agreed; she needed her family around her.

"What's bothering the King?" Jean asked, handing his portmanteau up to the driver. "He's hardly speaking . . . not just to me, but to anyone."

Petite relinquished baby Tito into the arms of his plump nursemaid, who jiggled the eleven-month-old and then headed back to the château. "We'll talk in the coach," Petite said, taking Marie-Anne's hand, "after this one goes to . . ." She closed her eyes to indicate sleep.

"What did you say?" the girl demanded, looking up at her mother. She wasn't yet two, and she was not only talking, but interrogating. The Little Advocate, they sometimes called her. "What did she say?" she asked her grandmother Françoise, her uncle Jean.

"Just that you're going on a very long trip," Petite said.

"I know that," she protested. "And I'm not going to go to sleep."

They had been in the coach for only a few minutes when Marie-Anne fell asleep in her grandmother's arms.

Jean gave Petite an inquiring look. "Well?"

Petite stared out the window. She didn't want a scene. "Promise you won't get upset."

"I promise." He placed his right hand over his heart.

"I'm considering leaving the King."

"What!"

"What?" Françoise echoed.

"Breaking off," Petite said. Suddenly it felt very real.

"You *can't*," Jean said.

"I have reason," Petite said evenly.

"Even if you did have reason, you couldn't. One: His Majesty wouldn't allow it. Two: *I* wouldn't allow it. Three: you'd have to leave your children."

"I'd take them with me," Petite said. They were passing the rock cliffs. She thought of the families living in caves. She felt she was in a cave herself, searching for a glimpse of light to show her the way out.

"Oh, and estrange them from their father the King," Jean said, taking a pinch of snuff, "ruin their lives, their future. That would be kind of you."

"Don't mock me, Jean," Petite warned, but she was discouraged by the truth of what he said. The children weren't hers—they belonged to Louis. Even a peasant woman had no right to her children: the law was the law, and the King's law even more so. Her daughter and son were of royal blood; they belonged to France.

"*I* happen to have an interest in this, remember?"

"Mother has a pension and you have Gabrielle," Petite said sharply. "And I have a duchy now." Truth was, she was considering living there. It was one of the reasons for the trip. She wanted to see the château, the estate, see what life there might entail.

"Jean, give her a chance to explain," Françoise said, moving Marie-Anne onto the seat between her and Petite. The girl moaned in her sleep, but nodded off again, her head in her grandmother's ample lap.

"Thank you, Mother," Petite said, putting her shawl over the child. "The King and I, we're—" She stopped, blinking back tears. "We're not . . ." Not *what?* What words could possibly describe such a rupture?

"Does this have to do with another woman?" Jean asked. "I certainly hope that that's not the case," he persisted, "because if that were just cause, there wouldn't be a marriage left standing."

Including your own, Petite wanted to say—but didn't. "Madame la Marquise de Montespan is with child by the king," Petite said evenly.

"Criminy." Even Jean sounded shocked.

"Isn't she married?" Françoise asked.

Petite nodded.

"Sacré Dieu," Jean said, shaking his head. "And to a madman."

Petite closed her eyes: the implications were overwhelming. Were Athénaïs's husband to find out, were the public to know . . .

"Are we there yet?" Marie-Anne asked, sitting up.

"Not yet, sweetheart." Petite pulled the child onto her lap and held her close. "But soon," she added, relieved to put an end to the discussion.

They rode in uncomfortable silence down the once-familiar roads, pulling, at last, through the gates of their old homestead. Petite surveyed the courtyard in wonder. It was both familiar and strange.

"Look how the trees have grown," Françoise said.

"And the weeds," Petite said.

"That should change now that I've found a good tenant," Jean said, jumping out. He kissed Petite's hand as he handed her down. "I seem always to be asking forgiveness," he said with a woebegone look.

"Oh, Jean," Petite said, moved by her brother's awkward apology.

He put his arm around her and they trekked across the weedy courtyard to the door of their childhood home.

MOST OF THE furnishings had been sold off and replaced with items of lesser quality, spare, but functional.

Françoise threw the mouse nest out of the old kitchen stove, and—once Jean got a spark going with a flint—she managed to start a fire. "Go down to the river for something to cook," she told her son as she cleaned off the familiar white table.

"Want to catch some eels?" Jean asked Marie-Anne, looking for something that might serve as a fishing stick.

"Yes!" the child said.

"Just like her mother used to do," Jean said with a wink, heading out.

"Watch her by the water, Jean," Petite called out after them. Marie-Anne was swinging on her uncle's arm, the two of them laughing.

PETITE'S OLD ROOM in the attic had been taken over by bats, so she made a bed for herself and Marie-Anne on a pallet in the sitting room. Late that night, she lay beside her daughter, listening to the gentle wheezing of her breath, feeling its warmth on her cheek. The night was still, silent but for the chorus of crickets. She stared into the dark. Her mother had taken the one lantern with her upstairs and they had no night candle. She thought she heard a noise, something moving. She remembered lying in the dark in her room under the eaves, listening for the Devil, fearing he was lurking under her bed, waiting for a chance to pounce. She thought of bone magic.

She felt for the locket she slept with, the locket with the bit of Marie-Anne's birth cord in it now, together with a strand of Tito's hair and Diablo's mane. Her trinity.

In the morning, Petite slipped out the back door and into the courtyard. The team of six coach horses standing in the paddock regarded her with curiosity. She stroked the nose of one of the horses and turned toward the barn.

The door hung off its hinges. She took a step inside. It was dark, the small window in the far wall boarded over. It took a moment for her to be able to see. The splintered walls of Diablo's stall had fallen in, and wood crates were stacked over the spot where her father had died. The cross was gone, the twitch. She heard creatures scurrying and backed out, into the light.

She walked around behind the barn: there, where her "convent" had been, was a pile of stone. It made her sad, seeing it thus, recalling her childish quest to follow in the footsteps of Saint Teresa. (How she had strayed.) She remembered her fright, burying the pin case. Was it still there? She crouched, pushing aside shriveled leaves, looking for something she could use as a tool. There was only a bent iron nail, but it was long. It would suffice. She stabbed it into the dirt. It glanced off stones. She sat back on her heels, checking her bearings—the wall of the barn, the stone outline of her hovel. She moved some of the rocks that had fallen in and tried again. She hit tin.

Petite brushed off the case and studied it. At times she'd wondered if it had been a dream, but now it all came back to her clearly: killing a toad and burying it under an anthill, taking its skeleton to the river at night. She had been only six years old—how did she have the courage? She'd been desperate to save Diablo's life. Now she was desperate once again, but it was her own life that needed to be saved.

She pried the case open. There were still traces of oil. *Bone magic.* Slowly, she made the sign of the cross over it. It was the Devil's power—but power, nonetheless. The power to tame, to make things right.

THEY LEFT FOR Vaujours shortly after, Jean riding his horse alongside the coach with his sword drawn—"for safety." They were heading into unknown parts. The rocking of the carriage quickly seduced both Françoise and Marie-Anne into sleep, leaving Petite with her thoughts. Obsessively, she reviewed the past in her mind—lies, she now knew. What *were* her choices?

The landscape was flat and barren, war-scarred still. They passed through a quarry and the remains of what must once have been a great forest. Men and women in rags worked the fields, children in tow. They stopped to stare, mouths agape to see the coach of a duchess go by.

They stopped at a ramshackle inn to refresh the horses. "The driver isn't sure which way to go from here," Jean said, leaning in the window.

"I have a survey," Petite said, handing him a rolled-up parchment.

"Holy. All that?" Jean traced the territory with his finger.

"Are we there yet?" Marie-Anne asked, yawning.

Sometime later the coach climbed out of a valley and into a scrubby terrain. A stone structure came into view, looming against the cloudless sky. A shrub rustled as wild creatures scurried out of sight.

"It has towers," Marie-Anne said. A goshawk took flight at their approach.

"It's a castle," Françoise said. "A small castle," she added as they got a better view.

A very small castle, Petite thought . . . and in ruins. Moss covered the remains of a stone staircase. Trees filled a roofless chamber and vines hung from the broken arches.

"Now I remember," Françoise said, taking Marie-Anne onto her lap. "Vaujours was where the Lady in White lived. Didn't she?"

"Yes, that's what I recall," Petite said as the coach jolted to a halt in what had been a courtyard, now overgrown with shrubs. To their right, the tumbledown castle. To their left, a pond.

"So that must be where she . . ." Françoise mouthed the words *drowned herself.*

Petite thought she heard a woman singing. "Did you hear that?"

"The frogs?" Françoise asked, tying on Marie-Anne's leather booties as the girl squirmed.

The woman's voice was a deep, sweet alto, both passionate and plaintive. Where was the voice coming from? They were so isolated.

"We can't stay here, Mother," Petite said, staring out at the pond, the still water.

"But we've come all this way."

"You can fix this place, you can make it nice." Jean jumped off his horse and tied the reins to his saddle horn, letting the horse loose to graze. "This turret is still intact," he added, relieving himself against the stone wall.

"She wants to leave, Jean," Françoise said.

"We should at least have a look around," Jean said as he did up his breeches.

JEAN WAS SHOWING Petite where an addition could be put onto the back of the structure, when Françoise appeared, a posy of flowers in one hand.

"Where's Marie-Anne?" Petite called out.

"Asleep in the coach," her mother said.

A wind picked up. "I'm going to check," Petite said, a prickly uneasiness coming over her.

She lifted her skirts and ran back to the courtyard. The door of the coach was open, the driver asleep on the roof with his hat over his face, the horses pulling at weeds. The coach was empty of all but their baskets, their travel clutter. Where was Marie-Anne? Petite scanned the cattails, the shrubby willows, the gently lapping water of the pond. And then she saw something that made her heart stop: a tiny hand, reaching above the surface.

"Jean!" Petite waded into the water, her leather boots leaden, dragging. *O Mary.* "Jean!" Petite felt a tendril, just a touch, and she lunged. She grasped her daughter's wrist. Marie-Anne was blue. Petite thrashed back to the shore with her child in her arms, praying with all her might: *O Mary, I am pleading, pleading, pleading.*

"Give her to me," Jean said. He laid Marie-Anne on the stones and pressed his hands into her tiny chest. A fountain of pond water spewed out of her mouth, into his face. "Good girl," he said, wiping his cheeks. "Keep it coming."

Marie-Anne began to wail.

"She'll be all right," Jean said, lifting her and handing her into Petite's arms.

"You're safe now, my sweet," Petite said, pressing the child to her heart. She noticed something clutched in her daughter's hand. Petite pried it free. Light glinted off the pin case.

"Mine," Marie-Anne wailed.

With a prayer and a curse, Petite heaved the case into the water, rocking her wailing daughter in her arms as it floated and then sank, out of sight.

"So, WHAT DO you think?" Françoise asked, back in the coach, the girl once again asleep on her lap, bundled in Petite's cloak.

"I don't know what to think, Mother," Petite said, her hand encircling Marie-Anne's thin ankle. Only that she had the Virgin to thank. And Jean. She closed her eyes, wincing against the memory of her daughter's hand sticking up out of the water.

"She said she saw a lady in a white dress, and that that was why she woke up, that the lady was singing to her—"

"I heard her too, remember?"

"So it must have been the ghost, just like they say, the ghost of the Lady in White."

"I don't know, Mother." Petite closed her eyes. The voice had been angelic. How could that be?

"Well, there's one thing *I* know," Françoise said with conviction.

"And what's that?" Petite asked, after a time.

"I'm never going back there. That's for sure."

"Me neither," Petite said, sniffing.

She felt her mother's hand on her own.

"Look," Françoise said, "just be patient. Accept this . . . this *other* interest. That's how to win him back. Really, you have to treat men like babies—even kings."

Chapter Thirty-Two

COURTIERS WERE PLEASED to be back in Paris for the new year, pleased to celebrate the city's transformation. The new street lights had everyone in raptures: night turned to day! The city was safer now, and with so many workers cobbling the roads, soon it would even be cleaner, as well. The muddy path along the Seine had been replaced by a tree-lined embankment called Le Cours. Already it had become a popular spot for the fashionable world to parade their finery.

Out of the public eye, Louis rented a house for Athénaïs for her confinement, and she disappeared from view. Secrecy was crucial. Louis, after all, was their Most Christian King. The day before Easter he confessed, touched for the Evil, and made the stations of the cross at both Notre-Dame and Hôtel-Dieu—a show of devotion never before seen in a king.

That morning, Petite sat shivering in the cold confessional, praying for guidance, a sign. In a week, the Court would return to Saint-Germain-en-Laye. In a week, Athénaïs would emerge from childbed, rejoin the Court there—rejoin Louis, and *her*.

She heard the priest enter, coughing. His breath through the grille smelled of garlic. "Forgive me, Father," she began as soon as he was settled, "for I have sinned." *Yes. Where even to begin?* "It has been two years since I last confessed. A year and a half ago I had another child." *Dear little Tito.*

The priest knew, of course. Louis had publicly legitimated their son the month before.

"I have malice in my heart against a woman I once loved as a sister." Petite paused, unsure how much she could reveal. "Because now my 'beloved' loves her as well."

"Ah," the priest said.

He knew the code, knew it was the King she meant, but mention of this "other" no doubt took him by surprise. "My health often prevents me from intimate congress," Petite went on, uncomfortable about addressing such a subject with a priest. One day she could walk for hours, the next she could not manage a step. Of late the complications had been increasing: irregular menses and pain in one leg. In hot weather, she had difficulty reading. Sometimes, but not always, she couldn't control an embroidery needle. "Even so, I cannot forgive."

"This is not an easy thing to resolve, certainly," the priest said, shifting in the creaky wooden chair.

Petite pressed her forehead against clenched fists. "I am lost, Father."

"Allow love to guide your actions."

"Even if those actions lead to Hell?" For both herself *and* Louis?

"The person of whom you speak—he is anointed by God," the priest said slowly, as if thinking it through himself. "In giving him comfort, you do not sin. We've talked of this before."

"Yes, Father."

"So, the same principle applies in allowing him comfort," he concluded.

Petite covered her mouth to stifle a sob.

"This is the Lord's realm, my child. You must be like the blind beggar on the corner. Love is your stick—let it guide you. The Lord will fill your cup, or not. It is not your province to understand, only to have faith. You have mistaken the true nature of your pain, both spiritual and physical. It is a gift from God. Be joyful, and give thanks."

"WE ARE TO regard her as family," Petite instructed Clorine, explaining the new arrangement. The renovated rooms in the château at Saint-Germain-en-Laye still smelled of paint. The suite had been made over into two apartments: one for Athénaïs and one for Petite, with a door—a secret door—connecting the two. That way, when Louis visited Athénaïs, he'd come and go through Petite's rooms. The courtiers would assume he was with Petite, the official maîtresse en titre. That way, there would be no suspicion.

"Sometimes His Majesty will stay here with me, and sometimes he will go there," Petite said, trying to sound matter-of-fact.

Clorine glared at the green-painted door.

Petite gave her a look. "I expect you to be gracious about this." It was a diabolical arrangement, yet she had agreed to it—agreed, in effect, to be the "cover" for Louis and Athénaïs. There were reasons, certainly—public opinion, the violent husband, Louis's needs—but reasons were no solace in the dark of night. Petite wasn't at all sure that she would be able to endure. She consoled herself that Louis loved her truly, and that the man who visited Athénaïs was not really Louis, but that other man: the King. "His Majesty must experience nothing but peace when he comes to call."

He called that very morning, after Mass, and sat in Petite's new "withdrawing" room holding a mug of mulled wine. Restless, he put the mug down and went to the window to look down at the courtyard, and then turned to examine the fixtures.

"They did a good job," he said, picking up a marble vase, examining it for flaws.

"I think so too," Petite said.

"Will it suit?"

Petite wasn't sure what he meant exactly. "It's lovely."

"My love, I want . . ." He put the vase down, taking care how he placed it. "It's my hope that you and the Marquise will be happy here together." He cleared his throat. "I would be most content if . . . if you could be friends again."

Petite's dish of tea clattered as she set it down. It seemed that more and more was required of her.

"You know, of course, that it would look suspect if there appeared to be any ill feeling between you, if you and the Marquise weren't often in company together, as you have been in the past." He cleared his throat a second time, visibly disquieted.

"I understand."

"I knew you would." He glanced at the pendulum clock.

"All . . . went well?" What little Petite knew of the birthing was through Clorine, who was acquainted with one of Athénaïs's maids.

"It was not without the usual trauma." Louis picked up his mug. The diamond in his ring twinkled. "Twins," he said. "A boy and a girl—but the boy stillborn."

"I'm so sorry," Petite said, knowing what a horror that must have been. "The girl, she's . . . ?"

"Well, apparently. She's with a nursemaid in Paris. Everything very hush-hush, of course." Louis shrugged. "It's a wonder I even know."

"And the mother?" Petite inquired (graciously, graciously).

Louis glanced back up at the clock. "I should go see."

ATHÉNAÏS SHOWED UP unexpectedly at Petite's Saturday-night reception. Fatigue was visible in her eyes.

"How are you managing?" Petite asked, taken aback by the sympathy she felt.

"Barely," she said, stepping into the sitting room.

"Why, if it isn't the goddess herself," the Duchesse de Nemours exclaimed in greeting. "Where have you been, Madame la Marquise? We can't tell you how boring it has been around here without you."

PETITE LIT CANDLES in anticipation of Louis's visits. She wanted to make sure that their time together was pleasant. She had hired four of Monsieur de Lully's protégés to play stringed instruments in the dressing room and arranged for their two children to be present (briefly).

"When you see His Majesty, you're to curtsy," Petite instructed her daughter, arranging the girl's ringlets. Marie-Anne was only two and a half, and spirited—quite like her father in that respect. With her dark, almond eyes, the girl was irresistible.

"Ow." Marie-Anne pulled away. "Don't, Mother."

"Don't, *please*," Petite instructed. "And if the King picks you up, be sure to kiss him on the cheek."

"It's prickly," Marie-Anne said.

"Shall I tell His Majesty how good you've been?" Petite made a point of regaling Louis with stories of their children's cleverness, noting how like her father they were.

"Tell him I draw monsters," Marie-Anne said, pulling a ribbon out of her hair.

"Show me a curtsy, Mademoiselle."

Marie-Anne shook her head with exaggerated vigor.

"Please, you make such a pretty one."

The child positioned her feet and picked up the hem of her dress. Solemnly, she looked down at her blue satin slippers.

"Bend your knees just a little," Petite said, repressing a smile. The girl could melt the hardest heart.

"Here he is, all cleaned up," Clorine announced, entering slowly, Tito clinging to her fingers. "We've got a surprise for you."

"He's walking?"

"We'll see," Clorine said, slipping her fingers out of the boy's hands. Ponderously, the baby took three steps.

Petite clapped.

"Hooray," Marie-Anne exclaimed, jumping up and down in her frog imitation. "Hooray! Hooray! Hooray!"

Petite scooped the boy up before he toppled. She'd been concerned that he might never walk, in truth. He was a small and somewhat fearful child—not the sturdy little warrior Charles had been, or plump and placid like baby Filoy—yet steadfast in his way. He had Louis's eyes.

"The cook has made a treat for you both," Petite said.

"Nun's biscuits?" Marie-Anne looked up hopefully, her fingers in her mouth. The heavenly scent filled the rooms.

"Ah, he's here," Petite said, hearing the commotion in the entry, footsteps. "I'll ring when to bring them in," she told Clorine. She handed the boy into her maid's arms.

"What smells so good?" Louis asked, entering. He propped his sword in a corner before embracing her. With a sigh, he sat back in his easy chair and put up his feet.

"A glass of rosa solis with that?" Petite asked, offering him the plate of biscuits. "Perhaps you'd like to see the children before they return to the Colberts." She rang for Clorine.

Louis's face brightened as Clorine ushered Marie-Anne and Tito into the room.

"I made a monster," Marie-Anne immediately announced.

"Show His Majesty your pretty curtsy, Mademoiselle," Petite whispered.

Biting her lip, the child arranged her feet and lifted her skirt.

"Knees, look down," Petite prompted, but it was no use.

Grinning, Louis put down his glass and opened his arms. The girl ran to him. "Do you have something for me, Mademoiselle Marie-Anne?" he asked, lifting her onto his lap.

She touched her lips to his cheek. "Prickly," she said, giggling.

Louis smiled, catching Petite's eye.

"Tito has something to show you," Petite said.

Clorine hovered over the boy as he took two steps.

Louis applauded. "I didn't know he was walking."

Petite nodded to Clorine. "Kisses goodbye now." Short . . . and sweet. "Madame Colbert will be waiting," she explained, refilling Louis's glass. The spiced golden cordial was believed to inflame lust.

"I'm sorry, my love, but I have to go." Louis took a sip before putting the glass back down on the side table, taking care to place a cup doily under it. "I'm expected."

"I understand," Petite said, her heart aching.

"I THINK SOMEONE'S taking your things," Clorine told Petite a few weeks later. "Day before yesterday your spangled head-rail disappeared, and this morning your tooth powder." She knew it wasn't one of the staff—she'd tested their honesty with coin. "And frankly, I think it's—" Clorine tilted her head toward the green door.

"Why would Madame la Marquise want tooth powder . . . or a head-rail for that matter?" Petite asked. "She never wears one."

"Don't you think it odd that things go missing after she's been here? I bet two sous that she's got them locked up in her secret cabinet."

"If you know of it, Clorine, it can't be all that secret."

BEFORE LONG, ATHÉNAÏS was pregnant again—"bagged," Clorine announced with disgust. "And we're not talking pheasants."

Louis was not the one to tell Petite. With her he talked about the children Marie-Anne and Tito, the Dauphin, hunting, horses and dogs. Then—with a sigh that had become characteristic—he'd say, "I'd best check on the Marquise."

Soon after, there would be the sound of china breaking.

For comfort, Louis turned to Petite. Even their lovemaking was "comfortable" now. Petite wanted more. She ordered a provocative gown made of fine silk and a fan of vermilion ostrich feathers. She ornamented her long curls with pearls and ribbons.

She sent Clorine to Paris with a shopping list: Venetian brocades, hand-painted stockings and—she flushed making this request—a certain (forbidden) book.

"It's a good thing I didn't get searched at the gate," Clorine exclaimed on return, her straw basket bulging. "That book."

"I didn't know you could read Latin." Petite was mortified.

"This isn't Latin," Clorine said, shaking *L'École des Filles* in front of her. "But there are words in it I'm happy to say I do not know."

"I thought it was a schoolbook," Petite lied, taking it from her.

"Some school." Clorine rolled her eyes and blew out a breath.

PRICK, LOVE STICK, *piss-instrument. Balls, arse.* Her cheeks flaming, Petite avoided the gaze of the Virgin as she read. *Cunt, clit. Bliss.*

LOUIS BEGAN TO visit Petite regularly. Sometimes he neglected to go through the green door at all.

"This is the second month you've missed, Madame," Clorine observed, studying the journal where she kept note of the household comings and goings, including her mistress's health, her menses and bowels.

"I know," Petite said with a smile. She'd experienced no nausea this time, and her health was strong again; she was enjoying her fullness.

Clorine frowned. "I hate to think what's going to happen when *she* finds out."

PETITE WAS WOKEN from a deep sleep. She thought she'd heard a scream—not the horse's cry that she still sometimes heard in the night, but that of a woman. A door slammed shut. It sounded close by.

"Clorine?" Petite called out, parting her bed curtains in alarm. She heard what sounded like hard heels on the wood floor. What was happening? The single candle set in the ox-horn lantern threw little light.

Petite was lighting another candle when Athénaïs came bolting into the room, her hand raised and Louis fast behind her.

"I'll murder her," she hissed, brandishing a knife.

Louis lunged for Athénaïs's hand and the knife clattered to the floor.

"And you too, you miserable excuse of a man!" Athénaïs cried as she tried to wrench free. "Swamp scum! Pig offal," she sobbed, confined now in Louis's strong arms. "You son of a bitch."

"Quiet," Louis murmured, as if soothing a child.

Two maids and a footman appeared at the door, like a family of ghosts in their nightcaps and smocks. "Retire," Louis commanded, and they disappeared. He sent Petite a look of exhausted relief, and ushered Athénaïs away.

"Mademoiselle?" Clorine came into the room carrying a night candle.

"Athénaïs just tried to kill me," Petite said shakily, picking up the rusted trench-knife. The double-edged blade was dull—but capable of harm, certainly.

"Zut! While I was asleep?"

"Just now," Petite said, dazed. She placed the knife on her bedside table and crawled back under the covers.

"I'll sleep in here tonight," Clorine said, closing her bed curtains.

"Yes," Petite whispered, her baby fluttering within her.

LOUIS RETURNED LATE the next morning. He looked as if he'd had little sleep. "She's tranquil now," he told Petite, pacing in front of the roaring fire, booted and spurred. "Blucher gave her vervain water and confined her to bed."

Petite was familiar with vervain. She'd helped her father gather it from the waste grounds in the full heat of summer. He had used vervain for a number of complaints—dropsy, gout, worms—but never for murderous intent.

"She wants to see you," Louis said, leaning against the mantel, his arms crossed over his chest.

Petite looked at him in disbelief. "Louis, she tried to kill me."

"She wouldn't have hurt you. Not really."

Petite looked away, short of breath. She'd seen the fury in Athénaïs's eyes, the knife in her fist.

"You know how it is when she's . . ." Louis put out his hands to indicate a big belly. "I should have told her in the morning. She's more emotional at night."

Petite made a look of derision. "Louis, I'm not—"

"This is not a request I make lightly, Louise," he said, his voice impatient now. "She's in danger of losing the child. Just call on her. It would only be for a few minutes—that's all I ask."

THE GREEN DOOR SHUT behind Petite. Athénaïs's rooms were much like her own—but for the decor, which was in an opulent Oriental style. A cat slunk under a side table as a maid appeared.

"The Marquise is expecting you," she said, shooing away the hissing cat. She led the way through a series of small chambers to a bedroom, where Athénaïs was propped up against red silk cushions with a bed-tray on her knees. A small gray parrot perched on the upholstered headboard behind her, a gold ring around one leg attached by a chain to the bedpost. Everything was red—the bed curtains, the carpet, the headboard. Even the crystal chandelier was draped in crimson gauze.

"Ah, there you are," Athénaïs said, wiping her lips with an embroidered hand-kerchief. "I don't know what came over me." She grimaced. "Can you forgive me? That awful Blucher insists I'm to stay in this bed for at least a week—until I get my humors balanced. He claims I'm dominated by the dry one, which puts me at risk for melancholy." She laughed.

The parrot opened its eyes and watched Petite steadily, weaving back and forth on its claws. Petite felt for her locket.

"Sit, sit. I won't bite." Athénaïs smiled ruefully.

Petite lowered herself onto a stool. "I can't be long."

Athénaïs reached for a bowl of sweetmeats set on top of a black enamel cabinet. "Try one of these. The little blue ones are delicious—minty." She popped one in her mouth. "Does it make me blue?" She stuck out her tongue.

Petite nodded, but did not smile. She took a candy from the bowl and sucked on it.

"You're angry."

"You came at me with a knife," Petite said.

"Please, don't be like that." Athénaïs reached for her hand, but Petite pulled back. "I love you. I'm sorry. Truly." She blinked back tears. "This arrangement isn't easy for either of us. You'd think he had a goddamn harem—a harem of two."

And both of us with child, Petite thought, *like broodmares with a stallion.*

"And Queen makes three," Athénaïs said cheerily, raising her glass.

"I don't feel well," Petite said, abruptly rising.

PETITE WENT TO BED as soon as she got back to her apartment. By the time Blucher arrived, it was clear she was miscarrying. Six and a quarter hours later, the ordeal was over.

"I'll inform the King, Mademoiselle de la Vallière?"

Petite nodded, tearfully. She had wanted this child.

On the third day, Petite began to run a fever. On the fourth, she suffered visions, the surface of things giving way, demons emerging out of the shadows, their reptilian tails flicking, eyes glowing.

O Lord, punish me not.

Clorine, praying out loud, applied cooling compresses to Petite's forehead, under her arms, between her legs.

"This happens, Your Majesty," Blucher explained to Louis. "The bringing forth of fruit before it is ripe causes disorder."

"Is she in danger?" Louis demanded, his voice betraying fear.

"Yes, Your Majesty."

Louis called in his doctor, who in turn called in two others—grave men in black robes and tall, pointed hats. They stood beside Petite's bed frowning. On only one thing did they agree: she was dying.

O Lord, my sins are beyond my strength, I am bowed down, I am crushed, my strength forsakes me . . .

"It is time to call in a priest, Your Majesty," Blucher informed Louis.

Help me, O Lord . . .

Soon Petite was surrounded by men in black—priests on one side of her bed, doctors on the other. The smell of incense filled the room, the sounds of monotonous intoning.

"I'm sorry, Your Majesty," Blucher told Louis as the doctors bowed out. "There is nothing more we can do." There was sadness in his voice, as well as resignation.

Forsake me not, O Lord!

Louis returned to Petite's bedside, pressed her hand to his lips. "I must leave you," he said.

Petite looked into his soft hazel eyes. *I loved you.* Once upon a time.

He laid his head on her belly, his back heaving. She ran her fingers through his hair. "Go," she whispered, her mouth dry, her lips cracked and swollen. A king must not be present when Death was near, not when the Devil was known to hover.

Petite looked down at her body. She was lying on the daybed, her mouth hanging open, her eyes open too, but unseeing. She was in her old chemise, the worn one edged at the neck with laces made by her aunt Angélique. One foot, the misshapen left one, was exposed. Clorine was on her knees by the bed, sobbing her heart out.

I've died, Petite thought with surprise. She felt clear, like the sparkling of a crystal. She looked about the room at the dusty candelabra, her beloved books, the statue of the Virgin on the prie-dieu.

Then, as if in a fever, she seemed to see the walls give way, and behind them was her father walking toward her, leading Diablo through a flowering meadow. He was wearing his stained leather jerkin.

"It's not yet time, little one," he told her, and turned away.

Chapter Thirty-Three

PETITE FOLLOWED A WINDING PATH across the meadow. She paused, reveling in the sounds of the crickets and bees, a solitary songbird singing. Clusters of butterflies zigzagged over tall grasses, waving in a breeze.

She surveyed the hills in the distance, the arc of the sun. It had been a long time since she had come this way, beyond the realm of the Court. Beyond the sound of hammers on stone, the whirling dust, the army of workers cursing, pushing wheelbarrows, cart wheels screeching. Beyond the reach of the stone monument Versaie was becoming. Had become.

Gray moss hung from the limbs of a solitary apple tree, its trunk humped with knots, one low branch splintered and reaching to the ground. She remembered the ancient tree: remembered reaching for its fruit. Remembered taking a bite, the flesh crisp and sweet. Long ago. She remembered handing an apple to Louis. He had laughed, juice on his chin. She remembered the passion of their embrace.

Had passion corrupted them? she wondered, making her way through the long grass. Corrupted *him?* Had passion led Louis into the Devil's realm of insatiable desire?

It looked as if deer had nested under the tree—or possibly unicorn, she thought, although they were rare. The apples were small yet. She picked one touched with rose, but it was too tart to eat. She remembered watering horses at a stream nearby, and spotted the path into the woods. Entering the cool of the shade, she heard water, smelled the fragrant wild mint that often clung to mossy banks. She followed the path through ferns to a stream overhung with tree branches, its banks flowered with purple loosestrife. There, she crouched and drank deeply, then plunged her face into the clear water.

Gone to the river.

Sitting back, drying her face with her skirt, she noticed horse tracks in the mud—wild horses, possibly: they were not shod. And rabbit, of course, deer. A hunter's paradise, she had called it. *Our paradise*, he had said.

No longer. Where forest had been, trees stood in tubs. Where brooks had meandered musically over rocks, fountains shot arrows of water into the air.

Quenched, Petite stood. She traced her path back onto the sunlit meadow. Following her shadow east, she emerged onto a rutted cart trail. Ducks quacked by a pond. Cows nearby grazed knee-deep in flowers. In the misty distance, she saw someone approaching.

Petite sat in the dandelions, watching from under the brim of her straw hat as the figure moved toward her. It was a black man, clothed in blue. "Azeem?" she called out to the gentler, standing.

He stopped before her and bowed. "It's not to do with your children," he said, seeing the alarm in her eyes. "It's something else."

He'd aged, but his skin was still smooth, unwrinkled. His build, although slight, had density now. He'd lost only one of his teeth, which were white as whalebone. He'd acquired a long, curly black beard, the ends of which he clasped with one hand as he spoke, reminding Petite of the way one held the tail of a medicined horse as it walked, to keep it from toppling.

"You came all this way," she said. Louis was taking the waters nearby at Encausse, so it hadn't to do with him, either.

"There's something you must see," he said gravely.

Petite heard the horse's scream as they approached the royal stables. Yearlings in a far field were stampeding, running in a tight cluster. In a paddock, broodmares were snorting, circling their foals. A colt still wobbly on its stiltlike legs got knocked off its feet. The wagon used to haul horses was on its side in the stud paddock. A howling dog lay by the gate, struggling to rise.

The big stable doors gaped open. Petite heard the scream again, followed by the sound of splintered timbers, men shouting. She could feel the pounding of the horse's hooves through the walls.

Azeem gestured *back, back*: stay behind him.

The scene inside was one of pandemonium. The horses in their stalls snorted, their mouths tight, necks rigid with fear, ears pricked and swiveling this way and that. Against a wall, two grooms huddled over a man stretched out on the stone floor. His face was bloodied, his nose askew. At the far end men were yelling over the pounding strikes of a horse's hooves as they tried to secure a thick beam against the bars.

The head of a White reared up and lunged, teeth bared.

Petite stepped closer, her heart faint. The horse had the thick neck of a stallion. He was of an imposing size, yet he moved with lightning agility, biting and kicking with fury.

"It's him, isn't it," Azeem said.

Petite nodded.

"He was caught in the wild," he said, "out beyond Chaillot. But now we can't get near him."

"Get me a musket," a man commanded.

It was the master of the horse. Petite stepped forward, her mouth dry. Azeem took hold of her arm. "I just want to look," she said.

She stood at the gate, staring through the iron bars. He was back in the shadows, pawing the boards. He was scarred across the chest, above the fetlock on his right foreleg and on his nose. He looked like an old warrior, the sole survivor of a thousand wars.

"Beloved," she whispered.

He pricked his ears, then snorted, tossing his head.

He was still a fine and fearsome creature, Petite thought, in awe of his savage beauty. "He needs to smell me," she said, turning back to Azeem.

"You can't go in there," he said with urgency.

I must, Petite thought.

"Shoot him," the master of the horse told the livestock man. A ragtag boy stood behind lugging a coil of hemp rope.

Before the man could load his gun—and before Azeem could stop her—Petite unbolted the gate and stepped into the stall.

The stallion stood in the shadows, legs splayed, head lowered, his ears pinned back. His chest was slick with sweat and blood. He regarded Petite with a fiery eye.

She took a step toward him. He pinned back his ears and reared, warning her clearly: *Do not come near. I will kill you.*

She bowed her head. He was cornered: she must not threaten him. She crouched down against the stall wall. *"Nec cesso, nec erro,"* she whispered. I do not slacken, I do not lose my way.

DIABLO DIDN'T ATTACK her—that was a victory, of sorts—but he was a wild creature, wilder than ever before. He wouldn't let her near, threatening to strike if she dared to approach.

In the days that followed, Petite sat for hours in a corner of his stall, tempting him with fragrant cut grass, handfuls of grain, bits of fruit. She tried to provoke his curiosity by curling into a ball in the sodden sawdust and holding very still, not breathing. The last Sunday in June, she took a different tack, nickering and blowing, talking to him in his language. He turned away with flattened ears.

Discouraged, she returned to her rooms in the château, to the suite she shared with Athénaïs. *Patience is the companion of wisdom,* her father had often said, quoting Saint Augustine. Diablo was stubborn, but she was stubborn too.

"You have a caller," Clorine announced as Petite came in the door. She was leaning over the two children, fastening their shoe buckles. "Madame Colbert isn't returning for Marie-Anne and Tito until later this afternoon," she said, standing, "so I thought I'd take them down to the canal."

"It's beautiful out," Petite said. She could hear Athénaïs's parrot through the wall. As in Saint-Germain-en-Laye, Fontaine Beleau and even in Paris now, they lived side by side, linked by a door. The King's harem. His seraglio. His private brothel.

"We're going to sail the boat," Marie-Anne announced, holding the elaborate wood construction Louis had given the children.

"And climb rocks," Tito said, climbing down off the bench and running into Petite's embrace, tolerating her kiss. "You smell good, Mother," he said, "like horses."

"There's a priest in there," Marie-Anne whispered. "I told him he could sit, but not in Father's chair."

"Remember Abbé Patin?" Clorine tied bonnets on the children.

"My tutor at Blois?" Petite asked, shaking out the hay and wood chips that always seemed to find a way into her petticoats. The Thunderer?

"C'est moi," Abbé Patin said, standing as Petite entered the sitting room. He was wearing a coarsely woven hooded tunic over a cowl, his graying hair covered by a crested linen cap.

"This is such a wonderful surprise," Petite told him. "I wouldn't have recognized you. You look like a monk."

"I am a monk," he said, laughing heartily.

"Please, sit." The sitting room was the only one that did not share a wall with Athénaïs. Consequently, it was the room Petite loved best. She had lined the walls with books.

"I couldn't. You're a duchess."

"Abbé Patin, *please*. We are all of us equals in the eyes of the Lord. Wasn't that one of your sermons? If anyone should be standing in reverence, it should be me. Make yourself comfortable and tell me how you came about this transformation."

He refused the armchair, instead pulling up the cherry-wood chair and straddling it backward, resting his chin on the back of his hands. "I inherited a dissolute ruin of a monastery in Soligny-la-Trappe."

"North of Paris?"

"A day's journey. I have been putting it in shape ever since, and in the process my soul, it would appear. I became a Cistercian about three years ago."

"Is that not a silent order?"

"Are you suggesting I'm talkative?" He grinned impishly.

He was a tall man, and his coarse brown habit was short on him, exposing dusty riding boots and spurs. "You still ride, Abbé Patin?" Petite asked, recalling the gallops they had enjoyed at Blois.

"Every chance I get. And you?"

"Health permitting."

"You were only a girl, yet you were the most daring rider I've ever known. I'm told there's a wild stallion here that no one but you dare approach."

"Where did you hear that?"

"Your fame goes before you."

Petite smiled wanly. At least it was not fame of another sort. "What brings you to Versaie?"

"Other than the sinful pleasure of a vigorous gallop on a summer Sabbath?" He held out his hands, palms up, as if supplicating Heaven. "In truth I came to see you. I'm in Paris fairly regularly on monastery business, and I learned, recently, that you very nearly passed away. I was so relieved to learn that you were still among us, I felt I should come to tell you so myself."

Petite was warmed by the Abbé's smile. He'd always been someone she could talk to openly—and she had the same feeling about him even now, after so much time had passed. "I believe I did die, in fact, Abbé Patin. I felt a radiant light."

"Ah," he said with interest.

"I saw my father." Tears sprang to her eyes. "And my horse—my beautiful White."

"You talked of this horse in your first Confession."

"You have a good memory. This horse has come back to me."

"The wild stallion people talk of?"

"Strange, don't you think?" Strange and miraculous, frightening and wonderful. "I'm so confused. You have come at a good time." Indeed, it struck her that he'd been sent as well. "After this—this *vision*, would you call it?—I feel a need for spiritual guidance. My confessor is—" She paused. Her confessor was more concerned with the King's pleasure than her salvation. "I need more than perpetual forgiveness," she said.

"You don't think I'd be forgiving?"

"I know you would be honest."

He sat back, frowning. "This is a grave request, you understand."

"Abbé Patin, you have been a good friend to me. I trust you—and I can't tell you how much that means to me right now."

"As your spiritual adviser I may be called to speak unpleasant truths."

"I understand." Petite began to choke up, and paused before asking, "You are, no doubt, aware of my . . . situation?"

"You mean with respect to His Majesty?"

It shamed her. Maîtresse en titre was a polite name for concubine, in truth. "I fear the Devil, Abbé Patin."

"As everyone should," he said. "He's a wily opponent, certainly, but—" He hesitated a moment before saying, with an exhale of breath, "But I believe you are mistaken: it's not the Devil you need to fear."

Petite was taken aback. She watched as he stood, suddenly restless.

"May I presume to speak in the capacity of your adviser now?" he asked finally, his hands clasped behind his back.

Petite nodded, curious yet apprehensive. There was an urgency in his manner.

"I have not been entirely candid with you, I confess," he said, turning the chair to face her and sitting down, like a schoolboy facing an examiner. "I came to Versaie to see you today because I've something to tell you—something of concern."

He touched the tips of his fingers together, his thumbs tucked under his chin. "There have been rumors among the Religious that magic is being used at Court. Not so much charms and chants, the often innocent nonsense lovesick girls indulge in, but truly evil doings—Black Masses, human sacrifices, poison . . . that type of thing."

"*Human* sacrifices?"

"Of a newborn," he said. "One prays it's only a story. Do you recall the arrest several years ago of a priest at Saint-Séverin in Paris?"

"I don't," Petite said, but uncertainly.

"It was in the twenty-fifth year of the King's reign," Abbé Patin said. "In the summer."

Petite frowned, recalling that there had been talk of a priest's arrest shortly before the fateful trip to Chambord. "Vaguely," she said. Saint-Séverin was a large church, not far from Notre-Dame in the Latin Quarter. She remembered thinking it impossible for such evil things to go on there.

"He was a wizard-priest, a poisoner as well as a sorcerer, eventually convicted of demonic practices—blood sacrifice of doves, incantations of the Gospel in the Bois de Boulogne, that type of thing. Punishable by death, of course, but he got off rather lightly—he was of the nobility and the judge was a cousin." Abbé Patin gave her a look of disgust. "He was condemned to a disciplinary establishment for priests, but even that was too harsh for him, apparently. With the help of a diviner in Paris—a woman by the name la Voisin—he managed to escape and hid in a monastery in the south, in Toulouse."

Madame la Voisin, the teller of fortunes. "Remember Nicole, Abbé Patin?"

"That noisy, charming scamp?" he asked with amused affection. "Of course."

"I'm told she's a Religious now, at a convent somewhere in the south."

Abbé Patin sputtered with surprise. "I could easily imagine you in such a vocation—but not Mademoiselle de Montalais."

Indeed, Petite thought. She sometimes longed for the silence of a contemplative life—its elemental purity. *It is my wish.* "I only mention Nicole because she went to Madame la Voisin for love charms. Many of the ladies of the Court have gone to her, I'm told—including the Marquise de Montespan."

Abbé Patin started. "She's actually talked of this?"

"Why?"

"Because it all ties together, I'm afraid. One of my nephews is a monk in the monastery in Toulouse where the wizard-priest was in hiding. The priest was something of a braggart, I gather: he claimed to have performed rituals for the Marquise. Nothing is known for sure," he said with emphasis. "I learned this secondhand and it's quite possibly unfounded, yet. . . . Yet my nephew is a credible source. According to him, the priest-wizard said that the Marquise de Montespan aimed to capture the interest of His Majesty. He even boasted that his charms had worked."

Petite put her head down, taking deep breaths. Athénaïs had used *sorcery* to seduce Louis? "I'm all right," she said, putting up her hand. Athénaïs was many things—jealous, spiteful, given to excess—but she was rigorous about her religious devotions, strict about never breaking a fast, always observing a holy day, never missing a Mass. How could someone so meticulous about her faith partake of Satanism? "I'm sorry," she said finally, sitting up. "I get these attacks now and then. They mean nothing," she said faintly, taking a moment to catch her breath. "Are you aware, Abbé Patin, that His Majesty and the Marquise are . . . ?"

Abbé Patin nodded. "There have been rumors about that, as well. I confess I am greatly concerned about His Majesty's soul."

Petite's eyes teared. *Yes.*

"As well as yours," he said, sitting forward, meeting her gaze. "Tell me. This can't be a . . . a *comfortable* arrangement for you, to say the least."

"I feel trapped," she confessed. "What are my choices? Most women in an unhappy situation take the veil—but what convent would even have me?"

"I am in a position to vouch for you."

He was serious, she realized. And so was *she*. "But what about my children, Abbé Patin—"

"You would still be a mother to them."

A better mother to them, Petite thought—a mother who did not live in sin.

"This will take time to explore, I know," Abbé Patin said, touching the tips of his fingers together. "You are a pure spirit in a—"

"I am far from innocent, Abbé Patin," Petite said heatedly, interrupting.

"On a secular level, certainly. However, in some people there is a purity of soul that cannot be sullied, and I see that in you."

Petite paused, her heart's blood pounding. Dare she confess? "There is something I never told you—something I've never told anyone." Her voice quavered.

"Do you wish to speak of it now?" he asked, perceiving her seriousness.

Petite pressed her palms together. If she didn't confess now . . . would she ever? "Have you ever heard of bone magic?"

"Is it something to do with horses? I've heard of toad magic, a ritual peasants use."

"It's similar, I believe." And then she told him everything: of killing the toad, grinding its bones and mixing it with oil, using it to gentle Diablo. "It was a miracle, Abbé Patin. The horse was vicious, and then—in a moment—he became the gentlest creature imaginable."

"I've seen you with horses. Have you considered that it wasn't the ritual that turned him?"

Petite shook her head. "I began hearing things, seeing the Devil's face in the night."

"Children often have such fears. You were young."

"But old enough to make a pact with the Devil, Abbé Patin. Not long after, my father died suddenly and the horse disappeared."

"Until now," he said.

"Until now," she echoed, thinking of Diablo, his wild beauty. What did it all mean? Her father, Diablo, and now Abbé Patin. Yet another trinity. "There is more," she said. "After I found out about the Marquise and the King—" She paused. She could not reveal the existence of Athénaïs's two children by Louis, even to Abbé Patin. "I wanted to kill her."

The Abbé grimaced. "That's understandable, frankly."

"And not long after, I came upon that oil again, in a pin case, and I thought . . . I thought I might try it—on Athénaïs, or even on His Majesty. I wanted that power, Abbé Patin. I wanted to bend them to my will, and I was willing— perfectly willing—to deal with the Devil again in order to do so."

Abbé Patin sat back, taking this in. "What stopped you?"

"My daughter." Petite's brave facade began to crumble. "She must have found the pin case in my basket. She nearly drowned." Petite covered her face with her hands. "If I had lost her . . ." *O Mary.* She dabbed her cheeks with her sleeves. "So, you see?" she said, her voice shaky.

"I do." His voice was tender.

Petite took a deep breath and sat up, meeting his eyes. "Tell me what I must do."

"To combat the Devil?" He opened his hands wide. "What you have just done. Evil is vanquished by bringing it into the light."

"It can't be that simple."

"You are right in that this process—of en*light*enment, I think of it—is far from simple. It takes time, and considerable courage. But then"—he smiled, his eyes warm and shining—"I happen to know that you are an exceptionally courageous woman."

The clock chimed. "Ah, I'm afraid that this is the hour when I turn into a manic horseman," he said with a grimace, standing. "I am expected in Paris." He took her hands in his. "Will you be . . . ?"

"Already you have been an enormous help to me, Abbé Patin," Petite said. She felt lifted of a great weight.

"We will talk of all this further, I assure you," he said, "but as to that other matter—"

Petite tilted her head toward Athénaïs's rooms.

He nodded. "Just be watchful. Do you understand?"

"I do."

"May God be with you," he said, making the sign of the cross over her.

PETITE SAT FOR a time after Abbé Patin left, staring into space, reveling in the relief she felt at having unburdened herself, as well as stupefied by what had been revealed, the possibility that Athénaïs may have used dark magic to achieve her aim.

Her thoughts were interrupted by the sound of running footsteps outside. She went to the balcony window, but could see nothing beyond the usual construction—the piles of rubble and stone, carts lined up, everything motionless for the Sabbath. She turned when she heard the entry door opening—Clorine and the children. And then she heard a woman's musical laugh.

"Louise, I'm sorry to disturb you, but I'm afraid that we must leave immediately," Athénaïs said, closing a Chinese paper parasol as she stepped into the room. Her golden underskirt glittered with diamond knot pins. "I've ordered up our coach." It was Petite's coach, in fact, but Athénaïs considered it theirs. "We have to go to Saint-Cloud."

"Now?" Petite asked as Clorine came in with Marie-Anne and Tito. Through the open window she heard running footsteps again, people calling out. "What has happened?" she asked, alarmed.

"Henriette is gravely ill."

"Poisoned, Mother," Marie-Anne said with enthusiasm.

"Don't say that," Petite cautioned, taking both Marie-Anne and Tito into her embrace. "What do you have in your mouth?" she asked her daughter.

"A sweetmeat," the girl said with a guilty squirm. "Madame Montespan gave it to me. Louis spat his out."

"It's a coriander comfit. Would you like one?" Athénaïs asked Petite, reaching through her skirts.

"No, thank you," Petite said, her voice drowned by Marie-Anne's squeals of protest as she pried the sweet out of her child's mouth.

"Your coach is out front," Clorine announced.

"Are you all right, Louise?" Athénaïs asked, standing over Petite, placing her gloved hand lightly on her shoulder. "You look pale."

The courtyard at Saint-Cloud was packed with coaches, with groups of drivers and valets standing about. It was late in the day but light still, the sun just setting.

"The King and Queen are here already," Petite said. In front of the entrance was the royal coach, hitched to eight bay horses.

"The world is here," Athénaïs said.

People were standing near the door in clusters. Petite recognized Madame Desbordes, one of Henriette's maids of honor, talking with Philippe's valet. Inside, she could see Prince de Condé talking to Marshal Turenne, Madame d'Épernon and Madame de la Fayette looking on. Monsieur Lauzun was leaning against the wall, under a wall sconce, looking woeful.

"We've just come from Versaie," Athénaïs announced, climbing the wide marble stairs with the help of a walking stick.

Madame Desbordes leaned forward in order to speak confidentially. "Have you heard? The Princess claims she's been poisoned."

Petite recoiled. Terrible cries of pain could be heard from within.

"By the glass of chicory water I mixed for her!" the woman said, pressing a nose cloth to her face.

Athénaïs frowned. "*You* gave her the water?"

"No, thank God. Madame de Gourdon gave it to her. Poor Henriette—such agony, but it's not poison, I know it. Monsieur had the water given to a dog, and I drank some myself from Madame's glass, just to prove it."

"You drank it?" Athénaïs persisted.

"It took Monsieur a while to realize that she might really be in danger and to call in a doctor. Now every doctor imaginable is here: Madame's, Monsieur's, even the King's is here from Versaie. All of them insist that it's nothing but an attack of colic—even as she writhes! Nobody knows what to do, not even His Majesty. Everybody but Madame Henriette—right from the start she said she was dying and that all she needed was a priest."

"Is it all right for us to go in?" Petite asked, stepping aside to make room for five musicians followed by pageboys carrying their instruments.

"If you can find room," Madame Desbordes said. "It's as crowded as opening day at the Saint-Germain Fair."

THE SCENE IN the dark chamber was chaotic, crowded with courtiers coming and going. Philippe was standing by a window staring over at his wife with a stricken look. The suffering Princess was stretched on a bed, her nightdress open, her fiery red hair in disorder. The Queen was on one side of the bed, Louis on the other, clutching Henriette's hand. Petite knew the instant she saw Henriette's face that the Princess did not have long to live. She looked like a bone-thin cadaver, gaunt and gray.

Louis glanced up at Petite and Athénaïs, following them with his eyes as they passed by and into the crowd. Petite's throat closed, seeing the anguish in his face.

Athénaïs tugged Petite's sleeve. People had shifted to give them a place. They stood for a time, praying along with all the others: "O Lord, we place our beloved Princess under your care and humbly ask that you restore her to health. Amen."

"I won't see the dawn, Your Majesty," Petite heard Henriette tell Louis. Her face was gleaming with perspiration, and her eyes were wild, yet there was a curious acceptance in her voice.

"That's not true," Louis told her, pleading.

Petite turned to hide her tears. Henriette was only twenty-six, her own age exactly.

"Do you think she's really dying?" Athénaïs whispered, clasping the cross that hung from her pendant.

"Yes," Petite said in a low voice, noticing the tiny key dangling beside the cross: it was silver, with a heart-shaped ring. Athénaïs often wore the cross and the key together. It had never occurred to Petite to wonder why. *Be watchful.*

"Do you think she was poisoned?" Athénaïs asked.

"I don't know," Petite said as the musicians tuned up. How sad to be a princess, she thought, to die so painfully on a public stage. "I'll be right back." She made her way through to where the musicians were standing. "Play a pavane by Aisne," she told them.

As the music began, the Princess looked at Petite, her eyes shimmering. Weakly, she raised one hand, signaling the musicians: *louder, faster.*

Petite edged her way back.

"I think I'm going to be sick," Athénaïs whispered.

Louis pulled away from the bed and moved to where three doctors stood in a window recess. "Are you just going to stand there and let her die?" he demanded, raising his voice.

The musicians stopped playing. But for Henriette's groans, the packed room was quiet.

The doctors stared down at the floor.

Louis returned to Henriette with tears in his eyes.

"Don't weep, Sire," she said. "You'll make me weep too."

"Turn to God," he said, kissing her forehead and then pulling away.

There was a stir among the courtiers as the King and Queen departed. They knew what it signified.

THE NEXT MORNING, back at Versaie, Petite walked to the stables in the rain. It was warm, and she was protected by a hooded cape. She felt like a monk, walking in the mist, thinking ominous thoughts. Thinking about Henriette, her short, sparkling life, her agonizing death. Thinking about the rumors.

Had Henriette been poisoned? she wondered, turning down the road that led to the stables. It seemed impossible—yet fear gave suspicion gravity. A poisoner could not be seen. Even the weapon was invisible. A person could be poisoned by something put on the rim of a cup, or into a glass of wine. Something sprinkled on a coat or wig could turn a person's skin yellow and make their hair fall out, rendering them unable to speak, even to make final Confession.

The Devil be gone, she whispered, crossing herself quickly, afraid of even thinking such thoughts.

The stable courtyard was congested. Coaches, carts and horses were being readied for the Court's sudden return to Paris, everything to be draped in black. Petite nodded sad acknowledgment to the grooms and entered the stable. She stood at the gate to Diablo's stall, her hand on the bolt. So many losses, she thought, tears welling. A paradise turned to Hell.

She glanced inside. Diablo was standing facing her, his small, sharp ears upright. She dried her cheeks with the edge of her skirt and slowly—cautiously—stepped in.

Diablo threw up his head.

She stood against the wall. *I know you, yet I know you not.* There was beauty in his wildness—in his resistance. She closed her eyes, thinking about her talk with Abbé Patin the day before—her confession. *Had* that spell been broken?

She heard a soft, throaty nicker and opened her eyes. Diablo took a step toward her. She closed her eyes again quickly, not daring to look at him, sensing his approach, his hooves rustling the straw bedding. She felt his warmth, felt him smelling her arm, her hair, her shoulder. Felt his whiskers tickling her cheek. Weeping, she sniffed.

He startled, yet hovered.

Petite slowly reached through her skirts to a crust of bread roll. She held it out, palm up, waiting. Knowing he would come.

Chapter Thirty-Four

PETITE SAT UP, roused from a troubled sleep. A dream lingered: of the royal carriage drawn by eight black horses caparisoned in black velvet and matching plumes. Of knights, varlets, henchmen in hoods, water-men and pages accompanying a long line of black-draped coaches, everyone in mourning. Of strangely silent herds of horses, kennels of dogs, carts loaded with cages of monkeys, parrots and other exotic pets following at the rear. Of peasants following, scooping up the rich leavings. And, at the very end, Diablo, a solitary white figure in a black landscape.

Where was she?

Paris, she remembered . . . but not in her little house facing the Palais Royale gardens. No, she was in the Tuileries now, in a new suite of elegant rooms—rooms side by side with Athénaïs's chambers.

What year was it? What season? February, 1671, the twenty-seventh year of the King's reign. Soon it would be Ash Wednesday, soon Lent.

That morning she had tended Diablo, who was kept isolated in a courtyard behind the royal stables near rue Saint-Honoré: a cruel captivity. She'd tried, yet again, to back him—but he would not have it.

In the afternoon Louis had come to her, and, still warm from her embrace, he'd gone to Athénaïs. He'd hinted, in jest of course—*of course*—that it would be more efficient to have them both together in one bed. "We wouldn't fit," Petite joked—for Athénaïs had acquired girth—but his offhand remark distressed her.

It was not yet midnight, to judge by the fire still burning in the grate. She felt weighted down with fatigue. Her nights were often sleepless, and what sleep she did get was disturbed by frightening dreams—of a serpent with a woman's face, her hair swept up in points, of a lean, muscular man in a loincloth, his eyes burning coals.

354

Her days were clouded with troubling thoughts as well, with fears and suspicions. She'd been losing things: an ivory fan, a lace mantilla. The disappearance of her father's rosary still grieved her. She suspected Athénaïs now, in all ways: was she taking Petite's belongings? Worse, was she practicing witchcraft—*on her?*

Petite pulled a fur wrap over her shoulders. It had been a dismal winter, haunted by Henriette's sudden death. An autopsy had proved that Henriette did not die of poisoning, but even so, people suspected otherwise, whispering of dark magic. There had been no festivals, no médianoche, no balls . . . until now, with the madness of carnival upon them. Soon there would be the annual Mardi Gras masquerade ball.

Petite went to the window and opened the shutters. The night was cloudless, the moon full and bright. Her rooms faced the Rabbit Warren, the public gardens reaching to the city wall. Along the banks of the Seine she could see a carriage light moving down Le Cours, but otherwise nothing, no sign of life, just the vague outline of the fountain and the rows of elm, cypress and mulberry trees. Beyond the wall were the wooded hills, open country.

Petite heard someone cough. She whirled in the dark, her heart racing. She was unstrung, no doubt; she'd been having dream spells again. Yet the cough sounded as if it had come from behind the door to the connecting passage—the door to Athénaïs's rooms.

It couldn't be Athénaïs. The moon was full and it was early in the evening yet. She would be out at the gaming tables. Sometimes Petite heard her and her waiting maid stumbling in after dawn, laughing and cursing.

Petite pressed her ear against the door's shellacked surface—the "green door," as she thought of it, even though it wasn't green in Paris. She knew how to be quiet and watchful, how to be patient and wait. She knew how to hold stone-still for a long time—this was her skill in hunting—so she held silent, waiting for a sound, but sensed no movement. Clasping her locket—her protection from the Devil—she creaked the door open. She would just have a look, put her fears to rest . . . and then sleep.

ATHÉNAÏS'S CHAMBERS WERE a mirror reflection of Petite's own: an antechamber, a room in which to receive guests, a bedchamber and dressing room, a closet for the maid. Cats skulked out of view as Petite crept into the withdrawing room. Two enormous candles had been left blazing; Athénaïs had a mortal fear of the dark.

The parrot stood on a gilded base, pecking at a cake. It regarded Petite with one eye.

"Que diable," it said—and then coughed.

Petite leaned against the wall, catching her breath. She should return to her room. She had no right.

Late the following evening, long after shutting in, Athénaïs entered Petite's room unannounced, emerging through the "green door" to ask Petite to tie her ribbons and adjust her gauzy train. Petite rose from a chair, startled. It was past midnight, and she was in her bedclothes. Unable to sleep, she had decided to read the *Divine Comedy* by the light of a lantern in preparation for talking to Abbé Patin in the morning.

"Nobody can tie a ribbon as well, darling," Athénaïs told Petite, giving her a kiss.

Petite did as requested; she didn't want a scene. Athénaïs thanked her, said a few words about the masquerade ball coming up and left to join the gaming tables in the Queen's salon.

"Who was that?" Clorine asked, coming to the door. The candlelight cast her face in ghoulish shadows.

Petite raised her lantern and looked about the room. "Clorine, wasn't there a blue jay's wing-feather with my ribbons?"

"The one for your riding hat? It was here." Clorine smirked. "Let me guess: Madame de Montespan was just here."

I could kill her, Petite thought, wondering what else Athénaïs might have taken.

It was well past midnight when Petite opened the door to what she guessed would be Athénaïs's bed-chamber. Holding her breath, she stepped in, then softly closed the door behind her.

It was another world, a world of Oriental voluptuousness: India shawls hung from crystal chandeliers, textured wall-panels decorated in chiaroscuro, images of men and women embracing in various states of undress. It was a harlot's opulent boudoir, flimsy gowns thrown in heaps on the red Turkey carpet, the bedclothes in disorder, everything draped in laced red silk. Yet, it was, in a perverse way, an altar as well, for there were candles burning before crosses, statues, icons. Most everything was silver: a massive silvered bed rested on the backs of two silver lions, its silver bedposts ornamented with white plumes. A silvered sofa covered in tigerskin was set opposite a silvered fire-grate. Even the toilette table was silvered. Lights reflected off all the surfaces like stars on a cloudless night.

Petite heard the night watchman outside call out one of the clock. She'd come looking for her own things, yet she felt like a thief. She glanced quickly over the clutter on the toilette table, the jars of pomade and power. Candle-grease and ashes were everywhere. Petite picked up a silver coffer: inside was a tangle of jeweled ornaments, a rich rat's nest of bracelets, armlets and necklets, trinkets of pearl, diamond, emerald and ruby. But no humble wooden rosary, no spangled head-rail, no feather. On the silvered side table close to the bed was a deck of smudged Tarot cards and two half-full glasses of what looked like a spirituous liquor. On the wall, candles dripped wax onto a black enamel cabinet. Petite tugged at its door, but it was locked.

She startled, thinking she saw something out of the corner of her eye, something on the bed, but then realized it was her own image: the headboard was a mirror. Tangled in the rumpled bedclothes, she saw a small leather whip with a silver handle.

Mercy. She should never have come. She began to back away, but saw necklaces hanging from a silvered peg: beaded laces, long strands of pearls, rubies, a necklace of gold shells, another of bear's teeth. There were also two rosaries, one with an ebony cross inlaid with mother-of-pearl, the other with black beads and a silver cross. Petite noticed the pendant Athénaïs often wore—the pendant with the cross and key, hanging from a gold chain.

The key. Petite unclasped the pendant from the chain. Crouching, she fumbled the silver key into the lock on the black enamel cabinet. It fit, and the mechanism gave way. She swung open the doors to reveal two sliding shelves. She then slid out the top one. There, on a bed of green felt, were locks of hair, a thimble of nail clippings, her head-rail and blue-striped ribbon. There was even a tin bracelet she hadn't yet missed.

She sat back on her heels. There was also a man's silk hose and a diamond-tipped hat pin. Might these be Louis's? Shoved into the back, she saw a mess of revolting things: a tiny dried-up heart (a bird's perhaps, she thought) and what looked like a tangle of entrails, small bones.

Petite slid out the lower shelf. There, behind an ornamental brass box and a paper packet, was her rosary of wooden beads. *Mary, I thank you.* She kissed it and draped it around her neck. Then she opened the paper packet. A hard blue sweetmeat rolled out. The color was unusual—and then she remembered: Athénaïs had given her one, just before she miscarried. Just before she almost died.

Trembling now, Petite opened the heavy brass box. Ashes? She put it to one side, took out the packet and securely locked the cabinet. With the pendant and packet in one hand and the brass box in the other she crept out.

"Damnation!" the parrot squawked as she groped her way back through the rooms.

PETITE'S BEDCHAMBER SMELLED refreshingly of the apple logs she burned in winter. The moon cast bright squares of light on the bare floor. Athénaïs would never know she'd been into her rooms: the cabinet was locked, and now *she* had the key. Nevertheless, she pushed a chair against the door and, shivering, placed the pendant, the brass box and the packet behind the four leather volumes of Virgil in the bookcase next to her prie-dieu. After a prayer—in gratitude, in fear—she returned to her big bed, curling up under the covers, clasping her father's rosary to her throat.

"THANK GOD, YOU'RE HERE," Petite said, taking Abbé Patin's hands.

"What's wrong?"

"I've been having . . . it's like a trembling of my heart. Palpitations, the doctor calls it." Her courage was failing her now. At Mass, sitting with Athénaïs (as was the custom), she'd dared to hold the wood-bead rosary in her hands. Athénaïs had stared.

"Tell me what this is about," Abbé Patin said, leading Petite to a chair and sitting down in the seat opposite.

Petite wrapped her shawl around her shoulders. "Remember I told you I almost died?"

"Yes," he said, "you saw your father."

"What I didn't tell you," Petite said, "was that shortly before I got so sick, I'd been with child. I . . . lost it."

"And as a result you got sick?"

"Yes, but not exactly." Petite withdrew her father's rosary from her skirt pocket. Running the wooden beads through her fingers, she told Abbé Patin about

Athénaïs giving her a comfit just before she lost the baby. "I went to the market this morning, before Mass, to consult with an herbalist there. She told me that the comfit contained chamaepitys—ground pine."

"Ah."

"You know the herb?" The herbalist had recognized it immediately as an abortive, one of Madame la Voisin's "remedies."

"I do." He grimaced. "It's strong. It can kill a woman, as well as—"

"I know."

Petite went to her bookcase and took down the volumes of Virgil. She placed the brass box on the table in front of the Abbé. "Tell me what you make of this."

He picked it up and examined it. "I believe it's from Saint-Séverin church," he said, indicating the double S's in the intricate design of the lid.

Petite nodded. She'd thought so, too. "It was in Madame de Montespan's possession."

From somewhere outside, a woman was singing the "Hymn of Adoration": *"Let all mortal flesh keep silence . . ."*

Hesitantly, he opened it. "Ashes," he said, touching the contents with his finger, then sniffing it. Wiping his finger on his cassock, he made the sign of the cross three times, then replaced the lid and sat back, frowning.

"Human ashes, the herbalist thought," Petite said. "Although of course she couldn't be sure."

"I didn't want to say, but yes, possibly, and—" He regarded the box with a look of uneasiness. "And likely from a Black Mass."

Petite covered her face with her hands. As a child, she had imagined the Devil as a monster with a scaly tail and pointed teeth. She had never guessed that the Devil might lurk in the cold, calculating heart of a beautiful woman.

"Have you informed His Majesty?" Abbé Patin asked.

"I'm to see him shortly." Petite doubted that Louis would listen. He had changed. Was it possible that Athénaïs was spinning enchantments around him even now? "I've been suffering attacks of ill health, and now I can't help but wonder if . . ." If Athénaïs was slowly poisoning her.

"You must be cautious," Abbé Patin said. "You are in a time of danger, of high emotion. This is the Devil's realm."

PETITE SLIPPED ON HER dressing gown and walked behind where Louis was relaxing on the silk-covered couch of ease. He'd taken his pleasure of her: now was the time. "Louis, there's something I need to tell you—something you should be aware of," she said, leaning over him, her arms around him.

"I'm not going to like this, am I?" he said, tilting his head back to look at her.

No, she thought. She came around and sat beside him. He'd developed wrinkles, frown lines, hints of gray. "Please, hear me out." She thought of the "Plaisirs de l'Île Enchantée" festival at Versaie, thought of the performance of the innocent knight battling the evil sorceress. She thought of the knight's ring, the ring with the power to destroy enchantment. If only she had such a ring now.

"I hope this hasn't to do with the White," he said. "We've been over all that before."

"No," Petite said forlornly. Diablo had refused to service three mares, and now, rather than having him shot and fed to dogs, the master of the horse wanted to pit him against a pride of lions, for public entertainment. "This goes back to when I was last with child. I ate something, a comfit. Then I lost the baby and almost died."

Louis nodded. "You never mentioned a comfit."

"I had an herbalist test one," she said, taking the woolen shawl from the arm of the couch and draping it around her shoulders. "It contains chamaepitys, an abortive."

Louis tilted his head to one side. "So you think that maybe that was why . . . ?"

"Yes: why I lost the child."

"And this is what you thought I wouldn't want to hear?"

"Louis, Athénaïs gave me that comfit."

He stiffened. "Are you suggesting she intentionally gave you something to make you abort?"

Petite nodded slowly. "Yes," she said. "A poison that near killed me."

"That's absurd," he said, standing.

"Louis," Petite said, looking up at him, imploring. His face had rounded over time. His eyes, once inquiring and curious, had taken on a hard certainty. He wore his authority like a mask. "Athénaïs came at me with a knife," she said evenly, trying to stay calm. "You were there. How can you say it's absurd?"

"Athénaïs has rages," he said, pacing now. "She's a passionate woman—but blowing up in a temper is not the same thing as giving someone poison."

"Louis, please listen to me. She's practicing black magic—"

"Have you lost your senses?" His lips turned down with ironic contempt. "—on *you!*"

"You are not to speak of such things, do you understand? I *forbid* it!" He raised his fist—a threat—then pressed it against his forehead in frustration. "You *must* abide," he said, his voice tremulous. "Athénaïs loves you like a sister."

Petite made a noise through her nose, a sound of contempt.

"Oh, for God's sake, you make her sound like a devil." The door slammed shut behind him.

Petite sat for a time in the silence, her trembling fingers resting on the cold marble top of her vanity. She heard the voice faintly sing, ". . . and with fear and trembling stand."

It's over, she thought. The finality of that realization gave her strength. There was only one path now, and she knew the way.

She stood and picked up the small blue jar, opened it. It was dry, as dry as the single leaf on the twig wedged into the mirror frame. She broke off the leaf and crumbled it. Then she opened her wooden keepsake box and withdrew the moth-eaten scarf. She used it to dry her tears before throwing it into the fire.

THE NURSERY WING of the Colbert household was even more chaotic than usual. There was to be a Mardi Gras fete at the house that afternoon, and the children were in a flurry of anticipation. Madame Colbert asked her daughter, eleven now, to take the toddler and two girls upstairs to listen to their brothers at their singing lessons, and quiet suddenly descended upon the sunny nursery littered with crowns, masks and lacy petticoats.

"You look handsome, Monsieur l'Admiral," Petite told her son. The three-year-old stood self-consciously in his costume: the cap, breeches and cape of an admiral. She shook Tito's hand formally. He appeared anxious about his sudden promotion into the adult world.

"Watch, Mother," Marie-Anne called out. She twirled about the room in her faerie costume, then staggered to a halt. She frowned down at her feet, and shifted them into a more orderly third position.

"Quiet now, Mademoiselle Marie-Anne," Madame Colbert said. "You'll wear yourself out before the party." Marie-Anne ran to her, clutching Madame Colbert around her ample waist. "Would you like to tell your mother what you did yesterday?" Madame Colbert asked, clucking like a pleased mother hen.

"You tell," the girl said.

"Marie-Anne allowed us to put her on a pony," Madame Colbert boasted.

"The one that bites," Marie-Anne said.

"Oh, only nibbles," Madame Colbert said, smiling down at the child. "And only now and then." She stroked the girl's head. "A bit fearful," she mouthed to Petite.

"What did you say?" Marie-Anne looked up at Madame Colbert.

"What did you say, Madame Colbert," Madame Colbert instructed.

"What did you say, Madame Colbert?" Marie-Anne grinned up at her, the fingers of one hand in her mouth.

"I said that you are riding quite well," Madame Colbert said, taking the girl's hand out of her mouth.

"You did not. Madame Colbert."

"I love your costume," Petite told her daughter.

"It sparkles," Tito said, solemnly watching.

"With diamonds," Marie-Anne said.

"Not real diamonds," Madame Colbert told her.

"What are you going to be?" Marie-Anne asked her mother, sucking on her fingers again.

"What are you going to be, *Mother*," Madame Colbert said.

"I'm going to be an angel," Petite said. *Was going to be.* "Are you cold, Monsieur l'Admiral?" she asked little Tito. The child was bent over double, rubbing his bare lower legs. It seemed strange not to see him in a long gown and traces.

"No," he said.

"That means yes," Madame Colbert whispered, taking a seat and pulling Marie-Anne onto her lap. She shifted to make room for the boy as well, her arms encircling them both. "Such *big* babies now."

"Jeanne's baby Albert is one year old," Marie-Anne announced, leaning back against Madame Colbert's soft bosom.

"One year, two months." Madame Colbert beamed at the mention of her first grandchild. "And fat as a quail."

"Poupée is married now and will have babies too," the girl said.

Madame Colbert raised her brows. "That's what we pray for." The second eldest Colbert daughter—nicknamed "Doll"—had married only a month before.

"Mother is married," Tito said.

"She's not," Marie-Anne said.

"She is," the boy persisted. "To our father the King."

"No." Marie-Anne was insistent. "She's like a . . . a *strumpet*."

"Marie-Anne!" Madame Colbert shook the girl. "What a thing to say."

Petite put her hand on Madame Colbert's arm. "Please." It had happened so quickly. She looked into her children's faces. They were too young to understand. "I want you both to know that I love you *very* much . . . and that you have nothing to be ashamed of."

"The finest mother in the world," Madame Colbert exclaimed, and—seeing that Petite was in danger of weeping—she ushered the two children into the care of a nursemaid. "There now," she said, joining Petite at the window. "How about I ring for a hot cordial?"

"Thank you, but no—I must be going."

"Yes, of course—there's the masquerade ball tonight. I confess that I rather prefer staying home with the children."

"I take great comfort in your care of them, Marie," Petite said, tearfully embracing her. She could hear the older boys' voices in their singing lesson, the laughter of children, footsteps on the floor above. "They couldn't have a finer home."

PETITE PEEKED IN at the children before leaving. She blew them a kiss, then left, in tears. She wasn't far from where Diablo was stabled. She needed to see him, to steady her nerves.

Diablo nickered as Petite approached his corral, a small enclosure of stone walls. She leaned on the railing. He was aging, but he still looked good as he ambled over to her. He allowed her near—to groom and care for him—but he remained wild at heart. He would not let her put a halter on him, much less allow her to back him. It broke her heart to see him caged . . . and soon, if the master of the horse had his way, he would be ignobly sacrificed for public amusement.

"I'm sorry," she said, cupping his whiskery muzzle, "I don't have anything for you."

SHE TOOK THE RIVER road back in order to avoid the Mardi Gras procession. The sun would soon set. Courtiers would be dressing for the ball—the first since Henriette's death. It would be a sad affair without her.

Petite stopped to watch the boats, the river traffic. *Gone to the river.* What had happened that early morning long ago? It disturbed her that she still could not recall. What she could remember—and all too vividly—was feeling so desperately miserable that she no longer wished to live.

And now? Now, if anything, she was even more desperately miserable. She headed for her rooms at the palace.

"I WILL NOT BE GOING to the ball," Petite announced to Clorine. Her maid was dressed as a fine lady in the topsy-turvy spirit of the day, with five patches on her cheeks. "So put away my costume." The feathered wings were propped over the back of a chair and her gown was spread out on the daybed.

"Are you not well?"

"I am not."

At Petite's request, Clorine made her a mug of a steaming herbal concoction and dressed her for bed. "Thank you," Petite said, lying back on the pillows. Clorine lingered at the door with a candle lantern in her hand. "Thank you for everything, Clorine," Petite said, closing her eyes.

She lay in the dark, listening to the night revelries, the drunken Mardi Gras brawls.

Waiting.

After the night watchman called out eleven of the clock—after she could be sure that Clorine had retired and was fast asleep—she opened her bed curtains and, taking the night candle, groped her way to the withdrawing room. Draped in a thick woolen shawl, she put some sticks on the embers and used the flame from her candle to light two others. She felt her way to the escritoire and took out a sheet of her best paper, the squid ink, a good quill.

Dear Clorine.

She paused, considering. It was not farewell. Clorine would do her laundry, bring her food and books. She would have her (or her mother, or Madame Colbert) bring the children to see her several times a week. Later, when the time was right,

364

she would begin negotiations with Gautier and arrange to provide Clorine with a handsome dowry. But this was far, far into the future.

The future.

She was stepping into a great unknown, and she thought for a moment of throwing the letter into the fire. Instead, she wrote out her intentions, sprinkled sand on the ink and shook the paper clean. *Now it's set*, she thought. She folded the paper and placed it on the felt cover of her escritoire, exactly in the center. *For Clorine*, she wrote in a careful hand.

Should I write a letter to Louis?

She loved him—still—but she did not love the man he had become. Had Athénaïs worked a spell on him? Or had he always been thus, and she blinded? Had she herself been under some type of enchantment?

No, she would not write. She was too angry, too bereft, her love for the man he had been still burning in her. *Amor indissolubilis*. Would she ever see an altar flame without thinking of him? Without thinking of her willing surrender, her passion? *Their* passion.

She pulled away from the desk and went to the fireplace, adding three small sticks to the flames. Then she pulled a rocking chair up close to the fire and sat rocking, indifferent to the Mardi Gras revelry in the gardens below, waiting for the sun to rise, for the long night to be over. She knew what she wanted now: to be free of sin. To be free of the Court, of Athénaïs . . . and yes, of the King.

I can't live without your love, she had told him, recalling the last time she had run . . . run to her death, run for her life.

AT THE FIRST HINT of light, Petite dressed and gathered up what remained of her treasures: her rosary and locket, the worn copy of Saint Teresa's *Life*. She put on her hooded fur-lined cloak and opened the door, wending her way down the dark halls and cold, echoing stairs.

The street was littered with festive refuse. A man sprawling belly-up in an alley moaned. Three men in costume called out to her: "Hey, girl, over here." One thrust his buttocks at her and tumbled over with the effort.

She headed toward the stable yards.

DIABLO STOOD AGAINST the red light of dawn. Petite thought of when she had first seen him, standing at the edge of a woods. *Sing ye!* He had that beauty still.

She had to get him out of the city—but how? He watched warily as she climbed up onto the stone wall. She kicked off her platform mules and let them drop. Then, crouching, she pushed open the gate. As Diablo bolted, she slipped onto his back, clutching mane and straddling him, her legs tight around his girth. He bucked, but she held on. "Easy, boy," she whispered, half laughing. It felt wonderful to be on him. "Ho, boy!" she said as he bucked down a narrow alley, heading north. "Ho," she repeated when he shied at a cat. Heading onto Rue Saint-Honoré, she sat back, her skirts bunched up around her thighs, and pressed him forward into a canter. He was skittish, but he surged down the cobbled street, ducking vegetable carts and laden water-carriers. Early-morning workers stood well back, watching in awe. An old woman waved her cane, cheering. At Saint-Roch cathedral, Petite guided Diablo into the Rabbit Warren and toward the river.

Diablo raced down the river road, picking up speed, his strong legs coursing. The air was cold and fresh, the dawn light sparkling on the gray water. The city wall, the porte de Conférence, was ahead. The barrier was down, and there were two coaches and a line of people waiting to go through, waiting for their papers to be checked. "Go," she whispered, clutching mane.

People cried out, fell over, scrambling to get out of their way. Diablo dodged an old couple and surged over the high barrier. *Sing ye!*

Ahead: the long road along the Seine, the road to Chaillot. The river on one side and the farms and woodlands on the other rushed by in a blur. Petite sat back. Diablo slowed to a relaxed canter. It hadn't been a dream.

"Ho, boy," she said, grinning, and he eased to a walk. She guided him to an isolated hillock, then halted. She fell forward onto his neck, feeling his warmth, smelling his clean horse scent. She recalled being a girl and lying thus, recalled thinking of what a miracle it was, such trust. Now they were both older, and both of them scarred. Both in need of rescue, salvation.

She was anxious about discovery, but she didn't want to rush. She needed time, if only a moment—a moment to last for eternity.

Grasping his mane, she slid down off his side. He was free now. He could run—yet he stood. He turned his head to her. His eyes—now blue, now dark, now flashing a hint of red—were all-seeing, all-knowing. No, it hadn't been a dream. She pressed her forehead to his. *Am I doing the right thing?* she asked herself, her eyes stinging. *Yes,* her heart answered.

There would be pain, she knew, the pain of loss—but she already knew such pain. She would always love Louis, love the good man at his core—the man hidden behind the King's mask. She saw that man still, laughing with their children.

Their children.

Petite fell to her knees in the grass, her head pressed into her fists. How could she do this? *O God,* she prayed. *Help me.* Diablo sniffed her back, his breath warm on her neck. She sat up. *I could turn back,* she thought. Be the mistress mother, the strumpet. Athénaïs's handmaiden.

No. She could not. No longer. She could not live that lie. Would not. *Nolo, nolebam, nolam.*

She imagined life in a convent—the peace of that existence. Her aunt Angélique's prayers would be answered. The children would come to visit, her mother, her brother and his giddy wife. Abbé Patin—of course. There would be bouquets of flowers and dishes of sugar-plums. There would be song.

And Louis? What would become of her children's father? There was so much that was good in him, so much that was strong and true; and yet such profound weakness. Petite would pray for him, pray that he resist Athénaïs's lure, see her for who she was. Petite was powerless to do more. She must leave the rest to God.

She lay back on the grass, looking up at the sky, listening to Diablo munching weeds nearby. Listening to the sounds of the world awaking. A solitary church bell rang, its sound pure, resonating in the clear morning air. A flock of birds took flight.

Sin was in her; she knew that. She had made a pact with the Devil; she was his. That would never change. But she would not give way this time: she would continue on her path. "*Nec cesso, nec erro,*" she said out loud: I do not slacken, I do not lose my way.

She stood and brushed off her cloak. Diablo raised his head and looked at her. She took out a crust of bread she had hidden away in the pocket under her petticoats. Holding it out, she smiled through her tears. He reached out his long neck, and she stroked his ears. "Ready, old man?" They had a distance yet to go.

She pulled herself up onto his back. The river water sparkled in the morning sun. *Gone to the river.* Her breath quickened as she remembered looking down into the dark water. What had saved her? What was saving her now?

She nudged Diablo forward with her legs. At the river road, he broke into a vigorous trot, and then leapt into a canter. Her cap flew off and her curls came loose. The morning air felt fresh on her cheeks.

She remembered, as a child, watching the Romany woman on horseback, remembered her standing on the cantering horse, her arms outstretched. But mostly she remembered the breathless excitement she had felt, her heartfelt wonder, believing that the world was before her.

And now, again: the world was before her.

Diablo's canter was steady, his back broad. *Now?* she asked herself. She grabbed mane with one hand and steadied herself on his shoulder with the other. *Yes.* Slowly, she brought her feet up under her, crouching. Diablo flicked back one ear, but held his steady pace. And then—slowly, slowly—she stood, balanced and reached out her arms.

Oh, the wind!

AT CHAILLOT, JUST beyond the convent, Petite slipped back down onto Diablo's back and slowed him to a walk. "Ho, boy," she said, sliding off him. She had done it!

He turned his nose to her. She stroked his nose, his muzzle, his ears. She stood for a long while, her face pressed into his neck, running her hands over him. *O Lord, this beautiful horse is your creation, please look over him, protect him. Amen.*

It was time. Soon the river road would become congested. "Go," she commanded, her heart aching. Diablo startled, but did not move. She slapped him on the haunches. "Go," she repeated, but with more urgency. He had to run, *escape.* He twirled, but turned toward her again in confusion. She broke a branch off a bush and shook it at him. "Go!" she begged, weeping.

He trotted off reluctantly, flicking his tail, but snorted and turned again to face her, his ears pricked forward. She waved the branch, whipping it through the air with whistling sounds. *Go! Go!* He reared up and twirled, bucking and twisting, and cantered off.

At the crest of a hillock, he stood motionless, sniffing the air. He raised his head and whinnied. From a distance, a horse answered. Shadows appeared at the edge of a far meadow: *horses*. With a jump and a buck, Diablo raced into the hills, his long tail high and waving.

Beloved.

The convent bells began to ring. Petite watched in rapt wonder until Diablo disappeared from sight. *A horse in the wild is a beautiful thing*, Louis had once said.

Yes, she thought, turning toward the iron gate of the convent, toward freedom.

Epilogue: Marie-Anne, June 6, 1710

I WAS ATTENDING TO my morning toilette at Versaie when the messenger was shown in: my mother was dying, he announced. "Thanks be to God," I said. The boy no doubt found that to be an unloving response, but my mother's suffering, in this, her sixty-fifth year, had been painful to witness. A strong, proud woman, she had weakened dramatically after she'd had to strip the convent chapel of its ornaments the year before to help finance my father's wars. I believe her dying began then: the crippling headaches, the back pain, her hands so twisted with rheumatism she could not hold a quill. And something more, I suspect: something inside, something ruptured.

I ordered my fastest carriage brought around, took up my walking stick. If only I had stayed the summer in Paris. But, selfishly, I had come with my father to Versaie, escaping the stink, the dirt and the heat. "Have them tell her I am on my way. Tell her I'm racing." It was ten past seven of the clock: at this moment my father would be in the ceremonial of his Grand Lever. With age, he'd become fixed in his daily routine—anything unexpected disturbed him. I decided to send word. In any case, I was anxious to get to Paris before my mother passed away.

In spite of the congestion on the road, we made good time, the horses always at a trot. I lowered the blinds to keep out the dust. I was thinking impious thoughts: the discomfort of wearing black in summer, the people who would have to be notified (the list sadly short: most everyone dead). I wondered if Carmelites allowed gravestones, and, if so, what I should have inscribed on it. I believe, in retrospect, that this was God's way of making distress tolerable: "the solace of minutia," my mother used to say.

Used to say. Already, in my mind, she'd passed. It was then that the tears came.

I am, people say, very like my father: we are known for our spirit, our stubbornness, and—yes—our cold heart. But this is just a facade. I believe we feel too much, my father and I, that we're capable of being felled by emotion, and for this reason we must keep it in check.

Death. Grief. How sad to be the survivor, I thought. My mother had outlived everyone, in spite of her sometimes frail health. Grandmother, Uncle Jean—both gone. Her confessor, the kindly Abbé Patin. My brother Tito: his death at sixteen on his first military campaign nearly killed her, I know.

What sort of funeral would the Carmelites require? I wondered. No doubt it would be austere. What a relief not to have to stage a royal production. la Grande Mademoiselle's funeral had been spectacularly offensive, the container of her entrails exploding, filling the church with such noxious smells that people were trampled in the rush for the door, everyone gasping for air. How fitting, somehow: the big Princess had always been an angry woman, especially after marrying Lauzun and suffering his abuse.

And how fitting, likewise, that the Marquise de Montespan had not been honored at all. If one were to believe the account (and I do), *her* entrails had been thrown to pigs. If there is a Heaven, she is not there, despite what my mother might say—my saintly mother who'd even consented to being the Marquise's spiritual director. No, regardless of my mother's counsel, I'm quite sure that that woman is in that other place, suffering for the pain she caused others. Suffering for the pain she caused my mother.

And Father: is he innocent of blame? Doubtful.

He is putting up a strong fight against age—still goes riding, still hunts, still, according to Madame de Maintenon's whispered complaints, insists on daily congress. (At seventy-two! Dieu merci I have not inherited his lust.)

Did he ever love my mother? I wish I knew. He is, curiously, a jealous and possessive man. He does not take rejection well; once my mother left, he rarely even spoke of her. Certainly, he never went to see her. "She is dead to me," he said—yet he allowed his gardener to send flowers to the convent every morning. Was this his wish? There were always flowers in the visitors' salon, extraordinary bouquets. In a rare moment of intimacy, he told me that she was the only woman who had ever truly loved *him*. It was one of those sad and somewhat uncomfortable revelations between a father and daughter, and I did not pursue it.

Love is rare at Court: that I do know. I count myself fortunate to have experienced it, as painful as it was to sit by my poor husband as he lay dying, covered in oozing pustules. Such was the price my dear prince paid for nursing me to health.

Oh, Death. I still mourn.

THUS MY THOUGHTS ran as I entered the cool of the convent. I waited in the visitors' parlor, wondering if I would even be allowed inside. The door opened, and a lay sister summoned me: Sister Nicole, my mother's friend.

I stepped through the door into the inner sanctum. The silence was profound. "Is she . . . ?"

"Thank God you've come," Sister Nicole whispered. Tears streamed down her cheeks.

I followed Sister Nicole through a labyrinth of porticos and courtyards. The gardens were lush, fragrant and bursting with color. We passed a music room, a library. It did not feel like a life of deprivation, and this was a comfort.

We came to an arched wood door, the entrance into the infirmary, the room in which my mother lay dying. "She just had Extreme Unction," Sister Nicole said in a low voice.

"Is she in pain?"

Sister Nicole nodded, pressing her lips together.

I braced myself, and entered the room.

My mother was laid out on a high bed in her heavy brown robes. She looked so small, stretched out thus. She'd always been something of a giant in my eyes.

I approached. Her eyes were closed, and she was making a low, drawn-out moan of pain, the plainsong of the dying. The nuns praying beside her stepped back.

She opened her eyes, her beautiful eyes. I touched her dry, stiffened fingers: how thin they were. Was I hurting her? I looked at Sister Nicole.

"She can no longer speak," Sister Nicole whispered.

"May I embrace her?"

Sister Nicole hesitated. "She must turn to God."

My mother shook her head.

"What is she saying?"

"I think she wants you to hold her."

373

Carefully—for I did not want to hurt her—I gathered my mother into my arms. She laid her cheek against my heart. I held her thus, until she passed.

I STAYED THAT NIGHT in the infirmary. Sister Nicole and I laid my mother out. I thought I would be repulsed by death, but my mother taught me otherwise. She looked at peace. The nuns came, one after another: I saw that they had been a family to her, saw that love was not rare in that place.

The next morning, we moved her bed—her bier—to the choir, and positioned it behind the grille for public viewing. There was already a large crowd waiting when the shutters were opened. I was surprised by the passionate reverence, although I shouldn't have been. For years, my cook had been bringing me songs written about my mother, verses people sang in the markets. It was said people regarded her as something of a saint, credited her with healing ailing animals—dogs, but mostly horses.

All that long day, humble men and women came with their reliquaries, their crosses and rosaries, their medals and holy images. The nuns would take them, touch them to my mother's folded hands, her forehead, her lips, and hand them back. This went on until after five in the evening.

I sat veiled, at her head, moved by the singing of the choir, the prayers, overwhelmed by the love these people had for my mother. When the clerics entered, a great cry went up.

"They're going to take her away now," Sister Nicole told me. "To bury her."

"May I go too?"

"Yes, but first: we want you to have this." She pressed a humble wooden rosary into my hands. "It was her father's."

I ran the worn beads through my fingers. "Thank you." I touched it to my mother's hand, her lips, and then kissed it myself.

"And one other thing," Sister Nicole said, handing me a brass locket on a gold chain.

The clasp was tarnished; I pried it open with my nail. Inside was a strand of white horsehair, and a lock of fine hair—the hair of a baby, likely—as well as some decayed matter. "Do you know what it signifies?"

Sister Nicole shook her head. "All I know is that she never went without it."

"Then she should have it with her now," I said, fastening the chain around my mother's neck. Her skin had a porcelain luster. *Sleep, little one.*

Author's Note

Mistress of the Sun is a work of imagination sparked by real-life events and personalities. In the seventeenth century, the roman à clef (novel with a key) became popular. These were novels about real people, disguised by false names. Most of my characters are based on real people (Louis, Louise, Athénaïs, Lauzun, Nicole). A few, however, are composite. Gautier is inspired by the real-life Monsieur le Duc de Saint-Aignan, but many liberties have been taken with that distinguished man's life. A number of "Religious" influenced Louise de la Vallière's avocation (Abbé Rancé, Jacques Bousset, Louis Bellefonds, Père César); I've combined them into one individual, Abbé Alphonse Patin, a composite of them all. Clorine was indeed the name of Louise de la Vallière's maid, but that is all that is known about her.

Louise de la Vallière was an extraordinary horsewoman—that's fact—and no doubt there were special horses in her life. However, nothing is known of them, and Diablo, therefore, is a fictional creation. A travel journal by Sebastiano, an Italian priest visiting Paris, describes seeing Louise de la Vallière vaulting, and mentions her teacher, a Moor. There was said to have been a whisperer—a "gentler"—at the Court of the Sun King, and it is possible that this gentler and the Moor were one and the same.

Louise de la Vallière's health is something of a mystery. She was an athletic woman, yet she suffered periods of disability (including the attack of blindness). I discussed what little is known with a doctor, who suggested that she might have had multiple sclerosis, a disease that existed but would not be identified until the late eighteenth century. It's only a guess, but it fits.

In order to recreate history in fiction, one must simplify. In "real life," there were more houses and palaces, more scandals, more loves, more entertainments, more journeys and war—but most of all there were simply more people: more children, relatives, friends and servants. The Marquis de Saint-Rémy had a daughter, Catherine, by his first marriage. She no doubt complicated Louise de la Vallière's life, but I chose not to have her complicate this novel. Gaston d'Orléans and his wife did in fact have a much-wanted son, born retarded, who died at two, before Louise joined the Orléans Court at Blois. When she did arrive, there was also a fourth Princess, Marie-Anne, who lived only three years. Cardinal Mazarin is not mentioned, in spite of his significant role both to the country, politically, and to the young King, personally. There were, as well, a number of delightfully eccentric individuals who are not mentioned. I reluctantly did not delve into the stories of Madame de Choisy and her cross-dressing son, the evil Olympe Mancini and her equally evil lover, the Marquis de Vardes, the famous courtesan Ninon, and the charmingly outspoken Princess Palentine . . . not to mention a vast array of underworld characters. No doubt some of these individuals will appear in future novels.

Although never convicted, Athénaïs, the Marquise de Montespan, remains suspected of the witchcraft hinted at in *Mistress of the Sun*. For those wishing to read more about the period, I highly recommend Antonia Fraser's *Love and Louis XIV*. For more information on my research and the writing process, please see my website: www.sandragulland.com.

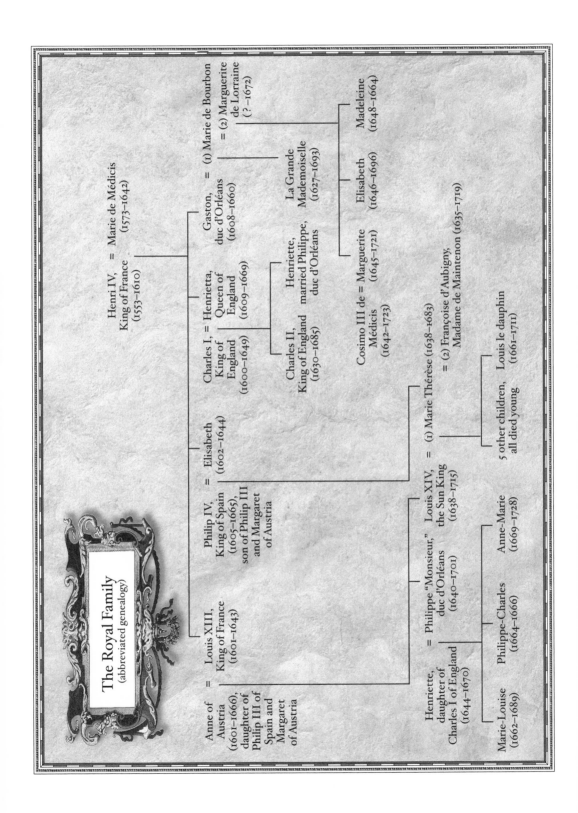

The Royal Family
(abbreviated genealogy)

Henri IV, = Marie de Médicis
King of France   (1573–1642)
(1553–1610)

Louis XIII, King of France (1601–1643) = Anne of Austria (1601–1666), daughter of Philip III of Spain and Margaret of Austria

Philip IV, King of Spain (1605–1665), son of Philip III and Margaret of Austria = Elisabeth (1602–1644)

Charles I, King of England (1600–1649) = Henrietta, Queen of England (1609–1669)

Gaston, duc d'Orléans (1608–1660) = (1) Marie de Bourbon
= (2) Marguerite de Lorraine (?–1672)

Charles II, King of England (1630–1685)

Henriette, married Philippe, duc d'Orléans

La Grande Mademoiselle (1627–1693)

Elisabeth (1646–1696)

Madeleine (1648–1664)

Cosimo III de' Médicis (1642–1723) = Marguerite (1645–1721)

Louis XIV, the Sun King (1638–1715) = (1) Marie Thérèse (1638–1683)
= (2) Françoise d'Aubigny; Madame de Maintenon (1635–1719)

Philippe "Monsieur," duc d'Orléans (1640–1701) = Henriette, daughter of Charles I of England (1644–1670)

5 other children, all died young

Louis le dauphin (1661–1711)

Marie-Louise (1662–1689)

Philippe-Charles (1664–1666)

Anne-Marie (1669–1728)

Glossary

amoroso a lover, a gallant

barley-hood a fit of ill humor brought on by drinking

barouch a horse-drawn carriage with four wheels. It has an outside seat for the driver and facing inside seats for two couples, with a folding top.

bratche a brat

branle a French dance that moves mainly from side to side. It is performed by couples in either a line or a circle.

cabriole a springing ballet step in which one leg is extended and the second leg is brought up to the first

capriole (in horsemanship) when a horse makes a high leap without moving forward, kicking its hind legs out together

carosse (or caroche) a luxurious carriage

carrefour a place where four roads meet

chime hours three, six, nine or twelve o'clock

close-stool a chamber pot enclosed within a stool or box; an early toilet

coat of plates a series of overlapping plates riveted onto a vest of leather

courante a dance characterized by running or gliding steps

covetise excessive desire, lust

deflourish to deprive (a woman) of her virginity

Fontaine Beleau the town of Fontainebleau in France, originally known by a variety of names: Fontaine Beleau, Fontaine Bello, Fontaine Belle Eau (all variations on "good water fountain"), Fontaine de Biaud (after Biaud, the original owner) and Fontaine Bleau (after "fontaine de Bleau," a spring discovered by a dog named Bleau)

frack lusty

galled sore from chafing

giglet a giddy, romping girl

gill-flirt a wanton or giddy young woman

gloom (v.) to look displeased, to frown or scowl

glout a sullen look; to be "in the glout" means to be sulking

hallali a bugle call

handfast (v.) to make a contract of marriage by joining hands

hugger-mugger in secret

Hungary water wine scented with rosemary flowers

jerkin a garment for a man's upper body, often made of leather

jeté (dance) a ballet step in which a spring is made from one foot to the other

justacorps a close-fitting body-coat reaching to the knees

King's Evil (or simply, the Evil) scrofula, tuberculosis of the lymph nodes of the neck

linsey-woolsey a coarse fabric of wool and flax

livre a unit of currency. Multiply by four to get its approximate equivalent in U.S. dollars today. France at this time did not have a central mint, and the value of currency varied from province to province. A Tournais livre, for example, was a quarter of the value of the Parisian livre.

lose his nature to be impotent

made (v.) (as in "to be made") to be pregnant

meddling in the context used here, sexual intercourse

médianoche—a midnight meal

minikin a dainty, sprightly girl

mouche a small patch worn on the face as an ornament or to conceal a blemish

nerval relating to or affecting the nerves

Palais d'Orléans today known as the Luxembourg Palace in Paris, where the French Senate meets

pas de bourrée (dance) a sideways step in which one foot crosses behind or in front of the other

pelerine a lace shoulder covering

petticoat breeches wide, pleated pants falling to the knee

pillion (as in "riding pillion") to ride a horse sitting on a "pillion"—a pad or cushion attached behind a saddle on which a second person can ride, usually seated sideways

pirouette (dance) multiple turns on one leg

pochette a small violin, often carried in a pocket by French dance masters

poke (n.) (clothing) a bag or small sack worn by women under petticoats

posset a spiced drink of hot sweetened milk curdled with wine or ale

prince or princess of the *blood* in France, paternal royal descendants

pure-finder someone who collects dung for use as an alkaline lye for steeping hides

quality rank or position in society

Religious (n.) a member of a religious order

rosa solis a liqueur made from the juice of the sundew plant, believed to be an aphrodisiac. Rosolio (or resoil) is still produced in Italy and Spain, though it no longer contains sundew.

rudded made red

seminal semen

snug a muff

stale (n.) (horses) a steady, old, sometimes blind horse; also called a "stalking" horse because deer have no fear of such an animal and the hunter can hide behind it and shoot over the horse's withers or under its belly

sou a unit of currency. Twenty sous equals one livre.

sullen-sick to be sick from ill-humor

swive for a man to copulate with a woman

toilette a towel or cloth; also used to put down on a dressing table (hence *toilette*)

touchy-headed slightly crazed, cranky

tucker (n.) (clothing) a piece of fabric worn by women to cover their bodice, often made of lace

tufter in stag hunting, a hound trained to drive the deer out of cover

uprise to rise from confinement after giving birth

varlet a menial, a groom

Versaie an early name for Versailles

voraginous resembling an abyss or whirlpool

vue a horn signal during a hunt, indicating that the hounds were still running

wet nurse a woman hired to suckle and nurse another woman's child. A "dry-nurse" is the woman who took care of and attended to a child but did not suckle it.

whitepot a type of custard or milk pudding

whitework embroidery worked in white thread on a white ground

young with child newly pregnant, in the early stage of pregnancy

Acknowledgments

Many have been midwife to this novel; as with elephants, it was an eight-year gestation. *Mistress of the Sun* would simply not exist without them:

My first reader, always, agent Jackie Kaiser.

My amazing editors, Iris Tupholme and Trish Todd, as well as Dan Semetanka and Fiona Foster.

My sharp and dedicated managing editor, Noelle Zitzer; production editor, Allegra Robinson; and copyeditors and proofreaders, Allyson Latta, Becky Vogan and Debbie Viets.

The members of my San Miguel writers' group, who cheered me lustily through a labyrinth of drafts: Susan McKinney and Beverly Donofrio.

The members of Wilno Women Writers: Pat Jeffries, Joanne Zommers and, especially, Jenifer McVaugh (who remembers my first creative attempt to tell this story *twenty* years ago).

My invaluable readers and consultants, in alphabetical order: Susanne Dunlop, Jude Holland, Gary McCollim, Mary Sharratt, Merilyn Simonds, Victoria Zackhein.

Two book clubs critiqued the manuscript: "Books Et Al" in Oakland, California (Chere Kelley, Akemy Nakatani, Robyn Papanek, Marianna Sheehan, Mary Sivila, Monique Binkley Smith, Leslie Tobler), and "19 girls and a boy(s)" in Toronto, Ontario (Carrie Gulland, Rebecca Snow, Fiona Tingley, Morwenna White, and Al Kellett).

A host of people extended their knowledge and help over the years: Nanci Clausson, for the use of her studio in a moment of creative desperation; Bruno and Anne Challamel, research assistants and consultants extraordinaire; Simone Lee, for access to a book on seventeenth-century horsemanship; Dr. John McErlean, for keeping me abreast; Dr. Rob Adams, for medical consultation; Dr. Karen Raber and Treva Tucker, for information on seventeenth-century horseback riding; Dr. Elizabeth Rapley, for consultation on life in seventeenth-century monasteries; scriptwriter Karl Schiffman, for plot wisdom; Bernard Turle, for a gift many years ago of a book on Versailles.

My historical guides: M. Ludart, through the historical mazes of Paris; Patrick Germain, through the châteaus of the Loire Valley (on horseback!); Ghislain Pons, tireless and knowledgable guide through Versailles.

And last, but *never* least, my biggest fans: Richard, Carrie and Chet.